Praise for

DAVID FENNELL

'A truly extraordinary crime novel . . . a gritty, dark thriller with
a serial killer of frightening proportions'
LYNDA LA PLANTE

'I flew through it . . . Tense, gripping and brilliantly inventive'
SIMON LELIC

'You couldn't ask for a more assured, if startlingly
graphic and gory, debut'
IRISH INDEPENDENT

'Unsettling, fast-paced, suspenseful and gripping . . . Excellent'
WILL DEAN

'A tense-as-hell, high-body count page turner, but a rarer thing too
—
one that's also full of genuine warmth and humanity'
WILLIAM SHAW

'A hair-raisingly dark thriller . . . you won't be able to put it down'
ARAMINTA HALL

'A blend of Lynda La Plante and Thomas Harris'
CRIME TIME

'A stunning start to what promises to be a fantastic new series . . .
layered, twisty and so deliciously dark'
M. W. CRAVEN

'David Fennell more than earns his place at the crime fiction table
with this superb exploration of a psychopath with the creepiest
modus operandi I've read in a long time'
FIONA CUMMINS

'A serial killer classic in the making . . . hooks you in and holds you
tight, right up to the extremely satisfying final page'
SUSI HOLLIDAY

David Fennell was born and raised in Belfast before leaving for London at the age of eighteen with £50 in one pocket and a dog-eared copy of Stephen King's *The Stand* in the other. He jobbed as a chef, waiter and bartender for several years before starting a career in writing for the software industry. He has been working in CyberSecurity for fourteen years and is a fierce advocate for information privacy. David has played rugby for Brighton and studied Creative Writing at the University of Sussex. He is married and he and his partner split their time between Central London and Brighton.

To find out more, visit his website: www.davidfennell.co.uk

Follow him on Twitter: @davyfennell

Also by David Fennell

The Art of Death

See
No Evil

DAVID FENNELL

ZAFFRE

First published in the UK in 2022 by
ZAFFRE
An imprint of Bonnier Books UK
4th Floor, Victoria House, Bloomsbury Square, London, WC1B 4DA
Owned by Bonnier Books
Sveavägen 56, Stockholm, Sweden

A CIP catalogue record for this book is
available from the British Library.

ISBN: 978-1-83877-666-4
Trade paperback ISBN: 978-1-83877-822-4

Also available as an ebook and an audiobook

1 3 5 7 9 10 8 6 4 2

Typeset by IDSUK (Data Connection) Ltd
Printed and bound in Great Britain by Clays Ltd, Elcograf S.p.A.

MIX
Paper from
responsible sources
FSC® C018072

Zaffre is an imprint of Bonnier Books UK
www.bonnierbooks.co.uk

For David H Headley

But if thine eye be evil, thy whole body shall be full of darkness. If therefore the light that is in thee be darkness, how great is that darkness!

Matthew 6:23

1

Friday, 2 January, St Martin's Court, Central London, evening

I T'S NOT THE FIRST TIME this week that Alfie McSweeney has the sense that he is being watched. He slows his pace and furtively slides his gaze up and down the narrow thoroughfare, his skin tingling as if a thousand ants are marching over his back and neck. Strangers pass quickly by. One bumps into him without apologising and is gone before Alfie has time to admonish him. Alfie scowls and looks above the crowds, his eyes sweeping every corner and shadow, but no one's looking his way. Yet still he cannot shift his unease. Scratching his temple, he wonders if his imagination has run away with him. *Wouldn't be the first time.* He takes a calming breath and smiles to himself to lift his spirits.

'That's better,' he whispers.

An icy breeze whistles down the court, penetrating the worn threads of his old overcoat. The temperature has dropped to one degree, or possibly lower, he thinks. Alfie is skint, with barely enough money to heat his tiny damp bedsit, and long ago become accustomed to the cold. Or at least, he thought he had. Tonight is different. Tonight feels as cold as death and it doesn't help that his blood is as thin as the cheap lager he's been drinking all afternoon.

He is distracted by the warm fragrance of freshly cooked seafood and garlic which floats from the half-open entrance to J. Sheekey's restaurant. A smart, well-heeled couple in their sixties are waving at the manager and some staff members, all smiles and air kisses as they leave.

Alfie narrows his gaze at the couple and feels his heart lift. *I know you. Both of you.* The man has a long face and is dressed like a dapper old country gentleman. The woman is thin with bony hands and wears brightly coloured blue eye shadow and pink lipstick, odd for a woman of her years, but hadn't she always made herself up that way? They huddle into each other, their breath forming a single white misty cloud. He hears the man say, 'I don't think I've tasted a finer lobster in the longest time. Truly, it was sublime.'

He recognises his voice and its cloying tone. *What's your name?*

The woman pulls on a pair of woollen gloves. 'And the wine. Oh, it was such a wonderful evening, dear. Thank you.' She links her arm in his.

He pats her hand. 'I'm so glad you enjoyed it. Let's get you home, shall we?'

Alfie's had a skinful today and doesn't want to give the wrong impression. He pockets his can of Tennent's Super, concealed inside a paper bag, brushes himself down and checks his breath, which seems a little ripe, but could be worse. Probably best to keep a little distance.

'Hello,' says Alfie.

The man's eyes flash in surprise as he meets Alfie's gaze for the briefest of moments before looking away with a tightened face.

Alfie opens his arms and smiles. 'It's me, Alfie. Alfie McSweeney.'

Frowning, they skirt around him without saying a word. Alfie blinks and watches, hoping they'll remember him, but they scurry down St Martin's Court and quickly hail a cab on Charing Cross Road. Alfie's shoulders slump and he feels a heaviness in his chest that weighs him down so much that he feels almost rooted to the spot. He taps his stubbly chin and for a moment wonders if he's actually invisible. A memory flashes and their names come to him. *Sid and Vera. I remember you . . .*

He notices someone standing at the entrance to St Martin's Court, where the couple had been only moments before.

Alfie feels his scalp prickling. 'Not you again,' he mutters.

He was right to be paranoid. Looking back at him is the stranger who has recently been watching and following him. As always, he is dressed in his filthy brown parka, baggy jeans and grubby red trainers. The parka is zipped all the way up, concealing his face within the dark hole of the hood. His stalker, Alfie had told Steve the barman at the Lamb and Flag. Steve had shot him a look that said, 'Who the fuck would stalk a drunken old loser like you?'

Alfie necks the remainder of the beer, drops the can to the ground and gives the stranger the finger as he crosses St Martin's Court, navigating his way through the interval crowd that begins to spill out from the rear doors of Wyndham's Theatre. He glances back and sees the man following, shuffling slowly behind him like the cripple he is. Alfie turns right onto Charing Cross

3

Road and hurries into Leicester Square tube station, merging with the crowd and descending the escalator to the busy platform deep under the ground. His chest is wheezing, and a cold sweat breaks out on his face. Alfie glances back and sighs with relief to see there is no sign of the freakshow following him. The train pulls up and he takes the Northern Line to Camden Town.

Alfie has a raging thirst when he arrives. He stops by a convenience shop run by a Turkish man called Omer, who is always courteous and does not judge him when he trades his coins for beer. He would prefer something stronger – whisky or rum – but his budget never stretches that far. Alfie picks up two cans and takes them to the counter.

'It's a cold one tonight, Alfie,' says Omer.

Alfie hands across the beers and his coins. 'Not half. These'll keep me warm, though.'

Omer rings them up on the till and slides them into a plastic bag. 'Have you eaten?' he asks.

'Just about to,' replies Alfie, glancing at the cans.

Omer smiles warmly at him. 'One moment.' He makes his way to the rear of the shop, grabs two sandwiches, a packet of crisps and a Snickers bar and puts them into the bag. 'A gift, my friend.'

A lump swells in Alfie's throat. 'I get my benefits next week; I can pay you back then.'

'No need, Alfie.'

Confusion swirls through him. Alfie cannot think of the last time anyone had been kind to him. A flash of his old life appears in his mind, when he was younger, when he was someone else, someone normal, someone's son, someone's friend – a teacher, a *shepherd*. He pushes the past from his mind as a knot in his stomach pulls and tightens hard. 'Thank you, Omer,' he mumbles, his eyes down.

'Goodnight, Alfie. You take care now.'

Alfie leaves the warmth of the shop, makes his way towards Regent's Canal and crosses onto the towpath, leaving behind the bustle and noise of Camden Market. He takes out a can of Tennent's Super and cracks it open. Swigging it back, he looks across the murky waters of Regent's Canal at the passing world: an arguing couple; a woman walking with her barking dog; two drunk men singing at the top of their voices. Alfie sighs. Omer's kindness and the sudden rush of memories had sucker punched him. He doesn't like dwelling on the past – too many bad memories. He shudders and shakes away the rising emotions. Finishing the can, he tosses it in the water and cracks open the second beer. Thank God for beer. Beer makes everything better.

Approaching Camden Street Bridge, he sees an orange tent underneath it. It has been there for about a week and more than likely belongs to a rough sleeper. There were many of them dotted around London, tents donated with sleeping bags by Good Samaritans for rough sleepers to see them through the winter. Poor sods.

He hears a sudden sound like something dropping into the water behind him. He jolts and turns to see a rippling on the surface of the canal. But there is no one around. He frowns and thinks he hears footfalls close by but can't see anyone. He feels something squeak and brush past his feet. A rat! 'Fuck!' he cries, jumping in fright and dropping the can. To his horror, it rolls to the edge of the towpath and falls into the canal. Alfie trembles with disbelief and, for a moment, considers how deep the canal is and if he could try and rescue it. But that is a dumb idea. Besides, the can would be more filthy canal water now than beer.

'Alfieee,' a voice hisses behind him.

Alfie feels the hairs on his neck stand on end. He turns and feels a hard thump on his temple that causes him to stumble sideways. Someone grabs his arm and pulls him away from the canal. His head is spinning and his knees give way. He feels himself being guided toward the tent and pushed inside it. He lifts his arms to fend off his attacker, but he is confused, weak from the blow and drunk too. He feels someone sitting on top of him and a hand squeezing his mouth and one of his nostrils closed, restricting his air. Something hard is inserted up his other nostril.

'Breathe,' says a voice.

Alfie doesn't want to, but he doesn't have a choice. He feels a clump of clawing, bitter powder shoot up his nose and down his throat. He chokes and his eyes water as his assailant squeezes his nose hard to prevent him expelling any of the powder.

He begins to feel a numbness and blinks. He tries to move his legs, but they seem weirdly heavy. His head is groggy and the numbness has spread through his body, making him feel like a slab of concrete, unable to move. He tries to speak but it's as if his mouth is stuffed with cotton wool.

The tent lights up with the dim glow of a small torch. Alfie can't move his head but he can see the dark hood of the filthy brown parka floating over him.

'See no evil, Alfie,' the stranger hisses. In one hand he is holding a nasal spray; in the other, a surgeon's scalpel.

6

Alfie wants to look away, but he can't move his head. He tries to scream, but his mouth is filled with drool now and his jaw feels solid and heavy like a brick.

His assailant takes out a phone, dials it and speaks to someone. 'McSweeney,' he says, placing the phone on the ground by Alfie's head.

Terror swarms through him as the stranger lowers the knife to his left eye. Alfie blinks and tries to close it, but the stranger digs the blade into the flesh and cuts around the socket. Alfie screams inside, his heart banging like a frightened hare's. He feels his eyeball being tugged and his head swirls as the stranger plucks it from the socket. He sees the blade lowering to his right eye, and then, before he passes out, Alfie hears the man on the phone speak a name.

A name from back then.

2

Monday 5 January, early morning

IN HER DREAM, DETECTIVE INSPECTOR Grace Archer is running through a decaying old hospital wearing only a ripped black dress. The walls close in around her and she is breathless, her heart pounding, her face clammy and hot with sweat. She is running for her life, pushing aside a battered gurney and a rolling, rusted wheelchair. The wounds on her hands are open and bleeding a trail of blood. Behind her she can hear his footfalls tearing after her.

He wants her and will stop at nothing to get her.

Just keep running.

She sprints down a dark hallway towards a closed door, her bare feet pounding a floor littered with shattered glass and used needles.

She turns. His face is hidden beneath a featureless mask with a bleeding @ symbol daubed over one eye. He is clutching his stomach, which is saturated with blood.

'Look what you did, Grace!' he cries, holding up his dripping red palms.

'You got what you deserved!' she shouts back.

The door is rigid. She pushes it using all her strength and, as it flies open, she tumbles forward to a stop at the edge of a swimming pool with swirling dark waters and the sweet, sickly smell of chemicals. Her feet teeter on the edge and she has to flail her arms to regain balance. She hears him roar, feels his bloody hands ram her forward. She falls, plummeting towards the dark waters below. Holding her breath, she crashes through the surface and sinks deep into the cold, cold water. Looking up she sees his masked face shimmer and then disappear. With a shred of hope, she kicks her legs, swims upwards, but hits something hard.

Glass!

Panic claws at her and she slams her fists into it, but it doesn't move.

Her heart pounds.

She swims to the left. More glass.

To her right. Glass!

Above, below and all around her are glass walls, closing in.

She is trapped inside a vitrine. She pounds and kicks the glass with her fists and feet, but there is nothing she can do. She is running out of oxygen and feels her head spinning.

A light appears at the base of the cabinet and two small hands appear, padding like feet across the surface of the glass. A pale face with a long nose and thin red lips smiles up at her.

Bernard Morrice.

Terror grips her like a fist and then she hears a voice calling her name. A voice from the past that fills her heart with hope. 'Graaace!' calls her father.

'Daddy! Daddy!' she cries out, but the chemical water floods her mouth and chokes and burns her throat.

Archer's eyes snap open and she bolts from her bed, gasping for breath, clutching her throat, her stomach almost lurching at the fetor of chemicals that seem to hang in the air as if they have travelled back from the nightmare she has just escaped.

'Grace . . .?'

Archer sees Grandad, dressed in his pyjamas and robe, standing in the doorway.

'You were dreaming again,' he says, his voice quiet, uncertain.

Her head is groggy from sleeping tablets and she sits back down on the bed. 'I'm fine, Grandad. It's just a dream, that's all.'

'You've been having them a lot recently.'

Archer sighs and rubs her temples.

'You were calling for your dad . . .'

Archer takes in two deep breaths.

'Did you see him in your dream? Was he there?'

'No, Grandad. I didn't see him.'

'Was – was *he* there?'

Archer knows Grandad will not allow Bernard Morrice's name to sully his lips, or be mentioned by anyone in his home. Morrice, the child serial killer who had abducted Archer eighteen years back when she was twelve years old. Her father was still warm in his grave when Morrice snatched her from his graveside and locked her in a filthy, muddy pit with a boy called Danny Jobson. Archer had thought she had learned to deal with that part of her life a long time ago. Yet three months ago she'd faced off against the artist-cum-serial killer called @nonymous who had come close to killing her; since then, it has seemed as if she was back at square one. She sighs and pushes Morrice and her dreams from her head.

'What time is it?' she asks, stretching her arms.

'Almost three in the morning.'

'I'm sorry I woke you.'

'That's OK. I was just worried about you, that's all.'

She looks up at him with a reassuring smile. 'I'm fine, really.'

'Are you sure?'

Archer crosses the room and embraces him. 'How could I not be with you here to look after me?'

He squeezes her back. 'I don't know what I'd do if anything ever happened to you,' he says, his voice quaking.

'You should get some sleep,' she replies in a calming tone and walks with him to his bedroom. He stops and reaches for the door frame to steady himself.

'I miss them so much . . . your dad and your grandma.'

'Me too, Grandad.'

'You know, after your dad died, she just gave up. She was never the same.' He stares blankly into his bedroom, the same room he had shared with his wife for all their married life.

DI Sam Archer had been executed as part of a series of gangland revenge murders in London eighteen years before and neither Archer nor her grandfather had ever quite got over the cold-blooded killing of her beloved father, his adored son. Although they had learned to adjust and accept he was no longer alive, even all these years later it's still raw.

'Get some sleep, Grandad, and I'll see you for breakfast.'

'Goodnight, sweetheart.'

'Goodnight, Grandad.'

Archer lies back in bed thinking about Grandad and how frail he is becoming in these, the early stages of dementia. She had taken a few days off work to look after him because he didn't eat when she wasn't around. Each night she would return and see that the food in the cupboards and fridge had not been touched. When she asked about it, he told her that he had no appetite, yet when she cooked for him, he ate like there was no tomorrow. It's as if he is two different people. His doctor had told her that this was quite typical for dementia sufferers and to just keep feeding him but this is becoming more challenging. Archer is returning to work in a few hours and often works long, late shifts. The time is coming for her to start thinking about extra care. She had enlisted Grandad's old pal and chess partner, Cosmo Mateo, to spend more time with him and ensure he ate, but Archer is now sure she's made the right decision. Despite Grandad's dementia diagnosis, Cosmo still allowed Grandad to make all the decisions. In short, Cosmo was a pushover, and if she was being totally honest with herself, as dizzy and forgetful as Grandad.

When the grey light of morning comes, Archer rises with a purpose and, after a hot invigorating shower, gets dressed. Returning to the bathroom she stands in front of the mirror, inserts her contact lenses and blinks them into place. At school she was teased about her different-coloured eyes: one blue, one green. A well-meaning supply teacher had pointed them out to the class as a way of educating them on what heterochromia was but this had unleashed a tide of teasing which became unbearable, until young Grace, who had never been one to suffer fools, cracked. She bloodied the lips and blackened the eyes of four boys and three girls from her year and gained a reputation and respect that she didn't much care for.

That was a long time ago.

She makes her way down to the kitchen and prepares breakfast.

'I'm just popping to the shop to get the morning papers,' calls Grandad from the hallway.

'You know I'm back at work this morning?'

'I remembered – and don't worry, I *will* eat today.'

'Promise?'

'Promise.'

'I'll be checking later.'

She hears him chuckle as he closes the front door.

Her phone rings with a call from DS Quinn, her partner, a smart, conscientious copper and no-nonsense Belfast man. Archer had been a detective with the NCA and had joined the Met three months back, replacing Andy Rees, a DI she had helped get sent down for corruption. As a result, her appointment had been unpopular and she'd been stonewalled by many of Rees's colleagues. Luckily for her, Quinn is no fan of corrupt coppers and was no friend to Rees. He was assigned to work with Archer on her first day and between them they had solved the murders committed by the killer who called himself @nonymous. With a caustic sense of humour and a grit and determination to match her own, Quinn has become a valued second to her.

'Good morning, Grace. How was your wee break?'

'A blast,' she says, dryly. 'I'm eager to come back to work.'

'Grand. I was just about to respond to a report of a fracas on the Strand. Care to join me? If you're free I can pick you up along the way.'

'I'm free. Come now.'

'On my way.'

Archer hurries to the fridge and ensures Grandad has enough food in for the day. Everything seems in order. She takes out her phone and types a message to him.

Grandad, called to work. Phone me if you need anything. Lots of food in the fridge :-) G X

Five minutes later Quinn pulls up outside. Archer grabs her peacoat and steps out into the chilly morning. A blanket of frost covers the road, pavement and rooftops of the brown-brick terraces of Roupell Street, a conservation area of preserved nineteenth-century terraces in the heart of London. Her breath forms before her and she feels the cold scratch at her scars.

Archer's experiences with Morrice and @nonymous had left her scarred, not just internally, but on her hands too. On the top of her left hand is a scar from the night she desperately used her bare hands to dig her way out of the collapsing, sodden pit that Morrice had trapped her in. On her right palm is a second scar, this one from the knife she had used to defend herself against @nonymous. Quinn had jokingly called them her 'unholy wounds'. She had not laughed, because in a strange way they almost were just that, her own personal stigmata. Despite Morrice being dead and @nonymous in prison, both killers had gained an almost mythical status among the fanatical followers of serial murderers.

Archer does not want to dwell on these wretched, ugly reminders. She has tried to adapt and come to think of them, not like the wounds of a passive priest in awe of a Messiah, but as notches on her skin marking the end of evil. It is the only way she can really come to terms with them.

She gets into the passenger seat. Quinn is wearing a beanie hat over his short dark-brown hair, a thick navy jumper and a suede bomber jacket. He looks across at her with what Klara, their colleague and friend, calls his 'don't fuck with me' baby blues. He smiles at her. 'Welcome back.'

'It's good to be back.'

3

QUINN TURNS LEFT ONTO DUNCANNON Street before speeding up the Strand. Moments later after passing the Savoy hotel, Quinn pulls carefully onto the pavement outside the Emporium, a stark contrast to the Savoy's grand opulence, and where one police vehicle is already parked.

Archer climbs out and assesses the premises. Sandwiched between a pound store and a fried-chicken takeaway, the Accessorise to Glamorise Emporium is a drab-looking store with grubby windows displaying dusty white polystyrene female busts wearing meretricious fascinators and gaudy gold necklaces inset with large stones of different colours. A faded yellow sign says: *Lovingly customised to your requirements.*

'A swanky establishment,' comments Quinn, dryly.

Archer hears shouting and is shocked to see two male uniforms she recognises as PCs Keith Hopkins and Nathan Watts, manhandle a distressed woman of colour, wearing a long pink cardigan.

'I just wanted my money back,' she cries, tears streaming down her cheeks.

A round man with a grey comb-over follows them and stands at the door with his arms folded. 'I want that bitch arrested! How dare she come into my shop and make accusations like that.'

Archer feels a rage boiling inside.

And then it all happens so quickly. Hopkins trips on his own feet pulling the woman down with his fellow officer. As if believing this is an act of aggression, Nathan Watts begins to wrestle her. The woman screams, but her voice is stifled as the other man reaches across her throat and begins to choke her. Quinn hurries behind him and peels his arm from the woman's neck. 'Just ease off the force there, mucker!'

Members of the public circle around, filming the scene with their phones. 'Oi! Leave her alone!' someone shouts. Other voices join in a chorus of outrage.

Archer crouches down and levels her gaze at Hopkins and Watts. Neither man looks at her. 'Stop this right now!' she bellows, as they continue to push and pull at the writhing, terrified woman.

'Get back, madam. This is a police matter!' says Hopkins.

Archer grabs his arm. 'You're applying unnecessary force to an unarmed woman, PC Watts!'

'I said back!' he snaps, twisting the woman's arms behind her back.

'My name is Detective Inspector Grace Archer. I won't ask you again. Release this woman.' Archer's tone is dark and cold.

'I think you two superheroes might want to listen to what DI Archer has just asked,' says Quinn.

Hopkins narrows his gaze at Archer, clocking her mismatched eyes. Realisation dawns on his puffy red face.

He releases his hold on the woman, a sneer of resentment flashing on his thin lips. His partner lets go too, but hovers nearby, twitching like a nervous hound waiting for a second chance to tear at the kill.

Archer takes the woman by the hand and helps her up. She is unsteady and weak from the exertion and force of the two men.

'I'm so sorry this has happened to you.'

The woman trembles and removes a paper tissue from the pocket of her cardigan, which she uses to wipe her eyes and nose. Underneath her cardigan, Archer notices she is wearing an NHS uniform.

'She was destroying property,' says the man with the comb-over.

The woman's eyes are wide with terror. 'I didn't touch anything! I only wanted my money back,' she repeats.

'And she resisted arrest,' adds Hopkins. 'Now, if you don't mind, we'll just take her along to the station.'

'And London can sleep soundly tonight,' says Quinn. 'Where would we be without big strong boys like you two?'

'What's your name?' Archer asks the woman.

'Dorothy Hayes.'

'Come with me, Dorothy. Let's get you home,' says Archer, escorting the woman away from the two policemen, and into the car. She closes the door and, turning to the two PCs, quietly but firmly says, 'I will have each of you for assault. Judging by the crowd you've attracted, that little show you just put on has already gone viral.'

An uncertain expression clouds the officers' faces.

'You two better leave,' says Quinn. 'But be aware that this is not over.'

Both officers climb into their car and leave quickly.

'What about the damage to my shop?' asks the shopkeeper, in an exasperated tone.

Archer takes out a contact card from her pocket. 'Get in touch with me, tomorrow, Mr . . .?'

'Goddard,' he replies, taking the card. 'Reckon I'll do just that.'

Archer climbs into the car. 'Where's home, Dorothy?'

'Vauxhall,' she replies quietly.

'DS Quinn and I can take you there, if you like.'

Dorothy sits trembling in the back seat, her head down.

'Dorothy, if you wish to make a complaint, I can help you,' Archer says.

The woman turns her gaze to the window. 'What would be the point?'

Quinn starts up the Volvo as Archer fastens her seatbelt.

'The police should be answerable for their actions. What just happened to you is wrong.'

'Do the police care? I don't think they do.'

'I do, and yes, most police do too.'

Dorothy snorts derisively. 'People like me, people like my daughter . . . we're invisible in this world. Invisible until something happens. Until we open our mouths and create a fuss. And then we get noticed. Then we get punished. All I wanted was a refund. I was polite to that man because I know he has a mean streak. He was mean to my daughter and she is the sweetest girl. The world is a cruel place full of cruel people like him – like the police.' Dorothy takes out a scrunched-up paper hanky from her sleeve and wipes her eyes. 'That man refused to give me my money back and when I wouldn't leave he phoned the police and began throwing jewellery, his own jewellery, onto the floor. He was blaming me as he spoke to the police.'

Archer catches Quinn's eyes in the rear-view mirror. She has no doubt Dorothy's story is true and feels her anger rising but keeps it in check.

Dorothy continues, 'He was happy to take my money. Yet when I returned his broken necklace he got angry, even called me a fat black bitch for my trouble.'

'I'm so sorry, Dorothy.'

'And as you witnessed with your police colleagues, that's what happens to people like me.'

'Dorothy, I won't let them get away with this, I promise you. I will speak to Goddard tomorrow . . .'

'Forget about him. He is nothing.'

Archer places her hand on Dorothy's. 'I'm so sorry. I will see to it personally those two officers are disciplined.'

On the drive back to Charing Cross Archer's phone rings from its mount on the dashboard. The number displayed is the Charing Cross Police Station. She answers, pressing the device's speaker button.

'DI Archer,' she answers.

'Grace, it's Clare.'

Archer's boss, DCI Clare Pierce is a sharp, twenty-year veteran of the Metropolitan Police. Pierce is ambitious and has strong connections in the upper echelons of management, and in Whitehall too, which often makes Archer wonder if her future lies at the Home Office. She is a hands-off investigator, which suits Archer, so receiving a direct call from her is almost never a good sign.

Archer and Quinn exchange a cautious glance.

'Clare, how can I help?'

'We were supposed to have a meeting this morning.'

'We were?'

'Have you been checking your emails?'

'Not during my time off, Clare. Sorry.'

'I thought that might be the case. Where are you now?'

'We're ten minutes away from the station.'

'Good. I'll let HR know you're on your way.'

'HR?'

'Don't be late.'

Pierce ends the call.

'What was that about?' asks Quinn.

'No idea,' lies Archer. 'I guess I'll soon find out.'

4

BETH HARPER WAKES TO THE sound of footsteps. Curled in the foetal position and still groggy from an uneasy sleep, she stretches her arm across to Ethan's side of the bed, but it's cold and empty. Heaving herself up she focuses her eyes in the gloom and scans the shadowy room for him but neither sees nor hears him.

'Ethan?' she calls, shivering, but he doesn't respond. As her mind clears she recalls the night before. An argument. She rubs her forehead. 'Shit!'

The glowing red numbers on the digital clock read 10.39 a.m. The restless night has caused her to sleep late and the room is cold, the silence deafening, broken by the creak of her neighbours' floorboards in the flat above. She slips on her dressing gown, tightens the belt and pulls open the curtains to reveal a sunny winter morning. Padding barefoot into the hallway she can't help but feel an empty sensation that feels like bitter loneliness. She rubs her elbows, leans against the wall and reflects on their argument. She had only wanted to know why he was spending less time with her in their flat. It was a simple enough question and she had asked nicely.

'I'm here now,' he had replied, petulantly.

'But you're not here all the time.'

'So?'

'Where are you going?'

He'd swallowed the last of his lager and crumpled the can in his fist. 'I'm doing stuff.'

'What stuff?'

'Fuck sake, Beth, what is this?!' he'd snapped, without looking at her.

She had flinched at his tone but wasn't prepared to back down yet. 'Just tell me what's going on . . . is there someone else?'

Ethan's neck and face had flushed crimson and it was then that he flipped, calling her a whore, a bitch, a cunt and every other obscenity men throw at women. She had always known him to be quick-tempered but lately he seemed out of control. To her shame she had crumpled and cried. Ethan had sat on the sofa, clenching his fists, his angry face turned away from her. She had gone to the bathroom, fixed her make-up, returned to the living room and apologised but he'd remained tense and trembling and she wondered if he was using again. She prayed he wasn't and sat beside him, stroking his back and soothing him.

'There isn't anyone else. I promise,' he'd told her.

'I believe you,' she replied.

He became aroused then and looked at her the way he did when he wanted to do *it*. She swallowed, knowing what this meant, but relented. After all, she loved him.

They've been together for almost nineteen months, which these days is not bad going. In the beginning he'd been wonderful and couldn't get enough of her, but recently she'd noticed a change in him, as if his interest in her was waning. Also, he had asked her to do kinky stuff in bed that freaked her out. She had refused but he bitched at her to stop being so 'vanilla', which was hurtful. Eventually she told him she would think about it but he had to give her some time.

Last night she had given in to him again and let him have his way. Once he was finished, he fell asleep and had clearly left in the middle of the night without a word.

She presses her lips together.

'Why not leave some money on the bedside table? I might as well be your whore!' she says out loud.

Her boyfriend before Ethan was Mark. He was nice and couldn't do enough for her, but she found that relationship too stifling. Nice just didn't cut it for her. She wanted something more, someone different to the boy next door she usually ended up with. She wanted a man with an edge, and she had found it with Ethan. He was good-looking in a sulky, boyish way and people swarmed around him as if he was some sort of celebrity, but he only seemed to ever have eyes for her. He was clever, funny and sexy, like a younger Leonardo DiCaprio. He was also well aware of this and used it to his advantage. When she met him, she had realised how bored she was in her relationship with Mark and allowed herself to be wooed by Ethan. She dumped Mark and began a fling with Ethan, which later tumbled into a boyfriend/girlfriend thing.

Their relationship had been going well until the last two months or so when he'd started mixing with an old friend of his, Adrian Boyne, who she didn't like one bit. Adrian made his money selling drugs and she wonders if Ethan is doing the same.

She walks to the kitchen. As usual, it's untidy with a stack of dirty dishes that she hasn't had the chance to clear.

Beth washes up and puts the dishes and pots away. Finishing her breakfast, she showers and gets ready for the start of her late shift. She hears a knock at the flat door.

'Beth, Ethan? Are you there?' calls her upstairs neighbour from the communal hallway.

Beth fixes an earring into her lobe as she crosses the hallway. Opening the flat door, she sees her neighbours, Sid and Vera, standing in the doorway. Vera is a tiny woman, five foot high with pencilled brows arching over eyelids daubed with a garish blue eye shadow and thin lips painted bright pink; colours that would cause a stir on a clown, never mind a woman of her age. Sid is tall, almost six foot and smiles benignly at Beth.

'Hi, guys. How are you?'

'Good,' replies Vera. She looks up at Beth expectantly, clearly waiting on an invitation to enter.

'I'm just about to leave for work,' says Beth.

Vera waves her arm dismissively and pushes her way in. 'We'll only be a moment, dear.'

Beth grits her teeth. 'I'm really running late. How can I help you?'

Vera is smiling and looking around the flat. 'Ethan here?'

'No, he's gone.'

Vera's smile disappears. 'Oh, that's a shame. I was hoping to talk to him. I would have called, but what with his phone going missing and all . . .'

Ethan's car had been broken into last week. He'd only left it for a few minutes. When he came back the window was smashed and his coat containing his phone and wallet were gone.

'I know,' replies Beth. 'He doesn't have a replacement phone yet. I don't know why.'

'Probably because phones aren't allowed at the place he's been going.'

Beth stiffens and frowns. 'What place? Where is he going?'

'You know that friend of ours we introduced him to? The one in Lewisham?'

Beth has a vague memory of Vera mentioning they had a friend in Lewisham but had no idea that Ethan had been introduced to him. 'No, I didn't know that. What's this about? Who is this friend and what is Ethan doing with him?'

Vera looks at her husband. 'Sid, we need to shop and Beth needs to get to work. Let's go.'

Sid obediently turns and exits the flat followed by Vera.

'Wait! Tell me where Ethan is.'

Vera stops, turns and faces Beth. Her make-up cracks as she smiles. 'Nothing to worry about, dear. Ethan will tell you. All in good time. You get to work now and have a good day.'

'But—'

'Goodbye, dear,' says Vera as she bustles Sid down the stairs and out of the building.

Beth watches them go and wonders just what Ethan is up to.

5

QUINN PULLS UP AT THE entrance to Charing Cross Police Station courtyard. As the gates slowly draw open, Archer sees DI Hicks, PCs Keith Hopkins and Nathan Watts, and a woman she doesn't recognise chatting together and smoking. DI Hicks and Archer are not the best of friends. He had been a close pal of DI Andy Rees and had never forgiven Archer for what she had done to his friend.

'Can't say I'm surprised to see that lot chumming it up together,' comments Quinn.

The woman has returned inside the building and the three officers turn to look at Archer. Fleetingly, she meets Hicks's gaze as Quinn drives past.

She makes her way up to the third floor and crosses to Pierce's glass cube, where the DCI, dressed in her customary fitted designer black suit, sits at her meeting table opposite a slender woman with a finishing-school posture. It's the same woman who had just been talking to Hicks, Hopkins and Watts.

Pierce's large raptor eyes catch Archer's. She nods, beckoning her to come straight in.

'Take a seat, please, Grace. This is Debbie Dickson from Human Resources.'

'Hello,' says Archer.

Debbie Dickson smells of cigarette smoke and smiles, or at least, seems to. Archer can't quite be sure. She takes stock of the woman. Her highlighted hair is styled into a pixie cut, with a heavy side-parted fringe that drapes over one eye like a curtain. Her smile is, at best, a grimace.

'Shall we crack on then?' urges DCI Pierce, glancing at her wristwatch.

Debbie begins. Her voice is small, but clipped and sharp. 'I'll get straight to the point. We understand that you have not been participating in your therapy sessions with Dr Abigail Hutchison, DI Archer.'

'No. I have not,' replies Archer who knows there is no point in denying it.

'May I enquire why you have not done so?'

'I don't feel the need for therapy.'

'I see.' Debbie's eyes flit to Pierce and back to Archer. 'Well, Grace, that just will not do.'

Archer bristles but holds her tongue.

'Considering what you went through last November with the attempt on your life, we think it wise you talk to a counsellor.'

'I'd rather not. I've had experience with therapists when I was a teenager and it's not pleasant.'

'But that was then. This is now.'

Archer considers this for a moment before replying. 'That doesn't really make sense.'

Debbie purses her lips and looks to Pierce for support; the DCI nods for her to carry on.

'Dr Abigail Hutchison is renowned in her field. She deals with all our special cases.'

'I hadn't realised I was a special case.' Archer's tone is sharp.

'It's not something we normally tell people.'

'Then why tell me?'

Debbie grimaces and avoids the question. 'I'm sure Clare would agree with me that urgent action is needed on this matter.' The DCI opens her mouth, but before she can respond Debbie adds, 'Especially considering the recent complaints from colleagues about your attitude?'

Archer feels her muscles tighten. Had she been the topic of conversation between Hicks, Hopkins and Watts during their cigarette break?

'Why have I not been informed about this?' asks Pierce.

'I'm sorry I didn't tell you sooner, Clare. It's only just been brought to my attention.'

'Brought to your attention when?' Pierce demands.

'Today. Unfortunately, I have not had the time to dig deeper into these allegations.'

'What allegations, exactly?' asks Archer.

'Some colleagues have felt intimidated by your behaviour.'

'Oh, for God's sake!' mutters Pierce.

Archer feels her heart sink. She has worked hard all her career and never faced any problems like this before. But that all changed when she joined Charing Cross Police Station. One of the consequences of being involved in getting rid of the corrupt DI Rees is that she now has enemies working in close proximity. She looks out across the office and sees DI Hicks looking her way with a satisfied smirk on his face.

'OK, let's hear the allegations,' says Pierce.

'Perhaps Grace would like to wait outside, before we—'

'That won't be necessary,' interrupts Pierce.

'But—'

'Oh, for Christ's sake! Just get on with it,' snaps Archer, but instantly regrets her reaction.

Debbie Dickson flinches, blushes and an awkward silence fills the room.

'I'm not sure there is any need for that type of outburst,' the HR woman finally says.

Pierce interjects. 'Debbie, we are all very busy and we are horribly short on staff. Can we press on? Please.'

'As you wish. This morning DI Archer attended a crime scene that was already well controlled. Two uniformed police officers, who shall remain nameless—'

'PC Hopkins and PC Watts,' interrupts Archer.

Debbie's face tightens. ' . . . reported being humiliated by DI Archer whilst trying to do their duty.'

'They were manhandling a middle-aged NHS worker, an unarmed woman of colour,' Archer says sharply. 'Yes, let me repeat, woman of colour, as if she were a dangerous criminal. She was clearly racially profiled and our boys in blue were unnecessarily violent, Debbie! How embarrassing will that be for the Met, considering it was filmed by several members of the public and I have no doubt is now online for all to see.'

Debbie sits rigid, jaw clenched. 'That's not what I was told.'

'Debbie,' says Pierce. 'If our male uniforms cannot show even a modicum of respect for women and people of colour, then we have a serious problem. Don't you think?'

'We already have a systemic problem with misogyny and racism,' adds Archer.

The HR Manager's eyes flare and Archer continues, 'That aside, I was not disrespectful to anyone.'

Debbie's lips thin. 'It was reported that you were aggressive and unnecessarily angry.'

Archer sighs and shakes her head.

'As a result, one of the officers is considering taking time off with stress rela—'

'You can't be serious!'

'I'm very serious, DI Archer. Our officers have enough to deal with already, without being humiliated in public by senior officers.'

'Check the online footage, Deb. It'll open your eyes.'

Debbie opens her mouth to speak but Pierce interjects, 'I can guarantee you, Debbie, Grace will ensure this will not happen again.'

Debbie's lips part in an insincere smile. 'Of course. In the meantime, Grace, I would suggest, with Clare's support, you begin your therapy with Dr Hutchison. Dr Hutchison can help you with your outbursts and any PTSD you might be experiencing.'

Archer meets Pierce's gaze. The DCI shakes her head furtively. Archer remains silent and is reminded of the increase in nightmares and sleepless nights she has had.

'Maybe it would be wise to put DI Archer on light duties until her therapy has—'

'No!' Pierce's voice is curt. 'I'm afraid that's out of the question as we're so short-staffed.' The DCI stands. 'Thank you, Debbie. I understand you are busy so let's say farewell for now.'

Debbie Dickson bites her lip then draws her head up. 'Of course. Should Grace's role change, do let me know and I will update her file.'

Pierce flashes a humourless smile and opens the office door.

'Naturally. Goodbye.' Debbie turns to leave, but stops and looks back. 'I forgot to mention, Grace, your first appointment with Dr Hutchison is on Wednesday at 4 p.m. Don't be late.'

Archer bites her tongue.

'You have Dr Hutchison's details. I'll email you your list of other appointments, Grace.'

'Very generous. Before you go, Debbie, I want you to know I'll be filing a complaint against Hopkins and Watts. You'll be hearing from me shortly – and you might not want to mention that to them when you're next having a quick ciggie out the back.'

The HR Manager's face reddens.

'Bye, Debbie,' says Pierce as she closes the glass door behind the HR Manager then turns to Archer. 'Debbie Dickson is an officious idiot,' Pierce sighs. 'That said, I do need you to start therapy. I don't want the weight of HR on my case confining you to non-operational duties.'

Archer knows she has no choice. 'I'll attend. I promise.'

'Dr Hutchison is one of the best, and a friend. We don't always get people of her level to support us.'

'Only "special cases"?'

'It's because I insisted on it, if you must know. If Debbie Dickson had her way you'd be taking a call with a psychology graduate.'

'I'm sorry, Clare. I didn't realise. I appreciate your care and support.'

'It's not easy asking for help – and it's even harder taking that first step to opening up in front of a stranger.' Pierce sits behind her desk and steeples her hands together. 'Trust me, I know.'

Pierce is a tough, uncompromising DCI and Archer wonders what she has experienced that would cause her to seek counselling support and hint, to Archer of all people, that she had been damaged.

'I'll be there on Wednesday.'

Pierce nods. 'Close the door on your way out, please.'

6

BRIAN BAILEY SITS ON THE end of the flowery blue sofa unaware that he is bouncing his knee up and down. He half watches the tedious shopping channel his wife Linda insists on viewing every week. The space between them is like a cold chasm. Linda is perched on the opposite end of the sofa like a stuffed owl, her knitting needles clicking like drumsticks.

He hears the show's presenters laugh and on cue Linda follows suit, choking out a dry cackle.

Brian mutters under his breath and in his peripheral vision sees her turn to look at him.

'What was that, dear?' she asks.

'Nothing, erm . . . nothing.'

'I do so wish you would stop doing that.'

He blinks and looks at her. 'Stop doing what?'

'That thing with your knee. It's really annoying.'

He stops bouncing his knee and folds his arms. Linda didn't often speak out of turn. Perhaps she senses his swelling impatience. 'Yes dear, sorry,' he replies.

The show breaks for a commercial.

Linda says, 'That was ever so funny. I do so love those two boys. They make me laugh out loud, they do.'

'You know I'm not much into that sort of thing.'

A pained expression flashes on his wife's face and for a brief moment he regrets expressing his opinion. She sets her knitting down in the space between them and pushes herself to the edge of the sofa. 'Well, I'm sorry, Brian. I don't have many pleasures in life, especially since the girls left home . . .'

'I know. I'm sorry.'

She shakes her head. 'No matter . . . Shall I make us a nice cup of tea?' she asks without looking at him.

An idea takes seed in his mind. 'Let me make it.'

Linda looks at him and beams brightly. 'Oh, that would be nice, thank you. I bought your favourite Bourbon creams today. We'll have some with our tea, shall we?'

'Of course,' he replies, furtively tapping his phone in his trouser pocket.

He forces a smile as he leaves the room and enters the kitchen across the unlit hallway. Filling the Russell Hobbs kettle with water, he peers through the window and sees what he thinks is a dark, hooded figure facing him. He stiffens, narrows his gaze and blinks but all he can see is his reflection in the glass. Shaking his head, he turns away and with one eye on the living room door, takes his mobile phone and chooses the ring tone option from the device's *Settings*. Edging towards the kitchen door, he plays the ring tone loud so that she can hear it.

'Oh, what now!' he says in a peeved tone.

'Who on earth is phoning at this time?' calls Linda. 'It's not one of the girls, is it?' she adds with concern in her voice.

'It's the office,' lies Brian.

'What do they want?'

He puts the phone to his ear. 'Brian Bailey,' he says, entering the living room and rubbing his neck. 'Hi, John, how can I help?'

'Who's John?' mouths a puzzled Linda.

He feigns an irritated expression and continues with his ruse. 'Oh no ... did you try and reboot it? ... I see ... What did Nigel say? ... He's gone home sick? ... I see, OK.' He sighs. 'Damn it, I'll have to come in ... No, it's no problem ...' Brian makes a sad face at his wife and shrugs. 'OK, John. I'll be there in thirty minutes tops. See you then. Bye-bye.'

'What's going on and who's John?' asks Linda.

'He's an intern, and thanks to Nigel clearing off home on the sick, John is on his own right now and one of our main servers has gone down. Looks serious. I need to go in straight away.'

'Oh, for pity's sake! It's late. Can't it wait until tomorrow?'

'I'm afraid not. That server processes all our donations. The charity could lose thousands,' he replies, marvelling at his ability to lie so blatantly.

Linda's shoulders slump. 'Oh, I suppose you'd better go then.'

'Don't wait up.' He leans across to kiss her goodbye. She purses her pale lips, but he diverts and pecks her cheek.

'What time will you be back?'

'Could be one hour, could be six. Who knows? I'll text you.'

From the cloakroom under the stairs, Brian pulls on his grey wool overcoat and grabs his car keys from the hall table. He shouts a final goodbye and hurries out the front door and into the chilly night. With a spring in his step, he hurries down to the roadside where his Ford Mondeo is parked. He hears footfalls close by and stops to look. His eyes scan the front garden and quiet street but he sees no one. Shrugging, he climbs into his car and starts up the engine. He turns up the heating and switches on Classic FM. As the windows demist, he places his palm close to his mouth and breathes on it to check his breath. It'll do.

With a tremor of excitement, Brian drives away from Linda and his 1930s semi.

Brian drives at a steady pace through the thin traffic on the A23 through London and almost thirty minutes later the towering white chimneys of Battersea Power Station loom on the skyline ahead. He drives by Battersea Park, glancing across at the main entrance where he sees a couple sharing a cigarette enter the park. He turns onto Prince of Wales Drive and looks for a parking space, indicating left when he sees the perfect spot in between a Mini Cooper and a red BMW coupe.

After a quick reverse park, he removes a pair of gloves from the glovebox, climbs out of the car and straightens his coat, acting natural, as if he is local. Pulling on the gloves, he starts to make his way across the road but halts when he sees a car approaching. He notices the driver's face is partially covered and that his eyes seem to stare directly back into his. Brian blushes, averts his gaze and waits for the car to pass. He wonders if the driver can see through him and knows why he is here. He swallows and for an instant thinks he might just go back home to Linda, but decides he's just being paranoid, as always. Pushing the doubts from his head, he crosses the road and enters the park via the small side gate.

The park is dark and full of shadows but it feels good to be here. There are trees on either side of the pathway and the excitement of the hunt surges through him as he moves cautiously through the thick of the timber, waiting, watching. Around him he hears the tread of quiet feet. The blood pounds in his ears and he sniffs the air but all he smells is the acrid stench of weed and cheap beer. Through the shrubs he sees the couple he saw at entrance earlier, sitting huddled together at the edge of the boating lake.

He backs into the shadows and heads deeper into the woods. Ten minutes pass and he stops at the perimeter near another pathway. A man is walking down it, his eyes scanning the area. He is young, not as young as Brian'd like, but beggars can't be choosers.

He emerges from the trees, startling the younger man.

Their eyes lock and Brian feels a tingling all over. Here is a kind of courtship, a discreet yet public mating ritual flecked with cautious signals and gestures, one that he is all too familiar with. Brian nods at the man and retreats into the shadows. The younger man hesitates, shifts uncomfortably on his feet and glances around to see if anyone is watching. There is no one.

Brian leads him through the uneven surface, weaving in and out of the bushes and flora to a sheltered clearing carpeted in moist woodchip. He feels himself hardening as he makes his way to the centre among the narrow beams of moonlight from the twisted bones of the branches overhead. He feels a sudden sharp pain in his toes and yelps.

'What is it?' asks the young man, nervously.

Brian looks down to see a jagged rock protruding out of the woodchip. 'It's nothing. I just banged my foot. That's all.'

The young man stands at edge of the clearing. He seems uncertain.

41

Brian gives him a reassuring smile and beckons him inside. After a moment he steps into the clearing, glancing behind him with a worried expression.

'I'm sure someone was following me.'

'Sometimes people like to watch.'

They are inches apart.

'What's your name?' asks Brian.

The younger man frowns. 'Who cares?'

Brian shrugs. 'Shall we start?' he says, licks his lips and leans forward to kiss him, but the man frowns and steps back.

'No kissing. I'm not into that.'

'What do you want to do then?'

'Just suck me off. Nothing else.'

Brian smiles and drops to his knees. 'Fine by me.'

The man's hands grip the sides of Brian's head in preparation.

Brian tries to unbutton his jeans, but his gloved hands make it awkward.

'Hurry up,' says the young man.

Brian slips off his gloves and begins loosening the buttons of the man's jeans. He hears the sound of a twig cracking but ignores it. Pulling down the man's trousers, he leans forward and takes him in his mouth. The young man jolts suddenly and wrenches his cock from Brian's mouth.

'What the fuck?' cries Brian.

He hears a thudding sound and looks across to see the man lying on the ground. 'What are you playing at?' he asks, but the man is still and does not respond.

'Brian Bailey,' says a cold breathy voice.

Brian jumps and turns to see a figure dressed in a dirty old parka with the hood zipped all the way up, hiding the face inside. He feels his spine ice over. 'I—I should really be going now.' He tries to stand but the man in the parka leans over, squeezes his neck and growls. 'Sit back down, Brian.'

Brian swallows and sits on the damp woodchip.

'Jesus loved you. Once.'

Brian feels his body shuddering all over. 'I-I'm not the person you think I am . . .'

The man removes something from his coat pocket and tosses it at Brian's feet. A mobile phone. 'Phone him.'

'I don't know who you want me to phone. I'm not that Brian Bailey. You're mistaken.'

The man circles behind him, crouches down and presses a scalpel into Brian's neck. 'Phone him,' he hisses.

'But . . .!'

'Do it!'

'OK, OK.' Shaking, he struggles to recall the number and somehow manages to. He presses the numbers on the keypad and dials.

'Put the call onto speaker.'

Brian does as he is instructed and they listen as the phone rings three times before being picked up. There is no greeting, only breathing followed by, 'Who is this?'

Brian's heart pounds. 'You promised me!'

'Brian?'

His assailant begins to remove one of Brian's shoes and tears the sock from his foot. Brian tries to crawl away but feels a hard blow to his temple which causes him to drop the phone. His head spins; his stomach is in knots and his chest begins to heave in sobs. 'I don't want to die!' he cries.

The man straddles him and shoves the sock roughly into his mouth and tapes it over with duct tape. From his pocket he removes what looks like a nasal spray bottle. He inserts it into

Brian's nostrils, squirts a powder inside and blocks his nose with his thumbs. 'Breathe,' he commands.

Brian shakes his head and trembles. He cannot breathe! The man releases his thumbs. Brian is desperate for air and has no choice but to inhale the powder.

Within minutes, Brian feels his head swimming. He blinks losing focus and after a moment sees something sharp and silver close to his eye. He tries to scream through his gag for someone, anyone to help. He feels the small knife press into his skin and squeezes his eyes shut. 'Noooo, preazze,' he tries to say, but his body is beginning to numb and feel heavy.

'See no evil, Brian.'

He feels the blade sink into and cut through the soft flesh around his eye. Confusion clouds his mind and then everything goes dark.

7

ARCHER AND QUINN ARE DRIVING to Battersea Park early on Tuesday morning following up on a call from a police officer, Jimmy Barnes, and a 999 call from the park-keeper.

'Jimmy said there are two bodies in a grim state.'

'Do we have ID?'

'Nothing yet.'

'What's with the tip?'

'Jimmy and I are buddies. He called me because he thought we might be better suited to this case after the @nonymous murders.'

'That doesn't bode well for what lies ahead.'

'My thoughts exactly.'

Quinn drives through the main entrance of the park on a road with sluggish morning joggers clogging the route. He revs his engine, and like a flock of startled pigeons, the runners begin to part.

Up ahead Archer can see the response car and, beside it, a sturdy uniformed officer with salt-and-pepper hair, who seems familiar. He is talking with a pot-bellied man dressed in the khaki outdoor clothing of a park-keeper. A second officer is sealing off an area of trees and bushes with police tape.

Quinn pulls over.

'Hey, Jimmy,' Quinn greets the officer. 'Grace, this is Sergeant Jimmy Barnes.'

'I think we may have met,' says Archer.

He smiles. 'That was a long time back and you were very young. I'm surprised you remember. I worked with your father for a time, just before he passed. He was a good man.'

'He was. Thank you.'

Barnes gestures to the man in khakis. 'Ma'am, this is Harold Richardson, the assistant head park-keeper.'

'I understand you found the bodies, Mr Richardson?'

'Yeah. I was passing by and thought I heard a phone ringing. I could hear crows squawking from the bushes and thought it wasn't a phone, it was the bloody birds. But then I heard it ringing again. I was certain it was coming from inside them bushes. I called "Hello" but no one answered. The phone continued to ring so I went to have a look, thinking someone had dropped it . . .' The park-keeper shudders and points to the bushes. 'Never seen anything like it in all my born days. Lying in there, they is . . .'

'Can you tell me what time you found them?'

'Around 7. I usually do my rounds of the park at that time, checking what I can before people arrive.'

'And did you see anyone else?'

'Just the usual joggers. No one suspicious, like.'

The second uniform cop joins them, a younger man with generously gelled spiky blond hair. Archer notices his face is drawn and pale.

Barnes turns to him. 'Radio for a local beat officer or two, Wayne. We need an extra pair of hands to keep the people away.'

'Will do, Jimmy.'

'Poor lad. It's his first week on the job and that scene has shaken him up.'

'He'll get used to it,' says Quinn.

'You might change your mind when you see what's in there.'

Archer looks towards where the park-keeper had pointed. 'Mr Richardson, can I ask what route you followed that took you to the bodies?'

He points to a growth of bushes behind the police tape. 'Just there.'

'We also took that route with Mr Richardson when we arrived,' adds Barnes.

'Thank you, Mr Richardson. We may need to talk to you again.'

'I have his contact details, ma'am,' says Barnes. 'I've also taken the liberty of calling in the CSI team. They gave an ETA of thirty minutes.'

Archer nods a thanks and looks back at the park-keeper. 'Not a word about this to anyone, Mr Richardson.'

'Not a word,' he repeats, tapping his nose.

As the park-keeper leaves to carry on his duties, Barnes says, 'I've never seen anything like it. It's just bizarre.'

'Has anyone reported anything suspicious?' asks Archer.

'Nothing yet, ma'am. We were waiting on some more officers before we do a door-to-door.'

'I can sort that out, if you and your partner keep people away,' replies Archer.

'We can do that.'

As the two officers watch over the site, Archer and Quinn suit up in PPE and grab a torch and evidence collection supply bag from the boot of the car. They make the short trip along the same route that Barnes and Richardson had taken through the shrubs and bushes to avoid decontamination of any other possible access points. It leads to a gloomy clearing sheltered by trees with their overhead skeletal branches. The ground is covered in thick moist woodchip and lying in the centre of it is a man with his trousers around his ankles. Archer looks towards the second man, who is further away in the shadows and points the torch beam. The second victim is lying on his back with his feet resting against the trunk of the tree. One of his feet is bare and his arms are outstretched. His throat has been cut and his eyes have been cut from their sockets, leaving two golf-ball-sized black holes. An inverted crucifix has been carved down the middle of his face and across his mouth and cheeks. In each of his outstretched hands sits an eyeball. Archer notices a clump of duct tape and what looks like the man's missing sock lying on the ground nearby.

'Jesus Christ!' exclaims Quinn.

Archer is thankful for the cold morning. On a warmer day the smell of blood and death in this confined, sheltered space would be horrific to deal with. She treads cautiously back towards the first corpse. He is wearing a blue blazer with a jumper underneath and his head is resting on a jagged rock protruding from the woodchip.

'Looks like he fell over and hit his head on the rock,' says Quinn.

Archer points to the other side of his head where his hair is matted and clotted with dried blood. 'Or someone clubbed him, he fell over and hit his head on the rock.'

'He's young. Looks to be in his early twenties,' says Quinn.

Archer notices a wallet poking out from the man's trouser pocket. She takes it out and opens it up. Inside are two credit cards, one debit card, a faded ID card and forty pounds in cash.

'Not a robbery then,' observes Quinn.

'It would appear not.'

Archer slides out the bank cards and ID card. 'His name is Justin Sykes. He works for Grafton's.'

Quinn crouches beside her and leans in to look at the ID card. 'They're a recruitment company. Finance, I think.'

Archer studies the grainy digital mugshot. 'It's definitely him.'

Placing the cards carefully back inside the wallet, she hands it to Quinn who inserts it into a plastic evidence bag.

She shines the beam on the dead man's face and head. 'No other cuts or bruises . . .' She points the light to his hands and wrists, which are also clear. Leaning in closer she sees something between the index finger and middle finger of his right hand. A hair, darker and longer than the hair on his head. Quinn fishes tweezers from the evidence supply bag and hands them across.

She glances across at the second corpse. 'Same colour as his friend's.'

'Looks like someone interrupted their playtime.'

Archer should, in theory, wait for the CSI team but she doesn't want to risk a sudden downpour of harsh winter rain compromising evidence. Quinn gives her a small plastic bag to store the strand.

She notices a phone, poking out from the side pocket of the dead man's blazer and eases it free. Pressing the screen, it lights up and reveals two text messages from someone called Joel Dean. There are also three missed calls from Dean and two from his mum.

Archer hands the bagged phone to Quinn and points the beam on the ground around the body, shining it near the dead man's feet. There are indents and copious amounts of dried blood in the woodchip leading across to the tree.

'He was murdered here at this spot and dragged to the tree,' says Archer.

They edge closer to the second victim and crouch down.

'Fuck,' whispers Quinn.

He is in his mid to late forties with a slim build and receding dark hair.

'Whoever did this really had it in for this bloke,' says Quinn.

Archer holds her gaze over the man's bloody hands. 'Look how his hands are tilted so that the eyes are looking back at his face.'

'Creepy. What do you think that means?'

'I don't know . . . yet.' Archer cocks her head and looks at the dead man's nose. 'Powder.'

'Cocaine?'

'Possibly.'

'The plot thickens.'

'He's wearing a wedding ring.'

Archer narrows her gaze at the blood-caked band on his wedding finger.

'Look,' says Quinn, pointing at the dead man's feet.

Archer points the beam and sees a broken Samsung smartphone with a cracked screen etched with dried blood and mud. She takes out her own phone, opens the camera app and snaps a picture. 'There's a pattern there. Could be the sole of a trainer,' she says.

'Aye, looks like the killer stamped it with his foot,' says Quinn. 'Was the victim phoning for help?'

Archer turns to look at Justin Sykes and then back at the eyeless man. 'Could be. I'd take a wild guess and say this guy was the target.'

'Jealous lover?'

'If so, then a *twisted* jealous lover who has a thing for eyes.'

'Perhaps Justin Sykes was in the wrong place at the wrong time.'

'Perhaps ...'

Archer leans across and carefully searches through the man's pockets and finds his wallet. Inside are credit cards with the name Brian Bailey. Among them is his driving licence. 'He lives in Norton Gardens in Norbury.'

After placing the cards back in the wallet, Quinn holds open a plastic evidence bag and Archer drops it inside. She then takes a picture of the eyeless man's face, steps back to take a second of his full body, followed by two shots of Justin Sykes. She then points the torch beam east across the clearing and sees a row of small, leafless bushes crushed and trampled forward. Looking back at where she and Quinn entered the scene, she regards their foot impressions, including the park-keeper's and Barnes'. She points the beam over the ground and sees splodges of blood on the woodchip. She follows the trail and sees a third and a fourth, leading out of the clearing. 'The killer left with blood on their shoe.'

From the bushes and the direction she and Quinn had entered the clearing, Archer hears a man and a woman talking and then laughing. She recognises Krish's voice.

Krish Anand is a Crime Scene Manager. Archer and Quinn had worked briefly with him three months back during the @nonymous murders. They had formed a good working relationship, which Archer is keen to grow.

Krish arrives, accompanied by a female colleague; both are suited in PPE and carrying large nylon bags.

'Krish!' says Quinn. 'Nice to see you dressed for the occasion.'

'I like to make the effort,' he replies.

'Hey, Krish,' says Archer.

'DI Archer. Nice to see you again.'

The CSI gestures to his colleague, a blonde woman in her early thirties with delicate features and intense eyes. 'This is MJ, my second in command and our next big rising star,' he beams.

'Nice to meet you, MJ,' says Archer.

'Likewise.' She turns to look at Quinn and smiles, demurely. 'Hello again, Harry.'

'MJ.'

An amused Archer looks quizzically from MJ to Quinn and wonders just how well they know each other.

Krish speaks. 'We were just talking to Jimmy Barn—' He stops abruptly, his gaze turning to the victims and lingering on the eyeless man. 'Wow! Jimmy said to be prepared, but I was not expecting this.'

'It's pretty grim,' says Quinn.

MJ pulls the hood over her head, tucking back her hair.

'So, what are your thoughts?' asks Krish.

'We're keeping an open mind for now. Could be a jealous lover, or the eyeless victim was a target and his companion got in the way.'

'Could be targets of a gay killer?' offers Krish.

'That's entirely possible,' replies Archer.

MJ makes her way across to the eyeless man, sets down her nylon bag and crouches beside him. 'This has an almost ritualistic feel about it. It's a kind of crucifixion.'

'Not a random kill, then?' asks Quinn.

'I doubt it. The killer clearly has skill with a knife. Those eyeholes are perfectly cut.'

'The inverted cross on the face,' says Krish. 'Could be satanic.'

'It could be the Petrine Cross,' says Archer.

'The Cross of St Peter? It could well be,' Quinn agrees as he hands across the evidence bags to Krish. 'This wallet we found inside the left breast pocket of the younger man. His name is Justin Sykes. He had a dark strand of hair on right hand between index finger and middle finger. May belong to the second victim. Sykes' phone was in his right trouser pocket. This Samsung belongs to the second victim. His name is Brian Bailey. It's clearly dead and we assume broken by the killer. I'd like to know what data is on there.'

'We'll get Digital Forensics to check that out for you. My team will be here any moment.'

'We'll get out of your way then,' says Archer.

'Thanks. I'll be in touch with what I find.'

'Thank you, Krish.'

'No slackin' on this one, Krish,' says Quinn with a wink.

Krish rolls his eyes. 'Get out of here.'

'Bye, MJ,' says Quinn.

'Bye,' she replies without looking up.

As they make their way back through the shrubs and bushes, Archer turns to Quinn. 'So she's the mystery woman you've been dating.'

'Grace, if you don't mind me saying you'd make a great detective.'

Archer smiles. 'One day perhaps. What's she like?'

'Early days yet but going good so far. I met her through Krish at the pub about a month ago.'

'Good.'

Quinn nods across the grass at a shiny black motorcycle parked by their car. 'Her wheels.'

'That's sexy.'

'Yeah. I thought so too.'

Archer sees Sergeant Barnes' partner standing guard at the other side of the police tape. He looks their way and nods. Quinn walks to the car and Archer pulls back the hood of her PPE and talks to the young officer. 'It's Wayne, isn't it?'

'Yes, ma'am. PC Wayne Bickley.'

Archer can hear a soft Northern lilt in his voice. 'Is that a Geordie accent?'

'It is, ma'am.'

'What brought you down to London?'

'I've always dreamt of coming to the big smoke. Never thought it would happen, but here I am.'

Archer unzips the paper overall and steps out of it. 'It's never easy seeing murder victims.'

Bickley rubs his neck. 'No, ma'am. You hear about murders but you just don't expect anything like that.'

'I'm sorry you had to see it. But you'll adapt and it will become easier.'

Bickley regards her and considers her words. 'That's what I'm afraid of.'

Archer notices Quinn walking from the car towards her. He is carrying her coat. She folds up the paper suit and shivers in the cold morning air.

'I'll be fine, ma'am, but I do appreciate your kind words.'

'Good luck to you, Wayne.'

He smiles warmly. 'Thank you.'

8

As Archer pulls on her coat she puts in a call for assistance and talks to DS Joely Tozer. Archer brings her up to date and asks her to gather whoever she can for a door-to-door of the surrounding area. She also asks her to organise two Family Liaison officers to meet her and Quinn at Brian Bailey's address.

'I want to ensure Mrs Bailey gets the right support from the Met at this difficult time.'

'I'll get that organised.'

'Thanks, Joely, and keep me up to date with anything.'

'Will do.'

Archer ends the call and after waving goodbye to Jimmy Barnes and PC Wayne Bickley, she and Quinn leave Battersea Park.

Quinn drives and Archer makes a second call, this time to Klara at Charing Cross Police Station. Klara Clark is a colleague and friend from Archer's years working at the National Crime Agency. She had started at the Met last week during Archer's time off, transferring from the NCA after the retirement of Archer's ex-boss, Charlie Bates. Bates had been a mentor and father figure for both of them, but his retirement had put the analyst in a difficult position with the new governor, who did not much like her 'sort'. It had not been proven, but it was rumoured that he'd said that he had no time for: 'fucking blokes that were now birds, however good they was at their job'. Archer had a word with DCI Pierce, who had taken a shine to Klara after the key role she'd played in the @nonymous investigation, and had no hesitation recruiting the analyst to her team in the Met. In Archer's opinion, Klara has no equal. A former child prodigy, she is a technical genius with the ability to understand criminal data like a fortune teller.

The phone picks up. 'Os here, criminal data engineer, state yo' business loud and clear,' sings Os Pike in what sounds like an amateur rap. Os, or Pikey, as he is known to his colleagues and mates, is a junior analyst on Archer's team. He is competent and keen to grow in his role, but in Archer's opinion still has a way to go.

'Good morning, Os!'

'Oh God! Ma'am . . . good morning . . . sorry, I was expecting a call from someone else.'

'What's a criminal data engineer?' she asks.

Quinn glances her way with one eyebrow arched.

'Erm, just a title for my rap . . . Erm, how was your break?'

'It was good, thank you. Is Klara there?'

'No, she has Met new-starter induction training today. Lucky Klara!'

'OK. I need some help from *you* in that case. Quinn and I were called to the scene of a double murder this morning and I need you to build me a profile on the victims.'

'Sure, absolutely.'

'Have you got something to write on?'

'One moment . . . yes. Fire away, ma'am.'

'The first victim's name is Justin Sykes. In his twenties, possibly lives in the Battersea area. Check the police DB obviously for any info and then check social media. Look at his Facebook, Instagram, Twitter, LinkedIn. What is his personality, habits, friends, where does he drink, eat, etc. Also check the name Joel Dean and what his connection is to Justin. The second victim is Brian Bailey from Norton Gardens, Norbury. Same checks for him. We'll be back at the station in thirty minutes depending on the traffic. We'll catch up then.'

'Yes, ma'am. Oh, one last thing. Someone just called and asked to speak to you urgently.'

'Who?'

'A Mal Jones. I said you were busy and to email me and I'd send it on.'

'Great. Thanks, Os.'

'I'll send it now.'

'Cheers.'

'Bye.'

'What's a criminal data engineer?' asks Quinn.

'No idea.'

'Sorry, I forgot to mention Klara is out today.'

'No worries.'

Archer's phone pings with Os's message containing an email from Mal Jones. She opens it.

Dear Detective Inspector Archer, Mal Jones here from the *Mal Jones Investigates* true crime podcast. Perhaps you've heard of it? I was wondering if we could meet

and talk? Cutting to the chase, during my research
I've come across some information to do with Bernard
Morrice that I'd like to share with you . . .

Archer swears under her breath and deletes the email
without reading on.

'Everything OK?' asks Quinn.

'Just some bullshit, that's all.'

The morning traffic is heavy and it takes the best part of an
hour to return to Charing Cross Police Station. Quinn parks
in Chandos Place on a vacant space outside a Mexican
restaurant. As they leave the car and enter the station, they pass
through the four sturdy columns that support the Corinthian
capitals, the same ones her father walked through every day
during his tenure as a DI. Archer gets a sense of her father's
presence. This isn't the first time, and although she is not the
superstitious type, she does feel the same reassurance that he
always managed to give her.

They make their way up the stairs to the third floor where
Archer and her team are based. The space is modern and
open plan with rows of computer monitors lighting up the
desks.

'How's it going, Os?' asks Archer.

'Hi, ma'am, Harry. Right, so Brian Bailey's wife, Linda,
phoned the police in the early hours and reported him missing.
She said she woke up around two and realised he wasn't in
bed. She phoned his mobile phone, and when that didn't pick
up, she dialled his office. One of the night workers answered
and told her that Brian had not come to the office.'

'Good. What else have you got?'

'Brian Bailey is forty-four, he and his wife have two teenage daughters. He doesn't have a social media presence, although I found him through Google. He is an IT manager who works for a Children's Charity called the Pogo Foundation, in Canary Wharf.'

'Great. Thanks, Os. And Justin Sykes?'

'Justin Robert Sykes of Rowena Crescent, originally from Reading. His parents still live there. Moved to Battersea three years ago. Shares a house with Tyler Green. Justin's gay and in a relationship with a Joel Dean, ten years older than him. I'd hazard a guess and say they had an open relationship.'

'What makes you think that?' asks Archer.

'Looking at their Facebook timelines they have been together for two years, yet both of their relationship statuses are specified as single. That said, from Joel Dean's Facebook especially, you could come to the conclusion that he is a single-ready-to-mingle gent. I'll show you what I mean.'

Os pages through several pictures depicting a bare-chested Joel Dean kissing different men at a club called the Horsemeat Disco.

Archer speaks. 'It seems likely Justin was cruising in Battersea Park when he was murdered. Their open relationship would tally with that.'

'Look at this.' Os plays a short video from the club. It shows Joel Dean with his tongue out at the camera. On his tongue is a pill. He turns to embrace another man and inserts his tongue in the man's mouth. The second man kisses him and swallows the pill. 'Job done!' Joel shouts at the camera, affecting a shaka 'hang loose' gesture with his hand.

'He's a dealer with "benefits",' jokes Quinn.

'There's something else about Joel,' says Os. 'I thought I'd look him up in our DB, just in case. He's been in trouble over the years.'

'For what?'

'Drug offences and GBH, apparently.'

'Dealing?'

'Pills, coke, weed, that sort of thing.'

'And the GBH?'

'He beat up an ex-partner, pulled a knife on him and threatened to kill him.'

'Our first suspect,' says Archer.

'We should pay him a visit,' confirms Quinn.

'I'll send you his address,' says Os.

'Thanks. After that we'll go see Mrs Bailey,' says Archer.

Archer turns to Quinn. 'I'm going to put a call into Thames Valley Police. Someone will need to visit Justin Sykes' parents. Harry, could you find out whatever you can about Joel Dean's ex-partner and that GHB incident?'

'On it now.'

9

ARCHER HAS TAKEN OVER THE driving of the unmarked Volvo and is mulling over Quinn's rundown of his conversation with Joel Dean's ex-partner, the victim of his GBH assault, an estate agent from Kensington called Adam Fry. Fry was apparently surprised to be called by the police for a private incident that he'd not given any thought to in years.

Quinn had reassured him there was nothing to be concerned about. Fry had been reluctant to share any details until Quinn requested that he come to the station immediately and bluffed him by saying he could send a response car to pick him up to speed things up, *thank you very much*. That had pressed Fry's panic button. Fry took the call to a private room in his '*place of work*' and opened up. He told Quinn that he and Dean had done a lot of drugs and alcohol together. Too much for two people with fiery personalities. The evening in question had been full on with emotions heightened by drugs and booze. To his regret it had ended with police involvement and he'd wished it hadn't. The whole affair was as much his fault as Dean's. Quinn had thanked him for his help and updated Archer, who was not yet ready to exclude Dean from the suspect list.

It's almost midday when Archer and Quinn arrive at Chiswick High Road and Mortlake House, an unprepossessing high-rise block situated behind an equally unprepossessing Halfords store. Archer glances at the note paper containing Joel Dean's flat number and rings the intercom button.

After a moment, she rings a second time, but still there is no response.

She presses the number next to his and waits.

A voice crackles on the speaker. 'Yes?' asks a woman.

'Hi, I'm looking for Joel Dean . . .?'

'You have the wrong flat. Press twenty-two.'

'There's no response.'

'Why are you asking me then?' she replies with an indignant note. 'I'm not his keeper.'

'My name is Detective Inspector Grace Archer. I'd like to talk to him.'

'If he's not answering that's probably a good indication he's not at home.'

The woman's sass grates on Archer.

'Perhaps you've seen him?'

'Why would I have seen him? I keep myself to myself. I don't spy on my neighbours.'

'Was he at home last night?'

'How would I know?'

Archer feels a gentle nudge from Quinn and sees him looking intently at a blue van parking up inside the residents' car park. The driver has short dark hair and a beard.

'That's him,' says Quinn.

The irritated neighbour mutters something indecipherable. The intercom makes a hissing and squawking sound before the connection is cut.

They watch the driver step out of the van. Archer recognises him from the Facebook profile Os had shown them earlier. He is a broad man, around five foot eleven, muscular with a paunch. He is wearing a washed-out navy polo shirt, heavy duty paint-spattered work trousers and battered black boots. A roll-up cigarette hangs from his lips. He lights it up, pulls an overcoat from the van and puts it on. He takes a phone from the pocket of his coat, scrolls through the contents of the screen and pockets it.

Walking towards the front entrance, he exhales a plume of blue smoke and nods a greeting at Archer and Quinn.

'Joel Dean?' asks Archer.

His eyes scan them for a moment before he asks, 'How can I help you?' He has a Northern accent. Mancunian.

Archer shows her ID. 'Detective Inspector Archer and this is Detective Sergeant Quinn.'

Dean drops the cigarette to the ground and extinguishes the remains with the sole of his boot. 'I'm all up to date with my parking fines,' he says.

'We'd like to talk to you about Justin Sykes.'

Dean frowns. 'What about him?'

'Can we go inside?'

Dean shakes his head and almost laughs. 'He's been caught, hasn't he? That's why he wasn't answering my calls or messages. Bloody idiot! I warned him. But he wouldn't listen.'

'What do you mean by "he's been caught"?' asks Archer.

Dean opens the front entrance with an electronic key fob. 'He has light fingers. Can't help himself. He's got away with it for years. So now he's been caught and he wants me to sort his shit out for him before his precious mother finds out.'

Archer and Quinn exchange a curious glance.

'It's nothing like that, Mr Dean.'

Dean's brow furrows. 'Oh? What is it then?'

'May we come in?'

He hesitates before responding. 'OK, but I don't have much time. I'm heading out shortly and need to eat.'

In the shabby lobby of the apartment block, Dean presses the lift button. 'I'm on the second floor,' he tells them.

The lift doors slide open revealing a coffin-sized space with barely enough room for two people. Archer feels her mouth drying. She glances at the stairs to her left and says, 'I'll meet you up there.'

'I can take the stairs if you prefer,' offers Quinn.

'No, you go ahead.'

Since Bernard Morrice abducted her and trapped her in a small dark pit, Archer has had a loathing and fear of confined spaces. She takes the stairwell, two at a time, and joins them as Dean unlocks his apartment door. It opens to a narrow, windowless hallway that almost makes Archer's stomach lurch. Dean turns on the light and leads them down to the living room. *It's only a short walk.* Archer puts her head down and pushes through with ease.

'If you don't mind, I need to use the bathroom,' says Dean.

'Sure,' replies Archer.

Archer is relieved the living room is bright and airy. She takes in the space, which is around twenty feet in length, ten feet wide. The room is masculine in its grey decor and lightly furnished with a sofa, a sideboard with a television on top and a dining table next to a window overlooking Halfords. Quinn picks up a framed photo from the sideboard, looks at it and then shows it to Archer. It's a shot of a smiling Justin and Joel.

The toilet flushes and moments later, Dean joins them.

'When was the last time you saw Justin?' asks Archer.

His gaze lingers in a frown as he considers his answer. 'I'm not sure why you would ask me that . . .'

'It would help us with our enquiries, Mr Dean,' she replies.

'Saturday evening – we were drinking in Soho.' Dean's eyes begin to shift from Archer's to Quinn's. 'There's something you're not telling me.'

'Did you talk to him yesterday?'

'No. Like I said, he was ignoring me. He does that sometimes.'

'Did you have a row?'

'Yes, on Saturday, at the end of our night out. We were both drunk.'

'What was the row about?'

'It was pathetic, really. I wanted to go clubbing. He didn't. I said the wrong thing.'

'Was there violence?' asks Quinn.

'No! Of course not.'

'Did you see or talk to Justin at any stage yesterday?' asks Archer.

Dean shakes his head. 'No. We exchanged a couple of shitty texts. He was pissed at me because of our row.'

'Mr Dean, the body of a young man was found in Battersea Park early this morning.'

Dean blinks, his mouth opens, but no words come out. He stares intently at them. 'Do you think it's Justin?'

'Until a formal identification is made, we cannot confirm that,' says Quinn.

Dean sits down on the sofa, his face pale. 'But it must be him – he hasn't been answering my calls or texts.'

65

'Where were you last night?' asks Archer.

'I was here, at home.'

'All evening?'

'Actually, no, I was at the gym for part of that time.'

'What gym do you go to?' asks Quinn.

'PureGym in Piccadilly.'

'Nice ... that's quite a hike from here.'

'Not really. It's minutes from the tube and I often have jobs in and around offices and apartments in that area. It's convenient.'

'Were you alone?'

'Yes. But there were other people there too ... A-am I a suspect?'

'What makes you ask that?' asks Quinn.

'Perhaps it's the way you're angling your questions.'

'We may need to talk to you again, Mr Dean,' interrupts Archer.

Dean squeezes his hands together. 'I can't believe this!'

'Could you give me your contact details, please?' asks Quinn. He tells them his number and Quinn types it into his phone. 'Please don't mention this to anyone for now. We'll be in touch.'

Archer gets a call from DS Tozer as she leaves Dean's flat.

'The door-to-door is underway. I also just wanted to let you know that the two officers are with Mrs Bailey now.'

'I thought they were going to wait for us?' Archer feels a knot of irritation.

'Sorry, Grace. Crossed wires. It's PCs Mel Andersen and Jill Banks. They're both smart, empathetic types. Mrs Bailey will be in good hands until you get there.'

'OK. Good to know. We're heading there now.'

10

ARCHER AND QUINN PULL UP behind a police vehicle at the Baileys' semi in Norton Gardens.

Archer rings the bell and moments later the black uniform of a police officer appears behind the mottled glass of the front door. A young, mixed-race woman greets them. Her name badge says Anderson.

'PC Anderson, I'm DI Archer and this is DS Quinn.'

The officer steps outside, leaving the door slightly ajar. 'Ma'am, DS Quinn.'

'What have you told Mrs Bailey?'

'Only that this involves her husband, and we don't know anything more than that. I told her you'd be here soon, and then we would know more.'

'Good work. Thank you.'

'I'll take you in.'

Archer and Quinn follow her through the living room, a cramped space with busy, flowered wallpaper and surfaces dominated with ceramic Victorian lady figurines and various crystal animals. Perched on a chintz sofa, Linda Bailey looks to be in her late forties with greying short hair, large glasses and an anxious expression. Sitting next to her is the second officer, a round woman with a kind face.

'Mrs Bailey, my name is Detective Inspector Grace Archer, and this is Detective Sergeant Harry Quinn.'

'What's happened to my husband?'

'I'm sorry to have to tell you that a body has been found that we believe to be your husband.'

The woman's face turns ashen. She is silent for a moment before asking. 'How can you be sure it's him?'

'At this stage we have yet to confirm—'

'Why are you not certain?' she interjects.

'The body will need to be identified.'

Linda Bailey blinks several times but does not reply.

'Do you know where your husband went last night, Mrs Bailey?'

'As I told the policewoman, he had to go into the office for a bit because a server had gone down. He's ... he's an IT manager.'

'What time was this?'

'Around ten thirty.'

'Did he say how long he would be gone for?'

'Two hours maybe. I didn't wait up. I went to bed just after eleven.'

'Did you talk to him after he left?'

'No, I was in bed.'

'Before he left, how did he seem to you?'

She frowns. 'What do you mean?'

'What was his mood?'

She seems puzzled. 'His mood? He didn't have one. He was just sitting here, watching television with me like he always does.' She looks suspiciously from Archer to Quinn and back again. 'I'm not sure why you're asking all these questions.'

'Do you think you could give me your husband's mobile number?' asks Archer.

She folds her arms. 'I'd really like to know what has happened to him.'

'I'm afraid we can't say anything at this time.'

Mrs Bailey's expression is a cross between confusion and irritation. After a moment she writes down the phone number on a piece of paper and hands it across.

'We appreciate your help, Mrs Bailey,' says Archer. She turns to PC Anderson. 'Could I ask you to organise an appointment for Mrs Bailey at the mortuary in Horseferry Road. Tomorrow, if possible.'

'Yes, ma'am. We'll take care of her.'

'Thank you, both, and thank you, Mrs Bailey.'

As they leave and walk down the steps and towards the car, Quinn says, 'I'm not sure she knows much about what happened.'

'Agreed.'

As they drive back to Battersea, Archer sends Brian Bailey's number to Os, requesting a report on calls in and out. Around thirty minutes later they arrive at Rowena Crescent, a gentrified Victorian street in Battersea. Quinn pulls up at a free space almost twenty metres away from Justin Sykes' address, a yellow-bricked terrace with the curtains drawn.

Archer raps the front door knocker. After no response she knocks again, harder this time.

'All right! All right!' comes a voice.

They hear the sound of feet on stairs. The front door opens and a half-dressed young man with an untidy mop of hair answers.

'What is it?' he asks stifling a yawn.

'Does Justin Sykes live here?' asks Archer.

'Yeah.' He folds his arms and shivers in the cold as he waits. His eyes roll over Archer and Quinn. 'Are you selling something?' he asks.

'No. May we come in?' asks Archer, presenting her ID.

He blinks in surprise at the ID, frowns and beckons them inside. 'Yeah, come in.' He takes them into the living room and opens the curtains in the bay window. It's an untidy space with a threadbare sofa and unwashed dinner plates on the coffee table.

'What's up? Is Justin in trouble?'

'What's your name?' asks Quinn.

'Tyler – Tyler Green.'

'Do you live here?' asks Quinn.

'Yeah, Justin and I share this place.'

'Do you mind if I call you Tyler?' asks Archer.

He rubs his arms and shakes his head. 'No.'

'When did you last see Justin?'

'Yesterday evening.'

'What time was that?'

'Around seven. He was cooking and I just got home after an afternoon out with friends.'

'Where'd you go?' asks Quinn.

'We just had a few beers in Soho.'

'What do you do?' asks Quinn.

'I work in finance. In the city.'

'Nice. What does Justin do?'

'He works in recruitment.'

Archer asks, 'He was cooking. Did you eat together?'

'Yeah, we do that sometimes. We take turns.'

'How did he seem to you?'

'Fine. Look, what's this about? Where is Justin?'

'What happened after you ate?'

'We watched some TV and I went to bed.' Green rubs his neck as he recalls the evening before. 'I heard the front door closing and looked out from my bedroom window. I saw him walking up the street but didn't hear him return. I assumed he'd gone to Joel's.'

'Joel Dean?' asks Quinn.

Tyler nods.

'Who is Joel?' asks Archer.

'Justin's boyfriend.'

'Have you heard from Joel?'

'No. We don't really talk.'

'Why is that?'

'We don't see eye to eye. He's a bit controlling. Takes advantage of Justin. Justin's getting a bit fed up with it too, but to be honest, he seems to just put up with it for an easy life. He needs to break up with him. I keep telling him that, but he doesn't listen. Joel is no good for him . . . well, they're not good for each other.'

A silence hangs between them for a moment.

'Could we check his bedroom?' asks Quinn.

Green frowns, hesitates and rubs his arms. 'Don't you need a warrant or something?'

'It would really help us, if we could just take a quick look,' Archer replies, reassuringly.

Green considers this for a moment before shrugging a confirmation.

71

Justin Sykes' bedroom is at the rear of house overlooking the back garden. The room is sparse in decor with a built-in wardrobe, a double bed, two bedside tables and a desk under the window. In contrast to the living room, it is neat with a hotel-like tidiness.

Green hovers outside. 'I'm the slob of the house. Justin is forever having a go at me,' he says with a smile.

Archer notices the bed has been made, yet on the duvet is the imprint of a body.

Quinn leans over and touches the top of the bed. 'Still warm,' he says.

'Is there anyone else here?' asks Archer.

Tyler's face turns crimson. 'No. No one. Just me.'

There is a framed photograph of a smiling Sykes standing hand in hand with a broader, bearded, hairy-chested man at what looks like a Pride march.

'That's Joel,' mutters Green.

'You're not too fond of Joel,' states Quinn.

Tyler folds his arms. 'It's not that, I just don't think he's right for Justin.'

Quinn nods his head but doesn't say anything.

Archer says, 'Tyler, we appreciate you talking to us and letting us take a look in Justin's room. Do you have contact details for Justin's mum?'

Green looks nervously from Archer to Quinn. 'He's OK, isn't he . . . Justin?'

'We really need to speak to Justin's mum.'

Green's forehead creases. 'Please tell me what's happened.'

'A body we believe is Justin Sykes has been found.'

Green leans against the wall, his face full of confusion and Quinn says, 'Listen, son, we're sorry. But we need the contact details of Justin's parents.'

He rubs the back of his neck. 'I'll dig them out.'

A few minutes later as they leave, Archer says, 'Tyler, please don't mention anything to his friends or family, especially on social media.'

'O-OK . . . H-how . . . how did he die?'

Quinn squeezes his shoulder. 'You'll hear from us by tomorrow. I promise.'

As they walk to the car Quinn asks, 'What did you think?'

'Unrequited love?'

'Aye. Do you think he's a suspect?'

'Who knows? He's certainly on the list. We'll figure that out in time.'

11

BETH HARPER IS SITTING AT her desk in the London Ambulance Call Centre scanning the summary of an emergency call she has just written. Satisfied, she presses the send button and submits the report to the system.

Taking off her headset, she leans back and stretches the muscles in her back and neck which feel like bunched-up cobbles. She steals a glance at the old clock on the wall. It says 5.55 p.m. Five minutes to shift change with her colleague, Leanne, who should be here any minute now.

Where has the day gone?

She has barely noticed the shift pass, which is largely down to how manic the hours have been triaging calls for the twenty-five ambulances that she has under her control.

'Hi, Beth,' comes a voice.

She looks across the centre to see Leanne peeling off her overcoat and walking towards the lockers. Beth smiles. Even in her ambulance greens, Leanne always manages to look good. Her shiny dark hair is pulled back into a ponytail and her face, as always, looks flawless without make-up.

'Hi, Leanne,' replies Beth with a wave.

'How's it been today?'

'Crazy. Jimmy said we had two thousand calls by four o'clock.'

'Wowzers! That's mad. Listen, are you OK to hang for a minute? I'm desperate to pee.'

'Sure. Take your time.'

Beth begins to tidy the desk for Leanne. She is about to log out of her system when a call comes through. She is eager to leave and hesitates before answering, but everyone else is busy and there is no sign of Leanne.

She presses the button and answers. 'Hello, London Ambulance Service. Is the patient breathing?'

She waits for the caller to speak, but there is only silence.

'Hello, is anyone there?' she asks.

'Please . . . please . . .' says a trembling, husky voice.

'Hello? Who is this?'

The caller is sobbing. 'I-I'm frightened!'

'Please tell me your name.'

All she hears is choking wet sobs and then the caller asks, 'What's your name?'

'My name is Beth.'

The callers voice trembles down the line. 'Beth . . .'

'Could you tell me what's happened and how we can help?'

'Help me!' the caller cries.

Beth opens up a new incident screen. 'Tell me your name and I can help you.'

'I'm bleeding,' says the caller, the voice seems harsher, more of a growl.

'Are you alone?'

'Yesss.'

'What caused the bleeding?'

The caller begins to groan and then cries out in pain.

Beth's pulse is racing, but she remains calm. 'Have you had an accident? Has someone hurt you? Please tell me what happened.'

'I cut myself. That's what happened. There's blood every-where. Fuuuck . . . it's everywhere!'

'Please could you give me your address and I will send an ambulance to your home?'

The caller begins to chuckle darkly. 'Do you really think I'm that stupid?'

Beth blinks, hesitating. 'If you're bleeding badly, you will need to see a medic.'

'I'd like to see you bleed.' The voice has become deeper, guttural and dry.

Beth feels her muscles tensing, the seeds of doubt growing. 'I'm trying to help you.'

'Help me?' The caller's tone is harsh and angry. 'What could the likes of you ever do to help me?'

Beth composes herself and feels torn between doing her duty as an emergency call handler and the victim of a crank. 'I can send an ambulance.'

'*I can send an ambulance?*' mimics the caller in a shrill voice, which slowly deepens to a harsh growl. 'I'm cutting myself right now, bitch. Three long deep cuts down my arms, one for each minute I have spent on this hopeless fucking call with you.'

Beth stiffens. 'I'm putting the phone down.'

'Oh, Beth, Beth, Beth. I hope you remember this call . . . Beth!' The caller spits her name, like a curse word. 'Because I'm coming for you, I know where you live, and I will *cut you too!*'

Beth disconnects the call and throws the headset on the desktop, her hands trembling. She swallows, takes three deep breaths and feels her heart pounding hard in her chest.

Around her, Beth's colleagues chatter into their headsets, their faces buried in monitors as they respond to the deluge of emergency calls.

'You're white as a sheet,' says Leanne, appearing beside her.

Beth jumps.

'I just had a weird call.'

Leanne is cleaning her headset with a cleansing wipe. 'Not Ethan again?'

Beth shakes her head. 'No, some crank. He threatened me, said he knew where I lived.'

'Oh, babes! They all say that. Don't let it get to you.'

Beth and her colleagues are forever getting crank calls. It comes with the job and there is nothing they can do about it. At training they were warned about them and even laughed at the examples that were acted out. They are employed to ensure that the people of London who need their help are kept safe and hopefully alive, until medical assistance arrives and takes over. It is a responsible and important job that not everyone is capable of doing, therefore, the odd, untraceable crank call is the least of their worries. But this feels different, like a personal attack.

'You should report it to Jimmy,' says Leanne.

Beth logs off her system and shudders. 'I'm just out of sorts today. I'll be fine, thanks. Anyway, I'm supposed to be meeting Ethan.'

'You look spooked. You should get home. Never mind Ethan. He's no good for you.'

Beth ignores Leanne's comment. 'He's asked me out.'

Leanne's lips tighten. 'He doesn't deserve you.'

Beth sighs. 'I better go.'

Leanne gently squeezes Beth's hand. 'Whatever you want, doesn't matter what it is or what time, you let me know. I'm here for you – always.'

'I know. Thank you.'

Leanne takes Beth's chair and logs into the phone. A call comes through immediately and Leanne connects her headset and puts it on. 'Maybe that's him again. I'll tell him to go fuck himself with his blade, shall I?' Leanne presses the answer button on her phone. 'Ambulance, how can I help you?' she says, blowing a kiss to Beth.

Beth smiles and walks to her locker where she retrieves her coat and bag and waves goodnight to her colleagues across the expansive office. She hurries to the changing rooms where she slips out of uniform and dresses in a fitted cream wool pullover, blue jeans and white Adidas trainers. After brushing her teeth, fixing her hair and make-up, Beth stuffs her uniform into her bag and leaves the warmth of the call centre building, emerging into the dark, quiet and cold streets. She shivers and sighs.

A harsh cough comes out of nowhere and startles her. She wrinkles her nose as a cloud of bitter smoke engulfs her and jumps as a man hurries by, almost knocking her out of the way.

'Hey!' she calls in irritation, but he hurries on without taking any notice and flicks his cigarette against a parked vehicle.

She hears a chuckling sound from somewhere close by and stiffens. Looking around, she scans the street, but she sees no one, just passing traffic and a cyclist hurtling by. She thinks of the crank call and feels a cloying paranoia. Most people know where the ambulance call centres are. Could her crank caller be waiting for her? She shakes her head and chides herself. *Pull yourself together, for God's sake.*

She walks quickly away, her eyes and ears alert. Arriving at Waterloo Station, she feels her hand being squeezed and flinches.

'Beth!'

Beth turns and is surprised to see Sid and Vera.

'Beth, dear, are you OK? You look very pale,' says Vera.

'Vera, Sid, hello . . . sorry, I don't mean to be rude. I didn't see you there. It's been a long day.'

'Don't be silly, dear. You have such a challenging job, taking all sorts of calls from people in need. We were just talking about that today, weren't we, Sid?'

You don't know the half of it.

Vera continues, 'We watched you leave this morning, didn't we, Sidney, and I said, "There she goes, off to save the lives of Londoners. What would we do without her? Doing her bit and Lord knows this city needs all the help it can get." Isn't that right, Sidney?'

Sid grunts an agreement as Vera narrows her eyes and looks around Beth. 'No Ethan tonight?'

'I'm just on my way to meet him now.'

'He's such a nice boy. Where are you meeting him?'

Vera is sweet and nice, but also one of the nosiest people Beth has ever met. ·

'In Lewisham.'

Vera and Sid exchange a knowing look that puzzles her. 'Lewisham, that's nice, dear. I'm glad to hear it. Nice place.'

Vera loops her arm into Sid's and smiles at Beth. 'We should get going.'

'Wait ...' Beth wants to ask them about the friend they introduced to Ethan.

'Give that cute boy a big kiss from me,' says Vera, hurrying off with her husband. 'Bye!'

Beth watches them leave and decides it's best to hear direct from Ethan anyway. She thinks of the crank call and shudders, unable to shake off the feeling that she is being watched. She takes the escalator down to the Underground, occasionally glancing behind her, ensuring that no one is following her.

What's got into you today? Stop being so weak and stupid.

She waits on the platform for several minutes before the Jubilee line train thunders out of the tunnel. The crowd thickens and Beth feels herself being herded closer to the platform edge. She pushes back, panic rising in her throat, and turns her face away from the train's blowback and overpowering reek of diesel and oil that fills her nose, mouth and lungs. She exhales in what seems a futile effort to expel the fumes from her lungs.

The carriage doors slide open and she steps inside, her eyes searching for an empty seat, but there are none. The doors bleep their warning before ruthlessly sliding shut.

The train jerks. Beth quickly seizes the grab pole as her fellow standing passengers stumble and knot together. The train makes a choking sound and rolls slowly forward, building momentum by the second. Whispers, laughter and the tinny blast of grime rap music chitters from cheap earphones.

The crank call is playing on her mind and she can't help looking at the strangers around her. Could one of them be the caller? *Stop it!* She clenches her jaw in frustration at her stupid anxiety and tries to push those thoughts from her mind.

The train stops at Canary Wharf and she pushes her way out with the crowd. Three suited men, laughing and clearly drunk, collide with her and shuffle around her, rubbing against her, their stale beer breath almost making her gag.

'Shorry, darlin', says one of them.

Beth hides her irritation and pushes away from them.

'You coulda pulled, mate!' says another. 'Go after her.'

They all laugh in unison.

Beth hurries away. She feels her heart pounding and retreats for a moment into a quiet spot in the shadows of the platform to gather herself.

She closes her eyes and gives herself a few moments to calm down as the crowds rush past close by. Above the din she hears a voice hissing like a snake's, 'Beeeeth.'

Beth startles and her eyes bolt open. She scans the passing herd, but no one is looking her way. She shudders and shakes her head. You're imagining things, she thinks as she joins the crowd and makes her way to Heron Quays.

12

Rose Grant's eyelids begin to flicker and close, shrouding and protecting her from the piercing white light. She shifts uneasily on top of the unfamiliar mattress. It feels hard and cold, almost like a stone slab. Her head spins a storm of confusion and a cavernous silence rips through her ears. She wants to scream, but her mouth will not open. For a moment it feels like time has stopped and the world has left her behind.

Trembling and frightened, she gathers what strength she has, snaps open her eyes and gasps at the blinding light. She squints and turns her head away. Her stomach lurches and she feels her temperature rising, hotter and hotter. Beads of sweat scurry on her forehead like insects and she feels as if she might pass out again.

Where am I?

She cannot remember.

Blinking, she sees a nasal spray bottle lying on the mattress near her face. It has a picture of a butterfly. A black butterfly.

She frowns. Using all her strength she pushes herself up and stops when she hears a voice. It's unfamiliar, more a warble, and she can't quite make out the words. Holding her hand over her eyes, she looks beyond the light and sees movement in the shadows. She narrows her gaze but everything is blurred.

Rose tries to speak but her mouth feels as though it's stuffed with cotton wool. Her stomach lurches again, harder this time, and she feels the bile rising in her throat. Unable to help herself, she doubles over and what seems like a waterfall spills from her mouth and splashes onto the blue-and-red rug at the side of the bed.

The voice again, this time closer, but no more comprehensible. She coughs and massages her tummy and flinches suddenly at a hand that appears close to her face. It's holding a bottle of water. Rose feels a little better after throwing up but has a raging thirst.

The voice speaks. Clearer now. 'Drink.'

Rose snatches the water from the hand and swallows a mouthful before greedily gulping down the contents from the plastic bottle and dropping it to the floor without thinking. Wiping her mouth she thinks that the water had a funny taste but can't be sure. A growing sense of despair overcomes her and ignites a terror that spreads through her body. Her breathing increases rapidly and all she can think of is to get out of this place. She tries to shift but feels heavy, as if she has been filled with sand, bags and bags of sand. Despite her rising temperature, her bottom half feels oddly cold. With much effort she manages to look down and sees goosebumps on her legs. Her tights and shoes are missing. Where can they be? Turning to the floor she sees the damp vomit stain. Her head swirls and she tumbles from the bed, hitting the floor with a thud. She can feel the warm vomit on her bare legs and her bag under her chest.

The voice is warbling again, 'Stay calm. It'll all be over soon.' She thinks that's what she hears.

The fall has woken something in her. She no longer feels full of sand. She pulls herself up but feels a firm grip on her arm. Confused, she looks back, her eyes struggling to focus. Blinking, her vision begins to clear. Panic awakens her like a surge of electricity and in a brief moment of clarity she lashes out at the hand and makes a run for the door. Pulling it open, she stumbles out into a corridor. Her head begins to spin again and the hallway seems to elongate before her.

'Wait!'

She won't. She hurries up the long hallway, swaying sideways and thudding against the walls. A stranger appears. He looks at her and says something she can't quite hear. Behind him she sees stairs. She pushes past and hurries down them, holding the banister firmly. She hears footsteps behind her and picks up her pace, relieved there is only one flight.

She hears voices joined together in song. They seem close yet faraway too.

Down at the cross
Where my saviour died
Down where for cleansing
From sin I cried
There to my heart
Was the blood applied
Glory to His name

She crosses an unfamiliar hallway and runs into what looks like a large kitchen. It's familiar and at the same it isn't. *What's happening to me?* Her head is spinning and she hears footsteps from where she's just come. Behind her is a narrow door. She pulls it open and sees a bucket, mops, a vacuum cleaner. She edges inside and closes the door behind her, waiting as the footsteps run by. Her stomach clenches and she thinks she is going to be sick again. She retches but nothing comes up. The small space is filled with stale smells. There is no air and she has to get out.

Opening the door she peers out. Everything seems to blur but she is sure no one is there. She eases out of the cupboard and walks cautiously to the rear of the kitchen. She can make out a large door, pulls it open and tumbles outside, where the ground is damp and cold on her soft feet. She is in a garden and sees trees nearby. She hurries towards them, trying her best not to fall over.

Nearby, she hears traffic and hurries toward it. Through a break in the trees she sees a wire fence. Behind her she hears voices. Shouting. Panic drives her on and she climbs the wire fence. She feels pointed parts of the wire tug at her skin but using all of her strength, Rose hauls herself up and over the fence, falling to the ground, slamming her head on the pavement. Groaning, she sits up and feels something warm run down her face. She shivers despite burning up inside.

'Rose!' someone calls.

Rose's heart sinks. She pushes herself up and runs clumsily away, glancing behind her every other second.

She has no idea where she is, but it's crowded and loud. She squints at her reflection in a shop window. It takes her a moment to see and feel the dismay at her unkempt appearance. She is only wearing a vomit-stained T-shirt and has no shoes. She shivers in the cold and notices a silhouette watching her on the other side of the street. Swallowing, she turns round, but the figure has melded into the crowd. She could have imagined it, but fear has kicked in again and she picks up her pace anyway.

She begins to feel sick again.

Something is wrong. Oh God. Something is wrong.

Red, yellow, green and blue lights from shops, cafés and bars seem to blur at the corner of her eyes. She feels dizzy and slows to a stop. Her ankles and knees wobble. Reaching across, she steadies herself against the bonnet of a parked car.

Her head spins.

What's happening to me?

The sound of a car horn screams at her and a man sitting inside winds down his window and shouts, 'Oi! Get off my fucking car!' Startled, she totters clumsily away and leans with her back against a phone box. Eyes wide, she takes in three deep breaths and massages her temples. She hasn't eaten much today. A tasteless egg sandwich. But there is nothing unusual about that. She's never been a big eater. Perhaps she's caught a virus, or something. After a few more breaths of cooling air, she feels a clarity with a rising horror. Had her water been spiked?

Rose wants to cry and shout for help, but a knocking sound distracts her. She turns to see an old woman with large glasses frowning up at her from inside the phone box. Rose realises she is blocking the phone box door and stands out of the way.

'Sorry,' says Rose.

The woman looks Rose up and down with a disapproving stare and mutters something she cannot hear.

The world seems to spiral around her. Terrified, Rose slips into the vacated phone box and slumps to the floor, her stomach turning violently at the sour stench of stale piss. Rose is overcome with the need to get out of that small space. Pushing open the door, her head woozy, her legs wobble and she falls on her hands and knees onto the cold hard pavement.

A man shouts, 'Watch out, darlin'!' and several people laugh. Their voices seem far away, but she knows they are close by.

She feels her stomach lurch and then spasm. She groans and starts retching, but nothing comes out.

'Disgusting!' someone spits as they hurry past.

Rose's lip trembles and she begins to cry. She has never felt so frightened. So hopeless. So alone. Her vision is blurring. 'Help me!' she cries.

'Hello,' comes a female voice. 'Are you OK?' Rose blinks her eyes and after a moment sees a pretty woman with pulled-back highlighted hair, large eyes and full pink lips. 'My name's Beth. What's your name?'

Rose tries to speak, but her mouth begins to salivate and drool runs down her chin.

'Shall I call you an ambulance?' asks the woman.

The woman's face seems to distort and melt. Rose steps back, horror surging through her. She wants to scream, but instead turns to run.

'Wait!' calls the woman.

Rose scrambles through the throng, colliding with people and pushing her way through. Someone shoves her and she spins onto the road and thankfully manages to not fall over. The road is clear of people and she starts to pick up her pace. Her heart is pounding and she begins to sprint. She keeps running and running, like she had done at school, winning the hundred metres. She smiles at the memory, at that happy time and does not see the car as it speeds towards her.

Rose feels an almighty shove and the wind flies out of her. She finds herself flying and spinning in the air. She thinks, one last time, of the medal she received and how proud her mum was before her body slams against something hard and everything goes dark.

13

BETH HAD HURRIED AFTER THE woman, peeking over shoulders and weaving through the bustling, but infuriatingly slow, pedestrians. She'd heard the horrible thudding sound first and then, as she emerged from the throng, gasped as she watched the young woman tumble like a rag doll over the car bonnet and fall to the ground, her head slamming on to the hard gritty surface.

Beth froze, her heart in her mouth. And the car did not stop. It continued driving.

A moment of hushed silence followed, broken by a scream and then voices shouting for someone to call an ambulance.

'Get her off the road,' someone called. 'The traffic can't get through.'

Another voice called, 'You can't move her. An ambulance is on its way!'

Beth's heart is pounding and she's relieved to hear an ambulance has been called. She stares at the woman who lies serenely on the road as if she had just decided on a whim to fall asleep there. Her large eyes are wide open, looking toward Beth, but they are lifeless, the eyes of a dead woman. Beth is used to dealing with emergencies like these, but only on the phone. This is the first time she has ever witnessed one.

The woman is wearing only a T-shirt, which she had been sick over. Beth thinks she must have been on drugs. Why else would she be acting so strangely, be so underdressed in this weather? The T-shirt has lifted in the accident and Beth can see she is wearing no knickers.

Everyone can see.

Beth flushes, feeling a deep mortification for the dead woman. She hears the whispering and snorting of two men next to her and feels an anger well up.

'Have you seen enough?' she says to the men.

They look away before hastily retreating into the crowd.

She knows it's wrong to touch the body before the police arrive, but she can't stand to see the woman so undignified in death. She hopes someone would do the same for her, if she were ever in this unfortunate position. Crouching beside the body, Beth pulls the woman's T-shirt over her exposed areas.

'Well done,' comes a female voice.

The dead woman is pretty, with dark hair. She looks to be in her late twenties, a few years younger than Beth.

'Oh God . . .' a man's voice says.

Beth sees a pool of blood shimmer like a dark red halo under the victim's head.

She shudders, turns away, and notices a teenage boy furtively slip his phone into his pocket. Had he just taken a picture of the dead woman? Beth can't be sure. The boy turns to look at her and she notices one of his eyelids droops lower than the other and an orange wooden crucifix hangs on his chest. He stares back and slowly runs his gaze up and down her body. Beth feels her spine icing over and looks away.

She hears the sound of a siren and sees the flashing blue lights of a police car as it emerges through the parting crowd. Two male uniformed cops get out from the front and a third man with thinning red hair follows from the back. A detective? she wonders. The uniformed policemen examine the body of the woman; the third man is preoccupied, his face caught in the glow of his phone.

An older woman with curly grey hair waves for attention at the policemen. 'I saw everything. That car didn't see her coming. She weren't right. Off her face, I'd say.'

'Did you see what type of car it was?' asks one of the officers, a barrel-chested man with a shaved head.

She considers his question before answering. 'No, can't say that I did.'

A second, unmarked, car arrives with flashing blue lights.

The man with the thinning red hair is leaning on the police car. He looks across at the new police vehicle and quickly pockets his phone. He turns to the shaven-headed policeman. 'Any witnesses, Keith?'

'Not yet, sir.'

'Good work. Keep at it,' he replies with a sudden air of authority that does not sound convincing.

Beth notices two female plain-clothed officers step out of the vehicle. One is stocky with short blonde hair and looks like she might be pregnant. The other is a thin woman with a waspish face.

'Tozer, Marian, we have this under control,' says the detective called Hicks.

'Anything we can do to help?' asks the blonde woman as she looks down at the body. Beth notices a flicker of sadness appear on her face.

Her colleague asks, 'Has anyone called an ambulance?'

'I was just about to do that, Tozer!' says Hicks.

Beth notices the two women exchange a look.

'I just heard on the radio that it's on the way,' says the shaven-headed officer called Keith.

The pregnant detective says something to Hicks that she cannot hear. His face tightens and she talks with her colleague for a moment and they both look upwards. Beth follows their gaze to a CCTV camera.

'It was a hit-and-run,' says the shaven-headed policeman.

DS Tozer's gaze turns back to the dead woman.

'What's your name?' she asks.

'Hopkins,' he replies, tersely.

'Do we have the car make or licence plate yet?'

'No.'

'No, *Sergeant*,' corrects the detective.

Beth notices his jaw tightening.

'DS Tozer,' interrupts Hicks. 'We'll handle this. You can go on your way.'

'Any witnesses?' she continues, ignoring him.

PC Hopkins points to the older woman. 'This lady saw everything.'

'Other witnesses?'

Hicks frowns. 'We just arrived seconds before you!' There is a hint of insolence in his tone that Tozer hasn't noticed or is ignoring. Beth thinks the latter.

'Have you checked the victim's ID?'

'She's only wearing a T-shirt! I doubt she even felt the car hit her . . . died happy and full of class A party gear by the look of it,' Hopkins says.

Beth feels a flare of anger at the policeman's crass, disrespectful words.

DS Tozer glares at him. She leans toward him and says something out of earshot that causes the officer to flinch. He then scurries to his car, grabs a police overcoat and drapes it over the body.

Tozer scans the crowd.

Beth steps forward. 'Excuse me. I saw her.'

'Hello,' says Tozer. 'Did you see what happened?'

'Yes. I tried to help her. She seemed distressed as if she was having a panic attack, or something.'

'Did you see the car?'

'Only briefly.'

'Did you make out what type of car it was?'

Beth feels a fool for not taking better notice. 'I'm afraid I didn't. It was a smallish car though. White. Like a three-door something.'

'A hatchback?'

'I think so, yes.'

'That's helpful. Did you happen to notice if she was alone?'

'As far as I could see.'

The detective nods her understanding. 'One of these officers will take your statement, if that's OK?'

'Yes. Of course.'

'I'm sure this has been a shock for you.'

Beth sighs. 'A little. I work for London Ambulance. You'd think we'd be used to this sort of thing.'

'You must come across accidents like this all the time.'

'Kind of, but not really. I work in the response centre.'

'That's a tough job.'

'It can be. But I love it.'

'It's probably best not to be alone tonight.'

'I'll be OK. I'm supposed to be meeting my boyfriend.'

'That's nice. Thanks for your help. Have a nice evening.'

'Thanks.'

DS Tozer turns to the policeman called Hopkins and gestures at Beth. 'PC Hopkins, this woman would like to make a statement.'

Beth looks back down at the body covered by the overcoat and wonders who she was. She feels an odd sense of being watched, as if eyes are boring into her. She shivers, looks along the crowd and stiffens at the sight of a shadowy figure wearing an orange crucifix that seems to dissipate into the dark folds of the crowd.

14

ARCHER HAS JUST FINISHED ON a call from DS Tozer who, along with most of the Met and the public, has seen yesterday's viral footage from the Strand of PCs Keith Hopkins and Nathan Watts manhandling innocent NHS worker, Dorothy Hayes. Tozer wanted to check in with Archer to see if her impression of Hopkins is in line with Archer's. Tozer told her what had happened at the hit-and-run in Lewisham. Hopkins had been cruelly dismissive about the dead woman, and Hicks had been less than helpful.

Archer sits quietly stewing over Hicks's fatuity and Hopkins' attitude towards Dorothy Hayes and the deceased woman. This has rattled her more than Hicks, whose ineptitude is wearing, but also commonplace and never surprising. There is much to say and judge about DI Hicks, but at least you always know where you are with him. He bears his predictability like a tall pointy dunce's hat that he unwittingly wears on his head. Instead of a D, a large P is scrawled in coloured crayon.

The officer's lack of empathy has also darkened her mood and makes her realise she must submit the paperwork for the disciplinary that she's been considering. Hopkins needs to be made an example of. Archer has encountered this behaviour many times before among certain male officers and has no time for it. Despite the Met's honourable intentions in rolling out the diversity programmes, the truth is, they seem to have made only a minor impact. According to Tozer, PC Keith Hopkins' attitude to the victim is just another example of an officer not paying attention during class, or just not caring. Archer thinks the latter. It's an insidious trait that appears to be growing among what seems a fraternity of mostly white heterosexual policemen. In Archer's view there is a low tolerance from this fraternity for those on the police radar who are black, brown, poor or immigrants.

The dead woman's job, if that was her job, is of no consequence. She deserves better.

Asshole.

As if reading her thoughts Quinn says, 'I've had a few dealings with Hopkins and his silent colleague in the past. They're what us feminists call toxic males. Plus, they're both shit cops.'

Archer feels herself relax a little as Quinn thankfully lightens the mood. She looks his way, eyebrows raised. 'Us feminists?'

'Us feminists,' he repeats.

Quinn turns left onto St George's Road where the traffic is bumper-to-bumper.

'So when did you become a feminist?'

'Grace, I feel a tad affronted that you did not know this about me already!'

'I humbly apologise if I've shaken your delicate sensibilities.'

'That's quite all right,' replies Quinn, with a wry look on his face. 'You know me. A big strong boy. I'll be fine. Anyway, lots of men are feminists. I was reading this article the other day . . .'

'Don't tell me – GQ magazine? *Men's Health*? *Esquire*?'

Quinn snorts. 'Am I detecting a hint of cynicism?'

Archer smiles. 'Never.'

'I found it online—'

Archer interjects. 'A true indication of the article's authenticity.'

'Yep. Turns out there are lots of out-and-proud famous male feminists.'

'I bet there are.'

'Harry Styles. Will Smith. Chris Hemsworth. Tom Hardy, to name a few.'

'Sounds like quite an elite male club.'

Quinn smiles. 'Think of us as your cheerleaders.'

'I can't imagine that lot shaking their pompoms for womanhood.'

Quinn laughs. 'Many people would pay good money to see that show.'

When they get back to the office, Os Pike is at his desk, DS Tozer and DC Phillips have their heads down too.

'Did you get that report on Brian Bailey's phone, Os?' asks Archer.

'Yes, ma'am,' he replies handing across several sheets.

'Thank you.'

'How did the door-to-door at Battersea Park go, Toze?' asks Archer.

'It didn't yield much, ma'am. People were glued to their televisions and didn't hear or see anything last night. I'm hoping we'll do better with the CCTV.'

'Let's hope so.'

'The press got wind and were sniffing around. I warned them off and also asked the park-keeper to keep schtum, but to be honest, I'm a bit concerned about him.'

'In what way?'

'He was fine when we arrived, but later I noticed him become withdrawn and jumpy, as if scared of his own shadow. I think he had a delayed reaction to what he discovered in the park?'

'We should get him some help. Check in on him. See how he is and make sure he hasn't spoken to anyone. Could you do that?'

'Of course.'

'Changing the subject ... not long now until you're off on maternity.'

'Just a few more days,' smiles Joely.

'You must be looking forward to it.'

'I am. But I'm nervous too.'

Archer smiles. 'I bet you are.'

'I hear DCI Pierce has found a temporary replacement.'

'Do you know who?' asks Archer.

'I'm afraid not.'

'I'm sure we'll find out soon enough.'

From across the office, Archer wheels an unused whiteboard beside her desk. Quinn finds a marker pen amongst the pile of papers on his desk and tosses it to Archer. In the centre of board she writes:

Brian Bailey.

Deceased. Murdered. Angled cut to jugular.

Eyes cut from face and placed in hands. Inverted cross carved into face. Ritualistic? Main target? Drugs?

She then draws a line out to the left and writes:

Justin Sykes.

Deceased. Murdered. Accidental?

She then draws a second line out to the left and writes:

Tyler Green

Flatmate. Friend. Lover? Suspect?

She draws a second line to the right and writes:

Joel Dean.

Boyfriend. Open relationship. Suspect?

History of drugs and minor violence.

Finally, she writes:

Linda Bailey. Wife of Brian. Suspect?

Archer drops the marker on the desk and folds her arms. She stares at the board as if waiting for the mystery to somehow solve itself.

'Do you think Linda Bailey capable of those murders?' asks Quinn.

'These days I am never surprised at what some people are capable of.'

Quinn considers this and then says, 'From our first meeting with Dean and Green, both men seemed overly fond of Justin. Do you think there is a motive for either of them?'

'The obvious conclusion at this stage is a crime of passion, certainly for Green and Dean. Perhaps even Mrs Bailey too. Who knows?'

'I agree. It's too early to draw conclusions.'

'I'll chase MJ up and see if she has anything.'

Archer scans through the names and numbers on Brian Bailey's phone records, but nothing stands out. She catches up with paperwork as Quinn eventually gets through to CSI. Moments later she hears him laugh into the phone. 'I'd like that . . . OK, see you later, bye.'

'How's MJ?' asks Archer.

'She's good. Her and Krish are still working on their findings and will have a report tomorrow end of day or Thursday latest. She did say that the powder on Brian Bailey's nose is ketamine.'

'Surprising. I'd suspected the powder might be cocaine to help with the sex drive, but ketamine is a horse tranquiliser.'

'Well, it's used recreationally, but I agree, an odd choice. But perhaps it's not. This type is a potent variety known on the streets as BK.'

'BK?'

'Butterfly Ketamine. Apparently it sucker punches you and makes you float like a butterfly. Available from all our usual dealer chums.'

'I see. Then it was possibly given to him against his will.'

'That may well be true.'

Archer works late, completing and submitting to Human Resources, the disciplinary recommendation forms against PC Keith Hopkins and PC Nathan Watts and their unwarranted use of force against an unarmed woman. Bringing this sort of action against fellow officers will make Archer deeply unpopular again, but she doesn't care. Hopkins and Watts broke all the rules and need to be made an example of. She includes a link to the viral videos. On a news website she notices a short front-page story on the two bodies found in Battersea Park. The headline reads:

Dogging Sex Murders in Battersea Park

Two male 'doggers' were found dead in bizarre circumstances in Battersea Park this morning. Both men, who remain unnamed, are believed to have been the victims of a twisted and bloody killer. A source at the park told us, 'I never saw nothing like it. One had his

100

trousers down and the other had his eyes cut out. I'll have nightmares for weeks.' There are no statements from the police at this stage. More on this story as it comes in.

It seems the press had caught up with the park-keeper and squeezed what they could from him. *Fuck!* It'd be all over the national news and social media sites by tomorrow morning. She can almost feel Pierce's spitting fury as she wakes up to the media onslaught, the tabloids scaremongering and declaring police incompetence. Best warn her. Archer opens up WhatsApp and composes a message to the DCI, telling her to expect the worst. She then switches off her phone. It's been a long day and now isn't the time to deal with an unruly tongue-lashing from her governor.

It's after nine. Archer cuts across the busy traffic of the Strand and walks down Villiers Street, lost in her thoughts about the investigation and the next steps for tomorrow. At the same time she listens cautiously to the light tread of the footsteps that have followed in her wake since leaving the station. Slowing her pace, she shoots a sideways look at a shop window which reflects the scene behind her and notices a shadow meld into the crowd. Picking up her pace she hurries on, weaving her way through the throng as she passes Victoria Embankment Gardens before climbing the steps to the Golden Jubilee Bridge.

With a cold wind pinching her skin, she slows halfway across and turns to scan the people behind her. There is no one looking her way. For a moment she thinks she has imagined the whole thing but decides not to take any chances. With her guard up, she hurries on, her muscles coiled and ready to respond to whoever comes at her.

She exits the lights of Waterloo Road, steps into the gloomy quiet of Exon Street and soon hears the echo of footfalls behind her, the same beat, the same light tread. A burst of anger and fear surges through her that someone has the nerve to follow her to her home, her sanctuary. Turning left onto Cornwall Road, she conceals herself in the shadows of a doorway opposite the barber shop on the corner of Roupell Street. She hears the footsteps shift into a sprint and in the shop window watches the silhouette of her pursuer take shape and form, turn the corner, panting. From the shadows Archer narrows her eyes. Her stalker is a young woman. She is peering down Cornwall Road, presumably looking for Archer.

'Why are you following me?' Archer asks, with an icy edge to her voice.

The woman jumps and stifles a scream. 'Oh my God! You frightened the life out of me.'

She is pretty with wavy dark hair and wears a long camel coat belted at the waist. Her hands are inked with black tattoos depicting delicate flowers and birds.

'Detective Inspector Archer, I'm sorry, I just wanted to talk. My name is Mallory Jones. I emailed your colleague.'

Archer is momentarily caught off guard. She had believed Mal Jones to be male. 'You're the researcher? Or to be more accurate, the True Crime Podcaster?' Archer's tone is sharp.

The woman smiles. 'That's me,' she says, holding out her hand.

Archer inches closer to her and, through gritted teeth, says, 'How dare you follow me home!'

'I'm sorry I just wanted—'

'Just to be clear, and I say this to every other hack that comes knocking, I have no intention of ever contributing to the glorification of that monster, or any killer for that matter, for the titillation of your listeners, or anyone else.'

Archer turns and crosses Cornwall Road.

'No, wait, please. It's not like that. I've come across information that you should know. I wanted to talk to you before going anywhere else.'

Archer feels her blood heating, but keeps her temper in check. 'There isn't anything I haven't heard already, Miss Jones. Now do us both a favour and go home!'

'DI Archer, ple—'

'Goodbye.'

Archer enters the warm amber glow of the Victorian street-lamp in Roupell Street. Ahead she sees the curly bare branches of the star jasmine that grows from a small hole in the pavement and nestles against the front wall of the two-storey house. It has been there for as long as she can remember and after her father's death, and her abduction by Bernard Morrice, she and Grandad tended the then little plant and he often compared its thriving and blossoming in impossible conditions to that of her own. It was his way of encouraging her to hang on, to not give up, especially when times were at their darkest. She focuses on it now and pushes any thoughts of Mallory Jones's cheap hack harassment from her mind.

The house is hot as she enters it. Grandad, who has been feeling the cold more than usual, has the heating turned up full.

'Is that you, Grace?' he calls, above canned TV laughter.

'Sure is,' she says, doing her best to sound cheerful.

Archer takes off her coat in the narrow hallway with the familiar smell of sandalwood. A candle with an image of the

Virgin flickers on the wall between the photographs of her Grandma, a dignified, handsome woman of Algerian-Jewish descent, and her father, DI Samuel David Archer.

She hangs the coat on a hook and enters the living room. Grandad is sitting on the sofa with a newspaper on his lap. He turns the paper over so that it faces down and smiles up at her. He is pale, his eyes red and tired behind his new round wire-framed glasses.

Archer feels a knot in her stomach. 'Grandad, are you OK?'

He shifts uneasily. 'Yes. I'm well,' he replies, unconvincingly. 'How was your day?'

Archer notices his hand resting firmly, almost protectively on the newspaper. She sits beside him on the sofa. 'It was fine. Same old,' she lies. Since her recent brush with death at the hands of the @nonymous killer, she cannot bring herself to go into details with Grandad, especially considering the young woman killed in a hit-and-run and the two murder victims in Battersea Park.

She diverts the topic. 'What are you watching?'

'Oh, some quiz show. I'm not sure what it is.'

'You look tired.'

'You too.'

'How's Cosmo?'

'Up to his usual tricks, as you can imagine.' Grandad chuckles. 'He wasn't very happy when I took out his bishop and trapped his king with my rook.'

Archer smiles. 'The Grand Master of Roupell Street has yet to meet his match.'

'I seem to remember you beating me a couple of times.'

'That was a long time ago. My skills are way too rusty now.'

Grandad regards her with tired eyes, saying nothing and after a moment reaches across and squeezes her hand.

'If only I had control over this terrible world like I do over a chessboard.'

Archer squeezes his hand back. 'Are you sure everything is OK?'

'Everything's fine. I'm just being old and silly.'

Grandad yawns and Archer follows suit.

'I think I'll go to bed, Grandad.'

He seems not to have heard her and is sitting quietly in thought. He looks up and blinks. 'Yes . . . OK, dear. Sleep well.'

She bends over and kisses him on the cheek. 'You too. Don't stay up too late.'

'I'll be in bed very soon.'

Archer smiles and climbs the stairs to the bathroom where she removes her contacts, cleanses her face and brushes her teeth. It's a relief to shed the skin of the day's clothes and pull on comfortable pyjamas. Switching off the light, she slips under the duvet and closes her eyes as she steadies her breathing. Sleep does not always come easy for her but she feels her muscles relaxing under the warm duvet. With the hope that she might have an uninterrupted night, she turns over on her side, curls into the foetal position and moments later falls into a restless sleep.

15

THE FOLLOWING MORNING, ARCHER IS preparing breakfast, taking comfort in the warm smell of toast that fills the kitchen. She stands too near to the kettle as it boils, steaming her glasses. Still groggy from sleep, she wipes the lenses with a sheet of kitchen roll before pouring the hot water into the teapot. In her dreams she was back on that cold, rainy night, digging her way out of the grave-like hole in the ground that Morrice had imprisoned her in. When she emerged from the soil, she saw Morrice, smiling at her and she had felt the sharp pain in her hands and looked down at them. Each one was muddy and bleeding and the deranged Morrice had laughed in her face. Archer had woken in a sweat and struggled to get back to sleep.

She shakes her head, not wanting to think about that time, and pushes all thoughts of it from her mind. She switches on the radio. The BBC news is running with a story on the Battersea Park murders and speculating wildly about a killer on the loose 'viciously slaughtering gay men'. She sighs and switches it off, her thoughts turning back to Morrice.

She hears Grandad talking on the landing then moments later his feet thunder on the stairs as he hurries down them.

'Breakfast is almost ready,' she calls, finally pushing the dream from her mind.

Through the kitchen doorway she sees him in the hallway, pulling on his coat.

'Where are you going at this time?' she asks.

'Morning, Grace. I-I'm getting fit. I've decided I need to exercise. I've been too lazy. Remember when I used to go down the gym teaching the young ones to box?'

'How could I forget. I was one of your pupils too.'

Grandad smiles at the memory. 'Yes, you were. And a fierce opponent too, I recall.'

'That was a long time ago.'

'How long ago was that, Grace? My memory . . . you know it's not what it was . . .'

'Sixteen, seventeen years back.'

'That long, eh. Do you still have your gloves?'

'Even if I did, they'd be a little small. Are you sure you don't want breakfast before you go?'

'No, thank you. I should get going. Walking is good for you, so I hear.'

'What's brought this on?'

'I need to be fit and strong again. For you, for us.'

Archer feels a swell of love, but also thinks this an unusual response, considering Grandad is in the early stages of dementia and is sometimes prone to random thoughts. She worries that he still has Morrice and @nonymous on his mind. 'I'm a grown woman. I can look after myself,' she says in a soft tone that she hopes will reassure him.

'I know, dear. I know. But . . . I'll just go for a brisk walk around St James's Park. You remember me and your Grandma used take you there for picnics?'

108

'I remember. They were good times.'

Grandad buttons up his coat. He has an unusual intensity to his manner and a determined look on his face that she has not seen for a long time. 'It'll be good for me. For us. I'm doing this for us.'

'Don't forget that new mobile phone I bought you.'

He smiles and pulls it from his coat pocket. 'Never leave home without it.'

'Were you talking to someone just now?'

He looks away and laughs nervously. 'To myself, Grace. Just to myself.'

He embraces her and she hugs him back. He feels so bony under his coat; his body seems to be shrinking, getting thinner by the day. 'Be careful out there today,' he tells her.

'You, too.'

He leaves the house, closing the front door behind him. Archer crosses into the living room and peers out the window at Grandad, striding with purpose up Roupell Street. She sees his old friend and chess partner, Cosmo, hurrying toward him. They begin talking at each other, gesticulating at the same time, breath like mini clouds of steam puffing rapidly from their mouths. After a moment they turn and leave the street together.

Archer returns to the kitchen. As she eats her toast and sips her tea, she tries to make sense of Grandad's behaviour. Had he been talking to Cosmo on the phone earlier? If so, why lie? She feels bad for suspecting him. After all, it is not unusual for him to talk to himself. But she cannot shake the feeling that he is up to something. Meeting Cosmo in the street like that was not a chance encounter. So why not mention it? She considers it for a moment and shrugs it off as something harmless. At least he is keeping occupied and getting out in the fresh air. Cosmo will look after him.

Clearing the breakfast dishes, she wipes the surfaces, gathers the crumbs and opens the kitchen bin. She sees the newspaper he had been reading when she came home last night, the one he had turned over when she walked into the living room. She takes it from the bin and sees an article has been torn away but there is no sign of the missing piece anywhere. Dropping the paper back in the bin, she makes her way to the bathroom and, as she brushes her teeth and fits her contact lenses, she ponders what Grandad and Cosmo might be up to.

Archer leaves Roupell Street and switches on her mobile phone, expecting an angry voice message from Pierce in response to Archer's warning about the park-keeper talking to the press. She is relieved there is no message. Instead, the DCI has replied with a one-word text in capital letters: FUCK! Archer pockets the phone and crosses the concrete walkway of Jubilee Bridge, her hands thrust deep in her coat pockets, her collar turned up to stave off the bitterly cold January morning. Below her, the River Thames spills across the capital like a streak of black oil dividing the city. A dank smell rises to her nostrils, a cocktail of decay, metal and slurry with traces perhaps, she wonders, of old bone and flesh?

She arrives at Charing Cross Police Station at eight thirty and is greeted by Enquiry Officer Mark Beattie.

'Morning, Grace.'

'Morning, Mark.'

'Ella Grant is downstairs, waiting to speak to someone.'

'Ella Grant?'

'She's the cousin of Rose Grant – that's the woman who was killed in the hit-and-run yesterday. She says Rose was reported missing two days ago. She's just been to identify the body and is understandably quite upset. There are no other female officers here yet so I thought maybe you could . . .'

'Yes, of course I'll talk to her.'

'She's waiting in interview room 3.'

Archer swallows. *Room 3 is tiny.*

'I'll go see her now.'

'The incident reports have been filed.'

'I'll take a look before I go down.'

'Thank you.'

Archer turns to leave.

'Oh, by the way, our new analyst has finished her induction training.' Beattie looks beyond Archer and across the third floor. She follows his gaze to the empty office next to DI Hicks's, where, through the glass panels, she sees Klara Clark, dressed in a fitted seventies era grey trouser suit, on her knees, untangling a spaghetti mess of cables. For a moment, Archer does not recognise her. Her hair is trimmed short at the sides and has been dyed a deep orange-red colour. A long quiff swirls from the top of her head like a burning flame. But there is no mistaking Klara Clark's gangly frame and the way her long fingers deftly unfurl the mess of cables.

Archer smiles.

As if sensing she is there, Klara Clark looks up, smiles and waves and as Archer enters the office, Klara stands and towers over her. She welcomes her with a hug. 'So good to see you, Grace.'

'Welcome back. We've missed you.'

'I missed you guys, too.'

'Your hair's amazing.'

'I was going for Ziggy Stardust androgyny realness.'

'I bet heads are turning.'

'I prefer to think they're spinning.'

Archer chuckles. 'I've no doubt. Listen, let's catch up later. I have to do some quick reading before an interview. Great to have you back.'

'Great to be back.'

Archer sits at her desk, logs on to the police system and opens the report filed by the two uniforms: Keith Hopkins and Nathan Watts, and signed off by Hicks. Eyewitnesses suggest the deceased had been behaving strangely as if she was 'high' and 'off her face'. In the second report, after the description of the dead woman was matched with Rose Grant's, two female officers had visited the woman's flat, which was unoccupied. A neighbour had directed them to Rose's mother's address in Victoria. Anne Grant was babysitting Rose's five-year-old daughter and the officers stayed with the distraught woman until her niece, Ella Grant, arrived. Archer sighs heavily at the loss of Rose, a young mother, a daughter, someone who was loved, and no doubt loved in return. The ANPR report has identified the vehicle as a white Peugeot 108, reported as stolen. The driver is yet to be identified.

Down on the ground floor, Archer checks the other interview rooms. To her dismay, they are all occupied. Standing outside room 3 she takes a deep breath and enters. She takes another breath as she extends her hand across the table to the red-eyed teary young woman wearing a green parka. Archer places her notebook and pen on the table and tries to ignore the walls and ceiling as they close in around her.

112

She focuses on Rose's cousin.

'Miss Grant, I'm Detective Inspector Grace Archer. I'm so sorry for your loss.'

Ella's hand is soft and warm. With her other hand she wipes her eyes with a soggy tissue.

'Can I get you anything to drink?'

Ella looks down and shakes her head. 'I can't believe she's gone. I was only talking to her last week. We were laughing about Lilly and some of things she says.'

'Lilly is her daughter?'

Ella nods. 'She's crushed, poor little thing. Adored her mum.'

'I'm so sorry, Ella.'

It takes a moment for Ella to compose herself. She sniffs and lifts her head to face Archer. 'What happened?' she asks, in a harsher tone. 'I only know what my aunt told me. I want to know direct from you.'

'I'm sorry to say it was a hit-and-run. The car in question had been stolen and—'

'Stolen? By who?'

'That, we don't know yet.'

Ella frowns and wrings her hands on the tabletop. 'What do mean you don't know?'

'These things can take time . . .'

'How much time?'

'It's hard to say. Can you tell me why Rose might have been running barefoot down Lewisham High Street?'

'That doesn't make sense. I mean, what was she doing in Lewisham and why would she be running? She never runs anywhere.'

'Ella, some witness accounts describe Rose's behaviour as that of someone who was on drugs.'

Ella's mouth opens, confusion clouds her face. 'No! That's not true. Rose doesn't do drugs. She rarely even drinks.'

Archer regards her for a moment, reading her face for an indication of a lie. But there is none.

Ella levels her gaze and through gritted teeth says, 'If it's drugs you want to know about you should talk to her ex-boyfriend.'

'Why is that?'

'He's a dealer, among other things.'

'What's his name?'

'Adrian Boyne. I wish she'd never met him.'

'But Rose was not a user?'

Ella shakes her head. 'No. She definitely wasn't and I don't trust him.'

'Do you think he might have given her something?'

'Wouldn't surprise me.'

'That's quite an accusation.'

Ella shrugs. 'I can't stand him.'

'Ella, what did Rose do for money?'

'She was an apprentice hairdresser. Earned a pittance.'

'Did she have other means of income?'

Ella seems to squirm and, after taking a breath, says, 'She was on the game. Sometimes . . . not always. Only when she was short of cash.'

'How did she meet her clients?'

'You'll have to ask Adrian that.'

'Why do you say that?'

'Because he was also her pimp.'

'Where does Adrian live?'

'Shoreditch.'

'His address?'

'Number 9 Virginia Road.'

Archer writes the address in her notebook.

'Are you going to talk to him?'

'Yes.'

Ella wipes her eyes.

'I'll keep you up to date with everything we find, Ella. The ANPR system may have a photograph of the driver.'

Ella nods. 'I should go now. I need to be with my aunt and Lilly.'

'Of course. Could you leave me your contact number?'

Archer makes a note of the number. 'Thank you for coming in today, Ella. I know this isn't easy.'

Archer walks Ella out of the station, glancing at the clock on the wall behind the receptionist. It's 9.10.

Ella stands outside under the portico and zips up her parka. 'Please find whoever's responsible.'

'I will do my best. I promise.'

Ella nods a goodbye, and walks down the steps, turning toward the Strand.

16

ARCHER AND QUINN ARE IN Klara's hub listening to the analyst's findings on Adrian Boyne.

'Adrian Boyne is twenty-eight years old. Essex born, lives in a shared house on Virginia Road in Shoreditch. He's had a few convictions as a teenager for drug possession. Nothing serious. He's a known peddler of narcotics but to what level we're not certain. He's had no recent convictions. Oh, and there's nothing about pimping.'

'Klara, has Hicks followed up with you or Os about yesterday's hit-and-run?' asks Archer.

'He hasn't asked either of us. Maybe he spoke to Marian or Joely.'

'Neither of them have heard from him. Seems Hicks is the lone wolf in this investigation. Which is code for nothing will be followed up this side of the century.'

'Actually, I think I overheard him talking with Felton about it this morning,' says Quinn.

'Good. We should go see Boyne and move things along,' says Archer. 'Did you talk to Krish?'

'Yeah, very briefly. He was still compiling the data for the report. He did tell me the victim had been dead around eight to ten hours.'

'OK. Could you look into CCTV around Battersea between nine o'clock onwards and see what you can find?'

'No worries. I'll make a start now.'

'Thanks, Klara.'

Archer and Quinn leave the station and pick up the Volvo, which is parked on Chandos Place. Archer sits silently in the passenger seat staring out at nothing in particular, thinking about her meeting with HR.

As Quinn drives east through Bloomsbury and Old Street, Archer feels an unsettling glumness at the prospect of starting therapy. Her last experience after her childhood abduction had been a mess. Not only had she gone over her abduction several times, or more, with the police, but she was being forced to do it again with a shrink, who had been an idiot. He had tried to encourage her to let it all out, to cry, to scream. 'You will feel better,' he'd shrilled, pushing her, needling her, doing his best to get a reaction.

Her blood had boiled.

Eventually, she gave him a reaction and blackened his eye.

For young Grace, it felt that the shrink was enjoying her experience a little too much. He was not helping her and she'd sworn she would never talk to another counsellor again. But Debbie Dickson's words echo in her mind, 'That was then. This is now.' As vexing as the HR Manager seems to be, perhaps there is some truth in her argument. Perhaps this time will be different.

Quinn has the heat turned up high. Archer begins to feel hot and uncomfortable. She unbuttons her coat and cracks open the window. The cold air nips her face and revives her.

They drive through Hackney, passing the refurbished Edwardian Old Street Magistrates Court. Quinn points to it. 'That old place is a hotel now. And a boutique one at that.'

'Yes, I'd heard. Apparently, the old jailhouse cells have been converted into bedrooms. You can stay in the same rooms once occupied by the Krays.'

'Very romantic.'

'That's progress for you.'

'Indeed it is. I hope they've redecorated.'

'I'd like to think they have.'

'By the way, how'd it go with Debs from HR?'

'Could have been better. She has a strange lack of empathy. For a Human Resources Manager, that is.'

'She's all heart, is our Debs. Likes things done her way. Best not to get on the wrong side of her.'

'Bit late for that.'

'I shouldn't worry too much. I get the sense Pierce has your back now. That's all that matters, unless things turn to shit with her.'

They say nothing for a moment before Archer asks, 'Do *you* think I'm angry?'

Quinn considers this for a moment before replying. 'No. Not in the slightest.'

'Do you think I'm quick to lose my temper?'

'Not especially. Is that what she said?'

'I lost it in the meeting at one stage. Also, either PC Hopkins or PC Watts put in a complaint about being humiliated by me at the Dorothy Hayes incident.'

Quinn shakes his head. 'I bet Hicks put him up to that.'

'That was my conclusion too.'

'Spineless dick!'

'I've been given a choice: therapy or a desk job.'

'Shit!'

'Debbie believes I'm a "special case".'

'What does that mean?'

Archer shrugs. 'Who knows?'

'I wouldn't pay any attention to that nonsense.'

They drive in silence for a few moments. Archer's mind is turning over with doubt about her ability to cope with what she has gone through. She glances at Quinn and after a moment quietly confesses, 'I see Morrice in my dreams sometimes. @nonymous, too.'

She exhales and feels a weight shifting. It feels good to say it out loud.

Archer senses Quinn looking at her. She does not meet his gaze and stares through the window at the passing traffic.

'That can't be fun.'

'Don't say anything to Pierce. This is my problem and I'll deal with it.'

'I understand.'

'I-I've never really spoken about what happened back then. Not since those early therapy sessions. It's easier to just forget.'

They say nothing for a moment.

'I'm also claustrophobic. Hate small spaces,' she admits. 'Since Morrice ...' Archer pauses. 'That's why I couldn't take the lift yesterday at Joel Dean's place.'

Quinn says evenly, 'We'll just have to avoid small spaces then.'

Archer nods. 'That would be helpful.'

'Anything else?'

'That's enough. Don't you think?'

'I do. While we're in the confessional ... I want you to know I ... I tried to kill myself. Once.'

Archer feels a tightening in her chest and looks across at Quinn who focuses on the road ahead, his expression fixed.

'Actually, it was twice but I prefer to think the first time doesn't count because it was half-hearted. I had filled my coat with rocks that weren't very heavy and then jumped into a river that turned out to be four feet deep. I was sixteen at the time and sat in the freezing water for ten minutes, feeling just so desolate and hopeless, before deciding I'd had enough of the cold. Also, I couldn't feel the bottom half of my body, which wasn't nice. The second time was last summer. I was at Brighton beach, alone. My son, Joshie, adored Brighton. We'd go there on day trips. He loved swimming and he was a strong swimmer for his age . . . fearless, too. Ironic, then, that it was water that took him from us.' Quinn sighs. 'I undressed at the water's edge and swam out as far as I could go. I stopped and let myself sink. I was broken and I missed Joshie so much . . . Also, I had some weird, fantastical notion that as I drowned I'd meet him again and join him in a utopian Disney-like underwater afterlife . . . Funny what grief does to your head. As I sank, I saw a crack in the clouds. A single beam of sunlight shone down and danced on the surface. Sounds utterly corny, I know, but the Catholic in me took that as a sign from Joshie to come to my senses and that it wasn't my time. I swam toward it, hoping to touch and feel his warmth, but the clouds passed and took him away. I broke the surface and the gravity of what I had just tried to do hit me then. I sobbed and felt so ashamed that Joshie might have seen me at my worst. Anyway, I was cold and beginning to feel weak and I swam back with a grim determination. I didn't think I was going to make it and almost killed myself swimming back, no joke intended.'

'I'm so sorry.'

'That I failed?' laughs Quinn.

'No!'

'Don't be. Suicide for the men in my family is a trait, like high cholesterol. We all have it. May get you one day. May not.'

'How are you now?'

'I'm good, thanks. I still have my moments, but I'm much better. It's a tough gig when you lose a kid. Guilt can be a killer – literally.'

'For what it's worth, I'm glad you're still here.'

'Yeah, me too.' Quinn points ahead. 'If I'm not mistaken, that's where Boyne lives.'

He turns into a narrow, shabby Victorian street and parks opposite a rundown mews house. There are bars on the windows, old sheets obscuring the upstairs glass and a locked gate protecting the front door.

'Boyne must have a lot to protect,' says Quinn.

The front door opens, followed by the gate which opens onto the street. Archer catches a glimpse of a slim man in a baggy white sweatshirt disappearing back inside.

'That's definitely Boyne,' says Quinn.

Seconds later, a large man wearing a branded baseball cap, dark glasses and carrying a backpack, steps out onto the street. He is a bull of man, more muscle than fat. He talks with Boyne, who fist bumps him when they part company. Boyne locks the gate and closes the door as the man walks up Virginia Road, passing the unmarked Volvo.

'Definitely on steroids,' observes Quinn.

'Doesn't want to be recognised, although with that bulk he'll need a bit more than sunglasses and a baseball cap.'

They step out of the car and cross the street to the gated entrance. Archer presses the doorbell and notices a sheet twitching on the window. She hears voices inside followed by footsteps on a wooden floor. The lock turns on the door and Boyne appears behind the gate. The fetid smell of cannabis wafts from inside the house. Boyne's eyes slide from Archer to Quinn.

'How may I help you, officers?'

Boyne is tall with short dark hair, a wide boy with an equally wide face and a streetwise confidence.

'No flies on you,' says Quinn.

'Adrian Boyne?' asks Archer.

'That's me.' He grins, revealing two front teeth and a left canine made from gold.

'I'm Detective Inspector Archer and this is Detective Sergeant Quinn. We'd like to talk to you, if you don't mind.'

'I'm kind of busy right now, officers.'

Quinn scrunches his face. 'Of course you are.'

'We won't take up much of your time,' says Archer. 'We just have a few questions.'

'About?'

Quinn blows out a breath.

'May we come in?' Archer asks, gently, but firmly.

Boyne narrows his gaze and looks up and down the street.

'Come on, junior, open the gate,' goads Quinn.

Boyne arches his eyebrows at Quinn and goes to shut the door.

'There's no one else, Mr Boyne,' says Archer. 'This is not a raid. We only want to talk to you about Rose Grant.'

He regards them momentarily before shrugging and unlocking the gate.

Quinn sniffs the air. 'Someone's having a nice time,' he comments.

'You're quite the comedian,' says Boyne derisively as he closes the gate and door behind them. 'People smoke weed. What can I say?' He shrugs, leads them into the living room which, to Archer's surprise, is much less shabby than the exterior suggests. An enormous flat screen television dominates the space. The walls are bare and painted a stylish ivory white, the sofa is a pale-grey modern L-shape, and a glossy white oblong coffee table sits centre stage. Ashtrays, cigarette papers and threads of tobacco litter the surface, including a bag of green weed that Boyne makes no attempt to hide. A newspaper lies on the floor below the table.

'I heard about Rose,' says Boyne. From his pocket he pulls out a pouch of Lambert and Butler and falls back on the sofa, legs wide, before reaching across and scooping a fag paper from the table.

'How did you know? It's not public knowledge.'

'Her cousin Ella called and gave me a right earful, as if it was all my fault. Silly cow!'

'When did you last see Rose?'

Quinn walks to the window and peers behind the sheet covering the glass.

'Last week. Wednesday, I think.' He rolls the tobacco swiftly and expertly between his long fingers.

'What did you talk about?'

Boyne glances at Archer, his brow furrowing. 'This and that.'

'Could you be more specific?'

He sighs and stares at the blank television screen. 'Life stuff. Her family. Her friends. She was short of money and needed some extra cash.'

'Did you give her any?'

'Didn't have any to give.'

'Seems like you're doing OK for yourself,' says Quinn, taking in the expensive furnishings.

Boyne does not respond.

'Did you know Rose worked as a prostitute?'

Boyne places the perfectly rolled cigarette into his mouth and begins to search his pockets. 'Everyone did. It weren't no secret.'

'How did Rose get her clients?' asks Archer.

Boyne rubs his nose. 'Either of you gotta light?' he asks.

'Neither of us smoke,' replies Quinn.

He begins to search the back of the sofa.

'How did Rose get her clients?'

He lifts the newspaper from the floor and looks underneath it. Nothing. He shrugs again and sets the paper on the coffee table. 'I dunno.'

'Have you ever introduced her to a client?'

Boyne tenses and meets her gaze. 'I'm not her pimp, if that's what you're implying.'

'She was your ex-girlfriend, wasn't she?' asks Quinn.

'Yeah – and?'

'You don't seem especially upset that she's dead,' observes Archer.

'It's sad, man. I'm upset. You just don't see it.' He bangs his chest with his fist. 'It's all inside.'

'Witnesses think Rose might have been on drugs. Would you know anything about that?' asks Quinn.

Archer's eyes are drawn to the newspaper.

Boyne sniggers. 'Is that what this is about?'

It's yesterday's paper. The same one Grandad had been reading. The same one he had turned over when she walked into the living room.

'You tell us?' asks Quinn.

'That's bullshit, man. OK, she was a hooker, but she had a daughter and a mum to support. She never took no drugs. That wasn't her thing. No way, man!'

Archer is only half listening. The paper is open on a page showing a grainy colour mugshot of a man smiling darkly. The small, bold headline has been underscored several times with red ink. She picks up the paper, reads the headline and swallows.

It can't be true!

She looks across at Boyne who is watching her curiously. She feels Quinn's gaze too and can sense his unease.

Archer shows the article to Boyne. 'Why is this headline underlined?' Her tone is cold.

His gaze flicks to the paper and back to Archer. 'I've no idea.'

The air crackles between them.

'This house, this furniture, this operation you have going. It's all his, isn't it?' says Archer.

Boyne's lips tighten. 'Whose?'

'The drugs you peddle. The pimping you claim not to be involved with. It's all his. It's all been waiting for him. For his return.'

Boyne shrugs and turns to Quinn. 'Don't know what she's on about, mate. Seriously . . .'

Quinn is watching Archer through hooded eyes.

Archer tosses the paper onto the coffee table. 'We'll be in touch, Mr Boyne.' She turns to leave.

A cloud darkens Archer's mood as they cross the street and climb into the Volvo. That headline and that mugshot have hit her like a punch to the stomach. Why did she not know about this? Why hadn't anyone told her? Her thoughts turn to

126

Grandad, who had hidden the article from her. He had been acting suspiciously. He was up to something. But what?

'What was that about?' asks Quinn.

Archer exhales.

'Frankie "Snow" White, the drug lord, the man who had my father murdered is being released from prison in the next few days . . .'

17

As QUINN DRIVES THEM BACK to Central London, Archer calls her old NCA governor and friend of her father, the now retired Charlie Bates. It was Charlie who had eventually nailed Frankie 'Snow' White, for drug offences, including supply and production.

'I'm sorry, Grace,' says Bates.

'How long have you known?'

He hesitates before answering. 'I found out last week that his application was being processed.'

'And you didn't think to tell me?'

'It was kept under wraps, "need to know", apparently. When I heard, I just didn't believe it at first and needed to be sure. The word was his application would be denied, so I didn't think much about it, but it seems the courts believe he's done his time and is ready for parole. As you know, even behind bars Snow is still well connected and knows many important people.'

'This is just so wrong, Charlie. He's responsible for so many murders, including Dad's.'

Bates sighs. 'I know, Grace. Every copper from back then, every brief and every backstreet drug dealer knew it. But it was never proved.'

'His businesses are still operational?'

'That's right. He still has money, power and influence, which will have helped expedite his release.'

Archer feels sick to her stomach.

'I may be retired but I'll be keeping a sharp eye on him, Grace. I can promise you that.'

'I have to go, Charlie.'

'If you need anything, you know where I am.'

'Sure . . .'

'Take care, Grace.'

'Bye, Charlie.'

They're driving through Holborn. Quinn eases on the brakes for the red lights and Archer's thoughts turn to Grandad. She searches for his number and dials it. The phone rings but goes straight to voicemail. She ends the call without leaving a message and wonders what Grandad and Cosmo are up to.

'You OK?' asks Quinn.

'Been better.'

'I'm sorry about White.'

'I should have seen it coming. He was never going to go away forever.'

'No, I suppose not.'

Archer turns her focus to Rose Grant and the meeting with Boyne. 'Rose Grant was allegedly on drugs,' she says, 'yet her cousin Ella categorically stated that she never touched them and that she barely drank. Boyne also says drugs weren't her thing.'

'Or perhaps Ella didn't know her cousin as well as she thought she did and Boyne supplied Rose. He could be lying to save his bacon.'

'Well, Boyne is connected to White. Clearly, he's running one of his operations. If we prove Boyne did supply Rose, we can at least get her justice and bang a nail in the coffin for White. We really need the post-mortem report, which could take a few days.'

'Aye, it could, or maybe we should pay Dr Kapur a call. See what he can do for us.'

Archer feels her pulse quickening. 'My thoughts exactly.'

'Grace, a small suggestion. This is far from protocol but ...'

Quinn pauses and seems unsure about continuing.

'I'm listening.'

'Dr Kapur is very fond of absinthe. Particularly Czechoslovakian absinthe.'

'Oh?'

'Perhaps we could take along a bottle. As a gift, you understand. Not for an afternoon soiree at the morgue.'

'Thanks for clarifying. I'm assuming that'll help us get a faster turnaround on the report?'

'It may speed things along. If not, we can head to the water's edge at Embankment and get sloshed.'

'Sounds delightful, but absinthe isn't really my poison. Let's grab a bottle and keep our fingers crossed that the good doctor will do the business.'

'Excellent. I'll stop off at Gerry's in Soho. I can usually get a discount there. Familiar smiling face, ya see.'

'I can believe it.'

To Archer and Quinn's disappointment, Czechoslovakian absinthe is out of stock at Gerry's Wine and Spirits.

The retailer is a round, red-faced man with a friendly demeanour. 'You could try the French Combier L'Entêté. It's from the Loire Valley and an award-winning product, also half the price of the Czech. I'll knock a fiver off for you, Harry.'

'Very generous of you. We'll take it.'

'That'll be £55.'

Archer and Quinn exchange glances. The pathologist clearly has expensive tastes.

'Looks like an old medicine bottle,' observes Archer, as the shopkeeper places it on the counter.

'He can stash it in his cabinet and no one will be any the wiser,' replies Quinn.

They arrive at the mortuary on Horseferry Road in Westminster, a late-Victorian three-storey block with a central stone arch containing two heavy panelled doors coated in years of deep red gloss. Quinn fiddles with the bottle, cradling it as if he were about to present a prize. Archer presses the intercom buzzer and waits.

Seconds later the speaker crackles followed by a long throat-clearing cough from the depths of the coroner's court. 'Hello,' says Dr Kapur.

'Hello, Dr Kapur, it's Detective Inspector Grace Archer and Detective Sergeant Quinn.'

'Do we have a meeting?' he asks, curtly.

'No,' replies Archer. 'We'd like to discuss a case with you. Urgently.'

'I'm quite busy. Can you make an appointment?'

Quinn leans into the speaker. 'We've brought absinthe!'

The pathologist is quiet for a moment, before asking, 'Czechoslovakian?'

'Not this time. Something better.'

Kapur clears his throat again before releasing the door and meets them on the ground floor, dressed in a grey suit, his face long, his expression serious. His eyes roll over the bottle in Quinn's hands.

'It looks like a medicine bottle,' he says.

'That's what we thought,' replies Quinn, brightly. 'It's French.'

'French!' The doctor blinks, the first and only sign of emotion Archer thinks she has seen from him.

'From the Loire Valley, no less.'

The doctor raises an eyebrow and takes the bottle from Quinn. 'I'll give it a try at the weekend. Thank you. How may I help?'

Archer speaks. 'Rose Grant was brought in yesterday after a hit-and-run in Lewisham. Witnesses claim she was on drugs. We'd like to know if they were right and, if so, what drugs she'd taken.'

'I see. Why the urgency?'

'There may be a connection to a cartel.'

Kapur considers this for a moment before saying, 'You will be aware that some narcotics don't remain in the system for long. Is there anything in particular I should be looking for?'

'If it's illegal, we'll take it,' answers Quinn.

'Very well. I will examine the subject today and call you as soon as I know more. Thank you for my . . . medicine. I have always wanted to visit the Loire Valley. Perhaps a few shots of this will shake me into booking a flight.'

'Let's hope so,' says Quinn.

'Thank you, Dr Kapur,' says Archer.

The historic Wimpole Street in Marylebone, with its storied Georgian and Edwardian mansions, is a drop-in centre for the rich seeking urgent body transformations with costly plastic surgery, teeth implants and unnaturally white Hollywood smiles. It's also a hub of mental health therapists. Life Coaching, Existential Therapy, Cognitive Behaviour Therapy and Eye Movement Desensitisation and Reprocessing – whatever they were – are all on the menu. Archer can't help but picture a clientele of flawlessly beautiful people with an inherent mental fragility.

Dr Abigail Hutchison's surgery, curiously named The Tree of Life, is located on the first floor of 85 Wimpole Street. The doctor is a specialist in both Cognitive Behaviour Therapy and Eye Movement Desensitisation and Reprocessing. Archer is not sure what to make of either of those.

The time is almost 4 p.m. and Archer, having completed her pre-therapy questionnaire, is seated in a dimly lit waiting room on an uncomfortable designer sofa that probably cost more than her monthly salary. The waiting room would have been the parlour of the house, back in the day. It is a large, square space with the walls, picture rails and woodwork all painted the same pale, chic grey. A wide and unused black marble fireplace is the focal point of the room and two tall bay windows overlook the late-afternoon gloom and the busy traffic and pedestrians of Wimpole Street. She wonders how the Met has the money to pay for counselling in a place like this. They bemoan the lack of funds to boost recruitment for an over-stretched workforce, yet somehow they can find an impressive budget to refurbish Charing Cross Police Station. Shelling out funds for therapies in Wimpole Street, of all places, seems an unnecessary expense but Pierce has insisted she come here. Archer recalls the recent conversation with HR Manager,

Debbie Dickson, feels a tremor of irritation and wonders if only 'special cases' get sent to special places.

She hears a door close softly shut and looks up to see a blonde woman pull on a black leather biking jacket. Archer quickly realises it's MJ. She looks across at Archer and their eyes widen and lock in a moment of mutual surprise.

'Hi,' says Archer.

'Hi,' replies MJ. She looks away, zips up her jacket and hurries out.

Guess I'm not the only special case.

Archer hears a door opening and the sound of soft footfalls approaching from the hall beyond it, and looks up to see a handsome woman dressed in a white blouse and tweed slacks. Her hair is a glossy pale brown with elegant silver threads that shimmer in the glow of the hallway light.

'Grace?' she asks, smiling impassively.

Archer's stomach tightens as she realises she is not prepared for this. She's been avoiding it for weeks and suddenly here she is, in front of a shrink, expected to offload.

I can't do this.

They shake hands. Hutchison's grip is warm and firm.

'Please come through.'

Archer follows her down a carpeted hallway to a panelled door labelled with the doctor's name. Hutchison allows Archer to go first and follows her inside, closing the door behind her.

The room is lit with soft amber lighting and candles. On the walls are old paintings of countryside landscapes and a thick white woollen rug seems to grow from the centre of the floor where a French-style brown leather sofa faces a matching armchair.

135

'Please make yourself comfortable. I can guarantee you that this sofa is much more comfortable than that slab of concrete in the waiting room.' The doctor speaks in a calm yet authoritative tone. 'Can I get you something to drink?'

Archer perches on the edge of the sofa, her hands clasped together, fingers entwined. 'No, thank you.'

Hutchison eases into the armchair, with a Moleskine notepad and pen, and looks across at Archer. After a moment, she says, 'I understand this appointment has been dropped in your lap.'

Archer doesn't respond.

'I've read your questionnaire answers. Aside from contact details there is not much there, but that's fine. I've never much like the questionnaires anyway. We can forego that and have an informal chat instead. Then I can make an assessment and recommend a course of therapy. How does that sound?'

'Fine,' shrugs Archer. She feels a petulance clawing at her from within and begins to shift uncomfortably.

'I'll ensure there's no charge to the Met for this session. A favour for Clare.'

Clare. DCI Pierce.

'I'm sure she'll be pleased.' Archer can hear the acidity in her tone and instantly regrets it.

'Perhaps.'

A moment of silence hangs in the air between them, which is broken by the doctor. 'What would you like to get out of today?'

'Do you have many clients from the Met?'

'A couple.'

'Only special cases?'

Hutchison considers Archer's question. 'I'm not sure how I would define a special case. All my clients are special, in their own way.'

Archer feels a growing discomfort and looks around for a clock, but there isn't one.

'So, what would you like to get out of today?' repeats Hutchison.

Archer leans back on the sofa. 'I really have no idea. As you mentioned, this appointment was dropped in my lap on Monday.'

'I understand and I'm sorry about that. Would you like to start and tell me why you are here?'

'I was told to come here.'

'Why do you think that is?'

Archer blinks at the question. 'Human Resources think I need help.'

'Do you think they're right?'

'No.'

'Do you know why Human Resources think you need help?'

'Someone made a complaint?'

'About you?'

'Yes.'

'Do you want to elaborate?'

'I had a disagreement with an idiot police officer.'

'I see. Could there be another reason why Human Resources recommended you for therapy?'

Archer wonders if she already knows her history.

'Has DCI Pierce mentioned anything about me?'

'She recommended that you see me, but she did not say why. Clare – DCI Pierce – is a professional hard nut, as you may well be aware, but she is also loyal and decent. That said, I recognised your name from the newspapers after the @nonymous killings so I know a little about you from that period and I also did some research.'

'That's terrific. What's your diagnosis, doctor?' snipes Archer.

'I don't have one. It might be good for us to talk and see if I can help. But you may not need any. Let's find out. Let's prove Human Resources wrong.'

Archer is not a fool and can see Hutchison is only trying to help, but for some reason she cannot deal with opening up right now. She feels her neck burning and her skin tingling. Despite the space in Hutchison's office, Archer feels an over-whelming sense of being confined.

She stands. 'I can't do this. It's a mistake. I don't need help. I'm fine. I have to go. I'm sorry to waste your time.'

Archer turns and walks toward the door.

'Grace, wait.'

Archer hesitates but feels herself shrivel inside. She feels hot and flustered, shakes her head and hurries out of the building and onto Wimpole Street where the cold air calms her down.

Her phone rings. It's Quinn.

'Hey, just wanted to update you on a couple of things. Are you OK to talk?'

'Sure.'

'Firstly, we found the stolen car that killed Rose Grant. It was abandoned at a petrol station in Finsbury Park. We got the driver and his mate on camera. They're in custody now. They're just a couple of stoned kids with no previous.'

'OK.'

'Also, Kapur called.'

'What did he say?'

'He said he doesn't have much to work with. Rose's stomach was empty. There is evidence from her mouth and clothes that she threw up just before she died and if she'd taken something, or was given something, it didn't stay down too long. He's going to organise checks on her blood and urine. But that may take some time. He's on it though.'

Archer sighs. 'OK. Thanks, Harry.'

'Are you coming back to the station?'

'I don't think so. I have some personal business at home to deal with.'

'No worries. Sorry about that terrible joke.'

'I'm slowly getting use to them.'

Quinn laughs. 'See you tomorrow.'

'Bye.'

18

RCHER NEEDS THE SPACE TO think and her usual way to do that is to lose herself in a long walk through the city streets. She buttons up her coat, raises the collar and plunges her hands deep into the warmth of the pockets. She walks up Wimpole Street, navigating the throng with her head down and a pang of regret for giving up on the session with Dr Hutchison so quickly. She should have stayed and proved her, Pierce and Debbie from HR wrong, but she had suddenly felt as trapped as she'd been in that pit in the earth that Morrice had imprisoned her in eighteen years ago. She shudders at the thought, but any sense of fear is fast vanquished by a surge of gratifying anger. *Fucking Morrice!* She had long learned to deal with the legacy of her abduction, which included the night-time visits in her dreams, and, in her waking hours, the occasional sightings in dark corners of the little man with pale skin and thin red lips, watching her, waiting to snatch her away and place her back inside that bug- and worm-filled hole.

Archer crosses at Henrietta Place and cuts through Chapel Place, passing St Peter's, a humble, deconsecrated Georgian chapel made from bricks and stone quoins. She wonders if Morrice's spectre lurks in the shadows of the old church or if he is peering down from the stone tower where three leering crows squawk at her.

Isn't *murder* the collective noun for crows? she wonders.

A murder of crows.

The irony is not lost on her.

Morrice can no longer touch her. She had, after all, ended his life. The child killer had been slain by a feral twelve-year-old Grace Archer. She has accepted that he will always be a phantom in her life, but what she struggles to accept is the other unspoken repercussion of her abduction.

Her claustrophobia. It is her Achilles' Heel.

Fucking Morrice!

She cannot tolerate tiny spaces. Even the thought of them makes her nauseous. And there are times when she becomes totally overwhelmed, her head spins and the pressure takes its toll, regardless of the dimensions of the space she occupies at that moment. Like it did in Dr Hutchison's office. Thankfully, these occurrences are rare.

Archer's failure to see the therapy session through will no doubt result in a backlash from DCI Pierce and Debbie Dickson. She can't think of that now, will deal with it when the time comes. There are other, more pressing matters, on her mind. The murders of Brian Bailey and Justin Sykes, Rose Grant's suspicious death, Frankie 'Snow' White's release from prison and Grandad's secrecy. There is too much occupying her head right now. Her thoughts focus on Grandad. Why had he kept the article from her and what are he and Cosmo up to?

Archer hesitates at the final stretch of Chapel Place which is horribly narrow and dark. She can't help but feel disappointed and challenges herself to ignore her reluctance, overcome her fears and go for it. She breathes slowly and quickens her pace.

Breathe. Breathe. Breathe.

She exits quickly onto a bustling Oxford Street, stands at the edge of the kerb and composes herself. Engines rumble, exhausts puff and horns blare. Buses ferry their huddled passengers slowly through the gridlocked traffic as Archer turns her thoughts to Frankie 'Snow' White.

Like Morrice and @nonymous, White is a name that burns forever in her soul. Morrice and @nonymous are like shadows, phantoms that haunt her but can no longer harm her, but White is the returning bogeyman, the bogeyman who will be free any day now.

It has never been proven that White gave the green light for her father's death. But everyone knows the gangland boss was responsible. The hit had all the hallmarks of White's chosen execution style: one single bullet through the temple at close range, swift and deadly. In her father's hand was a blank white business card with droplets of his blood on it, White's calling card. White was all about the theatre and liked to add little flourishes to his kills. It set him apart from the other gangland bosses, or so he thought. He had many killers in his employ. It was said that the hitman who murdered her father was a killer with a taste for blood. Literally. Ending life was his job and spatter was his kink. The thought makes Archer sick to her stomach. She wishes she knew who the killer was. What she would give—

Her phone pings with a text.

Grace, I'm sorry about this afternoon. If you change your mind I have a free slot open at 8 p.m. tomorrow evening. I will leave it open for you.
Take care, Abigail Hutchison.

Archer bites her lip but then deletes the message and pockets the phone.

The walk has taken her almost one hour by the time she arrives in Roupell Street, where she sees light through the crack in the curtains. She fishes out her keys, unlocks the door and steps inside.

'Grandad, I'm home,' she calls.

He does not respond.

She looks in the living room, but he's not there. There is a quietness about the space, the only sound is the ticking of the old Harris of Bath wall clock in the alcove beside the fireplace. The time is almost 5.20.

She calls upstairs, but still he does not reply. For peace of mind she checks his bedroom, but there's no sign of him.

There's only one place he could be at this time. At least, she hopes he might be there.

She leaves the house and heads toward the local pub, the King's Tavern. Situated on the corner of Roupell Street and Windmill Walk, the King's Tavern is a favourite haunt of Grandad's, and Archer's, for that matter. It is one of London's finer backstreet drinking dens which has been given a modern yet traditional makeover. Retaining almost all of its original features, the exterior is painted a classic dark grey, which for Archer makes the dim amber glow inside seem all the more inviting.

She peers through the windows, looking over the heads of the locals and end-of-the-working-day drinkers. She sees him sitting at a table with Cosmo, deep in conversation with a third man she doesn't recognise. He looks in his forties, a stern-looking type with a humourless demeanour and a hollow look in his eyes. Grandad is talking, but the man does not look at him. Amateur tattoos are etched on his hands and neck. Archer's a cop who's met many cons in her time. This guy, whoever he is, is one. Archer discreetly takes out her phone, zooms in and snaps a picture.

As she pockets her phone, the man stands, says something to Grandad and leaves the table.

Archer walks to the pub door and opens it for him. 'Evening,' she says, willing him to look at her.

He glances her way, frowns and walks past without responding.

'Have a good evening,' she calls after him.

He ignores her and walks quickly up Windmill Walk, disappearing into the shadows.

Archer swipes open her phone, selects the photograph of the man and texts it to Klara with the message:

Hi Klara, please could you do me a favour and run your face rec software on this bloke and find out who he is? Thanks G x

She enters the pub, which is cosy, familiar and welcoming with the sweet smell of hops and the gentle hum of voices and laughter. Grandad and Cosmo are leaning into each, gabbling away. Archer pulls up a chair and joins them. Startled, they both turn to look at her.

Archer looks from Grandad to Cosmo whose eyes flare for a second and then he smiles weakly.

'Hello, dear,' says Grandad. 'I didn't know you were coming here tonight.'

'I hadn't planned to. I was looking for you and you weren't at home, so I thought I'd check here.'

Grandad beams. 'And here you found me.'

'I better be going,' says Cosmo, rising from his seat.

'Please stay for one moment,' Archer says, gently, but firmly.

'How's your day been?' asks Grandad, brightly.

'Frankie White is being released from prison,' replies Archer.

Grandad's face darkens. 'So you know.'

Conscious of Grandad's fragile mind due to the curse that is early dementia, Archer evens her tone. 'It's in the papers, Grandad. Why didn't you mention it?'

'You've been through so much already. I didn't want you to have any unnecessary upset.'

'But how could I not find this out?'

Grandad has no answer for that.

'So why keep it from me?'

A fleeting look passes between Grandad and Cosmo.

Grandad shrugs.

'Who was that man?' she asks.

A silence falls across the table.

'I really have to go,' says Cosmo. 'Arlene will skin me alive if I'm not back for supper.'

Neither Archer or Grandad say anything as Cosmo ups and hurries out of the pub. Archer looks at Grandad, waiting for an answer. He meets her gaze with a troubled expression that is both defiant and angry.

'He was no one.'

Archer feels an overwhelming ache of sadness. The onset of Grandad's early stage dementia has shifted his moods, sometimes for the better, other times for the worse. When he is happy, he is full of joy, the same Grandad she knew as a child before everything turned upside down. And when he is sad,

146

he withdraws into his grief and becomes inconsolable that his wife and son are no longer alive. 'But they were only here yesterday! How can they can be dead already?' he protested once in confusion. He rarely gets angry. That just isn't part of his personality. Yet she is beginning to glimpse more flashes of a fury that seems long hidden in a bottle that is starting to crack.

His expression softens and he sighs. 'I'm sorry, Grace. I'm very tired. It's been a long day. Let's go home, shall we?'

Archer reaches across and takes his hand. He smiles sadly at her and squeezes her hand.

'How about I make us a risotto tonight?' she says.

'I'd love that. I'll open a bottle of Chenin Blanc. It was your grandma's favourite wine, did I ever tell you that?'

'Many times.'

Grandad hooks his arm inside Archer's elbow. 'I expect I did,' he replies. 'I expect I did.'

19

ARCHER JOLTS FROM A RESTLESS sleep, gasping for breath. The muscles in her back and arms coil like snakes as she calms her breathing and quietens the storm in her head, grateful to be back in the real world. Squinting at the digital clock on the bedside table, she groans at the glowing numbers. 04.59.

Too early.

It usually happens in quiet, dark places where she finds herself alone during an investigation; for instance, a night-time street or an abandoned building. She'll hear a footfall, or a creak, feel a cold breeze on her neck and sense one, or both of them, watching her from the shadows. Her ghosts.

She sighs, rests her forehead on her knees and thinks about Dr Hutchison. Perhaps she *does* need help. She gives herself a moment and then reaches across, switches on the lamp. From the bedside table she unfolds her tortoiseshell spectacles and checks her iPhone. There's a missed WhatsApp message from Klara.

Hi, Grace. I'm running the facial rec software on that photo. Should have a match tomorrow providing he is on

our DB. I've pulled together the footage from Battersea
Park CCTV and uploaded it to my encrypted server,
should you want to take a look before coming into work.
You know the password. :-) Kx

Archer spends the next two hours studying the files. The footage
contains video of Justin Sykes walking up Prince of Wales Drive
at 10.20 p.m. He slows and removes his phone from his trouser
pocket, looks at the screen and then puts it back into his pocket.
She guesses he is ignoring a call from Joel Dean or his mother.
He then walks through the side gate and disappears into the
darkness of the park where there is no CCTV. A little later in
the sequence, a Ford Mondeo pulls into a parking space. The
lights switch off and, moments after, Brian Bailey gets out and
walks casually across the road and into the side entrance of
Battersea Park. Almost fifteen minutes pass and there is no sign
of either man. A couple emerge from the entrance. They look
as if they might be holding cans of beer. After that there is
nothing. Klara has included footage from the park's main
entrance, although the quality is poor. There are various
nondescript people entering and leaving, including a hunched,
limping figure dressed in a parka, who shuffles slowly out of
the park. Klara has taken individual shots of each one and made
the pictures bigger and clearer, but they're not perfect.

Archer stretches and yawns. The spectre of Frankie White
appears in her thoughts and she thinks about drug dealer,
Adrian Boyne. Witnesses claimed Rose was behaving strangely
before she died, as if she was drunk or on drugs, and while Dr
Kapur had found no indication of either, was that accurate?
Had Rose been given the sort of drugs that don't stay in the

body for long? GHB? Rohypnol? She taps her lip with a finger. There is something here. A connection that Boyne is involved with. A connection to Frankie White also.

It's just after 7 a.m. when Archer closes the laptop and hauls her tired body out of bed and into the shower. She loses herself in the hot water soaping herself down with a revitalising L'Occitane citrus shower gel, a Christmas gift from Klara. She dries her hair in her bedroom, dresses in a khaki wool sweater, black jeans and brown brogue boots.

'Morning, Grace,' Grandad calls from the landing.

She peeks out at him. He is dressed in his blue pyjamas and rubbing sleep from his eyes.

'Morning, Grandad. How did you sleep?'

'Not bad, thanks. How about you?'

'I slept well,' she lies. 'Would you like something to eat?'

'Maybe just some tea and toast.' He stretches and yawns. 'I need to wake up with a good shower.'

'You do that and I'll fix us some breakfast.'

Archer finishes getting ready before heading down to the kitchen where she turns the timer dial to full on Grandad's toaster, an old retro chrome Dualit model from the seventies. The appliance normally needs two minutes to warm up before it can toast bread and is anything but efficient. Toast is rarely a golden brown, and if you're not careful, it's often smoking and charcoal black, but he can't bear to be parted from it despite Archer offering to buy him a new one. She can understand why, of course. Thousands of slices of toast have popped from it over the decades, feeding her dad as a boy and Archer too, when she visited and later came to live here. Grandad has an emotional attachment to it, as he does with this house.

151

She reaches across, switches on the radio and fills the kettle as the timer ticks. Removing a breadknife from the drawer, she places a loaf of bread on the cutting board. Grandad's default station, Radio 4, is broadcasting the end of the news.

'The bodies of two men found in Battersea Park have been named as Justin Sykes, a twenty-four-year-old recruitment specialist, and forty-four-year-old IT Manager, Brian Bailey. Police believe the men were murdered and are warning people in the area to be cautious. An investigation is underway.

'In other news, after serving an eighteen-year sentence, London drug cartel boss, Frankie "Snow" White is being released from prison today. White was jailed in 1999 for importing and distributing class A and class B drugs. White claims to be a changed man and is looking forward to spending quality time with his family . . . And now over to John for the weather . . . John . . .'

Archer squeezes the breadknife handle hard. With her free hand she switches off the radio. She hears Grandad whistling to himself upstairs in his bedroom and is thankful he is not here at this moment. Not that it really matters. They both know White is being released. If anything, Archer is relieved she and Grandad have broken the ice about the subject and can now openly talk about it.

In the office later that morning, Archer gathers Quinn, Klara, Os, DS Tozer and DC Marian Phillips in one of the conference rooms on the third floor.

'Grace,' says Tozer. 'The press are pushing us for an update on the murders.'

'Understood. We should have enough to make a statement by the end of this meeting. Do you think you could draft something and talk to them?'

'I'll get on it.'

Archer nods a thanks, plugs her laptop into the presentation screen and displays the footage of Bailey and Sykes entering Battersea Park. She then shows the enlarged, grainy images of people leaving the front entrance.

Before she delegates, Tozer raises her hand and says, 'Grace, Marian and I can look into those people if you like.'

'Thank you, Joely.' She rewinds the footage of the beer-drinking couple leaving the side entrance. 'Try and find these two – they must have seen or heard something.' Archer fast-forwards to the footage of the hunched, limping man in the parka. 'See if you can track this one down. You might have to check CCTV of the surrounding areas and follow their tracks.'

'We can do that. No probs.'

'Thank you, Joely, Marian.'

'Grace,' interrupts Quinn. 'Krish and MJ are here.'

Archer looks out through the glass door and sees Krish and MJ, dressed in their CSI uniforms, peering in at them. Krish wears an eager expression and is holding a file. 'I didn't know they were coming.'

'Sheesh! Sorry, ma'am,' says Os. 'I forgot to mention he called this morning.'

Quinn turns to Os with a wry smile. 'Not like you to forget something monumentally important, Os,' he says, playfully nudging the analyst in the ribs.

'Sorry, man. I'm hopeless sometimes.'

Archer beckons Krish and MJ inside.

'Morning all,' says Krish.

'Morning,' the team mumbles in reply.

'For those of you that don't know,' Krish says, 'this is my second in command, MJ.'

MJ smiles and raises her hand in a polite wave as she and Krish take their seats at the conference table.

'So, what have you got for us, Krish?' asks Archer.

'We have a footprint and some lovely DNA for you to follow up with, and a matching name for the phone we found. First up: as you may appreciate the woodchip makes it impossible to detect footprints. That said, we discovered eight different sets in total outside of the perimeter of the clearing. Discounting DI Archer and DS Quinn's protected feet, I matched the others with the boots of the park-keeper, Sergeant Barnes and PC Bickley. Three remained. Justin Sykes' Dr Martens shoes, one pair of size ten leather soles belonging to Brian Bailey and one pair of size nine trainers belonging to the killer, we presume.'

'Do you know what type of trainers?' asks Archer.

'Vans,' replies MJ as she takes two photos from the file and lays them out on the table. 'They have a distinctive waffle pattern on the sole of all their shoes.'

Krish adds, 'A brand typically used by skateboarders and other grungy millennials. The rubber sole prevents slipping on the board.'

'Could the killer be a grungy skateboarder type?' asks Os.

'Who knows?' replies Archer. 'Os, it'd be worth looking into Justin Sykes', Tyler Green's and Joel Dean's Facebook and Instagram accounts. Look for friends or anyone who might be wearing Vans.'

'Will do.'

Archer turns to Quinn. 'I recall Joel Dean was wearing boots. Did you notice any other footwear in his flat?'

Quinn takes a moment to consider this. 'I don't. I remember Tyler Green was in his socks, though. But neither of them seem the grungy skateboarder type.'

'I can check the footwear on the CCTV,' says Klara.

Archer nods a thanks.

Krish continues, 'Coming back to Justin Sykes, there is evidence that he was having oral sex performed on him by Brian Bailey.' He smiles at the CSI. 'MJ and I had a disagreement. MJ thinks my conclusion that oral sex was performed on Justin Sykes while he was alive is naive.'

All heads turn to look at MJ. She regards Krish with a cool detachment and a shrug of her shoulders.

'What a dark mind she has,' he says, beaming with what seems like pride, or a schoolboy crush. Archer is not quite sure.

'She may be right,' says Quinn.

Archer notices MJ glance at Quinn and the flash of a smile appears on her face.

Archer turns Krish's words over in her head and tries to figure out the scene with Justin, Brian Bailey and the Vans-wearing killer.

DC Phillips, who is often quiet, surprisingly offers her thoughts. 'Three men cottaging in Battersea Park. They seduce one man and kill him in a weird sex game.'

'Possible,' says Tozer.

'You mentioned about DNA and the phone,' Archer says to Krish.

'Yes. The killer left identical DNA on both the bodies and, more importantly, we found a match.' Krish slides out a photo from the file. The picture is of a man who looks to be in his late twenties. He has a medium build with short and scruffy spiked brown hair. He has a streetwise look about him and seems oddly familiar. His round face has a serious expression.

'His name is Ethan White,' says MJ.

Ethan White. Archer swallows and can't take her eyes from the picture.

MJ continues, 'He is also the owner of the phone you found . . .'

'What's the phone number?' asks Klara.

Krish tells her the number and her long fingers dance across her iPad. 'I'm just running a trace. One moment.'

'He has a string of old minor offences,' says Krish. 'Drug use, mainly, but it seems he's been clean for a few years, according to his file anyway. His family are connected . . .'

Archer interrupts. 'Ethan White is Frankie "Snow" White's grandson.'

A loud silence fills the room.

'Is that true?' asks Quinn in a concerned tone.

'I'm afraid it is,' replies MJ.

What on earth has Ethan White got to do with these murders?

'We need to talk to him immediately,' says Archer. 'Do you have an address?'

'The address on the system is out of date,' says Krish. 'But his family are in Bethnal Green.'

Klara speaks. 'A call was made from White's phone in the Battersea Park area at 23.06 on Sunday evening to a landline registered at Ladywell Playtower in Lewisham.'

Lewisham.

'That would have been the same time of the murders,' says MJ.

'Boom!' says Krish. 'What ace teamwork.'

Archer turns to Quinn. 'Rose Grant was killed in a hit-and-run in Lewisham.'

Quinn's brow furrows. 'Witnesses claimed she was off her face.'

'Drug dealer, Adrian Boyne, is Rose's ex . . .'

'He also works for Frankie White.'

Krish chips in, 'Erm . . . you've lost me.'

'I think they've made a connection between the White family and the hit-and-run,' says MJ.

'I think there's more to it than that,' says Archer. Logging into Instagram, she searches for Rose Grant and saves a picture of her to her phone. 'We need to find out where White lives and pay a visit to this Ladywell Playtower.' Archer scans the photos on Rose's page but finds nothing of interest.

'Isn't Ladywell Playtower derelict?' asks Quinn.

'Not anymore,' replies Klara, holding up the iPad. On the screen is a photograph of a Victorian red-brick building with gothic arches and a huge circular tower with a turret. 'This is Ladywell Playtower in Lewisham. It used to be a bathhouse and was bought last year to be redeveloped.'

'Into what?' asks Archer.

'Private homes, apparently.'

'Let's finish up and go straight there,' Archer says to Quinn.

'Sounds good to me.'

'Krish, MJ, is there anything else?'

'Nothing else from me,' Krish says. 'MJ?'

'I'm good, thanks.'

Archer addresses the team. 'Anyone unclear on what they have to do?'

There is mumble of no and a collective nodding of heads.

'Great. Thanks, Krish and MJ.'

The team, excluding Klara, leave the room and return to their desks.

'Grace, have you got a moment?' the analyst asks.

'Sure.'

'I have an update on that other matter. Pop over to my hub before you go.'

Archer smiles. 'I'll see you in a moment,' she says and Klara leaves.

Archer goes to grab her coat from over her chair, but stops when she notices DI Hicks, dressed in a brown suit and orange striped tie, stroll by, holding a Styrofoam mug of machine coffee. He looks in at her with a smirk before walking to his office and shutting the door.

'Give me a moment,' she says to Quinn, as she heads toward Hicks's office. She enters without knocking and closes the door behind her.

A startled Hicks glares at her. 'You might want to learn to knock before entering someone else's private office!'

Archer wrinkles her nose. The small space reeks of machine coffee and flatulence. She reopens the door to let some air in and levels her gaze at Hicks. 'That stunt you pulled with Human Resources is a new low, even for you.'

'What stunt would that be?' he replies, silkily.

'I won't forget it.'

A smug look uncoils on Hicks's face, creasing his shiny, pockmarked face.

Archer shakes her head and leaves, crossing into Klara's office, her muscles tense.

'Everything OK?' asks Klara.

'It's nothing. What did you find?'

'I didn't want to mention it in the meeting, but I got a match on that picture you sent me from the King's Tavern.' Klara opens up the Police National Computer and displays his details on the central monitor.

'His name is Troy Whitehead. He's had a few convictions for dealing and burglary, but nothing that would keep you awake at night. He doesn't seem to be employed, yet he does have an undisclosed income and lives comfortably in Gipsy Hill. I did some digging on his address and discovered he has links with a company called EncryptoTalk. They manufacture illegal phones with encrypted software that allows criminal organisations to talk with each other.'

'What is his connection to them?'

'I think he's a broker. He imports the phones and sells them on.'

Archer folds her arms and considers what business Grandad and Cosmo would have with a broker like Troy Whitehouse.

'Phones are one side of his business,' adds Klara. 'This delightful character also trades in firearms.'

20

ARCHER'S HEART SINKS WHEN KLARA tells her Troy Whitehouse deals in guns. Is it Grandad's intention to purchase a gun from Whitehouse? She looks at the profile picture of the grim-faced man with the tattooed tear under his eye and makes a note of his address.

'Thanks, Klara. Please don't mention this to anyone.'

'Of course.'

Archer pulls on her coat as she leaves with Quinn, her mind turning over with Klara's revelation. There is nothing she can do for the moment. She needs to focus and, first things first, they need to talk to Ethan White. The clouds part, revealing a cold clear blue sky. As they walk to the car, Quinn asks, 'Do you think the White family are mixed up with these murders?'

She sighs. 'I wouldn't be surprised.'

'Certainly seems that way. As for Ethan White, chances are he's with the family welcoming dear old grandad home and not at Lewisham.'

'Ifs he's not there, we'll crash the welcome home party.'

'Sounds like a plan.'

It takes the best part of an hour to navigate the heavy morning traffic and arrive at Ladywell Road, a busy thoroughfare lined with smart brown-brick Victorian terraced houses. Quinn slows as they approach their destination. Above the tall hedges that surround Ladywell Playtower is the red turret that seems so strikingly out of place among the narrow Lewisham townhouses. Quinn puts on his hazards and pulls over by the entrance, an intricately pattered tall wrought-iron gate with a rugged crucifix welded into the design. Archer narrows her gaze through the railings of the gate. The architecture is unashamedly Victorian gothic, the bricks a deep crimson that seem to shimmer in the winter sun. The windows are newly restored with stained glass giving it an ecclesiastical feel.

'The picture Klara showed us doesn't do it justice,' observes Quinn.

'It's quite something, isn't it?'

'Reminds me of those buildings you'd see on the cover of an old dark romance novel. You know the ones depicting a scary castle on a stormy night on the edge of a cliff with a maiden dressed in her long white nightie fleeing barefoot from whatever terror lurked inside?'

Archer chuckles. 'I remember them well.'

'My mum read them – and I'll happily admit, what with me being a feminist and all, that I read a few myself.'

'I'm not sure you could ever categorise those books as feminist literature.'

'That's very true. Did you read them?'

'One or two, but the stories never quite lived up to the promise of their covers.'

'Someone's home,' says Quinn, looking towards the gate.

Behind it, Archer sees a frail-looking woman with lank hair and pale skin shuffling barefoot along the grass. She is dressed in a thick orange jumper and a green, shapeless dress.

162

A horn distracts their attention. Quinn looks into the rear-view mirror and frowns. 'A bus coming in. Why doesn't he overtake?'

'Because we're parked in a bus stop, maybe?'

Quinn kills the hazards and indicates. 'Right, that'll be why.'

Archer unclips her seatbelt. 'I'll get out first and have a word with that woman. You find somewhere to park.'

Quinn pulls out and turns down a side street as the bus takes his place. The turret towers over the hedges and Archer thinks she sees someone watching her from behind the stained-glass windows. Behind her she half hears the hiss of the bus doors opening and pushes the gate forward, but it's locked; to her dismay there is no intercom, just a stainless-steel digital lock.

She calls through the gate, 'Hello!'

The woman turns to look.

'Hello,' repeats Archer. 'Please could you open the gate?'

The woman wrings her hands and glances furtively to her left and right.

'It's OK, I just want to talk.'

The woman approaches the gate and smiles. What remains of her teeth are brown and chipped. From the car, she had seemed in her forties, but up close, underneath the ravages of drug abuse, is a woman in her mid-thirties.

'What's your name?' asks Archer.

'Evie,' she replies quietly.

'Can you let me in, Evie?'

'Can I help you, friend?' comes a voice from behind her.

Archer turns and is surprised to see a young lad looking back at her, studying her with large, curious eyes, one of which, the right eye, has an eyelid that droops lower than the other. He turns to look at the woman called Evie and frowns at her. To Archer's disappointment, she hurries away.

Archer turns back to the lad. 'Can you help me?' she asks, sharply.

'You tell me,' he replies with an unsettling confidence. His age is difficult to place, and she thinks he might be in his early teens. His voice, although not as deep as an adult's, has a mature tone to it. Archer takes stock of him and has the sense that he is from a bygone era. His dark hair is cut short at the back and sides and combed neatly into a side parting and he wears old blue jeans, a grey flannel shirt buttoned up to the neck, and a tweed jacket. Hanging around his neck on a leather thong is a chipped wooden crucifix painted a burnt orange colour.

'Do you have a connection with this house?' asks Archer.

He does not respond.

'Who was that woman?'

'Do not concern yourself with that one. She is fallen.'

Archer raises her eyebrows. 'Fallen?'

'Have you come to pray?' he asks.

'Not today, thank you. I'd like to get past this gate and speak to whoever is inside.'

'What's your name?' he asks.

Archer produces her ID. 'Detective Inspector Archer.' Over his shoulder, she sees Quinn crossing the road.

'Have you come to be saved?'

Quinn arrives by Archer's side. 'All right?' he says, cheerily, looking at the boy and back to Archer.

'Detective Sergeant Quinn, this is . . .' Archer meets the young man's gaze and nods in the hope that he will at least introduce himself.

After a moment he says, 'My name is Kain. With a K.'

'No school today, Kain with a K?' asks Quinn.

'I come home for prayer at lunchtime.'

'Prayer, is it?' says Quinn in a surprised tone.

'What's your connection to this place?' asks Archer.

'I live here.'

'You must know Ethan White then?' asks Quinn.

Kain shrugs.

'Does he live here?'

Kain hesitates before saying, 'Ethan will soon be saved.'

Archer narrows her gaze at the boy and wonders what he means by that.

'I'm so glad to hear that,' says Quinn. 'Now, is he home?'

'I don't know.'

Archer takes out her phone and shows him the photo of Rose Grant. 'Do you recognise this woman? She was seen in this area on Tuesday.'

He blinks at the picture and shakes his head.

'Sure?' asks Archer.

'Yes.'

'Look again.'

A deep, authoritative voice with a Midlands accent bellows from the house, 'Kain, come inside!'

Archer looks in its direction and sees a man with dark, shoulder-length hair and round spectacles standing under a pointed arch. Behind him, the front door of the house is open and she can see a small gathering of men, women and children wearing crucifixes just like Kain's.

'Hello,' Archer calls. 'My name is Detective Inspector Grace Archer and this is Detective Sergeant Harry Quinn. May we come in?'

'It's prayer time.'

Kain enters a code in the digital lock and pushes open the gate.

'We need to talk to Ethan White, urgently.'

'Ethan is not here.'

'That's convenient,' mutters Quinn.

Before Kain can close the gate, Archer is inside with Quinn behind her. She walks up the short path and cannot shake the sense that she has stepped into a different world.

'This is private property, Detective Inspector,' says the man.

'What's your name?' asks Archer.

Kain circles around Archer and Quinn and stands beside the man, his head at shoulder height. 'He's the Father.'

The man puts his arm around Kain's shoulder and squeezes it gently. Archer takes stock of him. He has a sturdy build and is of average height; nevertheless he seems an imposing figure. Wearing an open-neck black shirt with the sleeves rolled up, she notices the fingers on both his hands are covered in thick silver rings. There are a mixture of designs from skulls, to runes to crucifixes.

Archer tries again. 'Mr . . .?'

'My name is Aaron.'

Quinn asks. 'Surname?'

'Are you investigating me for a crime?'

Conscious of time and an increasing lack of geniality, Archer says, 'Please excuse our manners. We would just like to talk with Ethan.'

'I'm afraid Ethan has been called away to be with his family.'

Of course he has.

'OK, thank you. Please let him know we called.'

'I'll be sure to tell him.'

166

Archer shows him the picture of Rose. 'Recognise this woman?'

He studies the picture for a moment before replying, 'I'm afraid not.'

'OK,' says Archer. She hands across her contact card and says, 'Aaron, can I just ask how many landlines you have?'

He frowns. 'Landlines?'

'Telephone lines. How many?'

'There is one telephone that we all share. We lead a very basic life here.'

'Ethan made a call to your landline on Sunday evening just after eleven. I don't suppose you took the call?'

He ponders the question before answering. 'No, I did not.'

Archer nods. 'We appreciate your time, thank you.' She turns to leave and hesitates. 'Oh, one last thing. Does the name Brian Bailey mean anything to you?'

Aaron hesitates before answering, 'No, I'm sorry.'

Archer smiles. 'Have a good day.'

They leave and make their way back to the car.

'They seem fun,' says Quinn. 'Not quite the type of people I would link with anyone from the White family.'

'Agreed.'

'Who do you think they are?'

'I really don't know. I'll get Klara to look into them.'

Quinn unlocks the car and they climb inside. 'Ready to crash the White family reunion?' he asks.

Archer pulls across her seatbelt and feels butterflies swarm in her stomach.

'I'd be lying if I said I was looking forward to it.'

'Are you sure you want to do this? I can haul someone else in to help me out.'

'No. I have to do this.'

'I don't think we should go in alone. I'll call Jimmy Barnes and his ward. They should be on shift and he owes me a favour.'

'Good idea.'

'OK. Bethnal Green?'

'Yes, Paradise Row.'

'OK. Bethnal Green, here we come. I hope they've splashed out on the canapés. I'll be writing a stiff letter if the blinis are not up to the standards of my sophisticated palate.'

21

ARCHER AND QUINN STAND OUTSIDE St John's Church on the corner of Bethnal Green Road and Roman Road. Opposite are the White family residences, three houses in the centre of Paradise Row, a train of tall Georgian terraces overlooking Paradise Gardens, a narrow public park presently decorated with bunting and lights and the current location of a party.

'No sign of Barnes yet,' says Quinn.

Archer's eyes are fixed on the scene.

A medium-sized marquee looms in the centre with signs saying *Welcome Home, Frankie* and *Welcome Home, Grandad*, among others. At the entrance, a long queue of scrubbed-up people, comprising men in cheap suits and shivering women in tight dresses and fake tans wait in line along the park's twisty path.

'His minions have come to pay their respects,' says Quinn.

Scattered throughout the park are pockets of people sipping champagne, beer or wine. Archer's stomach is in knots as she scans the faces. She thinks she glimpses Adrian Boyne, but if it was him, he has become lost in the melee. After a moment of searching she sees Ethan White standing near a group of people his age, at the opposite end of the park, talking on his phone. He looks up from the call and scans the area.

Archer wonders if Aaron or someone else at the Ladywell Playtower has tipped him off.

'I see him,' says Quinn.

'Me too.'

Archer hears the sound of an approaching siren and sees Barnes and Bickley speeding up Bethnal Green Road.

'Shall we make our move?'

'Let's do it.'

Quinn gestures for Barnes to pull over near the entrance to the park.

'Watch out for the meathead guarding the gate,' says Quinn as they weave through a break in the traffic and cross the road to the park entrance. The meathead in question is a thick-necked, bald-headed heavy with small cauliflower ears. He frowns at them as they approach.

'Private party!' he says blocking the entrance.

'It's a public park, Popeye,' says Quinn, holding up his ID. 'Police, move aside.'

Archer rolls her eyes. Quinn's mouth is going to make this more difficult than she's anticipated.

Archer presents her ID. 'Detective Inspector Archer.'

'Make an appointment,' responds the guard, gruffly.

In a calm voice, Archer tells him, 'We're not here to make trou—'

He cuts her off. 'I said, make an appointment.'

'What business have you got here?' comes a voice.

Archer turns to see a thin woman with glossy black hair pulled back into a long ponytail that sits like a snake on the shoulder of her scarlet designer suit. Some years back Archer had researched the White family, more out of a grim fascination than anything else. The woman's severe expression is a family trait inherited from her father. She is Janine White, Frankie's daughter and Ethan's mother.

Archer hears the police car doors closing and knows Barnes and Bickley are close by.

'We need to speak to one of your guests.'

'It's not a good time.'

'It's urgent,' replies Archer.

Janine White smiles thinly. 'Please leave.'

Adrian Boyne steps up beside Janine, holding a cigarette and a can of lager. 'DI Archer, welcome to the party. I see you brought your dog with you,' he says nodding at Quinn. 'Now, what can we do for you? It's a long wait for Mr White, at least thirty minutes.'

'Archer?' says Janine White, her eyes narrowing in on Archer's mismatched eyes.

'Detective Inspector,' corrects Archer.

'You've got a nerve coming here! If Frankie—'

'I'm not interested in him. Yet. It's your son we want to talk to.'

The shadow of a frown presses feebly through the Botox on her forehead. 'What do you want to talk to him for?'

'It's a police matter.'

Janine shakes her head. 'No way.' But Archer can see she is unsure and perhaps fearful. 'You can't talk to him. Not today.'

Archer does not want to stoke the fire any more. 'Let's not make this worse for him than it already is.'

Janine rubs her palms and looks beyond the marquee toward Ethan who is talking with a young blonde woman. Janine turns back to Archer and points. 'It took a lot of persuading to get him here today. You make it quick and don't upset my boy, you hear?'

Archer does hear but does not respond.

Janine scowls, takes out her phone and makes a call.

Archer sees Ethan answer his phone.

'DI Archer,' says Boyne. He gestures to four ominous-looking men in long dark coats dotted around the park, looking their way. 'No funny business today. Right now, this little spot of East End greenery is ours. Be very careful.'

Quinn replies, 'Wind your neck in, junior. We'll be outta here in five.'

Janine finishes the call and Archer sees a frowning Ethan White threading his way through the crowd. His mother meets him halfway. Janine is leaning into him waving her arms in what looks like a heated exchange. Ethan's face reddens and he shakes his head and pushes past her.

As he approaches the gate, Adrian Boyne says, 'You don't have to talk to them, mate.'

Ethan ignores him and looks between Archer and Quinn. 'What's this about?'

'Let's move away from the rabble, Ethan,' says Quinn.

The meathead is still blocking the gate. 'Let me out, Clem,' says Ethan.

Clem seems uncertain and looks to Janine for approval.

Archer notices Ethan's hands curling into fists. 'Open the fucking gate!' shouts Ethan, his face purple.

Janine nods at Clem, who opens the gate.

Ethan storms out and skirts around to the cobbled throughway of Paradise Row. Archer and Quinn follow him.

'We'd like you to come down to the station with us.'

Ethan stiffens and pales. '*What?* Why?'

'We just have some questions.'

'Questions about what?' Ethan shifts uncomfortably on his feet and becomes increasingly agitated.

'We'll explain down at the station.'

Ethan points a trembling finger at Archer and retreats. 'No, no, no! I've been good. I haven't done anything!'

'Ethan, what's going on?' says a voice.

Archer sees the young blonde woman he had been standing with earlier.

'I'm not going anywhere,' says Ethan.

A crowd starts to emerge from the park.

'What the hell's going on?' shouts Janine.

'Shit,' says Archer and looks to Barnes and Bickley. 'If you wouldn't mind . . .?'

Barnes eases his way forward and tries to calm Ethan, but he lashes out at the DS. Bickley is on him immediately and together he and his partner cuff Ethan and bundle him into the car.

Archer turns to Quinn; this is going to get ugly. 'We better hitch a ride.'

'Ethan! Ethan!' cries Janine.

Archer jumps into the passenger seat as Quinn and Bickley sandwich a sobbing Ethan in the back. They're surrounded by people kicking and slamming the car. Barnes switches on the siren and lights and drives slowly forward and down Paradise Row. He increases speed as the crowd thins and as they drive past the rear of the marquee, a crowd of people hurry toward the second gate leading onto Paradise Row. At the front of the throng, Archer sees him and swallows. Watching her through his square black-framed glasses, his lips parted, teeth clenched, eyes wild with fury, is Frankie White.

22

ARCHER IS BECOMING ANXIOUS, FEARING for Ethan White's state of mind, which does not seem as robust and in control as she hoped it might be. His sobbing has increased to petulant fury and verbal abuse, which leads to more sobbing. Barnes and Bickley haul him out of the car for processing at Charing Cross Police Station, and he fights with them, biting, scratching and spitting to get free from their grasp.

While White is being processed and given time to calm down, Archer takes five minutes to herself, standing alone in the cobbled courtyard of the station, thinking just how many cigarettes she would get through at this time if she were a smoker. Seeing Frankie White has unsettled her more than she expected. She has no doubt that when White's eyes met hers in the squad car he recognised her. She wonders what went on in his head when he saw her. Had he thought of her father, the man he'd had murdered eighteen years ago? Did he see her as stepping into DI Sam Archer's shoes, to bring an end to the White family business? Quite likely. For the present, though, Archer has a murder investigation to lead and Frankie White will have to wait.

Barnes appears. 'Ma'am, might be best to leave White in a cell for a bit. I've asked the custody officer to keep an eye on him.'

'Sounds good, Jimmy. Thanks so much for your help today.'

Barnes nods a thanks. 'Anytime.'

With time to kill, Archer makes a decision to nip a personal problem in the bud. Signing out a car, she drops Quinn a note to say she'll be back soon and heads west out of Central London.

Troy Whitehouse lives on the top end of Gipsy Hill, in a purpose-built flat within a seventies three-storey block peppered with satellite dishes. Whitehouse has the second-floor flat with a balcony overlooking Gipsy Hill and the A24. She watches it from across the road in the unmarked borrowed car. There is no sign of activity or lights behind the windows. She opens the car door, steps out into the cold afternoon and hurries across the road to catch the front door of the building, which has just been opened by a resident, an old woman struggling with an overfull shopping trolley.

'Let me help you,' says Archer, holding open the door.

'Oh, thank you, dear. That door is just getting too heavy for me.'

'It is a bit of a beast, isn't it?'

The woman chuckles. 'You can say that again.'

'Have a nice day.'

'You too.'

Archer makes her way up the concrete stairs two at a time. Outside Whitehouse's flat, she hesitates before pressing the bell. She could get into a lot of trouble for this, should anyone at the Met find out she's paid the broker a visit when no crime had been reported and there is no evidence of any wrongdoing. All she has is Klara's findings and her own conclusions about the man who'd had a meeting with Grandad and Cosmo. Archer only wants to find out what business Grandad has with him. After that, she'll warn him off. That's it. Nothing more. Nothing less. But a creeping doubt ebbs through her and for a second she has misgivings about Klara's findings. Perhaps her friend is wrong.

No.

Archer quickly dispels those thoughts from her mind. In all the years she's known Klara, the analyst has never been off the mark.

Archer rings the bell and waits, but there is no answer.

After a moment, she rings again, but again there is no response.

'Can I help you, dear?' comes a voice.

Archer turns to see the old woman she held the door open for, haul her shopping trolley over the steps and shuffle toward her. She is a stout lady, around five foot high, with curly grey hair and blue-framed spectacles on a chain.

'Hello, again. I'm looking for someone.'

'And who would that be?' the woman asks, fishing out her keys. She reaches across to Whitehouse's door, inserts a key and turns the lock.

'I'm looking for Troy,' Archer replies, as if he is an old friend.

'Do come inside.'

'That would be nice, thank you.'

Archer follows her inside to a hallway that is decorated in pure wall-to-wall Victoriana.

'I'm Troy's mother,' Archer's hostess announces. 'But you probably know that already.'

'Yes, indeed,' lies Archer.

At the end of the hallway is the entrance to the kitchen. Mrs Whitehouse pushes the trolley speedily toward it but stops before she reaches it and turns to face the wall. From her coat pocket, she fishes out a second set of keys, larger in size, and inserts one into a keyhole in the wall. She then slides across a panelled door and shoves the shopping trolley behind it. Pulling the door closed, she then locks the hidden door and drops the keys back into her pocket.

Unusual.

She looks back at Archer with a cunning, intelligent smile. 'Come down to the kitchen, dear, and we'll talk.'

Mrs Whitehouse sits at the small kitchen table and beckons Archer to sit opposite. She regards Archer for a moment before saying. 'Police, is it, dear?'

'Is it that obvious?'

'I could smell it off you, down at the main entrance.'

Archer regards the woman with caution. 'Have you had many dealings with the police?'

'I've a few years behind me.'

Archer can see there is more to Whitehouse's mother than meets the eye, and wonders what was in the shopping trolley that needed to be locked away so swiftly.

'Where's your son, Mrs Whitehouse?'

'He's out on business and won't return until tomorrow.'

'So you lied about him returning any moment?'

'Correct, dear. What do you want with him?'

'I want to talk to him.'

Mrs Whitehouse tilts her head. 'About?'

Archer regards her for a moment. 'As well as being his mother, would I be right in thinking you and Troy are also business associates?'

Mrs Whitehouse is a pro. She holds Archer's gaze, her body language and facial expressions give nothing away, except for the slightest of twitches below her left eye, when Archer asks the question.

Archer answers for her. 'I know what he does.'

Mrs Whitehouse knits her podgy pink hands together. 'I'm not sure what you mean.'

Archer has no appetite for games. 'For now, Mrs Whitehouse, I have no interest in you or your son, but I want you to give him a message from me. Tell him to stay far away from Jake Archer and Cosmo Mateo, or God help me, I will do everything in my power to put him behind bars.'

Mrs Whitehouse smiles thinly. 'I don't appreciate idle threats from anyone, least of all the Old Bill. That said, I'll see to it my Troy receives your message and ensure he breaks off all contact with the aforementioned gentlemen.'

Archer stands. 'Make sure that you do.'

'Goodbye, dear. Close the door on your way out, thank you.'

Archer exits the building feeling vexed, but also pleased that she has scored a small victory. She makes a decision to call at Cosmo's place later and get the full story. Cosmo is an easy-going man, who wants nothing more than an easy life. He won't be a hard nut to crack. He's decent and a good friend to Grandad, but in his younger years he mixed with the wrong sort and she wonders if it is through him that Grandad was introduced to Troy Whitehouse.

23

IT TOOK ALMOST TWO HOURS for Ethan White to calm down. Eventually they got him into an interview room, more out of exhaustion than anything else, Archer believes. She is alone with him at the interview table. His head is dipped, his eyes are puffy and red.

'Can I get you something to drink?' she asks, gently.

'Why am I here?' he replies, his voice dry and croaky.

Quinn enters the room carrying a manila folder with the report from the Battersea Park murders.

'We want to talk to you in connection with a crime,' replies Archer.

Quinn pulls up a chair beside Archer and unceremoniously slaps the folder on the tabletop. Ethan jerks and frowns at the folder.

'Your mother is here with the family solicitor,' Quinn tells him.

Ethan shakes his head. 'I told you, I got my own brief.'

'Your mother was very insistent. I promised her I'd remind you.'

Ethan sighs heavily through his nose and folds his arms.

There's a knock at the door.

Archer answers. Tianna Rowland, the custody officer, a sturdy woman in her thirties, greets her. 'Ma'am, Mr White's brief is here,' she says gesturing to the gentlemen on the other side of her. Archer is surprised to see Aaron from the Ladywell Playtower looking back at her.

'DI Archer,' he says.

He is carrying a battered brown briefcase and wears a smart tweed jacket, a grey flannel shirt buttoned to the neck. Hanging from a leather thong is a rugged silver crucifix, which rests on his broad chest. She steps outside the interview room and thanks Tianna, who leaves them.

Archer folds her arms. 'I still only know you as Aaron.'

'Cronin. Aaron Cronin.'

'Ethan called you to be his brief?'

'You seem surprised.'

'Are you a solicitor, Mr Cronin?'

'I am many things, DI Archer. If you don't mind, I would like to talk privately with my client before we start.'

Archer takes him through.

Ethan stands up, his face beaming. 'Father!' he cries.

Aaron crosses the room and opens his arms. 'My son,' he says as Ethan slumps into his embrace.

Archer and Quinn exchange an incredulous glance.

'How long do you need?' asks Archer.

'Ten minutes will be sufficient.'

'We'll be waiting outside.'

Quinn takes the file from the table and leaves with Archer, closing the door behind them.

'What was all that about?' asks Quinn.

'No idea.'

'He called him "Father". I can't imagine his real dad would be very impressed.'

'Ethan's father disappeared before he was born. Rumours are Frankie had him taken out for beating up his pregnant daughter.'

'Nice family.'

'They're a charming lot. What is more curious at this moment in time is Ethan's connection with Aaron.' Archer takes out her phone and makes a call. Klara picks up. 'Hey, Grace.'

'Hi, Klara, I need you to do some digging for me. Find out who Aaron Cronin is. He's in his forties, a solicitor.'

'Do you have an address?'

'Yes, same address as Ethan White's.'

'Lewisham, Ladywell Playtower?'

'Yeah. Find out what's going on there. It looks as though there's a communal home of religious people living there.'

'OK. I'll get on that now.'

'Thanks, Klara.'

'No worries. Talk later.'

'Bye.'

Archer hears the interview room door open and sees Aaron emerge and look their way. He nods at them and retreats back inside, leaving the door open. Archer and Quinn follow and sit opposite the two men. Archer notices Ethan's face is brighter and he seems more assured and relaxed. She also notices he is wearing an orange crucifix.

'OK, Ethan, let's begin,' says Quinn, sliding out a photograph of Brian Bailey from the folder across the table. 'Do you recognise this man?'

Ethan looks down at the picture and then leans forward for a closer look. After a moment of consideration he says, 'No.'

Archer looks at Aaron, who meets her gaze.

Quinn slides out a photo of Justin Sykes. 'Do you recognise this man?'

Ethan shakes his head. 'I ain't never seen this man before.'

Archer searches his face and body language for a sign of something that might indicate a lie but sees nothing.

'Where were you on Sunday evening?'

'Which Sunday evening?' he replies.

Quinn clarifies. 'Four nights ago Sunday evening. Where were you?'

'I was at the church.'

'At Ladywell Playtower?'

He smiles and shoots a glance at Aaron. 'That's not what it's called.'

'What *do* you call it?'

'The Blood of the Lamb Church. It's a sanctuary.'

'Were you at this sanctuary on Sunday night, Mr White?' presses Quinn.

'Yes, I was. I was there all weekend and didn't leave until this morning.' His face darkens for a moment. 'I didn't want to leave, but they insisted.'

'They?'

'My family.'

'Your mother, Janine?' asks Archer.

'Yeah. She wanted me home for Grandad's homecoming. But I wasn't interested. I *hate* him. I hate all of them and what they represent.'

'Which is what, exactly?'

Aaron interrupts. 'Let's stick to the matter at hand.'

Archer nods an agreement. 'Can you prove that you were at the church that night?'

'Yes. I was with my new family. We spent the whole night praying and singing.'

Archer catches his eye. 'Who is this new family, Ethan?'

He gestures at Aaron. 'Aaron is the Father, and we, the others, are his children.'

Archer's gaze flits between Aaron and Ethan, as she tries to get the measure of them. 'What sort of family is that, Ethan?'

Before he can respond, Aaron says, 'We have approximately forty witnesses of men, women and children who will tell you the same story. Ethan was with us in song and in prayer.'

'What time did this hooley finish?' asks Quinn.

'It was perhaps after 2 a.m.'

'That's very late for children to be out of bed.'

Ethan chuckles. 'The spirit of the Lord was with us that night. He was inside the Father, touching us, healing us. It was a miracle.'

'Well, here's the thing,' says Quinn. 'Both these men were murdered on Sunday night and it just so happens a call was made from your phone to the church from where they were found.'

Ethan frowns. 'I don't know how that could be. I don't know, haven't ever met either of those men.'

'There might be a more rational explanation,' offers Aaron.

Archer meets his gaze. 'What would that be?'

'You may check the police files on your computer system to corroborate my theory, but one week back Ethan's car was broken into and various items were stolen. That's correct, Ethan, is it not?'

'Yes, of course. My coat, wallet and my phone.'

'Perhaps the perpetrator of the crime made the call,' states Aaron.

'That's quite likely,' replies Quinn, dryly.

'It's an odd coincidence that the phone-thief-cum-murderer should dial the church's number on the night of the murders. Don't you think?' asks Archer.

Aaron shrugs.

'Someone in your church answered the call,' replies Quinn.

'I will ask my flock if anyone took the call.'

'Please do that,' replies Archer.

'Now, are we done?'

Archer and Quinn say nothing.

'Is that everything, DI Archer?' asks Aaron, as she gathers up the photographs. 'If you're not pressing charges, I think my client and I can go home now.'

'Thank you for your time,' says Archer.

'Before we finish . . . I think Ethan might be owed an apology. You put him under considerable stress and bundled him down here on suspicion of a crime he could never have committed.'

'Hang on a minute,' says Quinn, 'we asked him nicely and he refused to come. He—'

Archer interrupts. 'Ethan, we apologise for the inconvenience.'

Ethan looks at Aaron, who nods his head.

Ethan looks back at her. 'I suppose I can.'

Archer stands. 'Until next time.'

Aaron narrows his gaze at her as Quinn sees him and Ethan out of the interview room then Archer makes her way to the third floor. The interview has not been a total waste of time. For Archer it's shown what a smart liar Aaron can be.

'Grace!' calls DS Tozer, as Archer walks to her desk.

'Hi, Joely.'

'Marian and I spoke to the couple we saw on the Battersea Park CCTV. They don't remember hearing or seeing anything as they were both drunk. They also fessed up to being stoned.'

'Pointless trying to get them to remember anything.'

'I'm afraid so.'

'What about the parka-wearing man with the limp?'

'We followed his trail on CCTV, but lost it. We're still looking.'

'Thanks, Joely.'

24

I T'S 8 P.M. AND ARCHER is sitting on the sofa in Dr Abigail Hutchison's consulting room. The lights are dimmed and a scented candle burns with a pleasant citrus and pepper aroma.

'Please feel free to take off your coat,' Hutchison tells her.

Archer slides off her coat and rests it over the arm of the sofa.

'Can I get you something to drink?'

It's been a long day and Archer realises how thirsty she is. 'Water, please.'

The doctor pours Archer a glass of cool water from a jug and hands it to her. Archer takes a mouthful and swallows. After a moment she necks the remainder of the water.

Almost five hours have passed since she locked eyes with Frankie White and took his cherished and somewhat unstable grandson away from his family to be questioned about the murder of two men in Battersea Park. It seems Ethan has a sound alibi, but something is just not adding up. Why was his DNA found on the dead bodies of Brian Bailey and Justin Sykes? Is someone trying to frame him, or is he lying?

'I'm glad you came,' says Hutchison.

'I almost didn't.'

'You seem troubled.'

'A difficult day.'

Archer places the glass on the coffee table.

'I'm sorry.'

Archer stares blankly into the empty glass.

'Can I get you another?'

'No, thank you.'

They sit in silence for a moment before Hutchison asks, 'Why did you come back?'

Archer leans forward, stretching her back muscles and considers the question before meeting the doctor's gaze. 'You mentioned you know my history?'

'I know some things. The recent @nonymous investigation was all over the papers, so I know as much as any member of the public about that case. When Clare asked me to meet with you, she suggested I review the Bernard Morrice files.'

'Did you?'

'Yes.'

'They're quite something, aren't they?' Archer says sardonically.

'That's an understatement.'

'There's also a Bernard Morrice true crime podcast featuring yours truly. That will blow your mind. And apparently some new glory seeker is recording a new, updated Morrice podcast. He's never been so popular.'

'I found the first one a little too "sensational" for my tastes.'

Archer is not sure if she is irritated or not by the doctor's admission of listening to that 'sensational' podcast. 'Then you'll have heard my last therapist being interviewed as an exclusive?'

'Yes. I'm sorry about that, Grace.'

'So, you will understand why it's hard for me to trust therapists. I learned that a long time ago. That therapist was just another in a line of opportunists seeking a bag of coins for someone else's trauma.'

'I understand your reticence and can promise you that will not happen here. Your welfare is my priority. Not only that, I also care about my reputation and that of this clinic. I have taken years to build both.'

They regard each other for a moment. Archer has been burned in the past from all corners, but that has never stopped her doing what she needs to do.

'So *why* did you come back?' Hutchison repeats.

Archer tenses. She looks away and feels herself closing up inside.

She stands, rubs her hands on her hips and walks across the room. 'I'm wasting your time. I'm sorry. I should go. Where's my coat?' Archer scans the room looking for it.

'Grace . . .'

'My coat!'

'It's on the arm of the sofa.'

Archer crosses the room and grabs it, her hands tightening on the thick material. She pauses and closes her eyes. *Pull yourself together.*

'There's no pressure to continue, Grace,' Hutchison tells her in a soft tone.

Archer takes a breath, lowers herself to the sofa and takes a moment to gather herself. 'I'm sorry . . .'

'Take your time.'

'Three months ago, during the @nonymous murders, I almost lost my life after a confrontation with the killer. The experience opened old memories that I thought I'd learned to keep at bay. When I was abducted at the age of twelve, I was already dealing with the murder of my dad. The pain of losing him was just so hard to deal with and then – and then that monster . . .'

Archer closes her eyes and absent-mindedly rubs the scar on the back of her hand.

'My father was everything to me. After my mother left us, it was just Dad and me. It was hard at first, but we adjusted and became happy again.'

'What happened with your mother?'

'She left for someone called Michael. She has another family now.'

'Are you still in touch?'

'No. She's tried to contact me a few times but I have nothing to say to her. When Dad died she came to the funeral. She was heavily pregnant and kept her distance, more out of guilt than anything else, I thought. She spoke to me during the wake and told me she couldn't take me home because she and her new husband, Michael, were starting a family and they didn't have room. I told her that it never occurred to me that I would go anywhere with her. Grandad took me by the hand then and said that I was to come live with him and Grandma. He told Mum she should leave. She wished me luck – and that was the last time I saw her.'

'How do you feel about her now?'

'I resented her for a long time. It was illogical, but my teenage brain couldn't get the *Sliding Doors* idea out of my head. Had she stuck by and not left us, then he might still be alive. I don't think that now, obviously. I don't think much about her at all, if I'm honest.'

'Tell me about your father.'

Archer feels a warm glow inside. 'He was a good man. Kind, thoughtful, a loving father. When Mum left we became a very tight-knit unit with my grandparents. Dad sold our house because Mum wanted her share, so we downsized and moved to a small two-bedroom flat in Muswell Hill. It was a lovely old Victorian building that needed a lot of work; hence Dad could afford it and with help from Grandad was able to do it up. Dad was hard-working and ambitious. He wanted to do well and give me the best start in life that he could. He loved his job, but most of all he loved his family.'

'I can't imagine what it was like to lose him.'

'I was living my worst nightmare. That is, until Bernard Morrice came on the scene.'

'He approached you at your father's grave?'

'Yes. I was miserable and had left school early, skipping the last few lessons of the day. I missed Dad so much and wanted to talk to him. I made my way to the graveyard. It wasn't anything to look at. There was no stone at that time, just a wooden cross that Grandad had made. The grass hadn't grown over his grave yet.'

Hutchison's eyes flit to Archer's hands where her right thumb instinctively rubs the scar on the top of her left hand.

'I was alone and it was getting dark. There was a black Ford Escort van nearby. At first, I thought it was a hearse for children. That's what it seemed like to me. I wasn't wrong – it belonged to Morrice. He called to me across the graveyard, asking for help. I ignored him at first. I knew not to talk to strangers but despite being wary of him, I wasn't yet ready to leave Dad's grave. As you can imagine, Morrice was persistent.

He came scuttling across the graveyard like a spider, yet I wasn't afraid then. Nothing could be worse than what had already happened. How wrong I was . . .'

Archer sits back on the sofa and crosses her arms.

'He was a small man, not much taller than me. He asked whose grave it was and I told him. He gave his condolences, but all the while he had a hungry look in his eye that unnerved me and I decided to leave then. There was something about him that unsettled me, so I told him I was expected home and turned to leave. He lashed out at me then, punching me in the stomach. He was strong and the blow was such a shock. I doubled over in pain and fell over on to Dad's grave. Morrice then dragged me to his van where he bound my wrists and legs and gagged and taped my mouth. It was dusk by then and no one saw us. He took me away in his hearse and locked me in a pit in the ground with Danny Jobson.' Archer hesitates before continuing. 'You know all this already. I'm sorry.'

'Don't apologise. This is your time. We can talk about anything you wish.'

'I told Danny I would protect him, but I couldn't. As I slept, Morrice came and took Danny.' Archer rests her elbows on her knees and knits her fingers together. 'I-I felt responsible. I'd promised him I'd protect him, that we'd leave that place together, safe and well, but I failed.'

Hutchison opens her mouth to speak but Archer cuts her off. 'I know you're going to say it wasn't my fault. Logic has told me that many, many times over the years. Still, if only I hadn't slept . . .'

A veil of silence hangs between them for a moment.

'You said that your recent brush with death stirred up old memories. How does this manifest itself?'

'Morrice visits me in my dreams. I've learned to control my sleep by imagining I'm somewhere safe, somewhere idyllic and calm; it's like a kind of self-hypnosis.'

'And you can no longer do that?'

'Since the @nonymous incident, it's become harder.'

Archer talks with Hutchison about @nonymous and discusses some of the events that have happened over the past few days, including her run-in with the two officers during the Dorothy Hayes incident.

'The report filed against you by the officer . . . he said you were angry.'

'I had every reason to be.'

'Of course you did. I do feel that your experience with these killers has had a profound effect on you. Why wouldn't it? I get the sense that you're experiencing a growing anxiety. I could recommend that you take some time out.'

'No!' replies Archer.

'I thought you might say that. And if you have been able to put yourself into that safe place before you can do it again. Although it may take some time.'

'I'll keep trying.'

'Our time is nearly up. Will you come again next week?'

Archer sits forward, gathers her coat. 'I'll do my best.'

'Let me know. I'm here if you need me. Take care of yourself.'

'Thank you, Dr Hutchison.'

Archer leaves the consulting room, pulls on her coat and buttons it as she walks down the single flight of stairs. She feels a sense of optimism and determination that she had not felt before the appointment. It has not been a disaster in comparison to the therapy she received as a teen. She steps out into cold evening air and pulls up her collar. It felt odd talking out loud about her experiences with Morrice and @nonymous. They are subjects she always avoids. But what it's made her realise is how much the past has become a distraction – a distraction that she cannot allow to continue. Two men have been murdered and Frankie 'Snow' White is a free man. Archer has a lot on her mind.

She hears a pinging sound on her phone and takes it from her coat pocket. It's an alert on her calendar, a reminder to take Grandad to the hospital in the morning for an overdue MRI scan because of a series of dizzy spells he's been experiencing. While the episodes have thankfully passed, they nevertheless want to check and see if he's had a minor stroke. Precautionary, the GP had told her. The appointment had slipped her mind and she is grateful for having the foresight to put it in her calendar. She will have to take the morning off work. She has no choice and WhatsApps Quinn and Klara to cover for her.

25

ARCHER TAKES A DETOUR HOME and walks up Blackfriars Road, stopping at a recently built block of modern council flats. She presses Flat 9 on the intercom.

'Hello,' comes a familiar voice.

'Cosmo. It's Grace.'

After a pause he says, 'I'll . . . I'll be right down, Grace.'

Archer figures he does not want his wife to witness him being grilled by her.

Fair enough.

He appears moments later, looking sheepish. 'Hello, Grace – cold tonight. How are you?'

Archer cuts straight to the chase. 'Are you going to tell me what's been going on?'

Cosmo's bushy grey eyebrows rise in surprise. He shifts on his feet with a look of faux confusion. 'Not sure what you mean, Grace.'

Archer is not in the mood for this game. 'Why were you and Grandad talking with Troy Whitehouse last night in the King's Tavern?'

Cosmo's face drops. 'H-how did you know?'

Archer wonders if Grandad is not the only one with dementia.

'You weren't hard to miss.'

'Shit! I knew this was a damn fool's errand. Shit!'

Archer folds her arms, waiting with a patient front that she is just not feeling.

'How on earth did you get mixed up with Whitehouse?'

Cosmo looks away from her and begins to wring his hands together. 'Grace, I'm sorry. I didn't know what to do. Jake insisted and I thought he just wanted some muscle, you know?'

'Why would he want muscle from Whitehouse?'

A pained expression shrouds his face. 'I'm sorry, Grace. So sorry. I thought I could do better with Jake. I really did . . .'

Cosmo doesn't seem able to find the words.

'Tell me what Grandad wanted from Whitehouse.'

Cosmo shifts back and forth on his feet, avoiding Archer's gaze.

'Cosmo?'

Cosmo casts his eyes downward. 'A gun. He wanted a gun.'

Archer feels her stomach lurching.

Cosmo continues, 'Jake saw the article about Frankie White and went bananas. I've never seen him so upset, so angry. He cried, Grace, wept in my arms. We sat in St Patrick's for three hours and I thought being there might calm him down, but it seemed to do the opposite. He wanted to scream and tear the place down. Honestly, Grace, I thought he was about to have another stroke.'

'What was he planning to do with the gun?'

Archer suspects she knows what the answer to that question is but wants to hear it from Cosmo.

'He wants to shoot White. Kill him dead for what he's done.'

Archer closes her eyes and sighs.

Cosmo pulls his coat together to stay warm. 'He'll go mad at me for telling you.'

A chill runs down Archer's spine. She shudders in the cold and thrusts her hands deeper into her coat pockets in a vain attempt to warm them.

'There's something else. He kept going on about a secret – a secret that he'd just discovered.'

'What secret?'

'I don't know, but whatever it is, it's eating him alive, and I don't doubt it's to do with Frankie White.'

Archer's mind races.

'Promise you won't say anything, Grace!'

'I can't promise anything, but I will deal with this.'

'Grace . . .'

'I've already dealt with Troy Whitehouse. So don't contact him again, or anyone like him, Cosmo. Understood?'

'Understood. I'm sorry, Grace. Truly.'

Archer turns to leave.

'Wait! Grace, did you get Jake's money back?'

Archer frowns and looks back at Cosmo. 'How much did he pay?'

'Five hundred pounds.'

Archer swears under her breath. 'There's no chance, Cosmo. Whitehouse will deny all knowledge and I am most definitely not risking my job to follow up on five hundred quid of illegally spent money.'

She leaves Cosmo standing outside his block, crosses Blackfriars Road cautiously, dodging the oncoming traffic and conscious of the dark, angry cloud that begins to envelop the space around her.

Archer decides she cannot wait to discuss this with Grandad. She must confront him tonight. With Whitehouse removed from the picture she now needs Grandad to forget any idea of being involved with him. Her stomach is in knots. Since his diagnosis of early dementia, she has had to be conscious of his emotions which are, at times, brittle. She will need to tread on eggshells and be careful of her tone. As she loses herself in her thoughts and makes her way to Roupell Street, a plan begins to form in her head.

She enters the house and removes her coat; hanging it on the wall hook she hears the sound of crockery being cleaned in the kitchen sink.

'Is that you, Grace?'

'Hi, Grandad,' she replies, trying to sound cheerful.

She enters the kitchen and Grandad smiles at her as he empties the sink of soapy water and rinses his hands. Archer smiles back despite his face being pale and drawn, more so than usual.

'How was your day?' she asks.

He stops to think, his eyes seeming lost for a moment as he dries his hands. 'Fine. I visited your father and grandmother's graves. Gave them a little clean and tidy and chatted to both of them for a while.'

'That's nice, Grandad. I'm due a visit soon.' She picks up a tea towel and begins to dry the dishes.

Grandad wipes down the worktops in silence before saying her name. 'Grace?' His voice is quiet with a melancholic tone.

She meets his gaze. His eyes are watery and a little red and he says nothing for a moment.

'Grandad . . .' she urges.

'When I go, Grace . . . when I go . . . you will put me with your grandmother, won't you? I want to be buried with her.'

'Of course, Grandad. We've discussed this many times.'

He nods his head slowly and squeezes her arm. 'How about a nightcap?' He smiles at her, his face brighter. 'There's enough Pomerol for two left in that bottle in the cupboard. I'll pour, shall I?'

'Why not?'

Archer finishes drying the dishes and puts them away before joining Grandad on the sofa. He hands her a glass of Pomerol. 'No one makes wine like the French,' he says.

'Dad always loved French wine.'

'That's because he was part French, thanks to his mum.'

He raises his glass and Archer clinks hers against his. 'To both of them,' she says.

'Forever loved. Forever missed.'

They sit in silence for a moment, sipping the wine in the warm glow of the dying embers in the fireplace. Grandad seems relaxed and Archer feels loath to broach the subject of Troy Whitehouse, but she believes she has no choice.

'Grandad, there's something I need to talk to you about.'

'What's that, dear?'

'I was contacted by a colleague today,' she lies.

'Oh . . .?'

'There was a raid on a flat in London.' More lies.

'Oh dear. What did they find?'

'I can't really say. Nothing legal, as you might imagine.'

'Drugs, I expect.'

'The flat belonged to a man called Troy Whitehouse.'

Grandad considers this name for a moment before his face tightens. He does not meet her gaze.

'My colleague found the name of Jake Archer written in Troy Whitehouse's contact book.'

Grandad swallows. 'Goodness . . . d-did he have any other details like an address or another name?'

'Nothing else.'

Grandad blinks and takes a large swallow of wine.

'I'm sure there are many Jake Archers in London, but I wanted to check with you first. What with me being a Met Detective Inspector, I need them to eliminate you immediately.'

Eyes wide, Grandad looks at Archer. 'They can't think it's anything to do with you, can they?'

The penny has dropped for him and she knows he has come to realise the gravity of the situation and its implications for her. He can't seem to find the words and after a few moments looks at her with pleading eyes. 'I'm so sorry, Grace. I didn't realise. I'm so sorry.'

Archer rests her hand on his. 'It's taken care of. But, Grandad, I don't want you to talk to him or anyone like him again.'

'He owes me money.'

Archer shakes her head. 'That money is gone now.'

Grandad's shoulders slump and his body seems to sink into the sofa. 'I don't know what I was thinking.'

'Grandad, White's been released and there's nothing either of us can do about that now. That said, I need you to trust me. I am not finished with him, I can promise you that.'

Grandad's face darkens. 'He's a dangerous man, Grace. He knows some bad people. He . . . he . . .' Grandad looks away and closes his eyes.

'What is it?'

For a moment Archer thinks he is going to reveal the secret that Cosmo had mentioned, but to her disappointment, he doesn't. He shakes his head. 'I'm tired, dear. I'll go to bed, if you don't mind.'

They stand and he embraces her tightly. Easing away from her, Archer sees a face full of pain. *What is he hiding?* He seems lost for words and shuffles from the living room to the stairs.

'Remember we have your doctor's appointment in the morning.'

He pauses, but does not look back. 'Goodnight, Grace.'

Archer swallows as she watches him climb the stairs, his shoulders slumped, his back bent.

After brushing her teeth a little later, she leaves the bathroom and passes his bedroom, stopping for a moment when she hears him quietly sobbing. She feels a pang of guilt for bringing up the topic and for lying to him too. But what choice did she have? She could not allow him to continue this dangerous path with Troy Whitehouse. Treading lightly across to her room, Archer wonders again what the secret could be that Grandad is hiding.

26

ETH HARPER IS ALONE AND keeping warm under the duvet in the one-bedroom flat she shares with Ethan. Located in Spitalfields, East London, the flat is part of a large shabby Victorian building situated on the corner of Middlesex Street above a vaping store with the odd strapline of *Wellness begins within*, which is a contradiction in terms if ever she saw one.

She has barely settled herself since today's drama. The police had arrived and bundled Ethan into a police car and whisked him away like a common criminal. Why on earth had they done that and then let him go without charging him? She knows Ethan's family are 'far from normal'; his words, not hers, but Ethan is not like them. He's different. He doesn't even talk to his 'far from normal' family and only went to the party because of pressure from his Rottweiler mum, Janine.

Beth had waited for hours at Charing Cross Police Station under the icy gaze of Janine who clearly did not want her there – not that her opinion mattered to Beth. Anyway, it had been a complete waste of time. Suddenly Ethan was not there anymore, having been escorted out the back door by his solicitor and taken away. In the end she came home alone, confused and hurt, then had lain on their bed and cried herself dry.

She hears the creaking of floorboards in the flat above where their elderly neighbours, Sid and Vera, live. She hears their flat door open and close and Vera's shrill voice bossing Sid into submission.

'Just be careful on the stairs,' she says. 'You know what you're like on those old feet.'

She hears their footsteps on the communal stairs, followed by a light tapping at the flat door. Beth bites her thumb. *I don't really want to see anyone now, except for Ethan, that is.*

Vera calls through the door, 'Beth, open up. We have something for you.'

Beth doesn't move or make a sound. She has not been able to make sense of what happened today and still needs time to process it. But the truth is, she has no one else to talk to, so when Vera calls, 'We know you're in there,' Beth sighs and slides out of bed. Hurrying to the bathroom, she quickly splashes cold water on her puffy, tear-stained face and lightly runs a brush through her hair. The last thing she wants is for Sid and Vera to fuss over her. Crossing to the hallway, she opens the front door.

'Hi,' she says, trying to sound bright, but failing terribly.

Sid and Vera stare back at her with concerned expressions. Vera's hand is resting on her chest. In the other is an old flask with a tartan pattern.

'You poor thing!' says Vera, rushing forward and embracing her.

Beth is too surprised to say anything.

'I heard you crying.'

'Oh . . .'

Vera takes Beth by the hand. 'Let's talk, dear,' she says, stepping inside and pulling Beth towards the living room. 'Sid, close the door behind you. That draught is chilling my bones.'

'Righto.'

Vera steers Beth to the sofa and sits down, pats the seat next to her. 'Let's have a little chat, dear.'

Beth lowers herself to the sofa and rests her hands on her knees.

Vera smiles at her and squeezes her hand. 'We heard about Ethan.'

Beth feels a quiver in her tummy. 'But how could you?'

Before she answers, Vera looks at her husband who is standing over them, watching. 'Sid, dear, you're making the place look untidy. Sit down please.'

Sid obediently sits opposite on an armchair.

'We received a call today . . .'

'From Ethan?'

'No, dear, from someone else.'

'Who?'

'His solicitor.'

'Why did he call you?'

Vera glances at Sid and shrugs. 'We know him.'

'You know him?'

'We do.'

'I don't understand.'

'It's a long story,' replies Vera, smiling. 'Oh I forgot, I brought you this.' She presents the old tartan flask. 'It's that tea you like. You know, the blend I make myself. You said you enjoyed it.' Vera twists off the cap. 'Let me pour you some.'

Beth doesn't have the heart to tell Vera she hates her tea and that it smells like raw sewage.

Vera hands her the cup of steaming liquid. 'Go on. Drink.' Her eyes flash mischievously. 'I put a little something extra in. It'll help you.'

Beth wrinkles her nose. 'What have you put in it?'

'Nothing that'll kill ya. Go on, drink,' Vera says, pushing the tea closer to Beth's mouth.

Beth doesn't want to be rude and takes a sip. She has to admit this particular concoction tastes better than it smells.

'What did the solicitor say?' asks Beth.

'He said Ethan is fine and not to worry about him.' Vera smiles, leans across and pushes the cup back to Beth's mouth.

Beth pushes back. 'Is that all?'

Vera shrugs. 'You know what solicitors are like. They keep their cards close their chest.'

'But *where* is Ethan?'

Vera levels her gaze and beams. 'Let's do a deal. You drink your tea and I'll tell you everything we know.'

Beth is not sure she likes the sound of that but wants to know everything. Clutching her nose, she tilts her head back and swallows the tea.

'Ethan is staying with his solicitor,' Vera says.

'His solicitor? Where is he?'

'He's staying at his home in Lewisham. He's quite comfortable. No need to worry.'

Beth feels a lightness in her head. 'He's been spending a lot of time in Lewisham recently. He wouldn't say why.'

Vera taps the back of Beth's hand, as if she is a child. 'Don't worry about him.'

'I need to see him.'

'You seem tired, dear. Are you sure you're OK?'

A fog seems to lift in Beth's mind. She rubs her forehead and wishes she'd had more sleep.

'Ethan needs me. He ... he's fragile.'

'He's in good hands. Aaron will look after him.'

'Who?'

'Ethan's in a good place. A special place. Lots of people live there. Men, women ... children too. A spiritual place, if you like. A place to be free.'

'Free from what?'

'From the evils of this world.'

Beth's head feels heavy. She looks at Sid, who is smiling back at her. 'Where is this place?'

'It might be best to leave him for now.'

Beth can feel herself tensing, though at the same time her head begins to spin.

'You should sleep ... sleep ...'

Beth feels her eyes getting heavy. In moments they close and darkness comes.

27

ARCHER ORDERS AN UBER TO take Grandad to St Thomas's on Westminster Bridge Road. She chats with him and tries her best to perk him up, but he is quiet and subdued and she suspects he has not slept. His face is pale, his eyes red. The fact of Frankie White rejoining his family as a free man is eating away at him and she suspects it will for a long time to come.

While Grandad undergoes the MRI, Archer sits in the busy waiting area, paging through the online newspapers and the latest speculation about the Battersea Park murders. There is little to see. In fact, the column sizes have shrunk considerably in the four days since the bodies first hit the headlines. That story is old news now.

A call comes through from Klara. Archer feels the disapproving gaze of the people around her and turns away to face the wall as she swipes the phone and takes the call.

'Hi, Klara,' she says, quietly.

'Hey, Grace. Have I caught you at an awkward time?'

'I'm just waiting for Grandad at the hospital.'

'How's he doing?'

'He could be better.'

'I can call you later, if you prefer?'

She hears tutting from a man sitting next to hear and heads out to the corridor. 'It's no problem. What's up?'

'Harry and I have found some interesting stuff about Aaron Cronin. He's definitely a person of interest.'

'In what way?'

'I'll send you a link to YouTube where there's a video interview with him. Go to the eighteen-minute point – it'll give you some context.' Klara lowers her voice. 'I'll tell you more when I see you. DCI Pierce is loitering at my door. She wants something.'

'Understood.'

'Hope Jake is OK.'

'Thanks.'

'See you later.'

'Bye.'

Archer notices her seat is gone in the waiting room and decides to remain in the corridor, leaning on the wall next to an ancient fire extinguisher. Her phone pings with Klara's message containing the link to the YouTube file. Archer fishes her earbuds from her coat pocket and inserts them into her ears.

The film is a documentary about the Jesus Army made sixteen years ago in 2001, according to the description underneath the thumbnail. Archer presses play and, despite the ropey old video-tape picture quality and tinny sound, the film is watchable. It opens with five middle-aged men resembling suburban dads occupying the inside of a multicoloured bus parked outside a pub at night somewhere in Central London. Four of them, dressed in baggy jumpers, sit around a table rocking and talking with their eyes closed. The fifth man is standing and looking through the windows at three women standing outside the pub, sharing a cigarette. He is wearing a black leather jacket that looks as if it has been spray-painted with similar colours to the bus. Sewn on the shoulder is a large red military-style patch with *JESUS ARMY* written in bold letters. He raises his arms, opens his palms and aims them like an amateur stage conjurer at the women.

'Jesus, Lord,' he begins, in a thick South London accent, 'look at them, Lord, make them see inside themselves. Make them see that thing what is there, Lord, the power, show them your power, Lord, bring them to the bus, Lord Jesus, cause them to walk to the bus, Lord Jesus, cause them to see us and feel your power inside us, Lord Jesus . . .'

The other men begin to babble nonsense that Archer supposes is speaking in tongues. The volume of their voices increases, their hands rise and all five of them begin chanting like an unhinged coven of blokes with dodgy haircuts and bad knit-wear. After a few moments the women finish their cigarette and drop it to the ground. They look toward the bus, giggle and leave. The film cuts to another street scene with the same men standing around a homeless man praying. The narrator, a quietly spoken Scotsman, begins to speak.

'Over three thousand people in the Jesus Army, including these men, have given everything to this church. They've handed over all their possessions, their income too, and follow a strict set of rules that is meant to sever them from anything considered worldly.'

Archer is intrigued to watch more, but fast forwards to the eighteen-minute point specified by Klara. The camera focuses on a slim, nervous-looking young man in his teens, who is sitting on a tired-looking chintz sofa. The narrator, who remains off camera, is talking with him.

'What brought you to London?'

'I came to find my birth mum, but she was gone.'

'Where did she go?'

'Prison.'

'Who's been looking after you?'

'I've been in foster care.'

'Do your foster parents know you're here?'

The boy shrugs.

An off-camera voice says, 'We're going to phone them this morning.'

The camera pans across a shabby magnolia room to a man dressed in a khaki jumper with a red wooden cross around his neck. He is seated on an armchair, his hands resting on the arms, as if he is sitting on a throne. Archer recognises him immediately.

The narrator continues, 'Aaron is a "Shepherd", a mentor and senior member of the church.'

The camera pans back to the boy. 'Aaron is my shepherd, my friend, my true brother. He is the reason I want to stay. Isn't that right, Aaron?'

The camera swings back to Aaron and focuses on a close-up of his face, which has the rigid, unreadable quality of a hardened poker player. Aaron does not answer the question. The narrator asks, 'Aaron, you are soon to become one of the church elders. In fact, you will be the youngest elder ever appointed. That's quite an achievement.'

'It is no achievement. It is an appointment from the Lord Jesus himself.'

'Quite. I understand many elders take a new designation. Will you be adopting a new name for your new position in the church?'

Aaron does not reply and looks away as if bored by the conversation.

'Deliverance,' says the teenage boy. The camera turns to his smiling face. 'His name will be Deliverance.'

'That's an interesting choice of name. May I ask why you've taken it?'

'It seemed as good a name as any.'

'I see. Still . . .'

'Tell him,' urges the boy. 'Tell him why you chose it.'

Aaron seems to shift uncomfortably in his chair but does not answer.

'He is Deliverance. He will deliver us from evil!'

Archer hears Grandad's voice and turns to see him pulling on his coat as he emerges from a consultation room at the end of the corridor. Beside him, dressed in scrubs, is the doctor, a Mediterranean woman around her own age who chats away to him as though they are old friends. Archer is relieved to see Grandad seems in good spirits.

'There she is,' says Grandad, cheerily. 'This is my granddaughter, Grace. She's a Detective Inspector. Grace, this is Dr Gabris.'

Archer and the doctor exchange a smile and greeting.

'Well, we're all done for now. We'll get the results to your GP in a few weeks. If we need to see you sooner, we'll be in touch.'

'Thank you, Dr Gabris,' says Archer.

'You're welcome. Bye, Jake.'

'Bye-bye, Dr Gabris.'

'Have a good day.'

215

Archer loops her arm into Grandad's and walks with him towards the exit. 'How did it go?'

'Can't say I enjoyed it much, going inside that big machine.'

'I'm sorry you had to go through that again.'

'Makes you think,' he says, his eyes staring into the distance at nothing in particular.

'What about?'

'Just how fragile we are.'

Archer squeezes his arm. 'You're as strong as an ox.'

Grandad smiles at her. 'She was very nice. Dr Gabris, that is. She talked to me all the way through it, made sure I was OK.'

'Yes, she seemed very nice. I'm glad she looked after you.'

They walk in silence, navigating through the medical staff, porters, administrators and visitors, until they reach the exit.

Archer asks, 'Do you need anything from the shops?'

'I think I might just like to go home. I'm quite tired, and that MRI has wiped me out.'

'Let's get you home then.'

Archer hails a black cab outside the hospital and climbs inside after Grandad.

As they make their way back to Waterloo, Grandad looks up at the ice-blue sky. 'It's a nice day for the time of year.'

'It is,' replies Archer, but her mind is elsewhere, focusing on the man, the teenage boy in the video had described as a shepherd. *What is your story and just how are you connected to these murders?*

28

ETH STIRS AND TRIES TO open her eyes, but they
feel heavy, as if weighted down by two invisible thumbs.
Her head feels foggy and she has no sense of time or
place. It's as if she is waking from a deep sleep, yet within
moments she begins to feel her body again.

Around her, it's gloomy, but a slice of daylight from a crack
in the curtains reveals the familiarity of her own bedroom. She
slowly turns her head towards Ethan, but he is not there. Sliding
her arm along the surface of the mattress to his side of the bed,
she can feel it's cold and wonders where he could be. She listens
for him in the bathroom, or down the hallway in the kitchen,
but hears nothing. She tries to think and then the events of
yesterday begin to seep back into her head. The welcome home
party. The police. Charing Cross Police Station. Returning
home, alone. Vera and Sid.

She pushes herself onto her elbows, her mind swirling with
confusion. Looking down, she sees she is dressed in her bra
and pants, and not her pyjamas, which is unusual. She tries to
remember what happened but can't recall getting undressed,
never mind getting into bed. A memory flashes in her head.
Vera and Sid were here last night in the flat, concerned about

her, about Ethan. There is something else ... Beth rubs her temples but can't quite remember what it is.

The clock on the bedside table says 12.37 p.m. Dread surges through her. How can she have slept so late? She realises she doesn't know what shift she should be working. She'll have to check the calendar in the kitchen – that's if she can haul herself out of bed. With an effort, she pushes herself up but stands too quickly. Her head begins to spin, her knees buckle and she topples back onto the bed.

She presses the back of her hand against her forehead, checking if she might be hot with a fever, but it seems fine. Why is she feeling like this? Had she been drinking last night? She doesn't usually drink during the week. Wait ... she recalls an old flask with dents and a red tartan pattern. Vera's flask. Vera had given her something hot to drink. The clouds begin to clear and she sees her old neighbour, sweet and nice, pressing the cup to her lips, insisting she drink.

'I put a little something extra in,' Vera's voice echoes in her mind.

Beth is confused. What did she mean by 'something extra'? She feels a swelling anger. Has Vera drugged her with some-thing? That's so irresponsible. Why would she do that? The fog is clearing and she remembers Vera talking about Ethan. What did she say? She knew something about where he is staying. He is in Lewisham staying with ... with ... his solicitor! But where in Lewisham? Vera and Sid must know. Beth will ask them. They owe her.

She listens for their footsteps creaking on the floorboards above but doesn't hear anything. Beth takes a few deep breaths, stands and reaches for her pink dressing gown that's hanging from the hook on the bedroom door. Steadying herself against the door frame she makes her way to the kitchen and checks the puppy calendar on the wall above the kettle. To her relief, she is on the evening shift and has the whole afternoon to pull herself together, talk with Vera and Sid, and then find Ethan.

Under the hot shower Beth is relieved to feel her body start to waken. She thinks about Ethan and feels a twist of hurt in her stomach. She really can't understand why he hasn't talked to her. He *always* talks to her. She is his rock, he had once told her. He has gone through so much crap with his dreadful family. He is the black sheep – or the white sheep, as she likes to say. He isn't like them. He is sensitive, kind and as fragile as a glass egg. She loves that about him.

Beth blow dries and brushes her hair before dressing in jeans and a sweater. She makes a Nespresso coffee from the machine she and Ethan bought together and drinks it quickly, thankful for the much-needed buzz it gives her. She hates confrontations but feels ready to talk with her neighbours. Making her way to her flat door she stops for a moment, considering what to say to them before asking for the address in Lewisham where Ethan is staying. *What was in that drink? Did you drug me? Why did you do that?* She makes her way out of the flat and up the stairs. A thought occurs to her and she hesitates. *Did Sid and Vera put me to bed? Did* they *undress me?* She feels nauseous and grips the banister tightly. That isn't possible. Is it? Eyes wide, she looks up the stairwell to the glossy black door, the entrance to their spacious flat. A part of her thinks she should return to her place and think this through, but she doesn't have the time. She needs to see Ethan and they are her only connection. Composing herself, she hurries up the remaining stairs and politely knocks on the door. She waits with her ear to the door but hears nothing. She knocks again, louder. Nothing.

'Bugger,' she says.

She doesn't recall hearing them leave, but how the hell would she if she's been drugged!

She goes back to her flat, bites her thumb and wonders what to do. She notices some of Ethan's paperwork on the coffee table. Perhaps there's something there. She begins rifling through the pile of bills, statements, official letters, but there is nothing about Lewisham. She hurries into the bedroom and opens the drawers of his bedside cabinet, pulling everything out. Receipts, cash, photographs. She narrows in on something she doesn't recognise: a chipped wooden crucifix painted a burnt orange colour. Strange, but not helpful; she drops it back in the drawer.

The wicker wash basket is full to the brim and a pair of Ethan's jeans hang over the top. Beth takes them out and searches through the pockets. She feels a card in the back pocket and takes it out.

'Bingo!' she says.

Printed on the one side of the card is:

Aaron Cronin
Blood of the Lamb Church
Ladywell Playtower
Lewisham

29

ARCHER, QUINN AND KLARA ARE in the analyst's hub, rewatching a BBC report on the Jesus Army from two years ago. The reporter, a suited man with a serious expression, is talking outside a large mansion house in a rural location.

'The Jesus Army was formed here, in this house in Bugbrooke, during the 1970s, by Noel Stanton, a local businessman.' The video cuts to grainy footage of a man in his sixties with scruffy grey hair, preaching to an audience of what Quinn had called 'happy clappers'. The reporter continues, 'Stanton, pictured here in the late eighties was the church leader who pulled the strings of his flock. He was known to preach daily about the sins of the flesh, yet when he died, hundreds of people who grew up in the church contacted the police about the physical, sexual and emotional abuse they were subjected to.'

Archer stops the clip. 'So we know that since this scandal, the Jesus Army are no longer in operation.'

'That's correct,' says Klara. 'Although they rebranded as the Jesus Army and washed their hands of the scandal.'

'It'll take a lot to clean those hands,' says Quinn. 'Cronin distanced himself from the Jesus Army after the scandal. His mother died while he was in the church and not long after that, his father too. Cronin inherited the family home, a remote farmhouse in Northampton, ten miles north of a village called Creation, of all things. It was at the farmhouse that he set up a commune, which was like a mini branch of the Jesus Army. There isn't much info about them.'

'I'll see what I can track down,' says Klara.

Quinn continues, 'So the situation today is that Cronin has set up his own project, which he calls the Blood of the Lamb Church.'

'What's their purpose?'

'There's very little about them on the Internet,' says Klara. 'They're private, which might be because they are new. From what I can gather they're on a recruitment drive.'

'Do we know how many members they have?' asks Archer.

'I'd hazard a guess and say they're quite small, but numbers are rising.'

Archer picks up a black marker and begins writing the names of the players in the investigation, with living and dead, on the whiteboard: Brian Bailey, Justin Sykes, Ethan White, Aaron Cronin, Tyler Green, Josh Dean. With a red pen she underlines Aaron Cronin's name and Ethan White's too.

She turns to Klara and Quinn. 'Brian Bailey's murder has some sort of religious connotation. Therefore, I'm putting Aaron Cronin and Ethan White at the centre of this mystery. They're involved either directly, or indirectly.'

'Are we sidelining Tyler Green and Josh Dean?'

'For the moment. Unless either of you disagree, we should focus on Aaron Cronin and Ethan White.'

'I'm all for that,' says Quinn.

'Me too,' adds Klara.

'So, what else do we know about Cronin and the Jesus Army?'

'I did some digging on Cronin,' Klara answers. 'After school he left Northampton to study law at Durham. He practised for a few years before going into business as an entrepreneur. He had one start-up, a computer sales business that failed, and later a semi-successful publishing and printing business. In the documentary Cronin is asked why he joined the Jesus Army. He says he was invited to join them in 2001 by an old friend, Cameron Pollard, who was a church elder. Cronin said he wasn't much interested in religion until he saw what they were about.'

'He saw the light,' says Quinn, dryly.

'You might say that.'

'So, in a nutshell, Cronin jettisoned his businesses, left his parents and former life behind, joined the happy clappers, became a disciple and started moving up the ranks,' says Archer.

'Perfectly summed up.'

Quinn says, 'He had no prior interest in religion. A lawyer and businessman who pursued success, wealth and gives it all up for a life of prayer and abstinence? I don't buy it.'

'A glib question: did something happen to him or did he lose everything or have some sort of trauma?' Archer asks.

'There's nothing on record.'

'He wanted the power that came with this sort of position – and with that power comes wealth. He certainly has charisma. There's something about the way he carries himself that sets him apart from the others in the documentary and at Ladywell Playtower too. He has a presence and a confidence that the others don't have.'

'There was certainly evidence of worship from that teenage boy.'

'Cronin was less than cooperative with us and I'd bet your wages, Harry, he knows more about Brian Bailey than he's letting on.'

'Erm, thanks . . . and I agree.'

'Was Brian Bailey a member of the Jesus Army?' Archer asks Klara.

'I'll look into that today.'

'What about Cameron Pollard?'

'He's retired and lives in Islington.'

'We need to talk to Cronin again and Ethan White too. Something's not adding up there. But before that, let's pay Cameron Pollard a visit. Is he still active with the Jesus Army or any other church?'

'There's nothing online to indicate that he is. From what I could cobble together he's retired and lives alone in a smart-looking Edwardian brown-brick in Highbury Fields. I'll ping you the address.'

'Thanks.'

'I found one other name that might be worth following up. Another "shepherd" who was once on his way to being an elder but never quite made it. I checked the police records. He's now an ex-teacher in his mid-forties. Has had a few drunk and disorderly convictions, which may be why he no longer teaches.'

'What's his name?'

'Alfie McSweeney.'

'I'll get Toze and Marian to look for him. Thanks, Klara. Good work.'

30

I T'S ONLY BEEN THREE DAYS since Beth took the same
train to Lewisham and saw that poor young woman get
killed in a hit-and-run. She shudders at the memory. She
had been travelling there to meet Ethan then too. He had
something to tell her, he'd said, but he'd cancelled at the last
minute. Was it something to do with his solicitor or this church?

Beth focuses on Google Maps on her phone and navigates
her way towards Ladywell Road. Lewisham seems so ordinary
and almost suburban that she wonders why Ethan asked to meet
her here. He had not indicated why Lewisham and she'd assumed
he'd discovered some new flash restaurant or bar. When she
saw him the following day and she had expressed her annoyance
at the cancellation of their date, he had apologised but he was
in such a state about his mother's pressure to be at the family
do that she hadn't questioned why Lewisham, of all places.

Ahead she sees a large posh-looking red-brick house with a
turret rising above a spiked iron fence lined with tall hedges.
Checking her mobile she can see that it's Ladywell Playtower,
the place where Ethan is staying.

She thinks it a strange-looking place with an equally strange
name and wonders why it is called a playtower. What does that

even mean? A play place for children, maybe? It looks much too creepy for that. She arrives at a tall iron gate with a cross inside it. She pushes the gate, but it's locked. Peering through it she sees a teenage boy. He is wearing old jeans and a tweed blazer and is sitting on a stone bench using a short knife to carve the end of a stick into a point.

'Hello!' she calls.

The boy stops what he's doing and looks across at her with a curious expression. She notices one of his eyelids droops lower than the other and that he is wearing an orange cross similar to the one she found in Ethan's drawer.

Strange.

The teenager seems familiar and Beth realises he is the lad she encountered at the hit-and-run.

'Hello, I saw you the other day. There was an accident . . .'

'Weren't me,' he replies.

Beth is certain it was him and wonders why he would lie. 'Please can you let me in? I'm looking for Ethan White. He's my boyfriend – partner, actually. Apparently, he's staying here.'

The boy folds the knife away and slips it into his blazer pocket. He stands, turns and walks out of sight.

'Hello! Wait!' calls Beth, but the boy has gone. 'How rude,' she mutters.

Beth looks up at the house to see if anyone is at the windows.

'BOO!' someone cries.

Beth gasps and stumbles backward, her heart pounding.

The boy has jumped out from behind the hedge at the other side of the gate and is watching her with an intense gaze, like a hyena taking the measure of its prey.

'You gave me a fright!'

The boy smiles but says nothing.

Beth takes a calming breath. 'Can you let me in, please?'

'Not allowed.'

His eyes look her up and down and linger too long on her chest. Beth feels the hairs on her neck rising. 'What do you mean, you're not allowed?'

The boy shrugs.

'I need to speak with Ethan White. Can you get him for me, please?'

He shrugs again.

Beth narrows her eyes. 'Are you going to help me or not?'

'Maybe.'

Beth bites her lip and tries the nice approach. She smiles and asks, 'What's your name?'

'Kain. With a K.'

'Hello, Kain. My name is Beth. I'd very much like to speak to Ethan White. Please can you tell him Beth Harper is here and needs to talk with him.'

'Special day, today.'

Beth does not know what to say to that.

'*Ethan's* special day,' adds Kain.

Beth feels a knot in her stomach. 'What does that mean?'

'He's joining us. Here at the church.'

'What do you mean he's joining you at the church? You must be mistaken. Can't be Ethan. He's not even religious.'

'We all come here as sinners. In this house you'll find them all: fornicators, adulterers, murderers, thieves, homosexuals, whores. They're all here.'

Beth frowns. 'Which one are you then?' she asks.

'I'm just a sinner, like you. Like Ethan. But after today, Ethan will be reborn.'

'Can you let me in, please?' says Beth, and feels a sharp pain in her side. 'Ouch.' Looking down she sees Kain's stick poking through the gate at her ribs.

Kain laughs, a weird choking chuckle like a braying donkey.

Beth steps back, rubbing her side, unsure what to make of this weird kid. She notices something twitching in the side pocket of his blazer. She doesn't want to ask what that might be.

Kain stops laughing and presses his face against the gate. 'I'm sorry, Beth. I didn't mean to hurt you. Would you like to come in for Ethan's special day?' He smiles sweetly at her.

Beth hesitates.

'I can let you in, if you like.'

'Just keep that stick away from me.'

His mouth spreads to a grin, which is part goofy, part sinister . . . more the latter. 'I promise.' He unlocks the gate and pulls it open.

As it creaks open, Beth's instincts tell her to leave, but she can't abandon Ethan. He needs her, and she needs him. Besides, she wants to know what exactly this Kain had meant when he said Ethan is joining them and being reborn. She walks through the gate and into the grounds and can't help but feel she is stepping into another world. She notices the twitching in Kain's blazer pocket has intensified.

'What is that?' she asks.

Kain reaches into his pocket and removes a small Blue Tit. It chirps and struggles in the firm grip of his grubby hand.

'Why don't you let it go?' she asks.

Kain laughs and throws it in the air above her head.

Beth flinches and ducks and hears the thud of something hitting the ground behind her. She looks to see the bird hopping across the grass with one of its wings sticking out.

'It's broken its wing,' says Kain, as he bends over to lift it.

'Can't you take it to the vet?'

'I'll look after her,' he replies, placing it back into his pocket. Beth shudders.

'Follow me. It's about to start.'

Kain turns and walks towards the left side of the house away from the front entrance and the turret. Beth shifts uneasily, but nevertheless follows him. She can hear voices and hands clapping from inside the old Victorian building. As they approach the side entrance, a heavy steel door, the voices being to sing.

Down at the cross
Where my saviour died
Down where for cleansing
From sin I cried
There to my heart
Was the blood applied
Glory to His name

Kain pulls open the iron door and Beth feels the rush of a muggy heat. Stepping through she sees forty to fifty people gathered around an old swimming pool lit by tall candles on large gothic candlesticks, one at each corner of the pool. Her gaze focuses on the pool. It's not filled with water. It's blood! Beth's stomach lurches.

She feels Kain close by. He laughs and says, 'Don't be frightened. It's only a red dye.'

Beth is relieved, but only a little. This is just too weird.

I am so wondrously
Saved from my sin
Jesus so sweetly
Abides within
There at the cross
Where He took me in
Glory to His name

The crowd's voices quieten as a man emerges from them with his arms spread wide open.

'That's Aaron,' says Kain.

The man called Aaron is dressed in a white linen top with matching trousers and wears silver rings on all his fingers. The people begin to clap and cheer as he walks down a ramp and into the horrible bloody water, wading across and trailing his hands across the glossy red surface. He stops, turns to face them and raises his arms, his hands dripping with red liquid.

His congregation start to sing again. A different song, this time with a faster tempo.

Have you been to Jesus for the cleansing power?
Are you washed in the blood?
In the soul-cleansing blood of the Lamb?
Are your garments spotless; are they white as snow?
Are you washed in the blood of the Lamb?

A cheer erupts and Beth turns to see Ethan step from the crowd, dressed in similar white linens.

'Ethan!' calls Beth but he cannot hear her voice over the crowd.

He steps slowly down into the pool, shuddering and smiling as his feet touch the red water. Aaron embraces him, hugging him tightly like an old friend, staining the linen of his shirt with his red hands. The singers gather around the pool, obscuring her view. Beth makes her way forward, pushing through the crowd.

'Hello, dear,' comes a voice.

Beth turns to see Vera behind her, smiling pink-lipsticked mouth and clownish blue eye shadow. 'So nice to see you here.'

Beth blinks. 'What are you doing here?'

'Hello, Beth.' Sid's voice is behind her and suddenly both neighbours are hugging and squeezing her. 'Welcome, Beth, welcome.'

Beth squirms her way free from them and rounds on Vera. 'Please stop!'

Vera smiles back at her, seemingly unfazed by Beth's protest.

'What did you put in that tea last night?' asks Beth.

Vera waves a dismissive hand. 'Just a little something to help you sleep, dear. You were distressed.'

'Why would you do that?'

'Ethan White!' a voice bellows, echoing through the hall and interrupting their exchange.

Cheers and whoops holler across the vast interior.

Vera's papery hands grab Beth's. 'Come on, dear. It's about to start.' She pulls Beth to the edge of the pool. 'Watch. Aaron is about to save Ethan.'

'Save him from what?' snaps Beth.

Vera grins a cunning smile and does not reply.

Exasperated, Beth watches as the man called Aaron and Ethan stand waist-high in the water. Aaron stands at Ethan's side with both hands resting on his shoulders. Ethan's eyes are half-closed and he is smiling strangely, mouth half-open, as if he is drunk or high.

'Behold a sinner who has come for deliverance . . .' Aaron begins.

The crowd cheers.

'Ethan White, sinner, degenerate, crook . . .'

Beth feels her blood go cold at Aaron's words. None of them describe the Ethan she knows.

Aaron continues, ' . . . but no longer is he that person. He is a good man. A kind man. A man of Jesus. Ethan White, this is your new family. This is your new home. This is your new life. Do you relinquish your old ways?'

Ethan does not respond and Aaron places his hand on his chest. Ethan begins to tremble at his touch. 'Ethan, do you relinquish your old life?' repeats Aaron.

'I do,' replies Ethan.

More cheers from the audience.

'Are you ready to be washed by the blood of the Lamb?'

'I am!'

Aaron places Ethan's arms into a cross position on his chest. 'In the name of the authority that is all-powerful in heaven and on earth, I now baptise thee!'

With what seems like all his strength, he plunges Ethan into the red water and holds him under for almost ten seconds, before hauling him up again.

Ethan is like something from a horror movie. He is gasping for air, trembling yet smiling.

Aaron continues, 'Feel the power of Jesus in you, like a mantle it covers you, protecting you, making you strong,' He places his hand on Ethan's forehead. 'Be filled with the power of the Holy Spirit, be filled with the power of the Holy ...' Ethan's eyes seem to roll into the back of his head and he shivers and collapses, sinking under the water.

'Ethan!' cries Beth, but her cry is lost again by the hollering of the congregation speaking in tongues at the top of their voices.

Moments pass and Aaron is carrying a limp Ethan out of the pool and through the crowd. Beth tries to break through, but they are in a frenzy and she cannot get to Ethan. She calls his name, but Aaron takes him through a doorway with the congregation following.

She feels a tugging on her coat and turns to see Kain.

'You can't go with them,' he says.

She tries to pull away from him but his grip is firm. 'Get off me!'

'Forget him. He has already forgotten you.'

Beth hears the door slamming shut and turns to see that everyone has gone. She pulls away from Kain and runs to the door, but it is locked. Tears spring to her eyes. What the hell just happened?

31

CAMERON POLLARD'S HOME IS A tall brown-brick Georgian house on Highbury Terrace in North London. Archer and Quinn climb the tiled chequerboard steps to the front door. Archer presses the doorbell, waits; when there is no response, she rings a second time. Moments pass with no indication that anyone is home. She raps the door knocker three times and notices movement in the downstairs window of the house next door. A thin, grey-haired woman wearing pearls and a pink cardigan watches them keenly as she arranges the ornaments on her windowsill. Archer nods a hello and then leans across and peers through Pollard's ground-floor window. The front part of the room is a living area with neatly arranged Victorian antique furniture. The rear is a dining room with a mahogany table and eight baroque chairs, one of which is turned away from the table. A laptop lies closed on the tabletop.

She notices Quinn crouching down to peer through the letterbox. Within seconds he frowns, covers his mouth and nose and stumbles backward. 'Fucking hell!'

'Harry?'

Quinn looks up at her with watery eyes. 'You know that stench you get from a corpse that's been rotting with the heat turned up ridiculously high?'

'Shit!'

'You might want to take a look.'

Archer swallows and holds her mouth and nose as she crouches down and peers through the letterbox. She can feel the oppressive heat from the central heating on her face and smells a trace of the rancid odour as it seeps into her nostrils. Inside, the hallway is long with a glossy wooden floor leading up to a kitchen with tri-fold doors leading to the garden beyond. There is a half-light in the kitchen, the tri-fold doors draped in vertical blinds. Slices of daylight cut through the gloom and she sees an outstretched arm lying across the floor of the kitchen. Sitting inside the bloody claw-like fingers, stiff with rigor mortis, is an eyeball.

Archer closes the letterbox, takes out her phone and makes a call to the CSI team. She then calls her own team for urgent assistance.

She and Quinn split up to talk to the neighbours on either side of Pollard's house, to find out if they saw or heard anything, and also to look at the access to the rear of their houses.

'Is everything all right?' asks the thin woman in the pink cardigan, who has spent a long time arranging two ornaments on her windowsill and introduces herself as Mrs Wilson.

'We're just making some enquiries. When was the last time you saw Mr Pollard?' asks Archer.

Her fingers touch her cheek as she tries to remember. After a moment of consideration she says, 'Friday. I'm sure it was Friday. He normally goes to Waitrose and does his weekend shop. I saw him return with his bags.'

'What time was that?

'Around two thirty.'

'Was he alone?'

'Yes, which is normal for him. He doesn't have many friends. None that come to the house, anyway.'

'Did you hear any unusual noises from his home at any point? Arguing or shouting?'

Mrs Wilson ponders for a few long moments. 'No, I can't say that I did. Come to think of it, when I did see him he was hurrying up the steps, puffing and panting as if he was desperate to get home. He didn't look well. Most unlike him.'

'I don't suppose you noticed if there was someone else in the street at the time?'

Mrs Wilson looks away as she thinks this over. 'I don't recall anyone . . . then again, I do prefer to keep myself to myself and try not to pry into other people's business.'

Archer offers a wry smile. 'When was the last time you heard any kind of noise from next door?'

'I usually see Mr Pollard pottering around his garden, but now that I think about it the last time I saw and heard him was that Friday.'

'I don't suppose you have a set of keys for his house?'

'I'm afraid not.'

'Would any other neighbour hold a set of keys?'

'Not that I know of.'

Archer smiles. 'Thank you, Mrs Wilson.' She points towards the back door of the woman's kitchen. 'May I?'

'Please do.'

'Could I ask you to stay here, Mrs Wilson? Just in case.'

Mrs Wilson's eyes widen. 'Just in case of what?'

'Nothing to be alarmed about,' says Archer as she steps outside into the rear garden.

She sees Quinn climbing over the other neighbour's wall with his PPE shoe coverings on.

'Anything from the neighbour?' Archer calls to Quinn.

'Nothing. He's as deaf as a post!'

'What was that?' comes a man's voice.

Quinn looks back. 'Nothing, Mr Tomlinson. You wait inside. I'll be back shortly.'

'Did you get anything from your neighbour?' asks Quinn.

Archer pulls on her PPE boot covers, climbs over Mrs Wilson's wall and drops down on to the grass. 'The last time she saw him was on Friday and he was hurrying home and seemed stressed.'

'He was being followed?'

'More than likely.'

The grass ends with a paved patio leading to the tri-fold glass doors. They make their way towards them and peering through the blinds, see the decomposed body of the man with his eyes removed and a crucifix carved into his face. His throat is cut, his arms are outstretched and in each of his palms sits an eye looking back at him.

'A familiar scene,' says Quinn.

Archer takes out her phone and takes several shots as Quinn checks the doors.

'The key's still in the lock. The killer probably exited from the front.'

She crouches down and examines the patio for traces of anything the killer might have left behind: a discarded paper tissue, droplets of blood, a footprint, anything; there is nothing. Pollard's neighbour, Mrs Wilson, last saw and heard him one week ago, which means the length of time and the inclement weather will have compromised any evidence. That said, CSI can do a deeper examination when they get here. There is always a chance they'll find something.

Archer's phone rings with a call from Sergeant Barnes. 'Hey, Jimmy.'

'Hello, DI Archer. Wayne and I were nearby and got the call. We're outside, ma'am. CSI are here too.'

'Great. We'll be there in a moment.'

'Anything I can do to help?' comes an unfamiliar voice.

Archer turns to see the head of an elderly bald-headed man appear above the wall.

'Northing, Mr Tomlinson,' says Quinn, his voice raised.

'Is Cameron at home? I haven't spoken to him in a while. Did I mention that?' asks Mr Tomlinson.

'Actually, you did,' replies Quinn as he heaves himself back over the wall and escorts the elderly neighbour back into his house.

Archer makes her way back to Mrs Wilson's.

Jimmy Barnes and PC Wayne Bickley are outside chatting to MJ from the CSI team. A second squad car arrives with two female officers.

'On your own today, MJ?' asks Quinn as he emerges from Mr Tomlinson's house.

'Yes, just me today, H. Krish had to scoot over to Camden urgently.'

'Don't apologise. Camden is welcome to him.'

MJ smiles.

'Gather around, everyone,' says Archer. 'Jimmy, have you got an enforcer in your car?'

'We do, ma'am.'

'Good. Lying in the kitchen inside this house is the body of a man we believe is Cameron Pollard. It seems he has been murdered in the same way as Brian Bailey. MJ, once we get access, Harry and I will wait for you to give us the nod to join you.'

'Sounds good,' replies MJ.

'Jimmy, could you organise the door-to-door questioning of all the neighbours and get someone to stand guard?'

'Will do.'

'Thanks, Jimmy. Let's get the door open.'

Pollard's panelled front door is heavy and takes four hard pushes from the heavy red battering ram, the enforcer, before it opens. Jimmy and Wayne recoil at the fetid smell and retreat down the steps as MJ, covered in head-to-toe PPE, ascends into Pollard's home, laying down forensic floor plates all the way to the living room and then the kitchen. Archer watches with admiration as MJ steps respectfully between the living room and kitchen and around the body, placing numbered evidence markers as she goes. It takes her almost an hour to assess the scene, after which she looks back towards Archer and Quinn. 'You can come in now.'

Archer pulls on the hood of her PPE suit and fixes on her face mask. She is first across the stepping plates and into the kitchen and Quinn is behind her. They stand carefully around the body. Lying on the floor next to it is a mobile phone. Archer picks it up, but the battery is dead.

'I'll take this. I'm assuming a call was made before his death. Klara can look into it.'

MJ takes it from her and places it into a plastic bag.

'No question it's the same killer that took out Brian Bailey,' says Quinn. 'If I'm not mistaken, that powder on his nose is Butterfly Ketamine.'

'And it can't be a copycat because the public doesn't know about the nature of Bailey's injuries and death,' says MJ.

Archer scans the kitchen, which is clean and tidy with the exception of occasional splashes of blood spatter.

'Any sign of the murder weapon?' asks Quinn.

'Not yet.'

Archer notices a knife block on the worktop with all the knives present inside. One by one, she removes and examines them, but there are no traces of blood on any of them. She checks the drawers and cupboards, but there is nothing unusual. Walking down to the living room she looks at the skewed dining chair at the head of the table where the laptop is. 'Pollard was sitting here, working on his laptop; he hears a noise from the kitchen . . .' Archer flicks the living-room light switch on, but no light shines. She tries the hallway light, which does not come on either. There is a small cupboard in the hallway outside the kitchen. She opens it, sees the fuse box and continues, 'The killer turns off the lights. Pollard closes his laptop, steps into the hallway and meets his murderer.'

'Not a nice way to go. That's for sure,' says MJ.

'It's grim indeed,' replies Quinn.

'How did you find out about this guy?' asks MJ.

'Klara found his name in connection with a suspect,' Archer tells her.

'Does he have a connection to Brian Bailey?'

'Klara is working on that. Pollard has a history with the Jesus Army.'

241

MJ arches her eyebrows. 'Interesting. I wonder if that explains the inverted cross.'

'The Jesus Army used the regular cross, never an inverted one.'

'Do you think the killer might be anti-religious or anti-God?'

'It had crossed our minds,' says Quinn. 'Pardon the pun.'

Archer's phone rings. She makes her way down the hallway to the front door and answers it. 'DI Archer.'

'Hey, DI Archer. It's Krish.'

'Hi, Krish. I heard you were in Camden.'

'Yeah. I'm here now.'

'What's up?'

'There's another body, murdered and disfigured just like Brian Bailey. Eyes removed and a crucifix cut into the face.'

Archer holds her breath as she absorbs Krish's news.

'DI Archer?' asks Krish.

'Where are you exactly?'

'We're at Regent's Canal, under the Camden Street Bridge. Camden Police are here. I told them you're leading an investigation with a similar murder.'

'Who is the senior office on site?'

'Neha Rei.'

'Ask her to call me, please.'

'Will do.'

'Thanks, Krish. We'll be there shortly.'

32

ETH IS SITTING ON A stone bench at the side of the church, dabbing her wet eyes with a damp handkerchief. She has never felt so alone. So left out. So forgotten.

What the Hell just happened to Ethan?

She has just witnessed him undergoing some sort of weird baptism in a creepy old Victorian swimming bath, surrounded by mad people. She blows her nose into the paper hanky, which has got too many holes now to be of any further use. She drops it onto the bench and feels the isolation and hurt begin to smoulder and burn away to anger. The weird kid called Kain is sitting next to her, poking the soil with his stick and singing that same hymn those people had sung just before Ethan was baptised.

'Could you stop singing, please?' she asks.

He does what she asks, but then begins to rock back and forth on the bench as he pushes the stick further into the earth.

Beth's phone rings. It's Ethan's mum.

'Fuck!' she mutters.

She feels the boy stop and look her way.

Beth wonders whether to answer it or not. What will she say when she asks to speak to her precious son? Beth stares at

Janine's name on the screen. Queen fucking Janine. She smiles to herself and swipes open the call. 'What do you want, Janine?' she answers, surprising herself. She has never dared speak to Janine like this before.

She hears a gasp down the line. 'I beg your pardon?'

Beth sighs and chooses not to say anything.

'Hello?' asks Janine.

'What do you want, Janine?'

'How dare you talk to me like that.'

Beth looks towards Kain, who is watching her with a curious, unsettling gaze.

'I don't know what you got him messed up in but you have a lot to answer for, my girl,' says Janine.

'Ethan's an adult. He makes his own choices.'

'Ethan's not well. He needs help.'

'And whose fault is that, Janine?' snaps Beth.

'You little bitch! You have no idea who you're talking to.'

'I don't particularly care, Janine.'

The language on the phone turns blue as Janine launches into a tirade. Beth decides she's heard enough. 'Goodbye, Janine.'

'Wait! Tell him I want to talk to him. Please.'

'I can't. He's disappeared to be with his new friends. You should try them. In fact, why don't you come by? I'm sure they'd love to meet you.'

'What're you talking about?'

'Ask him yourself, Janine. Ethan makes his own decisions and, as of now, as far as I'm concerned, he's on his own.'

'Where is he?'

'At the Blood of the Lamb Church in Ladywell. He's there now.'

Before Janine can respond, Beth disconnects the call.

She sighs and thinks she sees someone looking at her through the stained-glass windows on the church tower.

'You should leave,' says Kain.

'I can't think of anything I would rather do.'

'There's a back gate. I can take you there. It'll take you close to the high street.'

Beth narrows her eyes at him and then decides, what does it matter?

'Follow me,' says Kain.

He leads her through a gloomy copse of trees with overgrown, untended bushes, a contrast to the neatly trimmed hedges at the front of the building. In the shadows she sees religious statues. There is one of Jesus with missing limbs. There are also stone angels, some with swords, some crying into their palms. There is even what looks like a moss-covered stone house, a mausoleum, with a spade leaning against it.

'It's peaceful here. Like a graveyard,' says Kain.

'It's creepy, like a graveyard,' replies Beth, who is not sure she is entirely comfortable going any further. 'Maybe we should just leave through the front gate.'

'No, we're nearly there.'

Beth shudders, glances at the spade again and wonders if this actually is a graveyard with dead people buried here.

'A little rose came scurrying through here,' says Kain.

Beth looks at him with a perplexed expression. 'What does that mean?'

'A little brown Rose, pretty she was, scurried through here and got squished by a car.'

Beth feels her skin crawling. Is he talking about Rose Grant?

'What was she doing here?'

'Trying to leave, is what she was doing here.'

'Why?'

'She wanted out, is what she wanted. And she got that all right.'

Kain starts to poke her inappropriately with his stick and laughs at the same time.

'Stop it, you little shit!'

His eyes flare, his jaw tightens, and he pokes her harder.

Beth tries to grab the stick. 'Stop it!'

'That's enough, Kain,' comes a deep voice.

Beth turns to see the man called Aaron in dry clothes, a black open-neck shirt and faded jeans, his hair still damp.

Kain runs to his side and hugs him. He strokes the boy's head. 'Your supper is waiting for you in the kitchen.'

'Can't I eat with the others?'

Aaron smiles benevolently at him. 'Not tonight. Your time will come.'

Kain nods and extracts himself from him.

'Why not say sorry to our guest, Kain?'

'But I didn't do anything.'

'You know the rules.'

Kain regards Beth with a tight expression. To her surprise, he then runs at her, throws his arms around her and squeezes hard. 'Sorry. I'm so sorry.'

Beth shifts uneasily in his grasp. She tries to prise his arms off. 'That's OK.'

'Your time will come too,' he whispers, before releasing himself.

Beth feels the hairs on her neck rising. 'What does that mean?' she asks, but he laughs and runs off towards the house. Did he think she was going to get baptised like Ethan? Fat chance.

'I'm sorry about Kain. He can be a little eccentric.'

'That's one way to describe him.'

Aaron smiles.

'He said Rose Grant was here. She came running through this garden or graveyard, whatever it is, just before she was killed.'

Aaron's smile fades from his face.

They stand in silence for a moment.

Beth swallows. 'Was Rose a member of this church?'

He does not respond. Instead, his eyes slide to the mausoleum and drop to the spade leaning against it.

'I'd like to speak to Ethan.'

'Of course you would.'

Beth wrings her hands together. 'I'd like to talk to him now, please.'

'He is at the house, eating supper.'

'I should go now.'

'Yes, you must.'

He retreats towards the mausoleum and, to Beth's astonishment, begins to sing out loud,

Have you been to Jesus for the cleansing power?
Are you washed in the blood?
In the soul-cleansing blood of the Lamb?
Are your garments spotless; are they white as snow?
Are you washed in the blood of the Lamb?

Beth feels her scalp prickling and wants to get as far away from this man as she can.

Making her way through the trees, Beth pauses as the singing stops. Her heart begins to pound. She hears the soft tread of footfalls somewhere to her left and runs but a blinding pain in her head causes her knees to buckle. She falls to the ground, confused and terrified. She hears a familiar voice say her name. She trembles and tries to get up, but a second blow like an iron fist propels her back down. A weak gasp, a dying breath, escapes from her mouth and then everything goes forever dark.

33

ARCHER CHOOSES NOT TO SAY anything about Krish's news to any of the team until she and Quinn are in the car and on their way to Camden. MJ, Jimmy and PC Bickley have their hands full plus she does not want to risk whispers of this latest murder finding their way to the wrong ears, like the press, for example.

'Mother of freaking Jesus! Are you kidding me?' says Quinn as he steps on the accelerator.

'I wish I was.'

Archer's phone rings.

'DI Archer, it's DC Neha Rei. PC Mel Anderson and I are here at the scene in Camden.'

Archer had worked with Neha Rei during the @nonymous murders. She is a reliable and up-and-coming officer who has recently been transferred to North London after being made a Detective Constable.

Archer puts the phone on speaker.

'Hi, Neha. Thanks for calling. What have you got?'

'Just after four today we responded to a call from a jogger who spotted bloodstains on a tent underneath Camden Street

Bridge. He found the body of a man inside. The dead man's eyes had been cut out and placed in his palms. It's grim, Grace.'

'Do you have an ID for the victim?'

'The name on his credit cards is Alfred McSweeney.'

'I guess we can call off the search for him then,' says Quinn.

'Thanks, Neha. DS Quinn and I will be there in ten minutes. Make sure the press are kept away.'

'Will do. Thanks, Grace. See you soon.'

They arrive in Camden and park near the entrance to the towpath alongside a marked response car, an ambulance and Krish's Land Rover. They hurry their way along the canal-side and within minutes see Krish waving to them from under the bridge. The area is sectioned off with police cordon tape and behind it is a white forensic tent. She spots DC Neha Rei talking to a pale-looking man in running gear with a blanket around his shoulders.

Neha looks across and catches Archer's eye. She says something to the witness, leaves him and approaches Archer and Quinn. 'Grace. Harry. We asked around. No one has seen anything. No one knows who the tent belongs to. But it's not unusual for a rough sleepers to just put them up without warning. This is a quiet, secluded area, especially at night. Mel spoke to a local shopkeeper, who said he knows Alfred, or Alfie as he calls him, spoke to him last Friday.'

'What time was that?'

'Around ten thirty.'

'Was he alone?'

'Yes.'

'OK. Good work. Thanks, Neha.'

'Also, the press are hanging around.'

'Has anyone spoken to them?'

'No – and they don't know the circumstances of the victim's death.'

'Good. Keep it that way and make sure the witness says nothing.'

'Will do.'

They join Krish inside the forensics tent where a bagged body rests on top of a stretcher with two medics standing by.

'Glad you guys are here,' says Krish. 'The pathologist has just gone and the paramedics are keen to get on.' He carefully unzips the body bag and peels open the top. 'He was lying with his arms outstretched, eyes in the palms, like Brian Bailey.'

Archer feels her stomach clenching. There are two dark cavernous holes where Alfie McSweeney's eyes used to be, and a crucifix carved into his bloated grey face. As with the other victims, there are traces of caked white powder on his nostrils.

'The pathologist estimates the time of death to be around five days or more,' says Krish.

'He's been in the tent all that time?' Archer shakes her head.

'It would seem so.'

'Surprised no one noticed the pong sooner,' says Krish.

'Perhaps people thought the pong was the "fragrant" waters of the canal,' says Quinn.

'Where are his eyes?' asks Archer.

'In a bag. Do you want to see them?' asks Krish.

Archer frowns. 'No, thank you.'

'Anything else in the tent?' asks Quinn.

'There was nothing that I could see. Just some uneaten sandwiches and crisps.

Archer turns to the medics. 'Thanks for waiting. You can take him now.'

Krish says, 'I'll get a forensics report to you as quick as I can.'

Archer nods a thanks.

'Cheers, mate,' says Quinn.

They say their goodbyes and make their way back to the car, Archer deep in thought.

Quinn says, 'If Alfie McSweeney walked across the towpath, against his will or not, considering what was about to be done to him, he must have been very drunk . . .'

'Or sedated.'

'Or both.'

'We need a toxicology report.'

'I'll get that sorted.'

'Could you get one for Cameron Pollard, too?'

They walk in silence for a moment, Archer's mind racing. 'All roads lead back to Aaron Cronin, I'm sure of it. We need to find out what links these three victims with him so let's get back to Charing Cross. We have some work ahead of us.'

Archer takes out her phone and calls Tozer. 'Alfie McSweeney's just been found dead. Murdered and disfigured like the others.'

'*What?*' she replies.

'Harry and I are on our way back to the station. Can you meet us there?'

'On my way.'

'See you later.'

They climb into the car and Archer calls Klara.

'Hey, Grace.'

'Hey.' Archer hears DCI Pierce's voice in the background. 'Are you with DCI Pierce?' she asks.

'Yes. I was just updating her on where we're at.'

'Put me on speaker, Klara. I need to speak to both of you.'

252

Archer hears Klara talk to the DCI as the phone clicks on to speaker mode.

'Grace,' says Pierce.

'We have two more murders identical to that of Brian Bailey.'

There's a moment of silence before Pierce cries, 'Fuck!'

Archer and Quinn exchange a look.

'*Fuck!*' repeats Pierce, louder this time. 'Don't tell me we have another fucking serial killer?'

'I can't answer that yet, Clare.'

'Fuck!'

Despite the DCI's distinct middle-class sensibilities, Archer sometimes wonders if she has a touch of Tourette's.

'Just like Brian Bailey, the victims are two middle-aged white men: Alfie McSweeney and Cameron Pollard. Harry and I are on our way back to the station now. Toze and Marian are on their way too.'

'I won't be here,' says Pierce, with a testy tone in her voice. 'I have a meeting with the Super. We'll talk when I'm done.'

'We'll need a bigger team.'

'Of course you do,' replies Pierce, dryly.

Archer suppresses a surge of rising anger. 'Ma'am, four men have been brutally murdered in Central London. Harry, Klara and I cannot solve this case with only occasional help from DS Tozer and DC Phillips. We need—'

Pierce cuts her off. 'I know exactly what is needed, DI Archer. I don't need to remind you the Super has a fucking phobia about dipping his fingers into his piggy bank to help keep the streets of London safe.'

'I'm well aware.'

253

'I will fight tooth and nail.'

'Thank you.'

A moment of silence passes before Klara whispers, 'She's just left the room.'

Archer hears the DCI's voice in the background as she storms back to her office, her loud 'Fuck!' audible even with the distance.

'I think she took the news well,' says Quinn.

'I think her day has just been ruined,' replies Klara. 'Listen, I have an update on Brian Bailey. I started watching the Jesus Army doc on YouTube and I was sure I recognised one of the men on the video in the opening scene on the bus. He's hard to make out and I had to freeze the film at the right point, but I'm sure it was him.'

'How sure is sure?' asks Quinn.

'Very sure. I also tracked down Aaron Cronin's old farm-house in Northampton. He sold it ten years ago to a woman called Esther Tilling. She set up a Mental Health Support Home for locals who have been through trauma. I checked out their website and found a page charting a history of the farm. Among them was a scanned photo of Aaron and some of his church friends, I assume. Bailey was among them, and the boy from the video – the one who called Cronin his "shepherd". He's in the photos too. Not just him, though. He has a twin brother by the look of it.'

'Are there any names?'

'Nothing that mentions either of the boys.'

'OK. Thanks, Klara.'

'See you both when you get back.'

'Will do.'

Archer hangs up.

'So, they're all ex J's Army,' says Quinn.

'Seems that way.'

Archer looks out the window at nothing in particular and starts to turn over the events of the investigation in her head trying her best to build a fuller picture of why these men were murdered.

At the station Archer and Quinn set up an incident room with the help of the team. Klara wheels in a large television screen and attaches a spare laptop to it, ensuring it has the necessary access and credentials to all the police systems they need. Quinn pins up a map of Central London on one wall, while DC Marian Phillips tapes mugshots of the victims to the whiteboard facing the front of the room.

DCI Pierce enters the room, scans it with narrow eyes and comments, 'That was quick.'

Archer is relieved to see she has calmed down. 'Clare, I'd like you to see this.'

Archer logs into the laptop, opens YouTube in a browser and brings up the documentary on the Jesus Army. The team sit around the table as the film begins. Klara is engrossed in her iPad, digging deep for whatever she can find. Archer focuses in on Aaron Cronin and his quiet charisma and charm that captivates not only the people around him, but the camera too.

When the film has finished, Archer says, 'The common denominator between Brian Bailey and Alfie McSweeney is they were both members of the Jesus Army back in the early two thousands.'

'And guess who one of the treasurers was?' says Klara looking up from her iPad.

Archer looks across at the analyst. 'Without sounding cynical I'd say it was someone with a very nice house in Islington or a newly restored listed building in Ladywell. I'm leaning towards Islington.'

'My money's on Pollard too,' adds Quinn.

'You're both correct. Cameron Pollard was the treasurer for the Jesus Army and, after the abuse scandal, like his friend Aaron Cronin, distanced himself from the organisation and moved to live in another commune with none other than Aaron himself.'

'His friend?'

'They're old friends according to the info on this website,' replies Klara.

'What sort of website is it?'

'It's a blog set up by an ex-member of the church. It's really old; the HTML is basic and the design looks like it is from the early two thousands. It seems to predate the abuse scandal.'

'Thanks, Klara.' Archer addresses the team. 'On the subject of the abuse scandal, I think we may have a motive for the murders. Perhaps Bailey, Pollard and McSweeney were abusers and someone has returned for revenge.'

'Returned at the same time as Aaron Cronin,' says Quinn.

'Please elaborate,' says Pierce.

'He's been lying low for almost sixteen years and suddenly he appears back in the public eye with the opening of his new church at what was the Ladywell Playtower, Lewisham,' replies Archer.

'He must have a few bob to spend on that church,' says Tozer.

Klara nods. 'The Jesus Army amassed millions of pounds during their tenure. I wonder if all of it was accounted for after the church fell apart. They make their money from donations and members surrender their incomes in exchange for a more spiritual life, one closer to God, or Jesus.'

'There's always a price to pay with that fella,' mutters Quinn.

'Is Cronin a suspect?' asks Pierce.

'He's certainly a person of interest.'

'Have you spoken to him yet?' adds Pierce.

'We met, briefly.' Archer looks at Quinn. 'We need a return visit.'

Quinn nods a confirmation.

Archer addresses the team. 'Let's gather whatever we can on McSweeney, Pollard, Bailey and Cronin. Toze and Marian, could you check out the CCTV leading up to McSweeney's and Pollard's deaths? Trace their steps and see if they spoke to anyone.'

'Yes, ma'am,' they say in unison.

'Klara, could you print the photos, text and whatever else is on the blog website? Drop me the link to it on text. I might be able to use it when we meet with Cronin.'

'Sure thing.'

Archer turns to Pierce. 'Ma'am, any news on staffing?'

'That was a conversation. He generously said he will look into it, but I don't see a problem. That said, he didn't take the news of the new murders as calmly as I did . . .'

Archer bites her tongue.

' . . . In fact, he lost his temper, which is very unlike him. A little unprofessional, if you ask me. Anyway, he's keeping a close eye on the investigation, so we need to move faster.'

'We're doing everything we can, ma'am,' replies Archer. 'And I'll work over the weekend.'

'I think that would be best.'

Archer turns to the team. 'OK, everyone. Any questions?'

There are none.

'OK. Good luck and keep in touch.'

34

I T'S CLOSE TO SIX WHEN Archer and Quinn arrive at the Blood of the Lamb Church. Beyond the tall iron gate, the shadows of the gothic tower tremble under the red-and-orange glow of the stained-glass windows. Archer can't help but feel a sense of fire and brimstone burning behind those walls.

'At least someone's home,' says Quinn.

Archer hears voices singing. 'Can you hear that?'

Quinn listens with his ear at the gate as if that would somehow make it clearer. 'Something about blood and Jesus and a cross is what I hear.'

Archer glances up at the top of the gate, which is almost seven foot high. 'There's no intercom, they have no phones, allegedly, and there's no one to let us in. We have one option.'

'Climb the gate?'

'We'll say it was open when we arrived.'

'I like your thinking.'

Archer hauls herself up the iron bars, inserting her foot on the crucifix and pulling herself to the top of the gate. Gripping tightly, she lowers herself down the other side, dropping midway down onto the path.

'Nice work,' says Quinn who leaps onto the gate and is surprisingly nimble for his stocky build.

'Very graceful,' comments Archer.

Using his hands, Quinn lightly brushes dust from his jacket. 'I have my moments.'

Archer knocks hard on the front door and after several attempts with no answer they make the decision to look for another way in. At the right side of the main house there is a broad steel black door.

'This must be the old entrance to the swimming pool,' says Archer, pulling on the handle. The door is locked. Quinn bangs it three times with his fist and places his ear to the steel, listening for someone approaching. 'They're still singing, somewhere inside.'

'Let's try the rear,' says Archer.

They turn a corner where there is a light spilling from what looks like a kitchen. Inside are three women in dowdy dresses and baggy jumpers, washing and drying pots and pans. 'Looks like Aaron Cronin has embraced the twenty-first century and made all women equal in the kitchen,' says Quinn, dryly.

'Can I help you?' comes a voice.

Archer turns to see Aaron Cronin emerge from the trees, wearing scuffed, soiled gardening gloves. Behind him is Ethan White, carrying a large spade over his shoulder.

'Hello, Mr Cronin. Ethan,' says Archer.

Ethan looks at them with hooded eyes and does not return the greeting.

'Bit late for gardening,' says Quinn.

Aaron tears off his gloves. 'Needs must.'

'That's a big old spade, Ethan,' adds Quinn. 'You guys must have *a big old* garden back there.'

Aaron places the gloves on the kitchen windowsill. 'How did you get in here?'

'Quite easily, as it happens,' says Quinn.

'Can we talk, Mr Cronin – privately?' Archer asks.

'It's not a good time.'

'You have two choices,' says Archer, who is not in the mood for his games. 'Here, in the comfort of your church, or down at the station. The choice is yours.'

Aaron regards her for a moment. 'Very well. We'll go into my office.' He turns to Ethan. 'Drop the spade in the toolshed, Ethan, and tidy up. We can catch up later.'

'Yes, Father.'

Aaron leads them into the kitchen, a dated functional space with stainless-steel worktops, a decrepit old range cooker and a weather-stained butcher's block, currently being scrubbed by one of the women. The women glance their way, but no greetings are exchanged.

'You and Ethan White have become close,' says Archer.

'He is one of us now.'

'Nice to see you filling that father role,' says Quinn. 'You know his real father met a nasty end? By the way, have you met Ethan's birth family? They're delightful. You guys are gonna to get on like a house on fire.'

Aaron says nothing and takes them through to the main hallway, which is sparsely decorated and, like the kitchen, is also dated with little character or charm. They follow him up the stairwell and across the landing to an old oak door which leads to his office. The space is circular in shape, with tall, stained-glass windows depicting unsettling stages of the crucifixion dominating the room. Bookshelves line the walls and a large antique mahogany leather-topped desk occupies the space below the tall, arched north-facing window. Archer notices a silver MacBook Pro and a Samsung phone resting on top of the desk.

'I love what you've done with the place!' says Quinn.

Aaron sits at his desk and pays no heed to Quinn's goading. He looks at Archer. 'Shall we begin?'

'We're still trying to figure out why a call was made to your landline from Ethan White's phone at the same time and location that Brian Bailey was murdered,' says Archer.

Aaron shrugs. 'I already told you: Ethan's phone was stolen.'

'Don't you think it strange that the thief who stole Ethan's phone should call you at the same time that Brian Bailey was murdered?'

'A misdialled number, perhaps?'

'When we last met you mentioned you didn't know Brian Bailey. Yet we have proof that you worked together in Northampton with the Jesus Army in 2001.'

Aaron steeples his fingers together. 'That's correct. He worked with us for a short period, helping out as a volunteer.'

'Why did you not mention this at the time?' asks Archer.

'His name had slipped my mind. I barely knew him. It was only when I saw the news reports that I remembered.'

Archer gestures at the laptop and phone. 'Is that where you get your news?'

'Sometimes.'

'You said no technology was allowed in the church.'

'Members surrender their devices when they come to live here.'

'But different rules apply to you?' Quinn says.

'Yes, we lead a basic life, yet we still need access to the internet. Someone might need a doctor's appointment, or need to complete a government form, or use social media to spread the word of our church. Such is the world we live in today.'

'What's your phone number, Aaron?' asks Quinn as he takes out his own phone. Cronin gives him his number and Quinn enters it into his phone.

'How well did you know Cameron Pollard and Alfie McSweeney?' asks Archer.

Aaron smiles. 'Cameron is an old friend. Alfie, I recall, was another volunteer. We had little to do with each other.'

'They're both dead. Disfigured and murdered in the same way as Brian Bailey.'

'I'm sorry to hear that,' he responds, dispassionately.

'If you don't mind me saying, you don't sound too sorry,' says Quinn.

'They're in the hands of their maker, now.'

'Aaron, three men linked to you, either directly or indirectly, have been murdered. Do you see why we might be pressing for more cooperation?' asks Archer.

'You have my full cooperation, DI Archer.'

Archer hears Quinn sigh heavily.

'When was the last time you spoke to Cameron Pollard?' asks Archer.

'It was last week, sometime.'

'Can you give me a precise date?'

'I couldn't say,' he replies coolly. 'I'll look into it and let you know.'

'Was it last Friday?'

Aaron considers this and replies, 'Yes, I believe it might have been.'

'Was it a face-to-face meeting or on the phone?' asks Quinn.

'Phone.'

'Did you call Mr Pollard or did he call you?'

'He called me.'

'What did you talk about?'

'We exchanged the usual pleasantries, caught up and said goodbye.'

'That's a lot of small talk for someone who doesn't really do small talk.'

Aaron remains silent.

'It's odd,' says Archer, 'that Mr Pollard should phone you on the same day he was murdered, like Brian Bailey.'

'A coincidence.'

'Has Alfie McSweeney been in contact with you?'

'No.'

'Who's killing these men, Aaron?'

Aaron shrugs. 'I wish I knew. We will pray for their souls, DI Archer.'

Archer hears voices shouting followed by a scream from beyond the office. Aaron bolts from behind his desk, but Archer and Quinn are ahead of him and already outside on the landing. Looking down Archer sees a crowd of people surrounding Ethan White who is on his knees, sobbing. She is surprised to see Janine White. She crouches down beside her son and Archer's heart sinks. Standing over them, flanked by two bull-necked skinhead bodyguards, is Frankie White. He looks up slowly, his gaze meeting hers, his thin lips curling in distaste.

'*Get out of here!*' shrieks Ethan, his face purple with rage, his eyes red with tears. 'I don't want you here! I'm not yours. I live here now. *Go away and leave me alone!*'

Archer hurries down the stairs but is swiftly overtaken by Aaron.

'What's the meaning of this?' he bellows.

Ethan breaks away from his mother's grasp. 'Ethan, wait!' Janine calls, but he runs to Aaron and wraps his arms around him.

Frankie White frowns at his grandson, his eyes darting between him and Aaron. 'What the fuck is going on here?'

'Take me away from them, Father, please!' begs Ethan.

Frankie White cocks his head, his eyes wide, his lips parted as if he is about to laugh. 'Father? You have got to be kidding me.'

'It's some sort of church, Dad,' says Janine. 'They've brainwashed him.'

White regards his grandson and then his eyes slide to Archer's. 'Been a few years since our paths crossed, girl. You was only little,' he says in a tone as if they were old friends.

'What are you doing here?' she asks, through gritted teeth.

Archer senses Quinn stand beside her.

'Backup is on the way, ma'am,' Quinn tells her.

'Ma'am?' says White. 'You've come a long way. Your old man would be proud.'

Archer feels her muscles tighten like a fist. 'You should leave,' she says.

'Is that what I should do? Right, tell me, *ma'am* . . .' White glances at his grandson. 'Are you responsible for this shitshow?'

'You're not welcome here,' says Aaron, asserting his authority.

'Just who the fuck are you, exactly?'

'This church is my private property. You are not welcome here.'

White rolls his eyes as if this is just an irksome inconvenience. 'Ethan,' says White. 'Your mother wants you home. Pick yourself up and let's go.'

Ethan shakes his head.

'This place is not good for you. You should be home with your family,' says Janine.

'These people are my family now.'

'Don't be stupid, son,' says White. 'We're your family; your proper family. Let's go.'

Ethan turns on his grandad. 'It's because of you and because of her and all the rest of you I'm here! You're all fucked up, every last one of you.'

'Bit harsh,' replies White.

'I've found somewhere that I belong, somewhere that accepts me for who I am.'

'*We* accept you,' says Janine.

'You *control* me. But not anymore.'

'Baby . . .'

'Just go, Mum. Just leave.'

Janine's face scrunches and she looks away as tears fill her eyes. Despite who she is, Archer can't help but feel sorry for her.

'Let's go, Dad,' says Janine, turning to leave.

Frankie White's jaw clenches and his gaze flits between Archer and Aaron. 'We ain't done yet.'

35

ARCHER IS SUBDUED ON THE drive back to Charing Cross. Although she'd remained calm during her encounter with Frankie White, her muscles feel coiled and stiff.

'That can't have been easy,' says Quinn, breaking the silence.

'No,' she replies, rubbing her neck.

'If you don't mind me saying, you came across as a badass DI who takes no shit from no one.'

Archer smiles, welcoming Quinn's humour and allowing it to ease her tension.

'It didn't feel that way. My heart was racing and I thought I was going to puke.'

'Like I said. It couldn't have been easy.'

'Do you fancy a beer?' asks Archer.

Quinn snorts. 'Always!'

'Let's drop the car off and head to the Salisbury.'

'Sounds good to me.'

They get to the Salisbury just before eight. Situated on the corner of St Martin's Lane and St Martin's Court, the Salisbury is an opulent late-Victorian pub with shimmering etched glass, a carved mahogany bar and ornamental art nouveau fittings throughout the interior. The crowd has thinned having drunk the dregs of their poison before pegging it last-minute to the theatres for the 7.30 start of whatever West End show awaits them.

Archer orders two pints of Stella, and joins Quinn in a quiet nook, a two-seater leather booth facing out to the bar.

'Cheers,' says Quinn, holding up his stemmed Stella pint glass.

'Cheers.' Archer clinks her glass against his and takes a mouthful of the cold amber liquid. It tastes good and she downs a second mouthful.

'So, thoughts on the crazy cult leader and his response to our questions?' asks Quinn.

'He's lying and hiding something, obviously. Three men he has a history with have been disfigured and murdered so Cronin is willingly – or unwillingly – at the centre of this, and he's brought Ethan White along for the ride.'

'Why Ethan White?'

'Don't know the answer to that yet. He's clearly fragile, maybe even broken, ripe for—'

'Being initiated into his crazy-bollocks Jesus cult?'

'It would seem so. Ethan could be useful to him. He was born into criminality. It's what he grew up with, pretty much all he knows.'

'Do you think Ethan turning his back on his family is a front?'

'I don't think he's that good an actor.'

'Do you think Ethan is the killer?'

'It's possible.'

'We need to get him in again at the station. We need to understand more about why he's involved with Aaron Cronin.'

'We should talk to his friends, his neighbours, his family . . . Actually, we'll skip the Whites for now.'

'At Frankie's homecoming party, Ethan was with a young woman. Could be his girlfriend.'

'I'll find out who she is.'

They drink up their pints and make their way outside.

'Thanks for the beer.'

'You're welcome.'

'Goodnight, Grace.'

'Goodnight, Harry.'

Archer unlocks the door to Grandad's house and is hit by a bitter haze of smoke from a small fire on the hall rug. She gasps and feels her heart pounding. 'Grandad!' she calls. 'Grandad!'

With relief she hears his voice. 'Grace?' He emerges from the living room with a sleepy expression. 'What's happened?' He waves the lingering smoke away from his face.

'Thank God, you're OK,' says Archer.

Shards of glass and melted wax lie on the floor, the remains of the candle Grandad kept beneath the photo of her dad. It has obviously overheated, cracked and fallen from the shelf. Archer picks up the welcome mat and beats down the flames until they are no more.

'Oh my,' says Grandad as he crouches down and reaches for the broken glass.

'Wait, Grandad. They might be hot. I'll get a dustpan and brush.'

From the kitchen, Archer grabs the plastic dustpan and brush from under the sink and begins sweeping up the mess.

'That's so strange,' says Grandad.

'I think it just overheated and exploded.'

He shakes his head. 'It's more than that, Grace.'

'What do you mean?'

269

Grandad is staring, his eyes wide, at the picture of her father on the shelf. 'Your dad did this. He's not happy. He's sent us a sign about that monster who's been freed. That murderer! We have to do something, Grace. We must.'

Archer feels a deep ache in her heart and wishes she could ease the pain he has never let go of.

'Oh, Grandad. I don't think he would want to burn us out of our home.'

Grandad smiles at her. 'He knew you wouldn't let that happen, Grace.'

Archer sighs. 'If it was Dad, then we can't give him the opportunity to cause any more fires. This carpet is toast.'

'I'll get a new one.'

'Promise me you'll not buy any more of those cheap candles? I'll buy you some battery ones tomorrow.'

'I promise,' he says with feeling.

With the mess cleaned and the smell dissipated, Grandad heads to bed and Archer sends a text to Klara.

Sorry to text you late on a Friday. Anything more from the blog site?

Hey Grace. No worries. I'm working at home with Bowie playing in the background, one hand on the keyboard and another swirling a cold glass of French Chardonnay.

LOL. Lucky you . . .

I've tried to make the photos clearer using Photoshop so that I can run them through the facial recognition software, but the results are not great because the pics are low res scans from fifteen years back. I'll keep working on them and let you know. Also, I cross-checked the names and numbers on Brian Bailey's phone records again and found nothing unusual. No contact with the church or any of the other victims.

OK. Thanks for doing that.

Are you working tomorrow?

Yeah. Much to catch up on.

OK, good. I'll join you. I had no plans anyway.

Only if you're sure.

I'm sure. :-) Oh, by the way. I saw a message come through from Tozer about a witness sighting of Rose Grant in Lewisham. High Street. He said she was seen running from rear of the Church of St Mary the Virgin. Unusual to run from a church on drugs, especially from one whose grounds back onto another 'church'.

Then Rose must have come from the Blood of the Lamb Church. Send me the witness details, Klara. I'll go see him tomorrow.

Sending them now.

Thanks X

Night x

Night x

36

OVER THE YEARS ARCHER HAS become accustomed to not sleeping all the way through the night, yet always, when her focus is on a case, her night terrors dissipate. The irony of how it takes the hunt for a brutal killer to get a good night's sleep is not lost on her. She considers what type of person that makes her and if overcoming her near-death experiences has somehow transformed her into a hunter. A question for Dr Hutchison, perhaps.

Exercise has always helped so most days she tries to run first thing in the morning before work, even in the dark, waking hours of a Saturday morning.

Running alongside the shimmering black waters of the Thames, Archer picks up her pace and pelts towards the looming giant Ferris wheel of the London Eye. She shoots past another jogger, a man who instantly increases his own pace and tries to catch up with her. Archer can hear him gaining ground and steadies her breathing. She bolts through the London Eye entrance, eyes on the path ahead, but her gaze is caught by a familiar profile sitting at a bench overlooking the Thames. He looks across at her and smiles.

'Hello, Grace,' says Charlie Bates.

Archer slows her pace, stops at the bench and catches her breath as the other jogger catches up and speeds past.

'What are you doing here?' asks Archer.

'Waiting on you.'

'How'd you know I'd be here?'

'You're a creature of habit, Grace. You always have been.'

'Nice to see you, Charlie, but you could have just dropped by the house, or called. This is a little clandestine, even for you.'

Charlie turns to look at the waters and seems deep in thought. 'I hear you had a run-in with Snow.'

Charlie always refers to Frankie White as Snow, a moniker White happily embraced to symbolise the millions he has made importing and selling cocaine, or at least that's his story. Charlie always refutes that tale. The truth is the name originates from the days of the White gang, made up of eight brothers and cousins, most of who are now either dead or in prison. Frankie was the tallest of the gang, at five foot eleven; the others barely reached five foot five. Frankie 'Snow' White and the seven dwarves, is what they were commonly known as. A true story, apparently.

'Good news gets around quick,' says Archer. 'We met yesterday under difficult circumstances for White whose grandson has joined a cult connected to the murders we're investigating.'

'I'd heard.'

Archer looks at her old boss. 'You're remarkably up to date for a man retired from the force.'

'I have my grapevine – and if it involves the Whites, then I want to know.' Charlie turns to look at her and snorts a laugh. 'I bet Snow took that well.'

Archer almost manages a smile herself but stops. 'I just hope he doesn't get in the way of the investigation.'

'How's it going?' Charlie asks.

'Four murders and little evidence of who is responsible, but I have my suspicions.'

'That's what I want to talk to you about. That, and something else.'

'The second "that" sounds ominous.'

Charlie shifts sideways on the bench to face Archer. 'Brian Bailey was an ex-copper, a DC, in Northampton at the same time this Aaron Cronin fella was being questioned about a missing boy.'

'A missing boy? How do you know this?'

'When I saw him on the news, I recognised his name and did some asking around. Bailey was as bent as a two-bob bit. He was also a nonce.'

'Do you have proof?'

'No. The nonce part is all hearsay, but here's the thing. The nick he worked in was in a small backwater town. They had one computer for word processing and all police reports were written on pen and paper. The kid was never found and the files on Cronin magically disappeared. By the time this was discovered, Bailey had left the police to go live in Cronin's commune. Anyway, an old DCI mate of mine, Leo Randle, was leading the investigation into the Apostle murders. Operation Deliverance, he called it.'

Deliverance.

'Leo was a troubled soul with alleged drug and alcohol problems.'

'Was?'

'That's the question we'd all like answered. Leo's been missing for over seventeen years now, presumed dead. He was obsessed with this case. It became like one of his addictions. He lived and breathed it. The last I'd heard he had a strong lead and was pursing it.'

'What was the lead?'

Charlie takes out a sealed brown envelope and hands it across. 'I was able to pull this together. It's some of the files that he kept on the investigation. There's also a photo of Aaron Cronin I found at Leo's house after he went missing. It'll give you something to think about. More children went missing, Grace. Find out what happened to those kids and it's likely you'll find out who Aaron Cronin really is.'

Archer takes the envelope.

'That's not all. Ethan White is still receiving his prescription from Adrian Boyne, who has it delivered to the Church. There is another connection to crack – Snow's drugs going into that church. In the envelope you'll also find some recent photos of Boyne and Ethan meeting in Ladywell to do a very indiscreet handover of a package.'

'Thank you, Charlie. I'm really grateful.'

'You're welcome. There's another reason I wanted to talk to you. Consider it a warning to watch your back.'

Archer raises her eyebrows. 'Why?'

'Snow is free, Grace. He's re-establishing his London empire, which has taken a beating from the Russians and Albanians during his incarceration. He wants his turf back and will do whatever it takes.'

'White going to war against the Russians and Albanians? Christ! That's all we need.'

'Precisely. He's managed to buy new relationships with some powerful people and some have literally opened doors for him. Prison doors, for a start. He's also recruiting, and he doesn't just recruit any old thug from the street. He likes them filthy, with raw turpitude sewn into the fabric of their being. They are crawling out of the sewers to work for him. Degenerates, psychopaths, killers. He collects them, always has done, and plays them like grubby chess pieces. He pays them well, gives them what they want: drugs, women, men, boys, girls, whatever it is, he'll supply it.'

Archer does not want to think about what lies ahead once White is seriously back in the game.

Charlie turns his gaze back to the water. 'He's also out to settle old scores.'

'What scores?'

Charlie shrugs. 'Where to begin? Well, for starters, I nailed him and he went down for fifteen years. He'll want payback.'

Archer regards her old boss. He had been a great copper in his day and in the latter part of his career, a solid, outspoken governor who got the kind of results his contemporaries envied. She realises now that after his retirement he seems a different person. He no longer has the safety net of the force and seems almost cast adrift.

'Can you go into a safe house for a time?'

'I could, but I won't. Besides, it not me I'm worried about.'

'What do you mean?'

'The drug sting operation last year resulting in, among others, DI Rees's arrest. That cost Snow a lot of money.'

'But they weren't Snow's drugs. They belonged to the Russians.'

'Snow had an arrangement with them.'

A cold river breeze whorls around Archer and she shivers.

'Snow is not the forgiving type, Grace. You know that as well as I do.'

Archer folds her arms, hugging herself to stay warm. 'I'm not afraid of him.'

'He has someone working for him in the Met. Someone tasked with keeping an eye on you.'

'Who?'

'I don't know, but I'm working on it.'

Archer thinks about who it could be. Hicks would be the obvious candidate.

'How well do you know your DS?' asks Charlie.

She feels her stomach clench. 'Why do you ask?'

'Do you trust him?'

Archer frowns. 'Yes, I do, but why ask about him and not anyone else?'

'He's just the closest person to you. I thought . . .'

'I trust him, Charlie.'

Charlie nods. 'I wasn't implying . . . sorry, Grace, you were always a good judge of character.'

They sit in silence for a moment. Archer feels her mood darkening even more. Charlie has planted a seed she could do without right now.

'Snow's time is coming, Grace, and he'll have his revenge. He always does. We need to be prepared.'

'How do you know all this, Charlie?'

'You don't get to be in my position by just rubbing shoulders with coppers. I have friends on the other side of the fence too.'

'I'm worried about you, Charlie.'

'Don't be. I'll be fine.' Charlie smiles. 'Like I said, I have "friends".' He shifts forward and pushes his stiff body slowly off the bench. Archer helps him up. 'Bloody hell. I'm too old to be sitting on cold benches in the middle of winter.' He smiles sadly at her. 'I wish things could have been better for you, Grace.'

Archer has no response to that. After a moment she says, 'I should go.'

'Me too. Let's keep in touch. It's important you let me know if you see anyone sniffing around.'

Archer nods. 'I will.'

'Take care of yourself, Grace.'

'You too, Charlie.'

Archer turns and begins a slow jog back to Roupell Street. Her jaw tightens as she thinks of Charlie's news about Frankie White's return and his potential vendetta against her. *The fucking nerve of that low life.* Archer quickens her pace into a sprint and bolts up the Embankment. She thinks about Grandad, the pain he carries and the secret he still hides. She thinks about his desperation to get an illegal firearm to kill Snow; the pistol easily bought from the Whitehouse family. In her darkest fantasy she imagines holding the gun to Snow's head and pulling the trigger. She has killed before and made the world a safer place. Why not do it again?

37

CHARLIE'S NEWS ABOUT SNOW TURNS over in Archer's head as the hot rain of the shower pummels the tight muscles under her smooth skin. Before starting with the Met, she had worked with Charlie at the National Crime Agency and played a pivotal role in bringing down a drug-trafficking operation of two tonnes of cocaine valued at £180 million. The sting had led to the arrests of Russian gang bosses, traffickers, dealers and members of the police force who had turned a blind eye or helped facilitate the haul, unnoticed, into the London docks. DI Andy Rees, who Archer arrested, had overseen the docks operation. A knot of worry twists inside her at Charlie's revelations about Snow's crack-smuggling arrangement with the Russians. There would be repercussions and she would need to be mindful and watch her back. For now, her thoughts turn to the investigation and she pushes Snow from her head, washing him away with soap and water.

She dries her hair, dresses and in the street below her bedroom window, sees Cosmo cross and knock on their door. He and Grandad intend taking a trip to Chinatown to see the lanterns that have been put up for the Chinese New Year.

Archer is grateful Cosmo is continuing to keep Grandad occupied, especially considering the hard time she had given him after the firearm incident. She hears them in the hallway downstairs, talking over each other without realising it. She smiles and wonders if Cosmo's memory is as bad as Grandad's. She listens in amusement as the two of them gabble away at each other on a range of topics, every single one forgotten when they stop for breath.

Archer opens the deceased DCI Randle's Operation Deliverance file. She feels her pulse quicken at the photo of Aaron. It's a black-and-white portrait shot that has been defaced with a red biro. Aaron's eyes have been scratched over in red ink and an inverted cross scribbled across his face. *Did Leo Randle do this?*

She pages through the remainder of the file, takes several shots of the contents, including names and locations, and sends them in a group text message to Klara and Quinn.

Morning both, I'm heading to Lewisham to interview a witness and will be with you around lunchtime. Here is some intel on the murders of four boys dating back to the late nineties. Strong links to Bailey and Cronin. See you both later. Grace.

Archer is on the overground to Ladywell, on the way to talk with the witness, a young American called Jackson Price who lives on Lewisham High Street. Ironically, the quickest route from the station to Jackson's flat is on foot past the Blood of the Lamb Church.

Archer approaches the tall iron gate and slows her pace. Sitting on a stone bench outside the main house is the boy called Kain.

Dressed in a thick grey tweed blazer, a blue buttoned-up shirt, with his hair neatly combed on top, shaved close at the sides and back, he could be from another time. In one hand he holds a carving knife, which he uses to sharpen the end of a stick. Archer wonders what he plans to do with that stick when he is done. She stops and watches him for a moment and wonders who he is and how he ended up here. With the instincts of a guard dog, his eyes look across and meet Archer's gaze. He has a cunning intelligence to him that she finds unsettling. He gets up from the bench and walks towards the gate, pocketing his knife.

'Hello, Kain,' says Archer.

'You can't come in,' he states.

'I'm just passing by.'

Kain slips the stick through the gate, gripping it like a spear with both hands, then presses his face against the bars. 'Where you going?'

'To meet someone.'

'Who?'

'No one you know.'

'I know a lot of people.'

'I'm sure you do.'

They stand in silence for a moment before Archer asks, 'How did you come to be here, living at this place?'

Kain frowns. 'It's my home.'

'Do your parents live here?'

'It's my home,' he repeats.

Archer knows she'll get nowhere and glances at his stick. 'Are you going hunting?'

He cocks his head, revealing the fist-sized burn on the side of his neck. 'Might do.'

'How did you get that scar?'

Kain does not reply.

'Did Aaron do that to you?'

Kain's one good eye flashes and he stiffens. 'You better move on, missy.'

Although there is something deeply troubling about Kain, Archer finds it hard not to crack a smile at being called 'missy' by this teenage throwback from the early part of the last century.

'Thank you, Kain. I think I'll do just that.'

Archer leaves him and makes her way down Ladywell Road. She hears the gate creak open behind her and looks back to see Kain's head peering out, watching her.

It takes five minutes for Archer to arrive at Lewisham High Street and Jackson Price's home, a flat above a newsagent in a shabby two-up-two-down building some locals embracing a new gentrified Lewisham might consider *undesirable*. Diagonally across the road is the Church of St Mary the Virgin. Jackson's flat is a perfect viewing spot.

The entrance is a heavy steel green door at the side of the building. She pushes it, but it doesn't budge. She knocks it hard three times, waits but no one answers. After a moment she hears footsteps descending and someone singing out loud.

The door opens and a tall young black man with large silver headphones covering his ears appears. He seems startled when he sees Archer but nevertheless smiles politely. 'All right. Can I help you?'

'Hi. Do you live here?'

'I'm afraid so,' he says, shrugging.

'That bad is it?'

'I'm sharing a tiny flat with someone I barely know. But needs must. Living here is a temporary arrangement, thank God.'

'Sounds grim.'

'At the very least it's handy to get to and from work.'

'Where do you work?'

'In the theatre, darling,' he replies, affecting a hammy response.

'You're an actor?'

'For my sins.'

'Would I have seen you in anything?'

'I'm in *Aladdin*, at the Prince Edward in Old Compton Street.'

'That's very cool.'

'Have you seen it?'

'I'm afraid not.'

He laughs heartily. 'Oh well. You should come along. It's a fun show.'

'I'd like that. Listen, I was wondering if you could help me.' Archer presents her ID. 'My name is Detective Inspector Grace Archer.'

'You're here for Jackson. He's my flatmate. He mentioned you were coming.'

'Is he home?'

'Yeah. He's grilling a tuna and cheese sandwich, which is why I'm leaving. Two foods that should never be eaten together.' Lewis steps outside and holds open the door. 'Flat 1, on the left.'

'Thanks,' says Archer. 'and good luck with *Aladdin*.'

'Cheers, oh and when you speak to Jack, could you tell him I said to make sure he leaves the window open so that the flat doesn't stink of cheesy fish.' He smiles widely and warmly.

'I'll make sure to do that.'

'Thanks!'

As she starts to climb the narrow dark stairs, she hesitates. Her throat dries and she feels dizzy. On the wall behind her is a timer light switch. She presses it. The stairwell brightens. Archer ignores the walls on either side that seem to close in on her and hurries upstairs, following the smell of warm tuna and melted cheese that fills the space.

She takes a calming breath and knocks twice on the flat door numbered 1.

The door opens and a tanned, blond-haired man in his mid-twenties appears, chewing part of a greasy-looking toasted tuna melt sandwich that he holds in one hand.

Archer presents her ID and introduces herself. 'Hello, Mr Price. I'm DI Archer.'

He swallows quickly, wipes his mouth with the back of his hand and says, 'Hi. Yes. I've been expecting you. Please come in,' he adds with a soft North American accent. 'And please, call me Jackson.'

He takes her through to a living-room-cum-bedroom with two old-fashioned lead windows overlooking Lewisham High Street. On the other side of the road is St Mary's.

'According to my colleague, you saw Rose Grant emerge from St Mary's?'

'Yeah, I was walking home and saw her. It was weird, like she was off her face on drugs or something.'

'What do you think she was doing at the church?'

'I have no clue. The church itself would have been closed and she was running from behind it.'

'Was she alone?'

'Yeah. It was just her. I thought nothing of it at the time. You see a lot of people drunk and off their heads around here, but I did wonder later if she was running from someone.'

'Why did you think that?'

'She kept looking behind her.'

'And you definitely saw no one?'

He pauses to consider this question. 'No, definitely not. It was only after I saw her face on the news that I called you guys.'

'Is there anything else you can think of that could help us?'

'Nothing that hasn't been reported already.'

'Thank you, Jackson. I appreciate you letting us know. I'll let you get back to your sandwich. By the way, your flatmate said not to forget to leave a window open to let out the smell of tuna and cheese.'

He laughs. 'Sure thing. He hates the smell, but I love it. Thanks for the reminder.'

Archer crosses Lewisham High Street at the lights and walks up the small drive to the wide porticoed entrance of the Church of St Mary the Virgin. She circles around the building to the grassy grounds at the rear, sheltered with trees, ferns, old tombs and monuments. Cutting through the grounds, she tries to imagine Rose Grant running through them. *Why were you running? What frightened you?* She scans the ground all around for any possible clue but sees nothing. Walking through the trees, she eventually comes to a shoulder-height fence made from iron railings. On the other side are the grounds of Aaron's church, which are thick with trees, but with just enough light to make out other grave-like monuments: stone angels with swords, weeping angels and crucified Christs. She wonders if the land could have been sold up and divided by the fence but thinks that unlikely. There is something about the other side of the fence that makes Archer think it more of an expensive garden collection of gothic graveyard memorabilia ravaged and stolen from an actual graveyard.

Something shimmers on the ground through the railings. Archer's eyes focus on it and through the green blades she sees the glitter of gold. Crouching down she sees a gold looped earring. Her heart skips and she takes out her phone and snaps photographs at different angles. Removing a pair of rubber gloves from her backpack, she pulls them on and, using a pen, reaches through the railings and lifts out the earring. She looks at it with a sense of hope and wonders if maybe, just maybe, it belonged to Rose.

38

I N THE INCIDENT ROOM LATER that day, after updating
the team on finding the earring in the grounds of the
church, Archer, Quinn and Klara re-examine the information contained within Charlie's envelope.

'That defaced photo of Cronin is quite telling,' says Klara.

'Does him justice,' adds Quinn.

'DCI Randle had his demons,' Archer tells them. 'Charlie
found the picture at Randle's home after he went missing. No
points for guessing who his number one suspect was.'

'What happened to Randle?' asks Quinn.

'No one knows.'

Together they review the contents of Charlie's file. There's
not enough yet to join the dots, but there is enough to spark
a discussion and build a file of data from police records and
old news reports. The envelope had also contained family photos
of the boys taken from a newspaper article written in 2001.'

'Jesus! Grim reading,' says Quinn, quietly, his face turned
in a frown.

Archer and Klara exchange a look.

'Are you OK to carry on, Harry?' asks Archer, conscious that
the murders of these four boys may have resurrected feelings
about his own son's death.

Quinn rubs his neck. 'I'm fine. Let's crack on.'

Archer takes the photos of the boys, tapes them to the white-board and writes their names next to them. 'Jesus had twelve disciples, his apostles. These are the victims of what the press called the Apostle Killer. They share the first names of six of the Apostles.'

Luke Jones

Matthew Hart

John Harris

Mark Smith

James Ryan

Simon Brent

'Anything stick out?' she asks.

'All of the boys were good-looking kids. Angelic, you might say,' says Klara.

'Yes, and each boy had the same disfigurements,' says Archer. 'Severe burns to their bodies as if they had been tortured with a hot poker. The scars are in the same areas of the body: the chest, back, buttocks, genitals, mouth and eyes.'

They sit in silence for a moment deep in their thoughts.

Quinn breaks the quiet. 'I remember reading about these killings back then. They freaked me out. They happened over a period of five years with a year apart, in different parts of the country.'

'The first boy reported missing was Luke Jones from Devon, in December, 1996,' says Archer. 'He'd been missing for a week and his body was found hidden under bushes in remote woods by police dogs. Just over one year later, Matthew Hart in Sussex didn't return home from school. He suffered similar injuries and died under the same circumstances. One year after that, John Harris in the New Forest and one year after him, Mark Smith in Aberdeen, followed by James Ryan in Blackpool; the last reported murder was Simon Brent in Doncaster in 2001.'

'Someone was travelling across the country,' notes Quinn. 'Someone possibly spreading the word of God?'

'My thoughts exactly,' replies Archer. 'We need to know where Cronin was during those years. Specifically, was he at or near the locations of the murders?'

'I'll get on to that today and work on it over the weekend.'

'Thanks, Klara,' says Archer. 'Two thousand and one was the year Simon Brent was killed as the last known victim of the Apostle Killer. It was around that time that Aaron Cronin joined the Jesus Army. The killings stopped after that, or to be more precise, no other bodies were found. It's quite possible the killings continued. Charlie mentioned another boy in Northampton that Cronin was questioned about during his tenure at the Jesus Army. Brian Bailey was a DC at the time, looking after the case. The police files conveniently went missing. Bailey later left the police force and joined Cronin at his commune.' Archer presents the photograph from the North Oak Mental Health Centre website that Klara had found. 'This photo is from the commune, taken in 2001 and shows McSweeney, Bailey, Pollard, an unknown man and woman – presumably a couple because their arms are linked and they are leaning into each other; also in the shot is Cronin and the two mystery boys. Twins, by the look of it.'

'One of them is the boy from the Jesus Army video,' says Quinn.

'Yes. What we need to know is who he is, and if he is the boy whose police file went missing. If so, is he missing and buried somewhere having suffered a similar fate to the others? Safe to assume he has the name of an Apostle.' Archer bites her lip and taps the tabletop absentmindedly. 'Klara, you mentioned Cronin's farmhouse had been bought by a local woman. What's her name?'

'She's called Esther Tilling and she runs the North Oak Mental Health Centre.'

'It might be worth talking to her.'

'Would you like me to call her?' asks Klara.

'No, I can do that. I'll talk with Northampton Police, too. Perhaps someone remembers the case.'

'I tried the facial recognition software on both boys and the mystery couple, but the photo quality is just too grainy,' says Klara. 'We may get something back from Cameron Pollard's laptop when Computer Forensics have finished with it.'

'When will that be?' asks Quinn.

'Monday, hopefully. MJ knows how important this is.'

'Perhaps you can give her a nudge later,' says Klara, with a wink.

'Got a date tonight, Harry?' smiles Archer.

'Maybe,' replies Quinn.

'How's it going?'

Quinn shrugs. 'It's OK, so far. I like her, but she's intense sometimes. Don't know why. Women are so mysterious.'

Klara laughs and Archer thinks about seeing MJ leaving Dr Hutchison's 'special cases' surgery. 'I imagine her job takes a toll.'

'I suppose it does,' replies Quinn, who seems elsewhere for a moment.

'So, coming back to our four victims,' says Archer. 'We know about the abuse claims directed at the Jesus Army. None of that is a secret. It's public knowledge. What we don't know is Aaron Cronin's involvement, or the involvement of the people in the photograph from Cronin's commune.'

'It's a safe bet they're all involved in something,' says Quinn.

'I've no doubt. All of us agree that Aaron Cronin is the number one suspect for the murder of those boys. If we're right, that makes him a serial murderer.'

'If we *are* right, then we need to find out if McSweeney, Pollard and Bailey were complicit in the murder of the Apostle boys,' says Klara.

'Absolutely, we do.'

'It seems a risk, or even fantastical, to have a troupe of killers travelling the country and killing boys without leaving a trace of evidence.'

'I agree,' says Archer. 'The murderer of the six boys clearly has a *type*. Sweet-looking boys with angelic faces, in this instance. The deaths are identical and, to me, have all the hallmarks of a serial killer and it's no coincidence that Pollard, Bailey and McSweeney were murdered in the same way, but whether it is the same killer is unlikely. Serial killers rarely stray from *type*.'

'Do we have a second serial killer then?' asks Quinn.

'I don't think our perpetrator is a serial killer.'

'What's the motive for the murders then?'

'It can only be one thing. Revenge.'

39

ARCHER, QUINN AND KLARA SPEND the remainder of Saturday trying to fit the pieces of the jigsaw together. They call it a night around eight and part company with the intention of spending Sunday working remotely from their homes and keeping in touch via a private WhatsApp group.

Archer gets nowhere with Northampton Police. They are polite enough but know nothing about any complaints made against a man they have never heard of and don't seem interested in finding out. When Archer presses them, they cite staff attrition and lack of records and say they can do no more. She also tries the North Oak Mental Health Centre, but the phone just rings out every time she calls. Her patience wears thin. When she parts with Quinn and Klara, she checks out a car from the pool, having made the decision that in the morning she will go on a long drive to search for answers. Quinn offers to come along, but she says no. His time will be better spent helping Klara.

She wakes up early on Sunday morning, feeling even more restless and eager to get going. She showers, dresses and checks the fridge to ensure Grandad has what he needs in provisions for the day ahead. She had already checked the night before, but guilt at leaving him on her day off, despite having committed to working, pushes her to check a second time. She grabs some cheese and ham from the fridge and makes him a sandwich for later. She also takes out a lasagne from the freezer and leaves it on the side to thaw. He can pop it in the microwave for his supper.

She notices his phone lying on the kitchen worktop and taps the screen to bring it out of sleep mode. As she suspects, the battery charge is low at 1 per cent. Grandad has been good at remembering to take his phone with him, but not so good at ensuring it is fully charged. Archer plugs it into the charger and writes him a note reminding him that she has gone to Northampton for the day and to call at any time if he needs to. She writes that she has left him a sandwich for lunch and a lasagne for supper. She leans the note against the kettle, grabs her coat and bag, and hurries out the door.

Outside, the morning is dark as night, the air cold and damp, marking a possible change in the recent short dry spell. Archer slips into the car, starts up the engine and fixes her mobile phone to the dashboard stand. Turning up the heat, she waits as the windows demist and thinks about Charlie's warning. *Snow's time is coming, Grace. He will have his revenge.* She feels her skin prickle. *Could Charlie be right?* Her eyes scan the street looking for something out of place, someone who should not be there. She curses Charlie for bringing this news and feels guilt at leaving Grandad to fend for himself while she is out of London. A moment of doubt makes her pause. She can't risk leaving him. She grips the steering wheel tightly and closes her eyes. Perhaps she can try emailing Esther Tilling or phoning again. No. That had already proved to be pointless. Best to go there and speak directly. She also can't bring herself to let Snow's perceived revenge, whether real or imaginary, get in the way of this investigation. Not for something that might not even happen. Besides, she thinks he has other stuff on his mind, his grandson, for starters. Archer decides she must make the trip north. As for Grandad, she'll call Cosmo later, ask him to check in on him. It's the least he can do.

Because of the early hour, the city roads are clear of traffic, although every red traffic light conspires to slow her progress. It takes almost thirty-five minutes to reach the North Circular and as she takes the slip road to the M1, Archer searches the radio stations for something to help pass the journey and stops on one playing Sam Cooke's 'A Change is Gonna Come', a favourite of her father's. Happy memories flood her crowded mind and she turns up the volume and applies a little pressure to the gas, increasing her speed as she joins the motorway and the dozens of red tail lights stretched out for miles in front of her.

One hour later, the darkness has lifted but the light is a stone grey. Archer notices her fuel is running low and swears under her breath. The general rule is that the previous users of the vehicle should top up the tank, but whoever had this car before her hasn't bothered. Just her luck. She pulls into the first services she comes to; an Esso Petrol station. Filling the tank, she notices sheets of rain approaching from the north and sighs. Driving in the rain is not her idea of a fun time. She pays for the petrol and stops for a cup of tea and hot croissant in the services café.

Opening up WhatsApp on her iPhone, she begins to type a message to Klara and Quinn.

Morning! Hope you both slept well. Just wanted to let you know I'm en route to Northampton. Stopped for a break and some petrol. Klara, I know the farmhouse is remote and suspect it may be difficult to find even with this SatNav. Are you free later to help me navigate? Harry, how was your date with MJ? :-)

Minutes pass before Klara responds.

Morning, Grace! I'm just out of the shower and getting dressed. Give me a call when you need me. I'll be ready. Never one to roll out a cliche, but I'm imagining Harry with a big smile and a post coital cigarette. LOL.

Quinn is typing.

Thank you both for your confidence. Less said about the date the better. Good to hear you're on your way. I'm heading out for a morning run to clear my head. Talk to you both laters!

Archer wonders if Quinn's date ended in a row and feels bad for him. She thinks about MJ and is not sure what to make of her. Archer has only really known her in a professional capacity and has already witnessed that she is as good at her job, if not better, than her boss, Krish. MJ seems nice enough, perhaps a little standoffish, but hasn't that accusation been levelled at

Archer many times before – and to every other strong woman succeeding in a traditionally male profession? Archer should make an effort to get to know her better. They would be working together a lot in the future so perhaps she should start building alliances and go for a drink.

Archer is on the road for over one hour with the wipers on full pelt as the rain pounds the narrow country roads. She passes through the village of Creation, which contains lines of black umbrellas, the people underneath hurrying towards an ancient church just up from the village green. She drives slowly, taking in its quiet, picturesque, old country charm, the opposite of what she is used to back in Central London. As she leaves Creation behind and enters rural Northampton-shire, she realises how right she is in thinking the SatNav would be useless. All it shows is the road ahead and acres of open land. Glancing at her phone, she notices the signal is slowly fading to zero bars.

'Fuck,' she says.

She decides her only option is to turn back and ask around the village. Perhaps someone there can give her precise directions. Archer stops at a crossroads and does a three-point turn, thankful the roads are quiet out here. As she arrives back at the village, she is relieved to see the rain easing and parks in a space near the village green. She gets out, stretches her limbs and breathes in the clean, damp air of the small town.

There is no one around and Archer has the impression everyone is at church. She walks toward it up a sharp incline and sees a man in his mid-twenties wearing a scruffy green parka approaching.

'Morning,' says Archer. 'I wonder if you can help me?'

'Morning,' says the man, smiling at her from inside his hood. He looks above her and raises his eyebrows. 'It's stopped raining,' he adds.

'Yes, it has.'

He pulls down his hood revealing an untidy mop of red hair. 'What can I do for you?'

'I'm a bit lost – or, to be more accurate, my SatNav seems to be confused.'

He chuckles. 'That can happen round here. Where are you looking to go?'

'Out of town to the North Oak Mental Health Centre. Do you know it?'

'You mean Esther's place?'

'You know Esther Tilling?'

'A little. Not much. I knew her daughter at school.'

'Then you should be able to point me in the right direction.'

'Sure I can. It's easier than you think. Just keep heading north past the church and out of the village. Go straight over the crossroads and follow the signs to the old Mackie place. Pass that on your left and keep driving until you see the North Oak sign on the right. It's easy to miss so keep your eyes open.'

'Thank you so much.'

'You're welcome.'

Archer regards him for a moment and asks, 'Were you brought up here?'

'Born and bred.'

Archer smiles and takes out her phone. 'I wonder if you can help me further?' She opens the picture of the people at Aaron's commune and uses her fingers to make it bigger. 'This photograph is from fifteen years back, taken at the farmhouse which was to become North Oak. Do you happen to recognise anyone?'

He leans in for a closer look, his eyes taking in each person. He frowns and rubs his chin. 'Hmm . . . for a moment I thought I did, but now I'm not so sure.'

'Who did you think you recognised?'

'The two boys. They seemed familiar, but I don't remember any twins here at that time. There were none at my school anyway.'

Archer pockets her phone. 'I appreciate you looking.'

'Sorry I couldn't be more helpful,' he says, pulling up his hood and glancing at the sky. 'More rain expected soon.'

Archer looks up at the clouds like bulbous battleships in the sky. 'Isn't it always?'

40

ARCHER'S TYRES CRUNCH ON THE gravel of the drive leading up to the North Oak Mental Health Centre. It's not at all what she is expecting and seems the opposite to the gleaming happy-looking repurposed farmhouse pictured on the website, which on reflection is clearly a Photoshopped version of the ominous old farmhouse before her. Archer can't put her finger on it. The house is not in any state of disrepair. In fact, it seems to have had a recent paint job, yet no matter how much work has been put into making over the building, it still somehow exudes an unnatural presence on the land.

She parks by a wind-combed tree with branches that claw away from the house. Switching off the engine, she steps out of the car and notices the curtains are drawn. She walks to the front door and raps the door knocker twice. She steps back, looks up and thinks she sees the curtains twitching.

'Hello!' she calls.

But no one answers.

She knocks louder this time and then places her ear against the rough wood of the front door.

She can hear whispering voices and then a stern older woman's voice, 'What do you want?'

'My name is Detective Inspector Grace Archer. I'm with the Met Police. Can we talk, please?'

More whispers.

The door is unlocked, opens, but remains chained. A sturdy woman in her seventies with short grey hair and a heavily lined face peers suspiciously through the crack in the door. She glances around her.

'I'm alone. I just want to ask a few questions.'

'You've no business comin' round here without phoning first.' Her voice has a croaky edge, which gives it a genderless quality.

'Actually, I did phone, but no one answered. Please. I've come a long way.'

More whispers behind the door. The woman sighs. 'All right then. But not for long. You hear?'

Archer nods respectfully.

The door closes. Archer hears the chain lock sliding across and then the door opens. Archer hesitates when she sees the woman holding a shotgun over the crook of her arm.

'Don't mind this. Can't be too careful here. We have women in trouble. Come inside then. You're lettin' all the heat out.'

Archer steps inside. The woman closes and locks the door behind her, revealing the second whisperer, a woman of a similar age. She is elegantly dressed, with a delicate face, lightly powdered. She smiles warmly and extends her hand.

'My name is Esther Tilling and this is Glynis Hughes.'

'Good to meet you, Mrs Tilling, Mrs Hughes.'

'Neither of us is married so you can drop the Mrs,' says Glynis, gruffly.

'Please accept my apologies.'

'You can just address us by our first names,' smiles Esther.

Archer nods.

'You've come all the way from London?' asks Esther.

'I have. I needed answers to questions, urgently.'

'A detective, you say?' asks Glynis, looking Archer up and down with suspicious eyes.

'That's right.'

'You don't look old enough . . .'

'Glynis!' chides Esther.

Glynis grumbles something indecipherable.

'I must admit I wasn't expecting a visit from the police today,' says Esther.

'I'm sorry. I did phone several times yesterday but there was no answer.'

'Oh, yes. The phone is in the office at the back of the house and we often don't hear it.'

'I see. I hope not to take up too much of your time.'

'Come through to the kitchen. Would you like some tea? Glynis has just made a pot.'

'Yes, please.'

Archer takes stock of the interior as she follows the two women. The hallway is dimly lit and warm with threadbare Persian-style runners on the floor and landscape paintings and faded photographs of days gone by. It has a cosy, welcoming feel to it.

'Hello,' comes a voice.

Archer looks up to see a bony woman sitting on the staircase, watching her with a curious gaze.

'Hello,' Archer replies.

'Are you the police?'

'Yes.'

'Are you here about—'

A croaky voice interrupts the exchange. 'Lizzie, let us deal with the police, thank you,' scolds Glynis. She gives Archer a wary stare. 'Come into the kitchen please, Miss Archer.'

Archer smiles at Lizzie, who stares back with an impassive expression.

Esther sits at the head of a large stripped-pine table with room enough to seat ten people. She smiles at Archer, laces her fingers together and rests them on the tabletop. The kitchen is wide and long with a bottle-green Aga. The floor is laid with worn dark-red tiles and there are dual-aspect windows looking out to views across lush green fields.

'It's not as grand as we'd like, but it's our home and home to those who need our help.'

'How long have you lived here?' asks Archer.

'Fifteen years or more. We got it at a good price because part of the property had suffered with fire damage.'

'Oh, I had no idea. What caused that?'

'Kids muckin' around,' says Glynis as she places a mug of tea and a plate of digestive biscuits on the table in front of Archer.

'Thank you.'

'What can we do for you, Detective Inspector?' asks Esther.

'I'm leading an investigation into a man called Aaron Cronin. I understand you might have had some dealings with him.'

Glynis mutters angrily under her breath. A loud silence falls over the kitchen for several moments before it's broken by Esther. 'Leave us, Glynis, please.'

Glynis frowns at Esther and hesitates. Esther gives her an encouraging nod and then Glynis sighs and leaves Archer and Esther alone.

'Sorry about that.'

'Don't be. From what I know Aaron Cronin can have that effect on some people.'

'Unfortunately, not enough people see him for the person he truly is.'

'What do you mean by that?'

Esther takes a sip of her tea. 'Tell me why you're here, and I'll tell you what I know.'

Archer explains about the murders in London.

'I saw the deaths reported on the news. A terrible business.'

'And you will know that each of those victims appears in a photo on the North Oak website.'

Esther considers this for a moment. 'I was aware, yes.'

'Did you not think to contact the police?'

'That picture was taken such a long time back ... I didn't think it important.'

'Fifteen years or more is not a long time.'

Esther knits her fingers together. 'I suppose not. But I really didn't think it important. I'm sorry.'

'Did you know any of the victims?'

She shakes her head. 'Not personally. I had known *of* them before we took over the farmhouse. But I never spoke to any of them. I only ever dealt with *him*.'

'Do you mean Aaron Cronin?'

Esther's face darkens. She nods.

'How well did you know him?'

'Well enough.'

'What do you mean by that?'

'I've lived in this area all my life, Detective Inspector. I grew up in Creation, left for university and returned many years later to teach at the local grammar school here. Aaron Cronin was one of my pupils. He was a shrewd boy, clever, studious, but always seemed to be without humour or empathy. He was neither popular nor unpopular. He had one of those Marmite personalities, you know? You either liked him or you didn't. When I first met him he seemed to be one of those boys who was a loner, someone a bit different. I was smart enough to not judge a book by its cover . . .' Esther looks away and seems lost in her thoughts for a moment. 'Never judge a book by its cover, but . . . such lame wisdom.' She turns to meet Archer's gaze and shrugs. 'He was developing a reputation.'

'What sort of reputation?'

'I never saw any evidence of this, but apparently he would bring dead animals to school; rabbits, mice, birds, the like.'

'Was this ever documented anywhere? By the school, or the police?'

'Teenage boys were always up to no good and that's what we put it down to. I did speak to him about it once and he told me the animals were already dead.'

'Did you believe him?'

'No. Some, like Glynis, said it was on account of his blood-line and being brought up in this place. Are you superstitious, Detective Inspector?'

'No.'

'I never thought I was but living in remote places like this can change your mind. When I was a child, this place had a bad history. Some of it's true. But a lot is myths and gossip, exaggerated over the years. Funny how these stories become legend and people believe in them.'

'So what happened here?'

'The farmhouse dates back to the 1830s and belonged to Jerah Cronin. He lived here with his wife, Nessa, his son, Thaddeus, and daughter, Lowena. He was a butcher. A very good one, by all accounts. It was a passion for him and his skills were the stuff of legend in these parts. He would butcher anything at times when meat was short: horses, dogs, foxes – you name it. Sometimes people's animals would go missing and whispers would circulate around the village. And then one day the local schoolteacher, Abagail Morgan, a friend of Nessa Cronin, shows up at Jerah's door asking why Lowena has not been at school. He tells her Nessa and Lowena upped and left them. She sees Thaddeus, a fourteen-year-old boy at that time, trembling on the floor of the kitchen. This very room, in fact. Abagail thinks Jerah is not himself but he does not appear to have the heart of a broken man, she surmises. He has the heart of a devil. Suspicion and fear ripple through the village, as you can imagine. Some idle gossip speculates that Abagail Morgan is his lover, but she is having none of that nonsense. She wants to know the truth and starts snooping around. Now Abagail's sight is not the best, but she sees Nessa and Lowena in the distance one evening, their dresses flapping in the wind. With a happy heart, she runs to them, calling their names. But they remain still as statues. As she draws closer, she realises how wrong she is. It's not them. It's two scarecrows, wearing their dresses. Dresses that have dark patches of blood and protruding through the weather-torn material she sees bone stripped of flesh.'

Archer feels her skin prickling.

'They came for him, Jerah, the police and villagers, but he hung himself inside the farmhouse before they could get to him. He left a note saying his family live on inside all of them and will continue to live on in their young'uns and their young'uns and so on. After that incident the farmhouse became shrouded in superstition. When Nessa and Lowena's bones were laid to rest, people began to tell stories of how they saw them running frightened through the woods, pursued by Jerah himself, his knives and a flaming poker. Which was all nonsense, of course. Anyway, Abagail took Thaddeus in and raised him as her own. When he was of age he returned here, married and raised a family. He always kept three scarecrows in his fields: a mother, a father and a girl. Each of them had stuffed-sack head with eyes and a smile burned into the face and the Cronin family continued to live here through the generations without a recurrence of Jerah's crimes. Aaron Cronin is the last of the line.' Esther sighs. 'It took a long time for this place to heal.'

'Do you think Aaron is like Jerah?'

'The Jerah in that story is the stuff of myth. I couldn't say.'

'Do you think Aaron is capable of murder?'

Esther levels her gaze with Archer and says, 'Without question.'

'Why do you say that?'

'I have no proof of anything. Only my instincts.'

'When Aaron Cronin was living here in the commune, there was a complaint raised about him to the police about inappropriate behaviour against a teenage boy. Do you know anything about that?'

Esther looks away and shakes her head. 'I'm afraid not.'

'Do you remember the Apostle killings?'

Esther shifts in her chair. 'Yes, I do.'

'What do you know about them?'

'Only what I read in the papers.'

'Then you will know the similarities with the murders of Brian Bailey and Matthew Pollard and the obvious connection with history of the Cronin family?'

'I did speak to a detective many years ago. He was leading the investigation into the Apostle killings.'

'DCI Leo Randle?'

Esther considers the name. 'Yes, that's him. I told him about the younger Aaron, and the history of the Cronin farm, much like I've just told you.'

'What were his thoughts?'

'It was a long time ago, but I do recall he was very interested in talking further with Aaron.'

'Can I ask when you met with him?'

'I don't recall the exact date, but I do know it was 1999.'

'Did he contact you at any time after that?'

She shakes her head. 'No.'

Archer takes out her phone and shows her the image from the website. 'Did you ever meet these twin boys?'

Esther folds her arms. 'Not really. They weren't here for very long, I recall.'

'Do you remember their names?'

Esther takes a moment and replies. 'I'm sure they were called Peter and Jude.'

Archer feels a fluttering in her belly. 'Do you know what happened to them?'

'Sadly, not.'

Archer points to the couple leaning into each other. 'Do you remember who these two are?'

'I do. His name is Sidney Robinson and she is his wife, Vera Robinson.'

'Do you remember anything about them?'

'Nothing, I'm afraid.'

Archer pockets her phone. 'Thank you, Esther. I appreciate you taking the time.'

They stand and walk to the hallway.

'What made you buy this house, considering its turbulent past?' asks Archer.

'I had the dream of healing this place and the land around it. I wanted to restore it to its former standing before the murders. I also wanted to create a place for people to come and get better.'

'You're a modern-day Abagail Morgan.'

Esther smiles as she opens the front door. 'I don't know about that.'

'Thank you for your time.' Archer hands her a contact card. 'If you think of anything else, please call me.'

'I will. Goodbye.'

'Bye.'

41

THE RAIN POURS DOWN AS Archer makes the journey south, leaving Esther Tilling and the North Oak Mental Health Centre behind her. She reflects on their conversation, in particular her revelations about Cronin's childhood cruelty to animals, a trait of so many other serial murderers before him, and no doubt after him too.

She approaches the M1 and pulls over into a lay-by and removes her iPhone from the dashboard stand. She opens the investigation team's WhatsApp group and begins typing a message instructing everyone to be in the incident room at 9 a.m. to follow up on new developments. Fixing the phone back on the dashboard, she then makes a three-way WhatsApp call to Quinn and Klara, using the speaker option. As the call rings, she indicates, checks to ensure the road is clear, pulls out and makes her way toward the motorway.

Quinn and Klara both answer within five rings.

'Hey. I wanted to bring you both up to date.'

'Just saw your message,' says Quinn.

'How'd it go?' asks Klara.

'Interesting . . .'

Archer gives them a summary of her meeting with Esther Tilling.

'Cronin's definitely our man,' says Quinn. 'We need to get him into the station pronto.'

'I agree. I'm going to push for that tomorrow. I also want to see Ethan White and the kid called Kain. I've been thinking about Cronin and DCI Randle and want you to consider this *what if* scenario. Esther Tilling tells Randle about young Aaron Cronin taking dead animals to school, animals she suspected he had killed. Randle has been chasing this killer for years without success. He's obsessed, angry, confrontational. He suggests to Cronin that it's not unusual for serial murderers in their youth to cut their teeth by killing animals. Cronin understands Randle has no evidence linking him to the Apostle murders, yet he knows Randle is on to him and will not let this go.'

'He kills Randle,' says Quinn.

'Yes.'

'If that's true,' says Klara, 'then Cronin has played a blinder. With Randle missing, the investigation into the Apostle killings ran out of steam and was consigned to cold cases, where it sits today.'

'Cunning bastard!' says Quinn.

'There have been no reported Apostle murders since 2001, when Randle went missing,' says Klara.

'The same time Cronin joined the Jesus Army.'

'Perhaps he saw the light and turned over a new leaf,' says Quinn, sardonically.

'There are two boys still unaccounted for: Peter and Jude,' says Archer. 'We need to find out what happened to them.

Also, Esther was able to give me the names of the couple in the photo.'

'Excellent!' says Klara.

'They are Sid and Vera Robinson.'

'That's all I need. I'll start getting my searches underway and hopefully have something later this evening.'

'We'll catch up tomorrow morning. Thanks, both. Have a great evening.'

'Drive safely,' says Klara.

'Will do.'

'I second that.'

'Bye, Harry.'

Archer calls Grandad.

'Hey, Grandad.'

'Hello, Grace. How are you?'

She is relieved to hear his voice in good spirits when he picks up. 'I'm doing good. I'm driving back from Northampton and just checking in. What are you up to?'

'I'm just having a glass of Chenin Blanc, what with it being Sunday and that.'

'Since when do you need it to be Sunday to have a glass of wine?'

Grandad chuckles. 'You know me so well.'

'Did Cosmo visit you today?'

'He did. He won some money on something, the horses, I think, so we went for lunch at the King's, roast beef with all the trimmings and a couple of pints.'

'You must be sozzled.'

'Not quite. And we had a nice time.'

Archer is sure she can hear a slight slur in his voice.

'That's nice. Listen, the weather isn't great and the traffic is slowing, so I don't know what time I'll be back. Hopefully, before seven.'

'I'll be here. Watch those roads.'

'I will. Bye, Grandad.'

'Bye, Grace.'

It's dark and just gone seven o'clock by the time Archer arrives in Charing Cross Station to drop off the car. After checking it in, she makes the journey home on foot, her collar up to keep the rain and cold from her neck. Today's revelations about young Aaron have lit a fire in her belly. There is much to think over and follow up with tomorrow.

42

A RCHER WAKES IN THE GLOOM to her phone vibrating on the bedside table. The screen glows in time to the vibration and its light reveals her glasses next to the clock. She reaches for them and clumsily puts them on. Blinking through the lenses, she sees the call is from DCI Pierce and instantly regrets not texting her personally with an update before this morning's meeting.

Pushing herself into a sitting position, she answers. 'Good morning, Clare. Sorry I've not been in touch. This weekend has been a bit of a whirlwind.'

'So I gather.' Archer pushes her fringe from her face and wonders how she knows. 'I heard you were in on Saturday and saw your message yesterday. I assumed you'd been working all weekend. Anyway, I wanted to let you know I cannot make it this morning.'

'I'm sorry to hear that.' Archer cuts straight to the chase. 'I want to bring Aaron Cronin in for questioning today, and two of his associates also. One is a child.'

'On what grounds?'

'I have no proof, but I believe Cronin is connected to the murders of Brian Bailey, Cameron Pollard and Alfie McSweeney.

I'm also sure he is the Apostle Killer. White is helping supply drugs, and the minor may be suffering abuse.'

'OK. Start from the beginning.'

Archer brings Pierce up to date on everything including her discovery of the earring in the Lewisham church yard and her trip to North Oak to meet with Esther Tilling. She leaves out the details of Charlie's help for the moment. She wants to be sure of the legality of having his information and needs to speak to Klara about figuring out a way to cover their tracks if questions are asked.

'I remember the Apostle murders,' reflects Pierce. 'Who doesn't? I worked with Leo Randle for a while. He had a mouth on him, but he was a good detective.' She sighs. 'It can be a small world being a copper.' Pierce says nothing for a moment before adding, 'Good work, DI Archer. If you're right about Cronin, then I expect you to do whatever it takes to nail that motherfucker.'

Archer blinks. Hearing profanities from Pierce's delicate mouth in her plummy accent is still something she is getting used to.

'I'll send a reply to your WhatsApp message to reinforce the urgency to the team.'

'Thanks, Clare.'

Archer is first to arrive at the office, followed by junior analyst, Os Clark.

'Morning, ma'am. How was your weekend?'

'Delightful, Os. Just delightful. How about you?'

Quinn appears, unzipping his jacket. 'Morning.'

'Morning, Harry,' says Archer.

Os continues, 'I was catching up on some studying recommended by Klara. Otherwise, it was OK. Morning, Haz!'

318

Klara's flame-red hair and smiling face appears over the heads of all the others streaming into the third-floor office.

'Talk of the devil,' says Archer.

'Morning all.'

The rest of the investigation team arrive and herd their way into the incident room and Archer stands at the front. 'I appreciate you being here on time at what is a critical point in the investigation. First up I'd like to thank Klara and Os for compiling the information for this investigation and keeping it located in a single online library that we can all easily access. Thanks, Klara and Os. Now, our focus today is to bring Aaron Cronin in for questioning in relation to the murders of Brian Bailey, Justin Sykes, Cameron Pollard and Alfie McSweeney. You all know the details of the murders and if you've read the latest files you'll know there is a possible link to the Apostle killings back in the late nineties/early noughties.'

'Are we nicking the Cronin fella for those murders too?' asks Hicks.

'We're not nicking anyone. We don't have proof of anything. We're just bringing him in for questioning.'

Archer catches Hicks look at DC Felton and roll his eyes.

'We have a witness who saw Rose Grant stumble from the rear of St Mary's the Virgin in Lewisham shortly before she was killed in a hit-and-run. This same church backs on the grounds of the Blood of the Lamb Church where I found an earring that matches one that Rose wore on the night she died. The toxicology report revealed traces of Butterfly Ketamine in her bloodstream. She was taking, or was given, BK. She was frightened and running from that place. I want to bring in Ethan White to question him about drugs and Cronin, amongst other subjects. Ethan is the grandson of Frankie White. He seems to be estranged from his family at the moment and has shacked up with Cronin and his cult.' Archer glances at Quinn. 'It's our belief that White is supplying drugs to Cronin's community, probably via his close mate, Adrian Boyne, who works for Ethan's grandad. This could be big. Any questions?'

There are none. Archer notices Klara frowning at her iPad.

'Finally, the last person we're bringing in is a boy called Kain. Kain is fourteen years old and has a burn mark on his neck that is not unlike the burn marks applied to victims of the Apostle Killer. If our suspicions are right about Cronin being the killer, then Kain could be our link to finding out.'

Klara's brow is furrowed, her expression pale. She raises her hand.

'Everything OK, Klara?' asks Archer.

'I just saw on the police feed that two bodies have been found in a building in Middlesex Street, Spitalfields. It's the same address where Sid and Vera Robinson live.'

Archer's heart sinks.

'Jesus!' says Quinn.

'That's not all. It's the same building where Ethan White's girlfriend, Beth Harper, lives.'

'Who's there now?'

'Sergeant Barnes. The Crime Scene team are on their way.'

Archer looks at Quinn. 'Better get going then.' She turns to Klara. 'Klara, you're the most up to date with everything. I know it's unusual, but could I ask you to finish off the briefing?'

'Sure.'

Archer addresses the room. 'Everyone, Klara will finish the briefing. DI Hicks, when Klara's done, please could I ask you to take whoever you need, travel to Lewisham and bring in Cronin, Ethan White and Kain?'

DI Hicks sniffs and rolls his shoulders. 'I can do that.'

'Thank you, I really appreciate it.'

'Yeah. OK. Whatever.'

Archer grits her teeth and looks at Quinn as they leave the incident room.

43

RCHER AND QUINN ARRIVE AT Middlesex Street where a dozen or more members of the public stand at the opposite side of the street watching nothing more than a building cordoned off with police tape. The doorway is covered by a white forensic tent. Quinn pulls over and parks the car in a loading bay for the time being. Archer gets out, opens the boot and retrieves a bag of new overalls. Walking to the building they duck under the police tape and make their way towards Jimmy Barnes and his partner, Wayne, who are keeping the public at bay. She hears the crowd's whispers of dismay and the chittering of excited speculation wondering who the dead person or people might be.

'Ma'am, Harry,' greets Barnes.

'What's the scoop, Jim?' asks Quinn.

'The vaping store manager noticed the side door's been slightly ajar since Saturday. He thought nothing of it but noticed a smell when he came to work this morning. He peered behind the door and found the body of an elderly occupant, one of his customers, he claims. The victim's face is all messed up and cut like the others. We got the call and found a second body upstairs. An elderly woman, who I assume is his wife.'

'Do you know their names?' asks Archer.

'The vape guy said the old boy's name is Sid Robinson. We haven't mentioned the second victim to him yet. He said he noticed a rough sleeper with a limp hanging around on Saturday night.'

'Did he say what he looked like?'

'He was wearing a filthy parka with the hood pulled up covering his face.'

'That's our man,' says Quinn.

'Thanks, Jimmy,' says Archer.

She hears Krish's voice from inside the tent. He's talking to someone in the building. When he stops, Archer calls, 'Krish, it's Grace and Harry.'

Krish appears through a slit in the tent, dressed in overalls and holding an iPad. 'Get dressed and come inside. MJ is almost done upstairs.'

'Bollocks,' mutters Quinn, as he unbags his PPE suit.

Archer regards him for a moment before asking, 'Everything all right?'

'Things are a little . . . strained.'

'Was the date a disaster?'

Quinn scoffs. 'The date never happened.'

'Oh, sorry to hear that.'

He shrugs. 'I'm not sure we're going to last long, to be honest.'

They pull up their hoods and fix on their masks. 'Perhaps there's still time,' says Archer, who isn't entirely sure what to advise, considering her own relationship track record.

Krish reappears. 'Ready for action?'

Archer and Quinn follow him inside. Behind the main entrance to the flats above the vaping store, they see the first body. The smell of decay and burnt flesh hangs in the air. The victim's eyes have been cut and removed and the characteristic inverted cross carved down the nose and across the mouth. Despite that, Archer can see that it is the same man from the photo.

'He's been dead a couple of days,' says Krish.

'He was pushed down the stairs by the look of it,' comments Quinn.

Archer nods and follows Krish up the stairs and past the first-floor flat. 'Are the other occupants home?'

'We tried, but no one answered. Jimmy was concerned and used a ram to break in. There was no one there.'

Archer thinks it odd that Jimmy would press ahead and do that without seeking permission but appreciates that he took the initiative.

'He was in there for a long time. I had to chase him out in the end, just in case we needed access.'

In the flat on the top floor, the curtains remain drawn, and the fetid smell of death hangs in the air. Spotlights have been erected inside, providing the necessary light for Krish and MJ to do their job. Transparent anti-contamination plates have been placed carefully on the floor, forming pathways to the different rooms.

'Probably best we start in the kitchen,' says Krish.

Treading carefully over the plates, they enter a narrow galley-style kitchen. There is a walnut cabinet on castors underneath a window overlooking the street. Krish wheels it across to face them. 'Do you know what this is?'

'A hostess trolley,' replies Archer.

'Exactly. My mum had one in the eighties. She used it for dinner parties. It was always a talking point with our guests.

One point of interest about the home of these two elderly victims that might come as a surprise is the array of class A drugs and other narcotics they keep in their hostess trolley.' Krish opens the cabinet doors. 'Cannabis, cocaine, LSD, Ecstasy, GHB, Rohypnol . . .'

'You're never too old to party,' quips Quinn.

'Are there any more?' asks Archer.

'We haven't come across any.'

'Let's go through to the bedroom.'

In single file they leave the kitchen and cross to the bedroom, a double room with a threadbare olive-green carpet and dark-blue wallpaper with a gold fleur-de-lis design. Archer stands at the foot of the bed and swallows at the sight before her.

'Jesus!' says Quinn.

The bed is covered with ruffled pink bedding. Lying on top if it is the corpse of an elderly woman, her face cut and scarred in the same manner as the previous victims. On the wall above the bed, Cronin's name has been burned into the paper a dozen times in disjointed large, charred black writing.

MJ is dusting a bedside table for prints. Archer notices a brief and curt nod between her and Quinn.

'It's quite something, isn't it?' says Krish.

'You can say that again,' says Quinn.

'It's quite something, isn't it?' repeats Krish.

'Funny guy.'

Archer takes a photo of the writing and hears MJ tutting as she goes about her work. Whether that is directed at Krish and Quinn's banter or her own efforts at dusting, she cannot tell.

'So, I'm pretty certain the deceased didn't die here,' says Krish.

He swipes open his iPad and shows them several close-up photographs of the hall carpet. 'I found strands of the victim's hair and smudges of make-up on the hallway carpet.'

'He dragged her by the feet across the floor?' says Archer.

'Looks like it.'

Krish shows them shots of the entrance. 'There are signs there of a struggle, overturned shoes, traces of defecation and spark burns from the blow torch. She was maimed and killed as soon as the killer was inside and then dragged here to make some sort of statement.'

Archer feels Quinn's gaze. 'This is a bit of a spanner in the works. All along we had Cronin pegged as the killer. If it's him, why would he write his name all over the wall. Why implicate himself?'

'Probably because he's a narcissist,' says MJ.

All heads turn to look her way.

'I've been keeping up with the case,' MJ adds, her eyes flitting to Quinn's.

Archer wonders if Quinn has been discussing it with her. 'I think that's a safe assumption.' She looks back at the charred letters on the wall above the bed. 'Let's talk to him and find out.'

'I'm all for that,' says Quinn.

'I'll compile my report and send it to you tomorrow, end of day earliest, or the day after, latest,' says Krish.

'Thanks, Krish. That would be helpful.'

'If you need anything else, let me know.'

'Cheers, mucker,' says Quinn.

'There's something else,' says MJ, her eyes turning to Krish.

Krish shifts on his feet and looks away from Archer and Quinn. 'Oh yeah ... that thing I have to tell you.'

Archer narrows her gaze as she waits for him to speak. 'What thing?'

'Erm, bit of an error that we will fix, I promise. I say error, more a fuck-up somewhere along the line.' Krish looks to MJ, his eyes wide.

'I'll tell them,' sighs MJ. 'Cameron Pollard's laptop has gone missing.'

'Are you kidding?' asks Archer.

MJ shakes her head. 'I wish I was. I checked it in on Friday after finishing at Pollard's, but for some reason it has disappeared from our exhibit store.'

Archer frowns, her gaze flitting in disbelief from MJ to Krish. 'How can that even happen?'

'It'll be there somewhere, among a pile of other laptops,' says Krish. 'We'll find it, I promise.'

'It's my fault,' says MJ. 'I'm so sorry.'

'Just do your best to find it.'

'We will.'

Archer's phone rings. It's Klara. The DI leaves the bedroom and takes it in the hallway. 'Hey, Klara.'

'Hey, Grace. Are you still at Middlesex Street?'

'Yeah, what's up?'

'I just caught a missing person report on Beth Harper. She hasn't been seen or heard from all weekend. She was supposed to work on Friday and the weekend and didn't show up. Her parents and friends have been trying to contact her but have got no response. Nothing from Ethan White, either. It's really out of character for her, apparently, and I checked her social media and there's no activity. I'm running a check on her mobile phone and will let you know what I get.'

'OK. Thanks for that. We'll take a look in their flat now and see what we can find. Listen, we have a witness who saw someone, a rough sleeper with a limp dressed in a filthy parka with the hood up. It's the same person from Battersea Park; I'm sure of it.'

'Great. I'll see what I can find on CCTV.'

'See you later.'

'Bye.'

Archer ends the calls.

'Everything OK?' asks Quinn.

'Beth Harper has been reported missing. I thought we'd look around her flat for a clue to where she might be.'

Inside Beth's flat the odour is thankfully easier on the nostrils. There is a ripeness from an unemptied kitchen bin, but overall there is a pleasant, flowery girl scent lingering in the air. Quinn takes one half of the flat, the bedroom and bathroom and store cupboard, while Archer concentrates on the living room and kitchen. She rifles through paperwork, half of it belonging to Ethan, but there is nothing of interest, mostly bills and letters from the council. Archer would be interested in seeing Ethan White's bank statement to see where his income is coming from; the White family, no doubt, and whatever drugs he is involved with selling. Despite White's recent commitment to whatever backward cult Aaron has created, he is still doing drugs. She could see it in the lines of his face, could smell the chemicals from his skin when he got overheated and angry. He is a troubled soul, promised some sort of salvation from a corrupt preacher with a skewed moral compass and Archer has no doubt this will not end well for Ethan White.

'Found something,' says Quinn. 'A crypto burner.'

She looks up to see him holding a mobile phone. She stands and takes it from him and examines it. 'This is an EncryptoTalk phone.'

'All the rage with the "bad guys" apparently,' comments Quinn, dryly.

'Well, it will certainly contain proof of whatever Ethan White's been up to.'

'Think Klara can crack it?'

'I hope so.'

Outside, Archer and Quinn peel off their overalls and dispose of them in waste bags from Quinn's car.

'I wonder where Beth Harper is,' Archer muses.

'Perhaps she had enough of White and made a clean break. Who could blame her?'

But Archer has an uneasy feeling. 'I'm not so sure. She's disappeared and isn't answering her phone. Something's definitely up.'

44

ARCHER GIVES THE BURNER PHONE to Klara to see what she can pull off it. With Cronin's file in hand, she joins Quinn in the basement video room where a live feed shows a poker-faced Aaron Cronin sitting quietly at a table.

'Rodders said he was quite agreeable and came along without fuss,' says Quinn. 'Said he'd been expecting us.'

Archer folds her arms. 'Then he'll be prepared and we should be on top of our game.'

'He's come prepared with signed witness statements from several people testifying to his whereabouts on the dates of the murders.'

'Of course he has,' says Archer, dryly.

'What did Klara say about the burner?'

'It's an old model and should be easy to crack.'

'That's good,' says Quinn, his eyes fixed on the screen.

'She also discovered a bit more about the Robinsons. They lived in Devon back in the nineties and ran a guest house. She searched online and came across an old resume belonging to Cronin. He worked there for a few months – and that's not all.

The guest house is ten miles away from where Luke Jones, the first victim of the Apostle Killer, was found.'

'Oh, wow! That's *big*.'

'We have nothing on him for those murders, so we can't bring any of that up.'

'Maybe indirectly we can.'

'The fact is, we know we'll not get any sort of confession, or arrest. He'll walk away today, or tomorrow, if we can keep him in, but at least he will be under pressure.'

They sit and watch Aaron Cronin for a few moments before making their way to the interview room and take their seats opposite him. Archer looks through her files without greeting him or making eye contact. She turns to Quinn and gives him the nod for the caution. When he is done, Archer begins. From the file she takes out the old photograph from his farm and slides it across the table.

'Brian Bailey, Alfie McSweeney and Cameron Pollard,' she says. 'All friends of yours, colleagues of the Jesus Army who lived with you in your commune in 2001. In the past two weeks the three of them have been murdered and disfigured. Do you know anything about their murders?'

Aaron breathes in through his nose and sighs. 'I do not.'

'You knew all three men?'

'Some more than others,' he replies in a bored, casual tone.

'You knew Brian Bailey.'

'Are you asking or telling me?'

'I'm telling you.'

'We didn't have much to do with each other.'

'Yet he lived with you at the commune for over a year. Are you expecting us to believe that, having lived under the same roof as him, the best you can tell us is that you didn't have much to do with each other? One might think you had something to hide.'

Aaron levels his gaze with Archer. 'I knew him. Just not as well as the others.'

'When was the last time you spoke with him?'

'I couldn't say – but years.'

'How many?'

He shrugs. 'Ten . . .?'

'Someone made a call to your church the same night Bailey died. By our calculations the call was near the time of his murder. Did you take this call from Brian Bailey?'

'I did not.'

'Then who did?'

'Someone else, I suppose.'

'Someone else? Who else uses the phone in your office, Aaron?'

'Everyone is free to use the phone, Detective Inspector. We are a free church, not a prison.'

'Why would anyone want to murder and disfigure Brian Bailey in such a brutal fashion?'

'I've no idea.'

'His disfigurements – and indeed, those of Alfie McSweeney and Cameron Pollard – are quite similar to those of the Apostle killings from the mid- to late-nineties. Do you remember the Apostle killings, Aaron?'

His eyes narrow. He pauses before answering. 'I don't know that I do.'

Archer feels herself bristling inside but remains composed.

'At the time of Cameron Pollard's murder, a call was made from his home to your church. Did you take the call?'

'I did not.'

'Do you know who did?'

'I do not.'

'When Alfie McSweeney was murdered, a call was made to your church, from a stolen phone belonging to Ethan White. Did you take that call?'

'I did not.'

'Who did?'

'I have no idea.'

'You seem quite in the dark about the murders of your friends, Aaron,' comments Archer.

His stony, expressionless eyes remained dark and without emotion. Archer has the sense of a cobra waiting to strike.

Quinn leans across and points to the picture and the couple leaning into each other. 'Do you know these two people?'

He glances at the photo. 'Sid and Vera Robinson.'

'That's correct, Sid and Vera Robinson. Very good. Did you work for them in Devon at their guest house back in 1997?'

He smiles. 'You've been doing your homework.'

'Is that a confirmation of working for Sid and Vera Robinson at their guest house in 1997?'

'Yes, I worked there for a few months.'

'You must have made quite an impression on the locals.'

He pauses. 'I'm not sure I understand.'

'It was just a comment. Coming back to Sid and Vera, when did you last talk to them?'

'On Friday. They came for Ethan's baptism and celebration.'

Quinn taps his fingers on the tabletop and stares inquisitively at Cronin. 'What's that all about?'

'I'm not sure I understand the question.'

'Rumour has it you baptise your "children" in a pool filled with water dyed blood red? That's a bit weird, isn't it?'

'Have you brought me here to quiz me on the practices of my church?'

'Humour me, and then we'll get back on track. I promise.'

'It's symbolic.'

'Of?'

'The Lamb.'

'OK, which "lamb" are we referring to here?'

Cronin sighs, but does not reply.

'It's the sacrificial lamb, isn't it? The blood of the lamb that washes away all the sins of humanity. All those terrible sins.'

A stark silence fills the air between them.

Archer breaks it. 'Sid and Vera Robinson were murdered. Their eyes were removed and their faces were disfigured on Saturday. The day after you saw them last.'

Aaron does not respond.

'Did you have a problem with any of these people, Aaron?' asks Quinn.

'I had no problem with any of them.'

'Why have they all been murdered?'

'I have no idea.'

'It's a strange coincidence that the adults in this picture, who lived with you in your commune, have all been murdered. All except you.'

'Yes, it is odd.'

'You don't seem to be particularly upset about the deaths.'

'I am. I just don't wear my heart on my sleeve.'

'There are two boys in the photos. Who are they?' asks Archer.

'I don't recall.'

'Try a bit harder, Aaron,' says Quinn.

'I really do not remember. There were many children back then.'

'I bet there were,' replies Quinn, harshly.

Archer notices the briefest flicker of irritation in Aaron's eyes.

'Let me throw a few names into the pot,' says Quinn. 'Were either of them called Matthew, or Mark, or Luke.'

'No.'

'How about Peter and Jude?'

'I don't know any of those names.'

'OK. Let's talk about Ethan White. How did you meet him?' asks Archer.

'Sid and Vera introduced us. They are – were – neighbours. They saw in Ethan a troubled soul who could be helped.'

Or manipulated, thinks Archer.

'When you met him, were you aware of his family's connections?'

'No. It was when we got to know each other better that he told me.'

'Did this concern you?'

'Not especially. I wanted to help Ethan. He was going through a dark time in his life.'

'Do you or anyone in your church take drugs?'

'I don't take drugs or drink alcohol. Neither are allowed on the premises.'

Archer slides out the picture of Rose Grant. 'Do you recognise this young woman? A witness saw her leave St Mary's the Virgin.'

'That is a different church to mine, Detective Inspector. She was obviously lurking in the grounds and taking drugs. I understand it's a bit of a hotspot for that kind of behaviour.'

'I didn't say she was taking drugs. It was never mentioned in the news or the papers. How would you even know that?'

'Isn't it what you are alluding to?'

'Is it?'

Silence.

Archer takes a second picture from the file. 'I found this earring in the grounds of your church.'

Aaron shrugs.

'It belonged to Rose Grant.'

'I have never met this young woman.'

Archer takes the photos back and places them inside the file, leaving it open long enough for him to catch a collage of the victims of the Apostle killings. After a pause she asks, 'Aaron, who is Kain and where are his parents?'

'Kain is a member of my church. As is his mother.'

'Who is his mother?'

'Her name is Evie Scudder.'

Archer recalls the frail-looking woman, the drug-abuser Kain had described as 'fallen'.

'Is Evie a drug user?'

'She was, but she has been cleansed.'

'By the blood of the lamb?' asks Quinn, sardonically.

'She is a proud member of our church.'

'I met her briefly and she didn't seem especially proud. In fact, she didn't seem especially anything. It's almost as if she is still using.'

'It takes a long time to get clean.'

'What's your relationship with Kain?'

'Until his mother is better, he is my ward.'

'How did he get that burn scar on his neck?'

'He had an accident.'

'In the church?'

'Apparently so.'

'How did that happen?'

'Kain is a wilful child, full of mischief and curiosity. It happened in our kitchens. It was unfortunate.'

'Does he have any other burn marks on his body?'

'I am not aware of any.'

Archer watches him in silence for a moment. 'OK. That'll do for now, Aaron. Thank you.'

'I hope I have helped in your investigations.'

Archer gathers the file and stands. 'We'll talk again.'

Archer and Quinn return to the video room.

'He's a good liar,' comments Quinn.

'He is as guilty as they come. We just don't have enough evidence.'

The door knocks and Klara enters. 'I accessed Ethan White's phone. There are several conversations between him and Adrian Boyne with Ethan asking for drugs, Butterfly Ketamine and coke, mainly. White also asked if Rose Grant was "available". According to the date on the text it was the same day that Rose was killed.'

'This is it! We've got Ethan White,' says Quinn.

'That's not all. Boyne also sent him the credentials for a porn site. Not just any porn site, either. One that specialises in rape. In particular, the rape of women who are intoxicated.'

'Jesus Christ!' says Quinn.

Archer feels her skin crawling.

45

ARCHER AND QUINN SIT OPPOSITE Ethan White who does not look at them. His expression is sulky, verging on pouty and his eyes, as always, are puffy and red. He seems remarkably calm considering the meltdown during his previous visit to Charing Cross. Despite that, Archer can sense a measure of tension as he wrings his hands, his eyes staring blankly at the tabletop. Aaron had described Ethan as a troubled soul, and considering the data Klara had uncovered on White's phone, Archer understands why.

'Hello, Ethan,' says Archer.

He does not respond.

'How are you feeling?'

No response.

'Can I get you something to drink?'

'Why have you brought me here again?' he says.

'We have some questions about Aaron Cronin and his church.'

He curls his lips and rolls his eyes.

'What's your relationship with Aaron Cronin?'

Ethan frowns as if he's just been asked the dumbest question ever. 'He's my saviour.'

'Why do you say that?'

'He has saved me.'

'In what way has he saved you?'

'I've been cleansed in the blood of the lamb.'

'What does that mean?'

'My soul has been cleansed. My sins have been washed away. I'm a new man, a different man, a good man, like Aaron.'

'That's just peachy to hear,' remarks Quinn. 'Now tell us, how did you meet him?'

'My neighbours, Sid and Vera, introduced us.'

'How did that introduction come about?'

'They thought it would be beneficial for me.'

'Did Sid and Vera think your soul needed cleansing?'

He frowns. 'No. They just thought we'd be good for each other.'

'Does Sid and Vera know of your family's connection with crime?' continues Quinn.

'It's no secret.'

'So Aaron also knew about your family from the get-go?'

'I suppose.'

'Ethan, does Aaron, or anyone in his church, take drugs?'

He blinks. 'How would I know?'

'Are you supplying drugs to the church, Ethan?'

'No!' he states with an affronted tone.

'Is your pal, Adrian Boyne, supplying drugs to the church?'

'No! Why would he?'

'That's a question we would like to know the answer to.'

White begins to shift awkwardly in his chair. 'You're asking the wrong person.'

Archer takes over. 'OK, Ethan,' she says gently. 'Coming back to Sid and Vera. Were you good friends?'

White's eyes slide suspiciously from Quinn to Archer and back to Quinn. After a moment he says, 'As friendly as neighbours can be. I thought them a bit mad at first, but they're wild. Some of the things they've done, the places they travelled. They had lots of stories to tell.'

Archer smiles. 'Like what?'

'It's not for me to say.'

'Do they sell drugs?'

White stiffens. 'How would I know?'

'You were friends, and neighbours. You must have seen them swap drugs for cash. Happens all the time these days. Little exchange here. Little exchange there. No one bats an eyelid. It's only drugs, after all.'

'I wouldn't know.'

'They keep a stash of drugs in their flat: cannabis, ketamine, coke, Es, heroin, speed, LSD . . . I could go on. On a nice little hostess trolley to boot. Perfect for wheeling out to clients.'

'I never saw them deal. It wasn't their thing.'

'What *was* their thing?'

'They indulge, like anyone else.'

'Bit old to take class As, aren't they? All that crack would surely interfere with their heart meds, blood pressure meds, arthritis meds, no?'

'They like to smoke weed. That's their thing.'

'*Was* their thing,' corrects Quinn.

White frowns. 'What does that mean?'

'Sid and Vera were murdered on Saturday.'

White's face goes ashen.

'Ethan, when did you last see them?'

'It . . . it was Friday, at the church. They came for my baptism. We talked then. They were happy for me.' He rubs his temples. 'I can't believe they're gone.'

'Do you know why anyone would want to murder them?'

He shakes his head.

Archer opens the folder on the tabletop and slides out a photo of Rose Grant. 'Do you know who this is?'

White furrows his brow and takes a few minutes to consider his answer. 'Rose.'

'How do you know her?'

'She was Adrian's girlfriend.'

'Adrian Boyne?'

'Yes.'

'Was she a member of the Blood of the Lamb Church?'

'No.'

'Then what was she doing there?'

White shakes his head and doesn't reply.

'Did you speak to her when she was at the church?'

Ethan blinks and folds his arms tightly.

'Ethan, did you speak to her when she was at the church?'

'She came to visit . . .' He leaves it hanging there.

'Who was she visiting, Ethan?'

He curls into himself and trembles. 'Me.'

'Were you close?'

'No.'

'Did she want to join the church?'

'No.'

'Then why was she visiting you?'

'She needed money.'

'Did she offer to sleep with you for money?'

'Yes.'

'Did you sleep with her?'

'No! No, I didn't, I swear.'

'Did you give her Butterfly Ketamine, Ethan?'

342

White's eyes flash. 'We were just having some fun.'

'But she took quite a lot of ketamine, didn't she?'

'She panicked and ran. I tried to look for her, but couldn't find her, and th-then I heard she was dead.'

'Who else knows Rose was at the church?'

'Kain. He helped me look for her.'

'Did Aaron know?'

'Yes. I had to tell him.'

Archer places the photo of Rose back into the folder.

'Ethan, where is Beth?'

He shrugs.

'Have you and Beth split up?'

'Not yet. I've been trying to, but she doesn't want to.'

'Because she cares for you?'

He nods. 'Yes.'

'Did you know she's missing?'

He frowns. 'No. I didn't. I swear.'

'When was the last time you spoke with her?'

He takes a moment to think. 'It was at my grandad's coming home party, right before you dragged me away.'

'And you've had no contact since?'

'None. Not even at my baptism.'

'Was Beth at your baptism?'

'I didn't know she was there. I would have talked with her.'

'If you didn't know she was there, how did you find out?'

'Kain told me.'

'What exactly did he tell you?'

'He told me she watched the baptism and that he showed her the gardens afterwards.'

'Did he see her leave?'

'I don't think so. Aaron was with her. Perhaps you could ask him.'

'Perhaps we could.' Archer looks at Quinn and gives him the nod.

'Ethan White, I'm arresting you for supplying class A drugs to Rose Grant on Tuesday, 6th January. You do not have to say anything, but it may harm your defence if you do not mention when questioned something which you later rely on in court. Anything you do say may be given in evidence. Do you understand?'

Ethan's face contorts and he shakes his head.

'Do you understand?' repeats Quinn.

'Yes.'

46

K AIN SITS AT THE TABLE in the interview room,
quietly humming to himself and tapping his fingers
together as if he is counting. He is dressed, as ever,
in the same style of clothes: a grey flannel shirt buttoned up to
the neck and a tweed jacket; hanging around his neck on a
leather thong is a chipped wooden crucifix painted a burnt
orange colour. Archer wonders if he has any actual modern
casual clothes. Beside him is a social worker, a dishevelled man
called Steve, who looks fresh out of college. He whispers some
words of reassurance to the boy, but Kain shows no interest
and continues humming.

'Hello, Kain,' says Archer. 'Can I get you something to drink?'

He does not respond.

'Kain, I'd just like to start by saying that there is nothing to
worry about. You're not in any trouble. We just want to ask
some questions about Aaron.'

Archer waits for a few moments, but he says nothing.

'Kain, could you please tell us how you and your mother
come to be members of the Blood of the Lamb Church?'

The boy stares blankly at his fingers, tapping rhythmically
to the tune.

After a moment Quinn speaks. 'What's that song you're humming? It's a hymn, isn't it? What's it called now . . . "Down at the Cross" . . .? "Onward, Christian Soldiers" . . .? "The Old Rugged Cross"?' Quinn looks to Archer. 'That one was never off the radio on a Sunday when I was growing up. Made me want to slit my wrists if I'm honest.'

'It isn't any of those,' interrupts Kain, frowning at Quinn. 'What's it called?'

Kain levels his gaze at Quinn, starts to tap a beat on the tabletop with his hand and begins to sing,

Have you been to Jesus for the cleansing power?
Are you washed in the blood of the Lamb?
Are you fully trusting in His grace this hour?
Are you washed in the blood of the Lamb?

Quinn smiles. 'I thought it might be that one. I bet it's a big hit at Aaron's church.'

Archer notices Kain's hands curling to fists. Quinn has riled him and broken the ice. She takes her chance and gently asks, 'How long have you been with the church, Kain?'

'Two years.'

'So, you would have been ten when you met Aaron?' asks Quinn.

'Twelve!' he replies, indignantly.

'My apologies,' says Quinn.

'How did you meet Aaron?' Archer asks again.

'He came to Bristol where we lived. I was in the cathedral, walkin' by myself while Mum was at the doctors'. She was always sick with takin' stuff she shouldn't. It was a sunny day and I stood there bathing in the coloured beams from the great rose

346

window. He spoke to me, asked me my name. He seemed gentle and kind and I didn't mind talking to him in the house of God. We must have sat there for nearly two hours, talkin' about this and that. It was so natural, like we'd known each other forever. He wanted to meet Mum, but I was embarrassed because she was a whore and a drug abuser. I didn't tell him that at the time. I just said no, we was busy and that, so we left the cathedral and I went home.'

He stops for a moment and hums quietly to himself as if deep in thought.

'Go on,' urges Archer, gently.

'The following day I was picking up Mum's prescription and I heard a man singing in the middle of town. He was singing "Are You Washed in the Blood of the Lamb?". His voice was loud and it made me stop what I was doing and thinking. I knew it was him and followed the direction of his voice through the crowds. He saw me and smiled, and I smiled back. We became friends, after that, and I told him everything about me and Mum. He said he could help her. Save her. He came to visit us and she liked him too. When he left Bristol four weeks later, we left with him.'

'Did Aaron save your mum?' asks Archer.

'She doesn't want to be saved. She is a woman, and weak.'

'I see. Did Aaron tell you she is weak?'

Kain shrugs and says, 'It's plain to see.'

'Has Aaron ever asked you to do something that you thought was unusual?'

'Like what?'

'I don't know. It's not for me to say or put words in your mouth. Think of something that might be unusual for the leader of a church to ask of his followers.'

347

Kain considers the question and shrugs. 'I can't think of anything.'

'Has Aaron ever hurt you?' asks Quinn.

'Aaron is a man of God. He is the Shepherd. He would never harm his flock.'

The Shepherd. Archer had heard him called that before, by the boy in the video.

'Kain, how did you get that burn scar on your neck?' asks Archer.

Kain stares down at the table and says nothing.

'Did someone do that to you?'

'It was an accident.'

'How did it happen?'

'It was nothing.'

'Kain, that is a serious burn. If someone is hurting you at the church, we can help you.'

'No one is hurting me.'

'We can take you out of there. Your mum too.'

His eyes flare. 'The church is my *home.*'

'Do you have any other scars like it on your body?'

Kain folds his arms. 'No!' he says emphatically.

Archer doesn't believe him and wonders if she can get his mother to agree to an examination. She takes out a photograph of Rose Grant from the file and places it in front of him. 'Do you recognise this woman?'

Kain looks down at the photo and says, 'Don't know her.'

'You've never seen this woman at the church?'

'No.'

Archer returns the photo to the file and takes out a picture of Beth Harper she had printed from Facebook. 'How about this woman? Do you recognise her?'

He regards the photo for a few moments. 'No.'

'Look again. Take your time.'

He leans in for a closer look, humming as his eyes roll across Beth's face. 'I don't know this one.'

'That's interesting. According to Ethan White you spoke to her during his baptism. You told him Beth had been there on the day.'

'He's wrong.'

'Aaron has taken a special interest in you, Kain. Why do you think that is?'

'He said he has looked into my soul and seen a kindred spirit. Someone just like him.'

Archer feels the hairs on her neck lifting. 'Thank you, Kain. We appreciate you talking with us. Steve will see you home.'

47

ARCHER, QUINN AND KLARA MEET to gather their thoughts. It's dark outside and the incident room sash windows seem like black mirrors reflecting the quiet unspoken anxiety that ripples between them.

Archer turns her gaze to the incident wall and studies it in the hope that something will spring out at her.

Quinn's voice interrupts her thoughts. 'Did you watch the interviews?' he asks Klara.

'I was working with Digital Forensics on White's phone and missed Cronin's obviously, but caught White's and Kain Scudder's.'

Archer's mind is elsewhere. 'We nicked Ethan White, but that's just one piece of the puzzle. Kain is lying about Rose and Beth and Beth is still missing. We're close – yet still so far.'

'I think we're getting there,' offers Quinn. 'We just need to put in more hours.'

Archer joins them at the table. 'Do either of you two have any plans this evening?'

'MJ and I were supposed to be meeting to figure things out, but something has come up, as it always does. She's avoiding me. We had a bit of ding-dong about losing Pollard's laptop.'

'Uh oh, bringing work issues home is never a good idea.'

'It was my fault. I was tired and moody, and MJ was being . . . MJ.'

'What does that mean?' asks Klara.

'Don't get me wrong, she's really great. She's funny, smart and sexy. It's just . . . sometimes, she's intense and I don't push it because I assume she's had a string of difficult relationships. I did ask her one time what was going on, but she went quiet. She's a bit of a closed book.'

'Sorry to hear that, Harry,' says Archer.

'Did you have your date on Saturday?' asks Klara.

'No, she cancelled that also. Listen, I should inform you I'm not normally this unlucky with women. You may be surprised to know that some women actually find me irresistible.'

Klara laughs. 'That doesn't surprise me one bit.'

'Anyway, it suits me. I wouldn't have been great company this evening because we still have so much work to do. Therefore, I'm in for the duration.'

'I have no plans,' adds Klara. 'I dredged the Internet and found a list of people associated with the Jesus Army documentary. I could make a start on calling them.'

'Thank you, both. So, let's summarise Aaron's interview. All his alibis stack up. We know he wasn't present for any of the murders, but that doesn't mean he wasn't involved. Esther Tilling, who taught him at school, was less than complimentary about him and thinks him capable of murder. But that's just her opinion. There seem to be more people who hold him in high regard.'

'Mostly the "children" of his cult,' says Quinn.

'Of course. Let's put all of that aside for the moment. For each murder, a call was made to his church. Someone answered those calls. The question is who? Odds on, it was Aaron. Why were the calls made to Aaron? Two possible reasons: one, he instigated the murders because the victims had something on him, knew he was the Apostle Killer, and were blackmailing him; two, the possibility that someone from his past, a survivor, wants revenge.'

Quinn nods. 'They're both plausible reasons. There's something weird about him that I cannot place my finger on. For a self-styled man of God, he has no empathy or remorse about the murders of his friends. In fact, he seems quite at ease with the whole thing.'

'That's right,' says Archer.

'Where does Ethan White fit in?' asks Klara.

'Ethan White is in a dark place. Estranged from his family, perhaps his girlfriend too; he's fragile and unstable. Aaron saw that and groomed him over time, feeding his fears and making him feel safe and wanted at his church.'

'A narcissistic cult leader,' comments Quinn.

'Exactly that. Plus, Ethan thinks he is leaving behind his damaged, corrupt family to join a blessed utopia, where all his past and present sins are wiped from the slate. What he doesn't realise is that he's signed up for a different kind of corrupt family.'

'What about Kain?' says Klara.

'He's an odd kid,' says Quinn. 'Not fragile like Ethan, but definitely damaged and easily manipulated. Worships Aaron.'

'Kain mentioned Aaron was the "Shepherd",' says Archer. 'It reminded me of that boy in the Jesus Army video. He said the same thing.'

'By the way, I sent an email earlier to the account of the film-maker. It's an outdated account and my email bounced back,' Klara tells her. 'I also found an old out-of-date phone number. I'll look deeper and check out his friends and colleagues and see if I can get anything from them.'

'Klara, I was just thinking,' says Quinn. 'Could we take a close-up of that boy from the video and load his picture into one of those face-ageing apps? See if we get an idea of what he might look like today.'

'Definitely worth a shot.'

'Good idea, Harry. Klara, Ethan said Beth Harper was present for his baptism on Friday. Do you think you could look into the CCTV from that afternoon and see what time she arrived and left?'

'Sure thing.'

'If you give me the list of contacts for the documentary, I can start phoning them.'

'I'll print them out.'

'It's going to be a long evening. Either of you want tea or coffee?'

'Not for me, thanks,' says Quinn. 'I'm famished. I'm going to pop out and grab something to eat. Can I get either of you anything?'

'Nothing for me,' say Klara.

'Just a sandwich. Something plain. Cheese'll be fine,' replies Archer, reaching into her purse.

'No worries. I'll get it.'

'Thanks.'

Archer notices Quinn make a call as he leaves. Klara has seen it too. 'Bet he's calling MJ,' she says.

Klara smiles. 'Of course he is.'

Quinn returns twenty minutes later, carrying a parcel in one hand and Tesco carrier in the other. 'Sorry, the queue at Tesco was ridiculous.'

'What's that?' asks Archer glancing at the parcel.

'Don't know. It was waiting for me at reception. Just been delivered by a courier.'

'Apology chocolates from MJ?' says Klara.

Quinn snorts. 'Yeah, right.'

'Harry,' says Klara, 'while you were out, I made a close-up screen capture of the boy in the video and did my best to refine the image using Photoshop software. It's not great, but it's not awful. Should be good enough for the face-ageing app. I've just sent you the file on WhatsApp.'

Quinn places the package and bag on the tabletop and takes out his mobile phone. 'Thanks, Klara. I downloaded the face-ageing app to my phone as I waited in Tesco. Felt myself ageing a decade in that queue, to be honest.'

Archer has the list of documentary contacts and begins phoning around, in the hope of getting a lead on who the boy might be.

Two hours pass by.

Klara is searching through the CCTV. 'Hey, I have the footage of Beth arriving at Ladywell Station in Lewisham.'

Archer and Quinn join her and watch the shots of Beth arriving at Ladywell, leaving and walking towards Ladywell Road and the Blood of the Lamb Church.

'I sped through to see what time she left, but there's nothing. Unless there's another exit.'

'Or she never left . . .' says Archer.

'What about Lewisham High Street?' asks Quinn. 'Maybe she exited the same way as Rose Grant.'

Archer thinks it unlikely, but figures there's nothing to lose in looking.

'I'll give it a go,' says Klara. 'How did you get on with the face app?'

'Take a look,' says Quinn, gesturing at the large TV screen. 'I used an HDMI adapter to connect my phone.'

On the screen is an adult version of the boy rendered from the Photoshopped screen capture supplied by Klara. Archer studies the face, narrowing her gaze.

'He seems familiar,' she says.

'Yeah, he does,' replies Quinn.

Archer makes her twelfth call to a man called Rob Smith in Lincoln. The phone rings. 'Hello,' comes a man's voice.

'Hello, could I speak to Rob Smith, please?'

A hesitation before the man answers. 'I'm not buying anything. I don't need windows, or insurance, nor am I prepared to hand over my bank details, for that matter.'

'Sorry, Mr Smith. My name is Detective Inspector Grace Archer and I'm with the Metropolitan Police.'

'Oh, aye? What can I do for you?'

'I'm phoning in connection with a documentary on the Jesus Army. Were you involved in the filming of it back in 2001?'

'Oh, yes. The one in London?'

'That's correct.'

Archer gestures for Quinn and Klara's attention and puts the phone onto speaker.

'I remember it well,' Smith continues. 'It was my first proper job as a cameraman. Is this anything to do with that missing policeman?'

'DCI Randle?'

'Yes, that's him.'

'Did you know DCI Randle?'

'Not really. I recall he was asking the crew questions. No one liked him much because he was pushy and smelled of booze.

356

I saw his picture in the newspaper with a small article reporting him missing. This was after we had finished filming the documentary.'

'Mr Smith, where did you film the documentary?'

'It was in South London somewhere in Clapham. The Jesus Army took over an old Edwardian house. I can dig out the address for you, if you like?'

'That would be helpful, thank you. I wanted to ask you if you remember a man who was part of the documentary. His name was Aaron Cronin. He was one of the church leaders.'

Smith makes a tutting sound. 'I remember him, all right. He was a strange one. The others were likeable enough, but that Aaron fella . . .? I just didn't like him.'

'Why was that?'

'He seemed OK at first, but all that changed when this kid came along. He became weird, after that. I couldn't put my finger on it.'

'Do you remember the kid's name?'

'Oh . . . it seems so long ago. Let me think . . .'

'Was it Peter or Jude?'

'Yes, that was it! Jude.'

'What was Aaron's relationship to Jude?'

'I don't recall. Although I remember thinking that Aaron became different when Jude arrived. He seemed uneasy, for some reason.'

'Why did you think that was?'

'I couldn't say. Jude seemed like a good kid, but then I caught them arguing once, when I popped out for a cigarette. Aaron had her by the scruff of the neck. I thought it wasn't right treating a young girl in that way.'

Archer feels her throat drying.

'Hello . . .?'

'You said *her*?'

'That's right. Jude, short for Judith.'

Her. Jude. Judith.

Archer turns to look at the rendered image of the boy from the video. Klara and Quinn are doing the same.

'Hello?' asks Smith.

'What happen to her?'

'Her foster parents came to collect her. Nice couple. Two women from Northampton. One was a teacher, I think.'

Esther and Glynis.

'Thank you, Mr Smith. Perhaps we can talk again. Soon. I appreciate your help.' Archer disconnects the call and turns to Quinn and Klara. Quinn's face is ashen.

Klara's fingers begin typing furiously on her keyboard then speaks in a rush. 'Judith Tilling, also known as Mary Judith, or MJ, adopted daughter of Esther Tilling. Changed her surname in 2003, from Brent.'

'Simon Brent was the last recorded victim of the Apostle Killer,' says Klara.

'In the Bible Simon and Peter are the same person,' says Quinn. 'Peter and Jude. Simon and MJ were twins.'

Archer glances at the parcel. *Chocolates from MJ.* It's almost the right size. 'What's inside the parcel?' she asks.

Quinn is rigid. He pulls open the packaging. Inside is a laptop with specks of blood.

'Pollard's laptop,' says Archer.

There is also folded a note on lined paper. Quinn reads it.

Dear Harry,
Everything you need for the investigation is in this laptop.
By the time you receive this, it will all be over. I'm sorry about
Justin Sykes. He was an innocent. I never meant to hurt him.
Forgive me.
MJ

'Jesus Christ!' says Quinn.

'Harry, call her. Find out where she is,' says Archer.

Archer opens the laptop, but it's password protected.

'I can sort that,' says Klara.

'She's not answering,' says Quinn.

'We need to move,' says Archer. 'Harry, go to MJ's house and see if she's there. You know how to talk to her. Calm her down. If she's not home, meet me at the church.' Archer grabs her coat. 'Klara, keep in touch, let us know what you find on the laptop.'

48

WITH THE SIREN WAILING AND the blue lights flashing, Archer races across London in the direction of Lewisham, dodging sluggish traffic as she clears Westminster Bridge. Her phone is perched on the dashboard and she presses the call button next to the Blood of the Lamb Church's phone number.

It rings and rings, but no one answers.

'Shit!'

The news of MJ being the killer has still not quite hit home. All along Aaron has been their prime suspect, yet today she's had confirmation that his alibis are sound. She has accepted that, although she strongly believes that the murders are still either directly or indirectly linked to him. She has suspected blackmail as the motive, but at the back of her mind, revenge has been taking root. MJ's involvement in the case, her access to police records, her knowledge of forensics and her vendetta against a cabal of men, one of them the Apostle Killer, makes her almost the perfect perpetrator. She never imagined that the murderer would be the twin sister of one of his victims and considers what suffering MJ must have endured to make her choose the path of a vicious revenge killer.

A call comes through on her phone. Grandad's name appears on the screen.

'Now's not the time, Grandad,' she whispers to herself, a finger hovering over the *Decline* call button, but guilt consumes her, and she answers. 'Hey, Grandad. Is everything OK?'

He pauses before answering, then, 'I-I couldn't wait to tell you this any longer.' His voice is croaky, slurred even, and she wonders if he's been drinking, or crying.

Ahead is a knot in the traffic, forcing her to slow. She swears under her breath as the cars slowly part to let her through.

'Grandad, could we catch up later? I'm a little busy.'

'Grace, I've tried to bring this up a couple of times but I've just not found the right moment.'

There is sadness in his tone and Archer hates herself for having even thought of declining the call, never mind forgetting the stress he is under with his dementia diagnosis.

'Things have been difficult between us since I tried to get that weapon. I know that now. It was selfish and stupid of me, Grace. I should have thought of you and your job, but I didn't, and I'll never forgive myself for what I did.'

'Grandad, please don't be sad about it. It's over and we sorted it.'

'I don't want there to be any more secrets between us.'

'Of course not.'

'I want you to know the true reason I did what I did.'

'Grandad, you don't need to explain. I understand it's been hard on you—'

'The thing is, Grace. You don't know the whole story. I didn't until a couple of days back.'

'What are you talking about, Grandad?'

'It's about him, that cockroach!' he spits.

Without saying his name, Archer knows he is referring to Frankie White.

'He had your father killed! I know you know this, who doesn't? It's just – it's just the man who killed your father is the same man who took you.'

Archer blinks as she tries to absorb what Grandad has just said.

'Bernard Morrice was on White's payroll. Morrice was the type of person that cockroach employs to do his dirty work. Part of his payment . . .' he pauses and Archer hears him weep quietly, ' . . . part of his payment for killing your father was to have you to do with whatever he pleased.'

Archer feels her head spin and focuses hard on the road ahead. 'How could you know this?'

'A young woman came to the house. I don't remember her name. A reporter, she said. Has tattoos on her hands and arms.'

Mallory Jones.

'She said she knew you and had been trying to talk to you. She seemed nice so I invited her in. She told me she interviewed someone who use to work for White. He told her about Morrice.'

Archer feels her stomach churning. Her siren is howling, but it seems as if it is somewhere far away. Her breathing is deep and sounds cavernous in her ears. A strange, hot sensation surges through her and she grits her teeth. Her hands tighten on the steering wheel as tears of rage squeeze slowly from her eyes.

'Grace . . .?'

So this is Grandad's secret.

She swallows. 'Grandad, I'm sorry but I'm working late and I have to go.'

'Bu—'

'I love you, Grandad.'

She hears him sob quietly and disconnects the call.

Her head is swirling with confusion and questions, but there is no time for any of that now. She turns right onto New Kent Road, which is thankfully not as gridlocked. Pushing all thoughts of this revelation from her head, she steps on the accelerator and continues towards Lewisham.

Almost ten minutes later she is speeding up Ladywell Road and her phone rings with a call from Quinn. She answers.

'She's not at home,' he says. 'I'm on my way to the church.'

'She'll be there, looking for Aaron. How long before you get here? I'm almost there.'

'Less than ten minutes.'

Straight ahead, Archer sees MJ's motorcycle. 'She's here.'

'See you! I'll call for backup.'

Archer sees people, disciples of the church, milling around on the pavement outside, looking back at their home. Some are on their knees, praying and crying. She follows their gaze and sees smoke rising from the turret.

The car skids to a halt and she jumps out and hurries into the crowd. 'What's happened?' she demands.

'A fire,' replies a young woman. 'Someone's started a fire and Aaron is still inside.'

'Has anyone called the fire brigade?'

'One of the neighbours has,' she replies.

Archer looks up at Aaron's windows and sees them glow vibrantly, fire raging behind them.

'Out of my way!' Archer commands and, despite the risk, bolts into the church. Inside the stench of diesel and smoke is everywhere. At the base of the stairs is a discarded petrol can.

Upstairs, she hears Aaron let out a guttural roar of fury from his office. Hurrying up the stairs she hears MJ cry out followed by a crashing and shattering of glass. Smoke billows from the office, but she runs inside. Through the dark clouds she sees MJ, dressed in her bike leathers, lying on the floor amongst broken glass. Her arms are raised, protecting herself from Kain, who is repeatedly stabbing at her with a small, bloody knife.

'Kain, stop! Stop!' shouts Archer.

Kain looks up with a surprised expression. He grins and brays with laughter. In that same moment, MJ kicks hard at his knee and despite the roar of the flames Grace hears it crack. Grunting, he begins to hop backwards and out of the office, his laughter trailing in his wake.

The smoke is gathering and the flames are spreading. Archer can hear Aaron's screams but can't see him.

MJ's leathers glisten with blood, her face is clammy. Archer crouches beside her. 'Can you walk?'

'I think so.'

In the distance Archer hears sirens approaching.

She helps MJ up and senses a shadow nearby.

'Where are you, you bitch?' roars Aaron.

Archer turns and sees Aaron, feels her stomach turning. He is rising from the smoke, his face twisted and bloody with two cavernous bleeding red holes where his eyes used to be. His hair is slick with some oily substance and his clothes are wet. Archer wonders if it's diesel.

'Over here!' shouts MJ.

'MJ, stop!' Archer hisses.

Horror squeezes Archer like a fist as Aaron turns in their direction and stumbles blindly towards them, his arms swinging monstrously through the smoky air.

'You fucking bitch!'

MJ leans on Archer. She is weak and pale, her breathing suddenly laboured. Archer steadies her but pauses at the click of a lighter. Before Archer can stop her, it's too late. MJ's arm is outstretched, the flame of the lighter licking Aaron's damp, bloody face.

'MJ, no!'

In seconds he is engulfed in flames and screams in terror and pain at the top his voice. The flames in the office roar in defiance.

'Let's get out of here,' cries Archer, taking most of MJ's weight.

Around them the church is crumbling as the fire begins to eat away at the interior. It's a slow haul down the stairs; MJ has lost a lot of blood with multiple stab wounds to her body.

'They were *all* complicit,' says MJ. 'All of them. They *had* to die. You understand, don't you? You, of all people.'

'Don't talk. You're weak. Keep your strength.'

'It's too late for me, Grace.'

Archer feels MJ's body shudder as she eases her down the stairs. 'Help is on its way.'

'I met DCI Leo Randle. Leo knew I was Simon's sister and he told me he knew what Aaron had done to Simon and all those other boys. He told me Aaron was a paedophile, that he murdered the boys out of shame for his feelings, that the only way Aaron could control his desire was to disfigure them and make them pay by removing their eyes so that they could look back upon their ruined beauty . . .'

MJ almost slips from her grasp and Archer tightens her grip. 'Almost there.'

' . . . Brian Bailey knew Simon was being abused and covered it up. I knew I had to do something. I followed Aaron to London when he joined the Jesus Army. Leo did too. That was the last time I saw him. He was going to bring Aaron to justice. But then Leo was gone too. I-I think Aaron killed him . . .'

With all her strength Archer helps MJ off the stairs and kneels with her on the floor of the entrance hall.

'I threatened to expose him and tell the police, but Esther and Glynis took me away. We had no proof, but they threatened Aaron, said that if Esther, Glynis or I were to die, then a legally witnessed letter containing allegations against him would be sent to the press and the police. He believed them – and I made a promise that one day Aaron and the others would pay for their crimes.'

MJ coughs. Dark blood spills from her mouth and her eyes roll back in her head. Panic swirls through Archer and outside she sees Quinn hurrying toward her. Behind him, fire service officers and medics arrive.

'We need help!' she screams.

'MJ!' cries Quinn, as he rushes to help Archer take her weight. 'You should have told me! We could have helped you.'

They carry her outside and into the front garden and let her slip gently to the soft grass as a medic arrives and take over.

'What's her name?' he asks.

'MJ,' replies Quinn, holding her hand as her eyes flicker open and she smiles weakly.

'I did it for S-Simon and the other A-Apostles. I did it for them . . .' Blood begins to pool in MJ's mouth and spill down her chin and cheeks.

Archer notices MJ's hand is clutching Quinn's as the medic tries to open her jacket and stop the bleeding, but she can see it is too late. MJ's eyes lock onto Quinn's and she tries to speak but can't find the strength. She gasps and then sighs, her final breath leaving her mouth forever.

49

A T THE END OF THE day on Wednesday, Archer is preparing for a meeting with DCI Pierce to go over the final summary before the wheels are set in motion to close down the investigation.

Archer is worried about Quinn. He is pale and unshaven with dark rings under his eyes. Quiet and withdrawn, he sits at his desk, staring at a blank computer screen, unaware of the disparaging whispers that have floated around him since MJ was revealed as the murderer.

Archer feels Klara's presence. 'Is Harry OK?' she asks, privately.

'I don't think so.'

'Should we say something?'

'I might take him out for a coffee, before our meeting with Pierce.'

'Good idea.'

Quinn had not refused her offer. 'Be good to get out for a bit,' he replied, flatly.

He walks in silence beside her, his hands tucked into his bomber jacket, his head down. Despite that, Archer admires how he deftly navigates the bustling streets.

'Pret on St Martin's Lane, OK?' she asks.

He nods his head. 'Sure.'

Archer finds a free booth in the corner by the entrance. 'You take a seat. I'll grab the drinks.'

Quinn sits obediently in the booth and turns to look outside, staring blankly at the window and his reflection, which he quickly turns away from.

With the drinks bought, she joins him at the table and places his coffee in front of him.

'Thanks,' he says, cupping it with his hands.

'How're you doing?'

He meets her gaze and shrugs. 'Been better.' His eyes drop to the coffee, his thumbs idly rubbing the lip of the plastic lid.

'I can meet Pierce on my own, if you want to head home.'

He shakes his head. 'I'd rather see this through, if you don't mind.'

'Of course.' Archer takes a sip of her tea, which is lukewarm and tasteless.

They sit in silence for a moment, before Quinn breaks it. 'I'm still trying to get my head around it.'

'I understand . . .'

'I mean, I knew she had her demons and everything. Who doesn't, right? I tried to ask her several times but she never told me anything about her past. She would go quiet and clam up, so I never pressed further. That would come in time, I thought, just assumed she'd had a few lousy relationships.' He shakes his head. 'I mean, in the job we deal with this shit all the time but I had no idea.' He rubs his face. 'Some detective!'

'I'm sorry, Harry.'

Quinn's face darkens. 'She should have come to me.'

'Perhaps she knew your sense of reason would plant doubts. And that's the last thing she wanted. For what it's worth, I think she was torn. I think she wanted to get closer to you, to confide in you, but just couldn't.'

They sit in silence, Quinn lost in his thoughts. A moment passes and he looks across at Archer with a curious expression. 'I hope you don't mind me asking, but do you – considering what happened to you as a kid – do you understand why she did what she did?'

Archer is caught off guard by Quinn's question. 'She murdered and mutilated her victims, Harry,' she replies tersely, taking out her phone and checking the time. She can feel Quinn's gaze. 'We should get back. Pierce is expecting us.'

Back in Charing Cross Station, Archer and Quinn are seated opposite DCI Pierce in her office.

Archer is talking. 'Before he set up his church, Aaron Cronin was head of a cabal of paedophiles, which included Brian Bailey, Cameron Pollard, Sid Robinson, Vera Robinson and Alfie McSweeney. Pollard's laptop revealed a cache of photographs and videos dating back to the late nineties. They contain obscene images of underage boys and girls with Bailey, the Robinsons, Pollard and McSweeney.'

DCI Pierce frowns and shakes her head. 'And Cronin?'

Quinn answers. 'We found scanned Polaroid shots of him with a knife in his hand, cradling the bloody, naked corpses of his young victims. We also found the remains of three boys in the grounds of the church. We're hoping to identify them in the next day or so.'

'I can't imagine what their families must have gone through, waiting, wondering. But to end like this . . .'

They sit in silence for a moment before the DCI asks, 'What else?'

'We think that because DCI Randle uncovered the truth, Aaron became paranoid and modified his modus operandi,' says Archer. 'Rather than killing them and leaving them to be found, he decided to dispose of the bodies instead.'

Pierce sighs heavily.

'The photos are proof that Aaron Cronin was the Apostle Killer,' says Archer. 'DCI Leo Randle knew this. Unfortunately, he made a fatal error by confronting Aaron.'

'What news from the search in South London?'

'The remains of a body were found buried in the basement of the house once owned by the Jesus Army. There was a wallet containing credit cards with Leo Randle's name.'

'Poor Leo . . .'

'I'm sorry.'

The DCI shakes her head. 'Let's move on. Tell me about MJ.'

'She's been working in CSI for eight years, and recently transferred to London around the same time as Aaron began forming his church. She was a rising star in Krish's team and popular with her colleagues but she led a double life. She dressed as rough sleeper and would shuffle around the streets, pretending to be lame, following her victims and watching their every move, calculating how and when she would strike. We've spent many, many hours going over CCTV and have found footage of her stalking each of her victims. After each killing the simply seemed to disappear into the streets – because as a member of the force, she knew the CCTV locations and was able to avoid it.'

'But she couldn't have completely disappeared! There are cameras everywhere.'

'That's right,' says Quinn. 'We have footage of MJ on her motorcycle returning home each night after a kill. She wore a backpack, which we discovered in her flat, that contains the parka, jeans and Vans trainers.'

'She killed Justin Sykes and he had no connection with any of this, I understand?'

'We believe that was an accident,' says Quinn. She clubbed him on the head with a blunt object. She didn't mean to kill him, but he fell over and banged his head on a rock. That finished him.'

Pierce sighs. 'I see. You knew MJ personally, Harry?'

'I did. We were in one of those on-off relationships.'

Pierce frowns. 'And you didn't suspect anything?'

'Nothing. I knew she was troubled, but never suspected she was a killer.'

'I understand that on the night she killed the Robinsons, you and MJ should have been on a date?'

'That's right. She was part of the investigation and I expect she saw we were moving faster than she anticipated. She had to strike fast before we found out the true nature of Aaron and his group.'

'I assume she never gave you any indication of her past or her relationship with Cronin?'

'Nothing.'

'Where was she getting the ketamine to drug her victims?'

'We found a pay-as-you-go phone with WhatsApp messages to a dealer linked to Frankie White's network,' replies Archer.

'And why was Ethan White's DNA on the bodies of Brian Bailey and Justin Sykes?'

'We assume she wanted to divert our attention to White as a suspect for the murders. The fact that he was Snow's grandson would have sparked our interest and did. It seems she broke into his car, stole his phone and gloves too.'

'Why withhold Pollard's laptop?'

'MJ had taken the laptop because it contained photographs of her with her brother, Simon. She knew that if we saw those pictures . . . well, the game would be up for her. Today we interviewed her adoptive parents, Esther Tilling and Glynis Hughes. Esther first met Simon and MJ when they moved to Creation with their mother, June Brent. June had become friendly with Aaron, after he took an interest in her kids. According to Esther, June was eccentric to the point of bonkers. She led a nomadic life, taking her kids from town to town, under the radar of the authorities. It was June who made MJ cut her hair and dress like a boy. She would proudly parade her "twin boys" around, under the names of Peter and Jude, unaware the growing interest Aaron was showing in them was dangerous.'

'Where is the mother now?'

'After Simon's death, she had a breakdown and tried to kill herself. She's been in psychiatric care ever since.'

'And Rose Grant and Beth Harper?'

'We found traces of Rose's DNA in Ethan White's bedroom and an earring in the rear garden and we think she escaped into St Mary's the Virgin and then into Lewisham High Street. We believe White drugged her, with the intention of raping her, and she was terrified. The illegal porn sites he subscribes to specialise in date rape and indicates a fixation on dominance over comatose women. He's being charged for that and also,

374

alongside his pal, Adrian Boyne, for supplying drugs. We found Beth Harper's body in a concealed crypt at the rear of the church. She'd been struck on the head with a blunt instrument and a spade was found in a shed with traces of her blood and hair. Ethan White's prints are all over the handle. He's been arrested for her murder, despite vehemently denying it.'

'Of course, he would. Anything else?'

'Kain Scudder.'

'The teenager who killed MJ?'

'He denies that charge. He claims that, during a fight, Aaron stabbed her with a large knife he kept in his desk. He told us MJ somehow got inside the church and took Aaron by surprise, knocking him unconscious with a hammer. He said the building was beginning to burn when he heard Aaron crying out. He ran to Aaron's office and saw him unconscious on the floor, his eyes cut from their sockets. He said MJ was dousing him in petrol and telling him he would burn in hell.'

'But you saw Kain repeatedly stab MJ?'

'He owns a small carving knife. He says he used it against MJ to save Aaron but when I got there, it was as though he was unhinged. Not just that, he was enjoying it too.'

'Where is he now?'

'In custody.'

'His mother?'

'In care. Seems Aaron was feeding her drug addiction to keep Kain as his pet.'

'You mentioned the possibility of abuse against him.'

'The doctor checked him over,' says Quinn. 'He has burns on his body consistent with the Apostle killings. We asked him how he got them, but he wouldn't tell us.'

'Why didn't Aaron kill Kain like the others?'

'Kain isn't like the other Apostle victims,' Archer replies. 'When we asked him why Aaron had taken a special interest in him, he told us Aaron had said, "I looked into your soul and I saw a kindred spirit. Someone just like me."'

'A chilling thought,' says Pierce.

'Indeed. The other Apostle victims were all sweet, innocent boys, with what the papers described as angelic good looks. Aaron hated them for that reason. They woke desires in him that he couldn't deal with. He was conflicted – consumed by lust while despising himself and his victims. The only way he could deal with it was to disfigure their faces and turn their own eyes back on them as a kind of message.'

'A message?'

'Revenge for having the nerve to awaken desires that he desperately wanted to hide away. *Look at you now. You can no longer hurt me.*'

They sit in silence for a moment as Pierce processes Archer and Quinn's summary.

'Thank you both and good work. Very good work. You've cracked two cases. What now? Will you celebrate?'

The last thing Archer can think of right now is a celebration drink. The complexity of this investigation, the death of Rose Grant, the murder of Beth Harper, and the historical killings of Luke Jones, Matthew Hart, John Harris, Mark Smith, James Ryan and Simon Brent weigh heavily on her mind. Equally, MJ's death has moved her more and the reveal of Grandad's secret is just the icing on a rancid cake.

Quinn shifts in his chair. 'I might just call it a night. Go home and get some sleep.'

'Yes, celebrate another time,' says Archer.

Quinn nods and turns to Pierce. 'Thank you, ma'am. Goodnight.'

'Goodnight.'

'Night, Harry,' says Archer.

Quinn leaves.

'How about you, Grace?' asks Pierce.

'I have an appointment with Dr Hutchison this evening.'

'Hope your sessions are going well.'

'It's my third,' replies Archer. 'Early days but, yes, I think so.'

'I'm happy to hear that. By the way, I have some good news for you.'

'Oh?'

'I spoke to HR today. The complaint made against you by PCs Hopkins and Watts has been dropped.'

'I bet Debbie's devastated.'

Pierce snorts. 'The footage from that incident proved you were right.'

'What about Hopkins and Watts?'

'Moved to non-operational duties. If it was up to me, I'd fire them, but they've been given a second chance. Maybe they can learn from this.'

'Maybe . . .'

'Don't let me keep you.'

'Goodnight, Clare.'

'Oh, one last thing. We have a new starter taking over from DS Tozer during her maternity.'

'Oh good. Anyone we know?'

'Yes, he's been helping you out on this investigation. He's in uniform and looking for a change of scenery. Jimmy Barnes.'

'Good choice.'

'Yes. I thought so. Good night, DI Archer.'

At her desk, Archer takes out her phone and makes a call. After four rings the call is answered. 'Hello.'

'Is that Dorothy?' asks Archer.

'Yes. Who is this, please?'

'Hi, Dorothy. This is Detective Inspector Grace Archer. We met recently after the police incident at the Strand.'

'I remember.'

'I just wanted to let you know that the two officers have been removed from active duty.'

'Oh, I didn't want anyone to lose their jobs!'

'That's very gracious of you, Dorothy, but they haven't lost their jobs. They've been given desk work.'

'I see.'

'I'm sorry again for what you went through.'

There's a pause before she answers, then, 'I hope they can learn from this.'

'I hope so too.'

'Thank you for letting me know.'

'If there is anything else I can help you with, just call Charing Cross and ask for me.'

'I will.'

'Bye, Dorothy.'

'Bye.'

50

ARCHER IS SITTING ON THE sofa in Dr Hutchison's consulting room. The lights are dimmed, the citrus and pepper candle is burning. She stares at the polished walnut coffee table and loses herself in its rich tones of pale and dark honey. Slowly, she exhales, and settles into the doctor's environment. On the outside she is calm, but inside she crackles with a rage that burns through her like a forest fire, decimating her emotions, her humanity.

She clears her throat, which is dry, and absentmindedly massages the scars on her hands.

'How has your week been?' asks Dr Hutchison as she pours Archer a glass of water.

She should be happier. She should be relieved. The world is a safer place now that the investigation is over and Aaron and his cabal are no more. Yet, she cannot feel anything. Grandad's revelation about Frankie 'Snow' White offering her to child serial killer Bernard Morrice as part payment for her father's murder is a punch that she has not yet recovered from. That aside, Charlie had warned her White has someone watching her on the inside. And she has no idea who that is.

'Grace . . .?' prompts Hutchison.

Archer snaps from her fugue. 'Sorry.' She searches for a suitable response and replies, 'Eventful,' which she instantly regrets because it sounds woefully glib.

She takes a sip of water.

Dr Hutchison relaxes into the armchair opposite and does not ask Archer to elaborate. She will have seen the news and be aware of the investigation, including the loss of MJ, one of her own clients.

'Last week we talked about your encounter with Frankie White and your night terrors with Bernard Morrice and @nonymous. How have things been since?'

'This investigation has been relentless. When this happens my focus on the case keeps the monsters from my door. My dreams, that is.'

'That's quite a silver lining.'

Archer places the water on a glass coaster on the coffee table. 'I wondered if we could talk about that night. The night that I escaped from Bernard Morrice.'

'Of course. We can talk about anything you like.'

Archer takes a few moments to gather her thoughts.

'Once Morrice abducted me from the graveyard, he drove me to his home and locked me into a pit with Danny Jobson inside. Danny was nine years old . . . nine years old . . .' Archer pauses before continuing. 'The pit was horrible. It was shallow and damp, the soil infested with bugs and worms so much so that the walls seemed to be constantly moving.

'Danny was filthy when I got there and it wasn't long before I was too. He was younger than me by three years and terrified. I was too, but I was more worried about him because he had asthma and his inhaler was running low.

'We became friends quickly, talked about our lives at home and what we would do when this nightmare was all over.'

Archer closes her eyes and sighs.

'On our last night together, the rain hammered down on the trapdoor. Danny's inhaler was empty. His breathing was laboured, his lungs wheezed. God, I'll never forget that sound ... I was so worried. I had to do something, anything to help him. I thought maybe I could appeal to Morrice somehow.

'I was able to push the trapdoor up just a little. Through the gap, I could see the light from his cottage. I shouted and shouted across to him until I was hoarse, but he ignored me, or maybe he couldn't hear me. Anyway, eventually, Danny told me to stop. He asked me sit with him and just keep him warm. I put my arms around him and pulled him close. He was freezing and trembling, felt as fragile as a little bird. He said, "Grace, if you get out before me, will you tell my mum and dad that I'm sorry? Tell them that I love them and they are the best mum and dad ever." I told him he could tell them himself, because I wasn't leaving without him. He smiled at that. We were so tired that we fell asleep, listening to the rain. When I woke up, he wasn't in the pit.'

Archer reaches for the glass and takes another swig of water.

'I panicked – and through the gap I saw Morrice carry Danny towards the cottage. I screamed at him to stop, but he ignored me. It was raining so heavily that water began to seep into the pit. It softened the walls and edges and I was able to start clawing at the disintegrating mud. My heart was pounding but I was spurred on by my fury at Morrice.'

Archer glances at the scar on the back of her left hand.

381

'I made the narrowest of holes and had to remove my coat to squeeze through. When I was free, I was shocked to see traffic in the distance. I thought we were so much further away from anything. I wanted to run to get help, but then I heard Danny coughing. My heart jumped and I didn't know what to do. Morrice was an adult; he might have been a small man but he was strong. I had to save Danny, I just had to try no matter what the cost. I remember looking down at my arms. They were covered in mud and I'd cut my hand, which was bleeding. My face and hair were wet and muddy too, but I didn't care. I knew I looked monstrous but, in a way, it felt like an armour. I ran to his cottage with no thought to what I was going to do. I remember finding it surprisingly neat and tidy inside. Everything was floral chintz: the carpets, curtains, rugs, wall-paper, the furniture. It was not at all what I was expecting, but then again, I hadn't given much thought to what the inside of his house was like. I could hear Morrice talking upstairs. I crept up the narrow stairs and across the landing I saw Danny sitting on an armchair. It was positioned at an angle and I couldn't see his face. Morrice wasn't there and I could hear water running in the bathroom. He was inside it, chatting away to himself. As quietly as I could I whispered Danny's name, but he didn't hear me. I climbed a few more steps, but still couldn't get his attention. So, I slipped off my shoes and tiptoed up the remainder of the stairs, across to the room. I lifted Danny's hand, tugged it and was relieved that it was still warm from me hugging him. But then I saw his face . . . His eyes were open and staring across the room at nothing. I whispered his name, but I knew it was too late. He was gone . . . I wanted to cry, but I couldn't.'

Archer closes her eyes and takes a calming breath.

'From the hallway, I heard the bathroom door open and Morrice's footsteps. He looked so puzzled when he saw the mud I had left on his carpet. He frowned at it and his eyes followed the trail to the room where I was with Danny. By the time he registered me, I was feet away, charging at him, screaming like a demon, and with all my strength I pushed him. We both fell down the narrow stairs, my filthy hands scratching at his pale face and thin red lips. I heard a snapping sound as we tumbled to the ground floor. He landed on top of me and I beat him, kicked him, pushed at him; but he didn't move. I managed to slip out from underneath him and scrabbled across the floor. Still, he didn't move. As I pushed myself up, I could see his neck was twisted – and knew then he was dead.'

Archer stares blankly across the room.

A moment passes before Hutchison asks, 'How did you feel after that?'

Archer hesitates before replying, 'Alive.'

They sit in silence for a moment.

'We lost a colleague this week. She was a patient here,' says Archer.

'Yes . . . I'm sorry.'

'I didn't know her very well and I regret not getting to know her better. She also had trauma in her childhood and, like me, her experience determined her career. We joined the police to make a difference in the hope that no one would go through what we, and those close to us, went through. But she chose a different path from me. She chose revenge and violence.'

Archer glances at the clock. It's almost eight and her appointment is drawing to a close.

'Do you think she made the right choice?' asks Hutchison.

'I believe she knew that it could have led to her death and that was a risk she was prepared for. Did she make the right choice? From a legal perspective, no. From her perspective, only she can answer that question.'

'What do you think she would say?'

'I think she'd say yes.'

'If she was still alive now, what would you say to her?'

Archer thinks of Frankie White offering her as currency to Bernard Morrice.

'I envy you.'

Dr Hutchison regards her for a moment. 'Come and see me next week. We can talk more.'

Archer stands and takes her coat from the stand next to the door.

'Thank you,' she says, pulling on her coat.

'Take care of yourself.'

Outside on Wimpole Street, Archer takes out her phone and makes a call. It rings four times before it's answered. 'Hello?'

'This is Detective Inspector Grace Archer. We need to talk.'

'I'm so glad you called. Just tell me where and when,' says Mallory Jones.

51

Four weeks later . . .

Feltham Remand Centre, Hounslow

RANKIE 'SNOW' WHITE HAD LONG ago learned to never expect much from his family. His brothers, when they were alive, had been a crushing mix of brainless hoodlums and deviants, so it's no surprise that his grandson has turned out much the same. It didn't help that Janine had got herself knocked up by a second-generation Mick, a smack dealer and user, who was the nearest thing East London had to a village idiot. Frankie had loathed him, was having none of that around his family and business. He'd had him discreetly taken care of, which upset his daughter no end and she'd begged Frankie to let her keep the baby. Reluctantly, Frankie had agreed. He wasn't a complete monster, after all, he'd told himself.

'Mr White,' comes a voice. Frankie looks up from his chair in reception, at the overweight uniformed remand officer.

'What is it?' he snaps.

'He's ready. If you'll just follow me.'

Frankie stands and straightens the sleeves of his Crombie coat. Through the window outside he notices a squad car pull up and park beside his Mercedes. He regards it with a wary expression before following the chubby officer. As they walk through three doors that have to be locked and relocked, Frankie sighs heavily at each one. 'Can we just get a fucking move on? I haven't got all day.'

'Yes, sir. Sorry,' replies the officer who drops the keys twice before reaching the room where he asks in an obsequious tone, 'Would you like me to come in with you?'

Frankie gives him a withering look. '*Would you like me to come in with you?*' he mimics in a squeaky voice. 'If I go to the toilet, do you want to come along and hold my fucking dick too?'

'No, sir. Sorry, that's not what I meant.'

'Open the door and do one!'

'Yes, sir.'

The officer opens the door. Frankie steps inside and shuts the door behind him.

He is sitting at the table watching as Frankie plants himself on the chair opposite.

'All right, son. They looking after you here?'

'Where's my mother?' replies Kain.

'We're looking after her, as I promised. So just trust me, OK?'

Kain frowns, causing his right eyelid to droop lower than normal. 'What is it you want?'

'I want you to testify that my grandson did not kill Beth Harper.'

'What makes you think he didn't?'

'He may be many things. A murderer isn't one of them. So, it's all been arranged. I'll provide you with a new brief. You'll tell him that Aaron Cronin killed her. Understood?'

Kain leans forward and rests his arms on the table. 'Mr White, Aaron did not kill Beth. Nor did Ethan.'

Frankie narrows his eyes.

Kain's mouth twists into a sly grin.

'You killed her.'

Kain starts to hum a tune, a hymn or something like it.

'Point the finger at Cronin and I'll ensure you and your mum are looked after. Perhaps you could come and work for me when you're released.'

Kain pauses before answering, 'How long will I be here for?'

'Not long. A few more weeks before moving on somewhere else. You'll get a small sentence and be out early next year. I'll see to that.'

'How can you be certain?'

'Because I'm me, kiddo.' Frankie sniffs and stands. 'Hang in there.'

It takes almost fifteen minutes for Frankie to get out of the building, which irritates him no end. As he walks to his Mercedes, he stops by the passenger door of the squad car, opens it and gets inside.

'Mr White. It's been a long time. How are you?' says Jimmy Barnes.

'Could be better, Jimmy. Could be better. Got your promotion, I hear.'

'Yes, sir. I'm now based in Charing Cross Road.'

Frankie sniffs and nods an approval.

'I'm sorry about your grandson, Mr White.'

'Never mind him. He's made his bed. Now, tell me what the fuck is going on, Jimmy? Once again she's fucked me over. I mean, what am I paying you and that other idiot for? What is the point of him?'

'DI Hicks has no spine, sir. He lost it when Andy Rees was sent down.'

'Well, he better fucking grow one, because I am on the fucking war path and I want that Archer cunt taken care of.'

'I'll talk to Hicks – and I'll personally see to Archer myself.'

Frankie opens the passenger door. 'See that you do, Detective Sergeant Barnes. See that you do . . .'

Acknowledgements

First up, the team at Zaffre who have been involved in the making, marketing and selling of this book. Thank you Ben Willis, Ciara Corrigan, Nick Stearn, Elise Burns, Vicky Joss and Eleanor Stammeijer.

Graham Bartlett for his wisdom on police procedure. The brilliant team at DHH Literary Agency for their flag waving and support, and Goldsboro Books for producing a stunning limited edition.

A big shout out to all the bloggers and reviewers who have supported me and continue to do so. And finally, a massive thank you to my agent and rock, the one, the only, Mr David H Headley.

If you enjoyed *See No Evil,*
why not join the
DAVID FENNELL READERS' CLUB?

When you sign up you'll receive an exclusive deleted scene,
plus news about upcoming books and exclusive behind-
the-scenes material. To join, simply visit:
bit.ly/DavidFennellClub

Keep reading for a letter from the author . . .

Hello!

Thank you so much for picking up *See No Evil*.

There's a scene in Alfred Hitchcock's *The Birds* where Mitch Brenner's mother, Lydia Brenner, visits her friend Dan at his home. She lets herself in and is surprised to find broken crockery and glass strewn across the kitchen. The camera follows Lydia as she tentatively makes her way up the hallway searching for her friend. She enters Dan's bedroom and finds it ravaged by violent birds. Lying on the floor is Dan, his pyjamas streaked with blood, his eyes pecked from their sockets, all that remains are gaping dark holes of congealed blood. Hitchcock frames Dan's face in two twitching close ups that add a dizzying horror to what we and Lydia see. When I first saw this at around eleven years old, I was traumatised and afterwards became terrified if I saw three or more stalking birds perched anywhere close by. Fortunately, that's no longer the case as I now love them, especially when they fly in and hang around my garden. Still, the visceral shock of that scene has never left me and was ever present as I wrote this book.

I knew when I sat down to write *See No Evil* that I had to up my game after the success of *The Art of Death*. The next book had to be darker, the killer as twisted and diabolical as @nonymous, but at the same time I needed a steady thread of heart, enough to keep the terror at bay while also making you, the reader, turn the pages rooting for Archer, Quinn, and of course, Grandad.

See No Evil is the most challenging book I have written to date. This was in part down to COVID lockdowns and the severe impact the pandemic had on all of our lives. A second,

391

and more personal reason, is my father, who like Grandad, has dementia. Almost all of Grandad's experiences are accounts of what my sister and I have experienced with our dad. These scenes have been emotional to write and have also provided a degree of therapy. I know these scenes will resonate with many readers who have experienced a loved one with dementia, and I hope that in some way they offer a shred of empathy to your own experiences.

If you would like to hear more about my books, you can visit **www.bit.ly/DavidFennellClub** where you can become part of the David Fennell Readers' Club. It only takes a few moments to sign up, there are no catches or costs.

Bonnier Zaffre will keep your data private and confidential, and it will never be passed on to a third party. We won't spam you with loads of emails, just get in touch now and again with news about my books, and you can unsubscribe any time you want.

And if you would like to get involved in a wider conversation about my books, please do review *See No Evil* on Amazon, on Goodreads, on any other e-store, on your own blog and social media accounts, or talk about it with friends, family or reader groups! Sharing your thoughts helps other readers, and I always enjoy hearing about what people experience from my writing.

Thank you again for reading *See No Evil*.

All my best,
David Fennell